THE ORBSTARS OF T'VARIN

By Barry M. Fellinger

Dedicated to the memory of David Joseph Gallant

Born August 7, 1963, died January 1994,

A dear friend and brother in the Lord.

A warrior in his own right,

Who now walks in T'var's land,

And beholds Him face to face.

"And so it was that in the early dawn of the ancient mists of time that

Manglor brought dusk to the infant world of T'varin."

- From "Ancient Histories of the Old World"

found in the Library of Glephas.

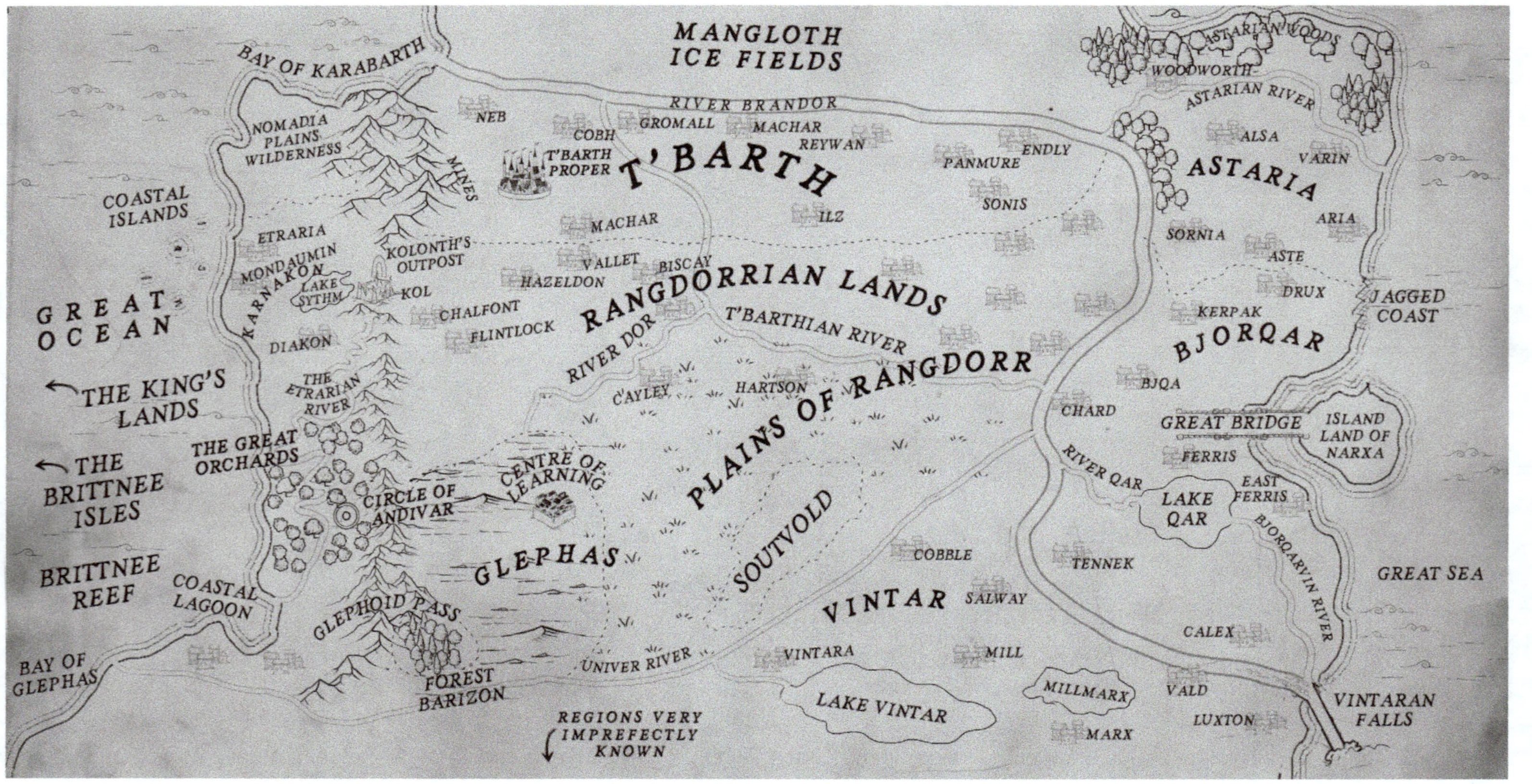
MANGLOTH ICE FIELDS
BAY OF KARABARTH
ASTARIAN WOODS
WOODWORTH
ASTARIAN RIVER
RIVER BRANDOR
NEB
COBH
GROMALL
MACHAR
REYWAN
ALSA
VARIN
NOMADIA PLAINS WILDERNESS
T'BARTH PROPER
T'BARTH
PANMURE
ENDLY
ASTARIA
COASTAL ISLANDS
MACHAR
ILZ
SONIS
ARIA
ETRARIA
KOLONTH'S OUTPOST
SORNIA
ASTE
MONDAUMIN
KARNAKON
LAKE SYTHM
KOL
VALLET
HAZELDON
BISCAY
RANGDORRIAN LANDS
DRUX
KERPAK
JAGGED COAST
GREAT OCEAN
CHALFONT
FLINTLOCK
RIVER DOR
T'BARTHIAN RIVER
BJORQAR
DIAKON
C'AYLEY
HARTSON
PLAINS OF RANGDORR
BJQA
THE KING'S LANDS
THE ETRARIAN RIVER
CHARD
GREAT BRIDGE
ISLAND LAND OF NARXA
THE GREAT ORCHARDS
CENTRE OF LEARNING
FERRIS
RIVER QAR
EAST FERRIS
THE BRITTNEE ISLES
CIRCLE OF ANDIVAR
SOUTVOLD
LAKE QAR
GLEPHAS
COBBLE
TENNEK
BJORQARVIN RIVER
BRITTNEE REEF
COASTAL LAGOON
VINTAR
SALWAY
GREAT SEA
GLEPHOID PASS
UNIVER RIVER
VINTARA
MILL
CALEX
BAY OF GLEPHAS
FOREST BARIZON
REGIONS VERY IMPERFECTLY KNOWN
LAKE VINTAR
MILLMARX
VALD
LUXTON
VINTARAN FALLS
MARX
MINES

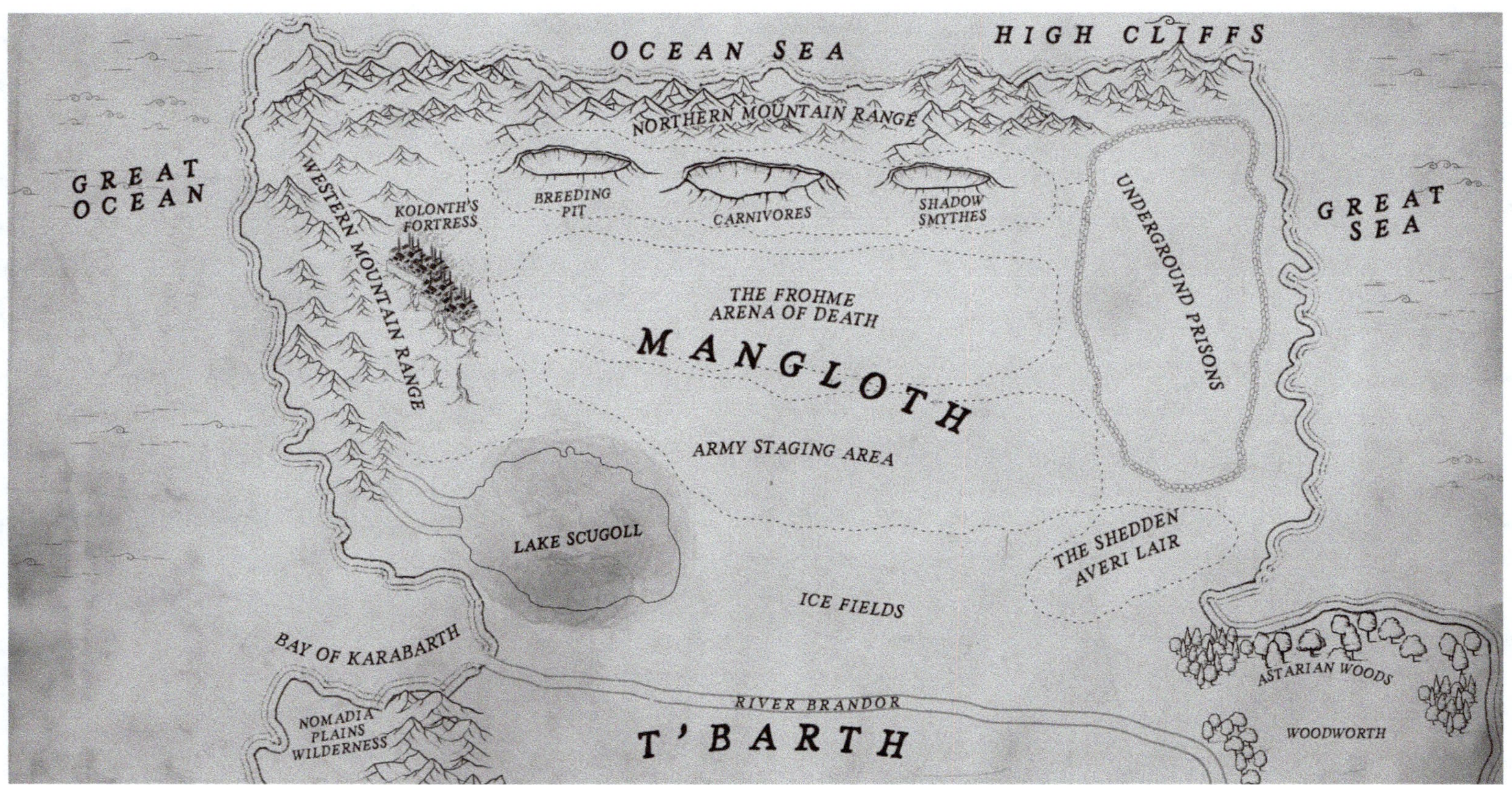

OCEAN SEA
HIGH CLIFFS
GREAT OCEAN
GREAT SEA
NORTHERN MOUNTAIN RANGE
WESTERN MOUNTAIN RANGE
KOLONTH'S FORTRESS
BREEDING PIT
CARNIVORES
SHADOW SMYTHES
UNDERGROUND PRISONS
THE FROHME ARENA OF DEATH
MANGLOTH
ARMY STAGING AREA
THE SHEDDEN AVERI LAIR
LAKE SCUGOLL
ICE FIELDS
BAY OF KARABARTH
NOMADIA PLAINS WILDERNESS
RIVER BRANDOR
T'BARTH
ASTARIAN WOODS
WOODWORTH

ENDINGS

Manglor continued his search for the precious jewel amid the endless passages and dank musty corridors of the Castle of Crystal. With the treasure, *the Orbstar,* in his possession, victory would be his and his insatiable hunger for dominion over all T'varin would finally be satisfied.

His shadowy cloak billowed about him every time a breeze wafted through as Manglor walked down yet another passageway. The fresh air it brought annoyed him, as did the furry rodents which scampered away at the sound of his approaching boots. Those that didn't move fast enough he squashed underfoot without a thought. At times, his height slowed his progress when some entranceways did not easily accommodate his tall frame, yet his determination drove him on in spite of these minor hindrances. He was relentless and would not allow anything to prevent him from achieving his goal.

He had been in the palace for a week, his enemies unaware, or so he thought, of both his location and the object of his quest. Outside, in the steadily driving rain, three dozen horsemen led by one lone figure on foot, approached the antiquated edifice. They had come silently, under cover of darkness, and so crossed the archaic covered Bridge that connected the domain of Bjorqar to the Island Land of Narxa, home to the Castle of Crystal.

The single, unarmed figure leading the small assemblage wore a seamless flowing white robe which shimmered with a soft warm glow. His sandalled feet made no sound, even in the midst of the downpour. He slowed His pace until the front line of the riders caught up to Him. He turned, revealing black hair flattened by the water and gentle green eyes that seemed to stare right through the troops and focus on something afar off.

He softly patted the horses on either side, as the troops surrounded Him and came to a halt. To those closest, there appeared to be a hint of sadness in their Sovereign's eyes.

"Orders, my Great King?" asked the leader of the twelve from Vintar, his face a mirror of both anticipation and worry. He wore the traditional garb of one his rank, a silver and gold cloak, a protective thick brown tunic, with matching pants of the same material and a wide brown leather belt around his waist that was home to a mix of knives and his longer sword blade.

"Let us attack now and drive the fiend into the open," urged the deep but decidedly female voice of the Chief Astarian Warrior Woman. If her hair was long, as was their custom, one could not tell due to the helm that covered most of her head and stopped just above her eyes. Although some might wonder how this did not affect their perception, the Astarians' fierceness in battle left no doubt about that concern.

Unlike the tightness of the Vintaran soldiers' uniforms, the Astarian tribeswomen wore their colourful clothing loose, allowing them as much free movement as possible. It was less armour-like and more practical, at least for their fighting style. Though others outside of their land, where visitors were few, may not have realized it, their clothing also served as their everyday dress; the variations of colours representing the different tribes of their homeland.

"Silence, comrades! What is your desire, my Liege?" The Captain of the men of Bjorqar's tone of voice betrayed his impatience for combat. His deep blue chainmail, like those of his troop, bore the insignia of their homeland on the breastplates and his posture reflected an eager readiness for a great battle.

"My desire, My desire," mused the Great King. "My wants are not of import - loftier purposes are at work here."

The small group moved forward, their leader now walking amongst them and remaining strangely silent. They reached the front part of the castle sooner than expected. It was a wide-open space, which in better times had been the site of an immense and beautiful garden. The crystal structure of the massive castle walls barely reflected anything, instead managed only to project the dreary image of the rain itself. The words were unspoken, but the thought that the once majestic castle had seen better days, hung over the group as they wondered what might come next.

All eyes turned to their King, awaiting His order. Decisively, slowly, brow furrowed in thoughtful concentration as though listening to an unseen voice, the King said, "I must go alone."

"But my Liege," several in the group cried out together. "That's madness, You cannot! It is folly."

The King cut them off, raising His hand for silence.

"It is of no use; I must face him unaided."

An expression of angry frustration passed over His face and no one dared question Him after that moment.

"What of us?" a voice broke the silence.

The King raised His hand, signalling for attention.

"Leaders, you will camp out here for the night. The rainfall will not end soon; the downpour will yet grow worse. You will find shelter to your left, with rock outcroppings large enough to shield the full party from the storm. Listen well! Everyone is to spend the night there. Under no circumstances shall anyone now follow Me or cross into the castle. At the first sign of the morning star, before dawn breaks, three soldiers, one from each of your three lands, are to enter the castle by a side door which you shall find carved in the rocks. The entranceway will turn visible with the fading light of the star."

The directions elicited some murmurings amongst the group until the King raised His hand, making it clear He was not yet finished. "The three of you must pass through and travel the passageway until you come to its end in a chamber in the castle. There, you will find..." The King hesitated as if about to give a longer explanation but then changed His mind. "What you must find. Once done, leave the room by the stairway to your left, through the other door to the chamber. Do not depart the same way you came into the room."

He continued, "Ascend the stairs and they will bring you to the front portals of the castle where you may leave. Leave at once and do not turn back. Once outside, rejoin your comrades. You are all to keep your distance from the castle, regardless of what you see or hear. Once the three appointed ones return to you, no one is to approach the castle. Heed My instructions and you will all be together outside the castle as the first rays of sunlight gleam over the horizon."

"And when dawn comes, where will You be, my Lord?" asked the Chief of the Astarians.

"I will be where I need to be and the dawn will bring what it must," the King declared in such an ominous tone of voice that no one could bring themselves to question Him any further. Many feared they would suffer a sleepless night puzzling over the riddle of His reply.

To their horror and surprise, their King turned abruptly and with a determined stride, walked without hesitation toward the palace entrance. His orders had been so forceful, and spoken with such authority, none presumed to chase after Him.

Manglor noticed the storm's increase in intensity as it pelted heavily against the castle's old walls. He smiled as though the storm was his own doing and, relentless, he carried on with his investigation. He sensed his goal was not far off. He refused to give in to weariness, for he believed he was close. His pale-yellow eyes glowed with anticipation for every fibre of his being told him that the Orbstar must be close at hand. "One more room, one more corridor, one more passage and it will be mine."

Breathing in the stale air and wiping the long strands of his now dirty blond hair from his eyes, the sweat on his forehead glistened in the dim light of his torch. Peering through the next doorway, he saw a faint blue glow coming from a table in the centre of the room. The table bore strange markings but Manglor did not notice them, so intent was he on the origin of the glow: the Orbstar. In less than a moment, he clutched the gem in his greedy hands.

"At last," he rejoiced. "At last, victory is within my grasp. I will take my place as rightful ruler of this world and thus fulfil my oath and my destiny."

"It will destroy you, Manglor."

Manglor's face fell in startled recognition. He turned to see the one person he didn't expect.

"So, You have come, my Liege," he mocked. "I see You have come unaccompanied. You are a fool! I will use this gift to end even You!"

"I say again: the Orbstar will be your destruction, Manglor. Return it to Me, come back to Me, let us make things as they once were."

"Never, *NEVER*, I will *never* be Your slave again!" cried Manglor in a frenzy. He raised the Orbstar and held it above his head. "I will no longer be subservient to Your whims, to Your ways. You may have doomed this world, Pretender, but it is my destiny to make things right, to transform this world and free its people from Your yoke of bondage. I will never be Your servant; I MUST BE *MASTER*!"

"Careful, Manglor, you know not what you do," cautioned the King, His hands out, palms up in a gesture of extended peace.

"You are so very wrong, *my Lord*. Your tyranny over this world is ended. You are now finite and at my mercy, of which I have none and I will now be infinite. I know exactly what I do. *DIE!*" Manglor shouted.

The glow of the Orbstar became increasingly bright, responding to the growing amount of hatred in Manglor's voice. As he held the gem high above his head, a beam of pure white light shot forth from the Orbstar, straight into the King's heart, piercing flesh and bone, leaving naught but a gaping hole in His chest. He collapsed onto the floor. His body lay still, blood-stained, wrapped in the bonds of death.

Manglor's triumphant cackle reverberated throughout the empty castle and into the night sky. Above the noise of the wind and rain, the troops nestled under the shelter shivered and their steeds paced restlessly, the ground trembling underfoot.

Manglor gave one last glance at the crumpled heap on the floor, smiled and strode from the room. He climbed the stairs outside the chamber and on the fifth level, returned to the small room which had been his headquarters during his week's pursuit.

"A fruitful work after all," he said. "Now to use my time wisely, studying this priceless jewel and making plans as the new, true and uncontestable monarch of T'varin. Lackey no more, this is now my domain."

Outside, as the night wore on, sleep would not come for most. The few who could sleep caught it only in snatches, being disturbed by nightmares. They would repeatedly awaken in a dense sweat and feel the chill of night settling deep into their bones. The tempest raged on, parodying some furious battle being fought both in the skies above them as well as deep in the ground far below.

"This does not feel right," the Bjorqarn Captain frowned, speaking quietly to his fellow leaders.

"Aye. I wish He would have taken some of us with Him. I do not like this at all. Why bring us only to leave us behind?" The Astarian Warrior Woman, stared ahead at the Castle ruins, unsheathing her sword to make a point. "He knows we all would fight for Him,no matter what."

"I do not always understand Him or His ways." The Vintaran commander's perplexed tone and raised hands with open palms demonstrated his confusion. "Sometimes trusting He knows best is hard."

"Very hard indeed," agreed the other two. The Captains huddled together, continuing to speak quietly to each other. They gave worried looks to the castle and then to their troops. A cloud of indecision hovered above them, as did an intangible evil, felt but not seen. It pervaded the night, a gloomy weight upon them all. Then, from the depths of the castle, came an eerie malevolent laugh, resonating enough to confirm their cruellest fears. All prayed that dawn would come swiftly.

Shortly before the first light of day, the rain slowed. A warm, soothing breeze began to blow off The Great Sea, forcing the night's storm clouds to vacate the sky. Soon, only the last few predawn stars were visible and the company breathed a sigh of relief. Even so, to the trained soldiers' ears, the morning air was unusually still; sounds of birds, or other animal life, completely absent.

The Captains had debated all through the night who they would choose from their companies to enter the castle as the King had commanded. They would have gone themselves, but they had not been given that option. In this early hour, they chose: Stalwart Culbeth of Vintar, Unwavering Anarate of Astaria and Unshakable Loxtwqar of Bjorqar. The three selected were honoured with these titles when their Captains called them out, the rest of the troops relieved, for all suspected that something menacing waited inside the castle and each remembered the hideous laugh echoing during the night.

Dawn began to break and the waning light of the morning star reminded them of their duty.

"Look!" exclaimed Culbeth. "Just as the King said, the door can be seen amidst the rocks. Quick now, before our way vanishes with the passing of the morning star."

"We are with you, comrade," said Anarate, as she and Loxtwqar hurried to help him pull open the door. They could open it only wide enough for one person at a time to fit through. The task was extremely gruelling and the door resisted every effort of their wills to be pulled further ajar.

"It doesn't seem to want us to discover what treasures hide inside," said Culbeth.

"I doubt you'll find treasure in that ancient ruin, good Culbeth," said his Captain. "Now best fortunes, you three. Meanwhile, we will ride to where our King ordered us. We will watch you escort Him out."

"That is to be hoped, my Lord," said Anarate.

Yet the uneasy feeling in their hearts warned that this might be a vain hope. The three passed through the doorway, their way lit by what little sunshine came in. Travelling forward, they soon realized the way was becoming brighter, not dimmer. They noticed a light from an unknown source grow brighter the closer they got to what must have been the castle interior. They had no idea how long it would take to reach their destination, nor what waited for them. They felt only a churning emptiness in their stomachs, that even drawing their swords would not abate.

The three lost track of time as they walked on and would have been hard pressed to say if they had been walking minutes or hours. Each new twist and turn they encountered only made it more challenging to count time. A sudden bend in their route told them they were directly underneath the castle. They saw an archway leading into a vast room, with another door at the far end. Barely noticeable through the opposite door was the outline of a winding staircase. They glanced at one another.

With haste, stealthily, swords still drawn, they made their way to the opening of the chamber. Culbeth and Anarate stood on either side of the door while Loxtwqar passed through. His muffled cry caused the other two to rush in, swords prepared to strike down whatever foe awaited them. There was no foe. There was no fight. There was only a vision beyond their vilest imaginings. Bloodied and collapsed on the floor, lay the lifeless body of their Great King.

"This! This is what we must see?" lamented Culbeth.

"This is Manglor's doing!" fumed Loxtwqar.

"No doubt and the villain shall pay dearly for this unspeakable crime with his wretched life," said Anarate, choking back the tears.

"What does this mean? How can this be? The Great King is dead," said Culbeth. "Shall now the entirety of T'varin fall beneath the oppressor's heel?"

"Come, there is no time to debate this here, we must leave with haste and warn our comrades. Something is going to happen. Do you not feel it? Listen! There is a rumbling noise from the depths of this cursed place," said Loxtwqar. "I fear the very stones we stand on are shaking in terror and will crumble, taking us with them if we tarry here too long."

"You are right, Brother. Let us make haste and rejoin our comrades as we were told to do," agreed Anarate.

"Halt! We must *not* leave His body amidst these ruins," said Culbeth. "We can't leave Him behind and..."

"We must, my friend," said Loxtwqar. "There is no time for anything else, we *must* move on. We have done our duty as the King commanded. We have found what He said we would find. We must leave as He told us."

The three raced through the door on the other side of the chamber and found the stairway as described. They flew up the steps, their swords at the ready should they meet their enemy. Their hearts weighed down and their faces tear-stained, they emerged through the front gates of the castle. They quickly reached their comrades, who were gathered near the front greenery of the castle. The castle that was now the tomb of their Great King.

When they rounded the last corner, Manglor heard their racing footfalls on the stairwell from his secluded chamber. He peered out the window to observe two men and a woman running to a gathering of fellow warriors. Manglor wished he could have overheard their conversation, but by the pain and confusion reflected on their faces, he guessed they now understood that their frail champion, their useless King, was no more.

How they had gained entrance to the castle without him knowing was not important. In fact, they were not significant at all. Nothing was, for he had the Orbstar, and with it, all T'varin was now his. The troops outside would soon bow to him and give him their allegiance. Or they could join their King.

"What news does the dawn bring, Culbeth?" asked his Captain, his face showing his victorious anticipation.

"Dawn brings ill fortune, Commander."

"Ill fortune is too feeble a phrase," said Loxtwqar, his head down in grief.

"What did you find, Sister?" asked the Chief of the Warrior Women.

"That we had to live to see this day," said Anarate, shaking her head, tears filling her eyes, causing her sisters to stare in astonishment.

"What? Speak clearly now," their leaders commanded.

"Inside, we followed as our Lord said, and found...and we found... we found His fallen and wounded, blood-stained body lying on the floor of the chamber He bade us enter," answered Culbeth, holding back his sobs.

"Whose? Manglor's? The fiend is finally dead!"

"If only 'twere so. No, sirs, not Manglor, T'var, T'var is dead."

"Impossible!" wailed the soldiers standing near enough to hear the report from their comrades.

"Unbelievable! You've been deceived. Some trick or illusion of Manglor's!"

"No, Captains. This is no deception; we have seen Him with our own eyes and felt no life in Him."

"Dead, He was dead!"

"No this is foolishness, one cannot kill the Lord of all T'varin, He is..."

Manglor had exited the castle in time to overhear the last words of their grief, arms waving in excitement, eyes glowing with both hatred and victory, determined to be the one to share the dread truth to these soon-to-be subjects of his wrath.

"*FOOLISHNESS INDEED!*" His harsh voice bellowed out above the discord of the gathered troops. "Your buffoon-like comrades are quite correct. T'var is dead, by my hand! Manglor is victor; your Great King is no more. I have slain Him and now I will slay you, unless, of course, you repent and swear fealty to me, your new King and legitimate Sovereign of all this world. Then perhaps I will allow you to live. Some of you, anyway."

Manglor's taunt was hideous at best, terrifying at worst. As one, the troops turned to face Manglor, swords out, ready to charge, waiting only for the signal from their Captains. The leaders looked to each other and then to Manglor who smirked at their pointless efforts.

"Very well. You have sealed your own fates!"

With an air of grim satisfaction, Manglor lifted the Orbstar above his head, the same way he had done only hours before. He felt the power of the gem building in his hands, focusing the energy of his will, intent on bringing immediate oblivion to all who stood before him. He readied to release the bolt of death, but their doom never came.

A quiet grumbling sounded from the castle behind them. The same quaking that the trio had experienced in the dark chamber only moments earlier. The vibration escalated, rising louder until the ground under their feet shook with such fury, everyone, including Manglor, had to fight to maintain their balance.

The clamour came unmistakably from the castle. All turned, Manglor too, to witness the walls of the castle shuddering furiously as though unseen giant hands were trying to pick it up and rip the structure apart. The entire castle buckled and in mere moments it crashed into ruin, an enormous heap of rubble left in its place. One last enormous crack resounded as the weight of the fallen castle forced much of its remains deep into the ground and then followed nothing but an eerie silence.

Manglor turned to face the small contingent before him. The troops from the three realms thought this was all Manglor's doing and the mark of their fate. All hope was lost.

"There your King lies, buried under tons of debris, entombed in the cursed castle He once created! See what reward you have for being in

His service; death at my hands. The Orbstar will annihilate you, just as it did Him. He is dead, and since you cannot be trusted to be loyal to the new Lord of T'varin, you may now join your dead King."

Suddenly the air was filled with a strange and sweet perfume, along with words that were music to the ears.

"Not quite Manglor, not quite dead at all," said an all-too familiar voice.

Unbelieving eyes turned to witness a striking regal shape walk out from the castle ruins, in a gleaming white robe, shimmering as though new. It was T'var. T'var the Great King!

The glow of the rising sun cast a golden aura around Him as He strode forth, tall, carefree and laughing. His laugh made their hearts leap for joy. Manglor stared, helplessly transfixed, eyes focused on his sworn enemy.

T'var drew closer. He spoke with a voice that was fresh and radiant, yet ageless and full of wisdom, ancient beyond measure. A voice tender and soothing, while still resolute and strong, resounded across all T'varin.

"You have done Me a favour, Manglor, and I thank you. You killed Me and in so doing have allowed Me to once and for all conquer death, the greatest enemy of T'varin's people. Yes, a greater enemy than even you, Manglor. My people no longer need fear death as before." His voice rose in volume as He spoke and now it reached its crescendo as He said, "I HAVE CONQUERED THE LAST ENEMY. *FOREVER!* DEATH IS SLAIN. YOU NEED FEAR IT NO MORE!"

T'var stretched out His arm in the direction of Manglor and pointed at the Orbstar still clenched in Manglor's hand. Manglor stared in helpless fascination as an invisible power pulled the jewel from his grasp, lifting it into the air, where it hung suspended between himself and T'var. A stream of colour burst forth from the Orbstar, assuming the form of a rainbow, enveloping both Manglor and T'var in a blaze of radiance, hiding them from sight.

The contingent of soldiers gazed in amazement as first red, then blue, green and violet shimmered around the two figures who at first became hidden, then partly visible, in the shifting colours. What quickly became apparent to those looking on, was during each change of hue, T'var intensified in brightness, almost as if He became more solid, if that were possible. Simultaneously, Manglor's shape decreased, not quite thinner, but more transparent, less real.

Within the Orbstar's coloured hues, Manglor's very essence seemed to be dissipating. In fact, some thought Manglor was being absorbed into the Orbstar itself. Neither Manglor nor T'var spoke. Suddenly it was all over. The colours vanished. Only T'var stood, solitary, smiling triumphantly. Manglor was simply not there, taken captive into the Orbstar which dropped obediently into T'var's waiting open hand. Manglor had become a prisoner in that which he so desperately had sought to possess.

With an almost cheerful grin on His face, as though concealing some special secret, T'var turned toward the ruins of the Castle of Crystal and carelessly tossed the Orbstar into the midst of the fallen debris. The soldiers gasped and a few ran to where the Orbstar had fallen, but their diligent exploration revealed no evidence of the jewel. They wondered if they had imagined the whole scene and giving up their hunt, reassembled with their comrades. Thus, the memory of the Orbstar faded into obscurity; its role in the defeat of Manglor eventually forgotten over the vast ages of time.

T'var turned His back on the castle ruins and began walking toward the road that led to the Bridge which connected the Island Land of Narxa to the mainland. The Captains, following T'var's lead, ordered their troops into formation, resolving to keep pace.

T'var was already far ahead by the time they were underway and to the horsemen, their Liege was visible only as a distant shadow as He began the crossing of the Bridge. They spurred their mounts on to keep up with their King, but it was no use; the closer they would get, the farther away T'var seemed to be. At last, they caught up to Him at the place where the mist-covered Bridge met the shore, guarded by the giant statues of an older age long gone. Their minds filled with questions but they found they could not speak and heard only T'var address the statues, "Call me when the Warriors Three are in their time of need."

At that, T'var turned to the soldiers, raising His hands in a farewell gesture. His voice, still vibrant and pure, rang out, "Remember well what you have heard and seen this day. You need dread death no more for I am *DEATHSLAYER* and Manglor is *VANQUISHED.*"

Then T'var seemed to grow larger than life as He spoke, "This is My charge to you. Share the words of My triumph with the whole of T'varin and to all your descendants who will come after you. Death is now the entrance way to My lands for those who willingly choose to love and follow Me with all their heart and soul. All must still experience death, but for My loyal followers it will never be the end, only the beginning of a new life in My eternal domain. Shout this truth far and wide, loudly and long."

T'var turned once more toward the Bridge, His parting words a promise, "I will return when T'varin has need of Me again. Do not doubt, do not fear. I will return." T'var took a few more strides into the rapidly receding mist and vanished with it.

CHAPTER ONE
THE WARRIORS THREE

The fading remnants of sunlight glinted off the golden hilts of the Sonswords and danced in the lengthening shadows. The intricate flowing script embossed on the silver sheaths in which the swords rested, captured the final light of dusk, surrounding the trio in a deep amber aura.

Except for the sound from the hoofbeats of their horses, the three warriors, Randak, his sister Wandarr and their companion Barak, traversed the King's Highway in silence. Each remained absorbed with their own thoughts as the way grew darker and less certain with each league. They found a sheltered area to the left of the road and camped there for the night. Sleep came swiftly and soon the three were deep within dreams full of their own hopes, past losses and future victories.

Dawn's light came too soon but the sleepers arose quickly and quietly. Their steeds were much refreshed after the night's rest. They had been ridden long and hard but some special quality of that quiet glade where they spent the night erased all trace of weariness.

"We have travelled a great distance already," said Barak, wiping the sweat from his brow as he mounted his chestnut brown charger, Evad. "How far, my Brother-friend?"

"We are now on the borders of what Wandarr and I once called home, Rangdorr, or as it is better known, The Rangdorrian Lands," Randak said as he commanded his golden palomino, Jip, onward. Pointing with one free hand, he explained, "I prefer the fuller name for it truly expresses the vastness of our homeland. Before you now are the flats of our wide Plains which go on farther than the eye can see. We must travel across the centre of them and then into the westernmost border's edge. It is there our enemy has one of his strongholds and if your information is correct, Kolonth himself may be there and I deem tha-," but Randak cut his words short and tears glistened on his face in the early morning light.

"What is the matter?" Barak, turned to the blond-haired, muscular man, though the shortest of their trio.

"Desolate, desolate, all is desolation," cried Randak in despair. "The countryside, though lacking in hills and valleys, was once rich with vegetation and the fields were golden wheat in its season and so many other crops which supplied sustenance to all of T'varin. Even the animals are gone, slaughtered by his troops. Now what's left is only ashes enshrouded in mist and reeks of a vile substance, no doubt one of Kolonth's creation."

Now he openly wept, his words broken up by his grief. "Once a sight to make your eyes marvel and your heart to give thanks to T'var. Now I see and smell only the blackness of the Enemy's filth. His minions have marched across, not caring where they stepped, leaving only ruin in their wake."

"I am sorry," said Barak, grieving for his friend's loss.

Kolonth. He whose name would strike fear into the fiercest. First-born and only child born of Manglor. Prince of Evil, Rebel of the King's

Kingdom, High Cleric of the Unholy Priests of Manglor. He who hated the world and yet lusted after it for his own. Unlike his sire who sought dominion over T'varin to right perceived wrongs, Kolonth was all chaos and destruction, tyranny and devastation.

Barak, too, remembered the pain of the day he returned to find that his home also no longer existed. Kolonth's forces were swift and merciless. After encountering these two new friends, he vowed in that moment to join them, find and destroy the monster, should it take them a thousand lifetimes to do so.

"I wish you had visited my land in better days," said Randak, "It was…it was…"

"It was home," finished Barak. "I know. I too, remember this unwelcome taste. We shall make the evil one pay."

"How many days ride to the stronghold?" interrupted the third rider in their group, bringing her white steed to a halt. Both turned in response to the rich voice of their companion, her long auburn hair flowing in the breeze, complementing her slim build. Her name was Wandarr, sister of Randak and unspoken love of Barak.

The trio was close, almost functioning as one. Barak still recalled the day their eyes first met. He had been weeping by the lake near the site of his shattered village. In fact, his being away from his home, seeking to meditate in his favourite secluded place by the quiet waters, caused him to miss the carnage of Kolonth's soldiers and most likely spared his life.

When Barak had arrived home from his meditation, he discovered the murder and devastation of his people and his village. He ran blindly in both anger and terror, yelling words without meaning and shaking his fists. Unwittingly, he found himself back at his place of solace. There, after sobbing uncontrollably in his grief, he cried out that his own life should be taken as well. He begged and pleaded that the King would strike him dead where he sat.

Without warning, a Starborn Sentinel appeared to him, its presence overpowering, as was its great height. Taller than anything Barak had ever seen in his life, it was garbed in golden armour, from head to sandalled feet. Even its hair was of the same colour. The sword it held out before it was both long and aflame, while its wide, oval eyes burned with the intensity of a white-hot fire. Barak would have sworn that he had seen its face at the time, yet he could never actually describe it to anyone.

"Mourn not," it commanded. "Hope has not perished, for it rides white and golden steeds."

At first, Barak thought it merely a vision created by the delirium of his emotions, except for Randak and Wandarr coming upon him in the next moment. The Warrior vanished but Barak's and Wandarr's eyes connected. To him, she was a revitalizing vision of loveliness in a world of gloom. A greater comfort lay in seeing the white and golden steeds that these two strangers rode. At least his sanity had not completely left him.

Barak regarded the two warriors. The man was clad in a deep brown tunic, while the woman wore one of pale green, their knee-high laced riding boots similar in style, but of different colours, his black and hers brown. Both wore matching golden-coloured belts that held the scabbards for their swords. The man appeared short in stature but with a strong build from a life of physical labour. The man brushed his long blond hair from his forehead as he spoke, revealing flashing blue eyes and occasionally a bright smile would cross his face, though his often-furrowed brow disclosed that he carried a great burden.

The woman, Barak noted, possessed the same blue eyes as the man, identifying them as possibly related, though she stood slightly taller than him. Yet, apparent from barely a slight glance, she was grown strong and lean, well-equipped to carry herself quite capably in any battle. Her long, auburn tresses flowed freely, dissimilar to the man's, whose hair was tied in the back.

Barak noted that in contrast to her fellow rider, there still persisted a look that he could only describe as brightness and optimism. It struck him how different she was from her companion, who had the toil of years so visible upon his features. Barak listened intently to their tale, still in awe both of the recent visitation by the Starborn One, as well as the arrival, as if on cue, of these two strangers, siblings actually, whose names he learned were Randak and Wandarr.

He discovered even more as the two explained their mission and quest to him. "Barak, we have continued to chase the armies of the fiend Kolonth throughout the lands of T'varin and warn those places we come across who have not yet been touched by his evil, of the threat to come and the importance of loving and serving T'var," Randak's fierce anger embodied his words until he fell silent, seemingly overtaken by grief.

His sister's tone was sombre, but lacking Randak's fury. "Yet always we arrive too late to prevent the destruction the Evil Lord revels in. At times, we reached cities, towns and villages we thought safe. Many of these places either unaware of Kolonth or ignorant of the rumours of his works."

Barak's words were accusatory, though not directed at the siblings. "Thus has my village Luxton and all of Vintar fallen. Perhaps if our leaders had listened."

"Sadly, Vintar is not alone. It has been thus in so many places we tried to warn."

Wandarr described their earnest pleading with the leaders to act and construct defences. How they would tell of the devastation they witnessed elsewhere and of the hideous fates which awaited Kolonth's captives. She related the sad truth that more often than not, with few exceptions, their warnings went unheeded, dismissed as a story with which to frighten young children into behaving.

Though Randak's ire was not abated, he found his voice. "We consistently find Kolonth's emissaries one or two steps ahead of us. These subtle ones work behind the scenes to deceive and lull people into a state of apathy and unpreparedness. They complete their work well; most people live unconcerned with events in the world outside their own little sphere. They foolishly consider themselves too insignificant to rate any Ruler's attention, evil or otherwise.

"You speak truthfully, Brother. In fact, Barak, through the lies and deceptions of the Evil One's servants, not only do they no longer believe in Kolonth's existence but they also no longer believe in the King's either. Oh yes, some still acknowledge Him in traditions, outward forms and civil ceremonies, but to most, T'var remains nothing but an obscure story, a legend, based on older myths from a time long past and any truth in it long forgotten."

"I fear our leaders were likely so deceived as well," Barak's tears ran freely down his cheeks. "Our neutrality meant nothing. Perhaps if you had stayed and fought? Yet you would have been only two alone and would have had no allies. No doubt our people did not pick up arms, protesting proudly to the foe that our neutral status should make Vintar exempt. I am just as certain they perished screaming, perhaps begging for mercy. It is still too fresh to think about." Barak walked a short distance, sat down in the dirt, leaned up against a tree and turned his head away to hide his sobbing.

*   *   *

Giving Barak some space, Randak and Wandarr, each in their own way, reflected on how far they had come and all the trials along the way. In the beginning, Randak alone, then later joined by his sister, travelled to as many towns in the Rangdorrian Lands as possible to speak their message. They believed the best way to obey T'var's Will was by warning the populace of the approaching danger. This became their sacred mission and what the inhabitants of the towns and cities and those of other countries decided to do with the message was their own responsibility alone. Too often, Randak and Wandarr suffered jeering and mocking and so left to warn people elsewhere. At the same time, they sought clues to the location of their enemy's current stronghold, for it was rumoured Kolonth moved through the lands he determined to destroy, sometimes before and other times, after his troops had wreaked their havoc. Establishing a hidden temporary fortress or lair close to each of his targets in turn, Kolonth had the perfect vantage point from which to watch his carefully laid plans and manipulations come to life. If they could only discover Kolonth's current hiding place, they hoped to finally confront their nemesis face to face.

Their message had been mostly mocked and ridiculed in Barak's land as well and with no indication of Kolonth's presence, they had left. Less than half a day's ride away, they turned to see smoke rising behind them. Feeling a strong compulsion to return lest there be any survivors they could help, they rode back to that last village, where once again their warnings had been spurned. Thus, they came upon Barak in his hour of woe.

They saw through Barak's anguish, the potential of a warrior for the King. Wandarr saw something else as well, something she sensed when their eyes first locked. Something beyond Barak's physical appearance; tall, chiselled features in a sturdy face that suited his short golden-brown hair, rich hazel eyes that drew her in and the form of one who spent much time swimming against the currents and building strength. Perhaps all that time in the outdoors accounted for his slightly darker skin tone. All these she took in at first glance but still something more on a deeper level intrigued her and not just his slight Vintaran accent, the southeastern inflection often detectable when he spoke.

She felt drawn to Barak and he to her, even as he and Randak had a strong feeling that they would become brothers-in-arms. Knowing it would cause an unexpected delay in their hunt for Kolonth, Randak was hesitant at first to have a third join him and Wandarr but between his sister's prodding and his own instincts that it was the right thing to do, he gave in and Barak's training began. It took but a week for Barak to be trained in the use of Randak's Sonsword, for he possessed no weapon of his own.

Randak and Wandarr took turns explaining the Sonswords to Barak, who listened intently to their instructions.

"The Sonswords are powerful. It is as though the Hand of T'var is directly upon us as we fight. It is a merging of us with Him, and Him with the Sword, as though He directs our hands."

"It is a powerful anointing that comes upon us in battle and none can withstand us. It is as though through the recognition of our own frailty, the power of T'var is magnified upon us. We can inflict harm on our enemies but a protective shield surrounds us as we fight, keeping their weapons at bay."

"We have discovered that so far, not even the strongest of Kolonth's magiks can penetrate it. As long as we focus on this triune union, no harm can befall us."

"Beware though, even the slightest distraction that takes our focus off T'var and the battle at hand can make us vulnerable to injury or worse."

Barak took all this in and though he had many questions, he thought it best to wait and think on them some more before asking. He also trained on Randak's horse Jip, for riding such a magnificent creature was foreign to him. However, Barak was a quick learner, for his wrath fuelled him and with Randak's skilled teaching, Barak's lessons in both swordplay and horsemanship soon ended. Yet now all three wondered how he could manage to join Barak and Wandarr with no weapon or mount of his own when the time for battle came.

An important question meaning there was only one thing for the three to do: patiently await the direction and response of the King. They waited in silence, seeking guidance, each meditating and communing with the one called T'var, Randak the most anxious, lest they lose Kolonth's trail. They sought direction as to whether Barak was actually to join them and if so, how and with what. They beseeched T'var that if this was meant to be, that Barak be equipped with what was needed to partake in the battles against Kolonth's forces. At the moment, with no ride, no weapons, no protective armour of any sort, he would likely be dead before his first battle even began.

They spent a full day and then another half a day in petition with no response. At noon, during the second day with the sun at its highest peak, a Starborn Sentinel appeared to them. Enormous and dazzling in the King's own Light, it shone more brilliant than the sun at its fullness.

"Greetings! Greetings from the King, and more than only salutations from T'var. Gifts for the new warrior, the first two fashioned in the smithies of Oldentime. A Sonsword, like your comrades' and receive also this steed from the pastures of T'var. His name is Evad, worthy to rival Randak's Jip and Wandarr's Nayr, for they share the same lineage."

"Oh!" marvelled Barak, at a loss for words.

The Sonsword, like Randak's though not identical, fit Barak's grip as though made specifically for his left hand. Distinct from Wandarr's Sonsword, which was embedded with an emerald gem just above the hilt and Randak's which had a fiery sapphire, Barak's Sonsword held a topaz, smooth and deep in hue. His horse, a chestnut charger such as he longed for as a little child.

"Treasure these and use them well in your battle against the darkness which seeks to swallow all of T'varin. Now you are bid to go, carry on your mission to spread the message of warning to those who will listen and to those who won't. Blessings of T'var be upon you, all three."

With those last words, the Warrior vanished and the three could remember little of his visit or of his appearance. All appreciated the sense of a comforting, powerful presence that allowed them to have the most restful sleep any had experienced for a long time.

Their peaceful slumber was not to be repeated. Kolonth had bent even some of the wild and untamed things of land and air to his will, using them as his eyes and ears everywhere, so he soon learned of their encounter with the Starborn. Now three hunted him, not two and he knew of the prophecy passed down from long ago. *The Prophecy of Hope* said that three would be his downfall.

So, where before he had no fear of Randak and Wandarr, the addition of this new warrior gave him concern, minor perhaps, but concern, nonetheless. Still, he thought it best to brook no chances and carefully devised how to bring about a successful endgame, smiling at his own craftiness.

*   *   *

While the trio rested in the next village along their way, Kolonth prepared his strategy, one he trusted would eliminate all three and thwart any foolish prophecy of his downfall from ever being fulfilled. From his outpost, a rebuilt watchtower within Rangdorr, near the now-lifeless town of Kol, situated close to the border of Karnakon, he sent his fastest messengers to relay his plans to his forces that were still within Vintar.

The watchtower itself dated back to the days of Manglor, and Kolonth had engaged both his soldiers and his prisoners, used as slave labour, to reconstruct the tower according to his own designs. It provided him with the perfect vantage point from which to monitor already fallen T'barth to the north, the progress of his troops as they rampaged through the Rangdorrian Lands and soon, to the west, when the next stage of his plan began to take shape: the fate of Karnakon.

Scarcely before the three warriors left Barak's ruined village of Luxton, they were attacked and Barak's mettle was put to the test. It kept on like this throughout their journey out of Vintar as the trio endured more assaults, drove off Kolonth's bands, killing many of the foe, only to repeat the same affair a few days later. Randak was fed up. "These delays are frustrating and beyond that, they concern me greatly. I worry that Kolonth holds some hidden purpose behind these annoying skirmishes."

"Perhaps he means to tire us out to the point of exhaustion, before revealing his full evil machinations, and knows we will not have the where-withal to fight back," ventured Barak, who busied himself with setting up wood for the evening fire.

"Perhaps. Though I must wonder if Kolonth has something else at play here. He is not always predictable." Wandarr found herself quietly staring at Barak as she spoke.

Barak smiled as he turned to face Wandarr. Realizing he was aware that she had been staring and caught slightly off guard, she spoke the first words that came to mind. "You did surprisingly well in your first few forays. In spite of your short amount of training, you easily disarm and dispatch your foes in combat like a seasoned warrior. Not even any injuries on you! For which I...we...are most thankful."

"As am I, Wandarr, thanks be to T'var."

Wandarr noticed Randak's grin as he looked from her to Barak. Nor did she fail to see Barak smile in return which left her feeling both awkward and happy. Barak kindly took the attention off her to save any embarrassment.

"Randak, let's hope your unease is misplaced and there is nothing diabolical of Kolonth's yet to manifest."

"We shall see," Randak was still not convinced, though in the moment he found himself more curious about what the future might hold for his sister and Barak, at least if he was reading things right. Those thoughts he kept to himself, recognizing they could be a dangerous distraction, especially in the heat of battle.

As it turned out a few days later, there was no time for any distractions, for just outside of the decimated town of Vald, a place where cousins of Barak had lived, the enemy engaged them in a surprisingly ferocious attack.

Afterwards, the three debriefed how the battle played out. "Perhaps your unease was not wrong, Brother, just delayed."

"At least they gave us a few days rest before today's brutal attack," Barak rubbed his sword arm, for it had endured a long and active workout.

"Though I wonder, why so intense compared to the smaller forays? Why so many more of Kolonth's foot soldiers this time and only a couple Captains on horseback? What are they up to? Was this to have a battle of a longer duration with more fighting yet to come our way?" Randak shook his head in frustration.

"Perhaps a test of our mettle? Maybe Kolonth is testing our endurance? Is it possible he knows of me and is testing to see what kind of threat we represent now that we are three?" Barak wondered aloud.

"We have lots of questions and few answers. Praise King, though! We were ultimately victorious and the enemy routed, though they seemed to engage in a planned retreat. One thought of already far ahead of time. Do you not think that odd?" Wandarr spoke thoughtfully, looking from her brother to Barak for a response.

"There was a great deal that was strange about that battle my Sister, though we won, somehow it feels like mayhap we did not. Yet here we are. Praise T'var, we survive to fight again, although we did not escape without some bruises and aching muscles. I do think it is time to use some healing ointment on ourselves."

"Agreed Randak, though I just realized what we possess may be the last of it. The Rangdorrian Lands are bereft of it now, thanks to Kolonth's foul doings."

"Yes, we may have to use it sparingly," Randak grew quiet, his face dour and sad, though it went unnoticed by Barak.

"I have no idea what you two are talking about. Do you have some magiks' healing powers or something?" Barak joked. Randak's current disposition caused him to cast a stern glare in Barak's direction, though Barak's obvious discomfort and innocent, *"What did I say wrong?"* look, caused even Randak's mood to lighten and he ended up laughing at Barak's unease.

That evening, the trio sat on the ground rubbing healing ointment on each other's difficult to reach bruises and sore muscles. The ointment, a derivative from plants found in abundance in Randak and Wandarr's homeland was known to work rapidly, not only easing aches and pains but also regenerating damaged skin and combatting fatigue.

Both men had removed their shirts and Barak now rubbed ointment on Randak's sore shoulders. "This medicine is amazing. We have none of this in Vintar, nor have I ever heard of it. What do you call it?"

Originally Barak had thought of positioning himself so he could administer the healing balm to Wandarr, but on reflection, thought it more appropriate for her brother to do that. He was not ready to be so forward quite yet.

"Ointment," laughed Wandarr. "Or healing ointment."

"It goes by many different names," Randak paused as he enjoyed the feeling of the ointment working its way into his shoulders thanks to Barak's thorough application of the balm. "I can feel it working even now easing the soreness in my shoulders. Thank you, my friend."

"My pleasure, Randak. What other names does it get called by?"

"Oh, too many to list. Most just say ointment. Now where does it hurt?" Wandarr laughed for she startled Barak, moving to sit directly behind him, ointment already on her fingers, ready to rub it in to wherever he indicated.

"Relax, Barak, relax! You are so tense!"

"Sorry, you startled me, Wandarr."

"Take a few deep breaths to help yourself relax and tell me where to apply the ointment. It works more effectively and quicker when one is at ease. Would you like me to start with your shoulders and then you can tell me where else to rub it in?"

"Sure, that's fine. I promise to relax and thank you." Barak closed his eyes and concentrated on calming his body as he felt the healing ointment burning deep into his shoulders. He didn't mind the sensation at all. The three slept well that night and even with taking turns to be on watch, all felt refreshed come morning.

Four days later, as they broke fast to eat their morning meal, Randak looked to his companions. "How strange is this now. We are well rested and we have seen no sign of adversaries for these past few days. What do you two make of this? Surely Kolonth knows we track him?"

"I am sure he has not given up on us, Randak. We draw closer to his stronghold with each day."

"Well, I for one, am pleased by this turn of events, though I am cautious of what this might forebode."

"So, Barak, you are a cautious optimist, but not a pessimist like my sometimes dour brother?" Wandarr teased.

"At least the battles have been good practice for me. I really learned a great deal through those marginal skirmishes. You must know the ruin of my homeland still weighs fresh on my mind. Sometimes it's as if any pain I inflict on those responsible lessens my own. And by the way Randak, I don't think you are dour at all! No offence to your sister."

"Why thank you Barak and I feel your pain. I know all too well of which you speak."

"No offense taken, Barak and I said sometimes, not constantly dour."

"So perhaps I am the optimist after all! Though, like Randak, I too wonder what Kolonth's strategy is about. There is something we are missing I think, but I know not what."

"Yes, I agree, pessimism and optimism aside, let's be realistic and not let our guard down."

"Especially now, Brother. Our journey from Barak's Vintar has now brought us to where we are about to cross the border into what's left of our homeland," choking as she declared it, causing Barak to look at both siblings astride their steeds. These two who had quickly become close friends and comrades in arms, freely shed tears and now Barak along with them. He saw Randak's clenched fists and heard his almost inaudible angry whisper, "He will pay."

*   *   *

The trio were not wrong. Kolonth was employing a plan. A strategy in every encounter where his forces engaged them. He wanted not only to measure their might, but to determine how serious of a threat these three might be to him. Most importantly, he needed to know, if they and that damnable *Prophecy of Hope* were one and the same. Kolonth did not like what he was learning. Not at all.

In fact, word spread by the few of Kolonth's forces who had firsthand experience in these forays, that when the trio would do battle to-gether in harmony, the power of T'var upon them manifested such that none could withstand them. Whether this was an excuse for their defeat, a simple lie or only partial truth, these reports bothered Kolonth more than he dared admit.

One of his malformed lackeys whose designation he could not remember and did not care to, had requested to enter the room where Kolonth currently sat, ruminating about next steps in his plans. The being was another failed experiment of the breeding pits but remained sentient enough to provide some useful service. The pitiful creature was obviously nervous, meaning whatever it was about to report on, Kolonth would not like.

Kolonth rose from his chair as the servant drew closer, barking, "What? You have a report?"

The flunky started shaking, fearful of looking into its Master's face.

"Stop quivering and look at me." Kolonth's patience was already at an end. "Report! Tell me what is so important you disturb my thoughts."

"Sss-ssorry master," the creature's fork-like tongue moved in and out of its mouth, causing a hissing noise each time it spoke, which remind-ed Kolonth of the servant's name.

"Ah, Snake, my faithful servant, what delicious news do you bring me?" Kolonth mocked, though the creature mistook the words for encour-agement.

"Thank you, Master, yes, Master, we thought you would want to know, the trio is about to cross the border into the decimated Rangdorrian Lands. They appear to be moving forward towards this stronghold, though are still many days away."

"I see..." Kolonth spoke the words calmly, though fury burned within. "And what do you think of this report, my faithful servant?"

"Oh, Master, I am not wise enough to know these things."

"I asked you what you think, not how wise you are. Tell me."

"I... I...," it stuttered, until blurting out, "It must mean the *Prophecy of Hope* is coming true, I fear. Many of our troops who encountered them and some of your other followers are saying the same. Saying the same." The servant couldn't help itself. "It may be the end! All is lost, Master. If the Prophecy, the trio, if it's them..." It was now in such a fright it couldn't keep itself from rambling, terrified of the wrath it had just raised. "Sorry, Master, it's all true, isn't it? It's all true."

Kolonth was incensed beyond measure, his rage escalating, transforming his face into a dark storm cloud of scorn and fury, his voice the thunder. Snake fell prostrate on the floor, pleading for mercy and forgiveness.

"Oh, Master I am ssss...orry... ss...sorry, Master."

"Truth? Truth? I am your only truth, Snake. I am Truth! Remember that. Not some damnable false prophecy. Not some heroic trio that is doomed to die by my hand. Not a false pretender, nor a myth about Him returning some day. I will make that all come to naught! I will be the true sovereign over all T'varin! Do you understand me, you miserable bag of deformed flesh? I am Truth! Your only Truth. You will obey me. Believe me. Serve me!"

"Oh yes, I shall, Master. You are the Truth. You are all. Sssorry, ssooo sssorry, Master."

"Ah, Snake, thank you, my faithful servant. Remind me, do you have a family?"

"Oh yes, of course, Master. I have twins: a boy and a girl. Almost five years of age now, Master."

"What of your partner? The one who birthed your children?"

"Oh Master, remember, she perished while giving birth to them."

"You live here in this stronghold with them, don't you Snake? Always keeping it ready for me should I choose to visit, don't you?"

"Yes, Master, of course, Master, why do you ask?" As limited as Snake's mental faculties were, it was becoming suspicious of where this line of questioning was going.

"Well, Snake, you say your twins murdered their mother, killed her in childbirth, so don't you think they should have to pay for that? That's only fair isn't it, Snake?"

"Oh no, Master, it wasn't like that. No, not at all, please Master, don't harm…"

"Bring them both to me, I need to feed and I may need a sacrifice for a ritual soon."

Snake thought that at the moment, the only thing worse than his Master's hideous smile was the terrifying hunger in his voice.

"Oh no, Master, I won't do it, I won't! I won't. No, Master, you will not harm my children, I won't let you. I will stop you."

"Stop me!" Kolonth broke out into laughter. "Stop me? You vile, worthless, useless creature!"

Snake rushed at Kolonth determined to do whatever it took to safeguard his children. In this matter, Kolonth was correct; Snake was useless. As soon as Snake was within reach, Kolonth picked him up, stared into his eyes, partially draining his soul, whispering, "You know what Snake? Your children are mine. Not in the way you think I mean, but truly mine. You see, your pathetic partner was anxious to please her Master. She accepted me willingly when I planted my seed within her."

Snake was beside himself, "Please stop teasing, Master. Not true! She would have told me."

"Oh Snake, she couldn't, because I made her forget. That is why she thought the twins were yours. But that was the lie. Her labour broke the spell though. Don't you know why their mother died in childbirth? Not because of the burden of having twins, but because when she knew the truth, she couldn't bear the thought that she would be the one to bring my offspring into the world," Kolonth smile was infuriating.

"No, Master, that's not true, Master," Snake squirmed to free himself in defiance.

Kolonth was enjoying himself too much to even think of letting go. He brought his captive ear's closer, whispering his torment. "Yes Snake, it is all true."

Snake was trembling, attempting to shake his fists, crying, "No, Master, untrue, too cruel, why are you so cruel to me, Master? I have served you loyally. It's not true! They are my childr…"

"No, Snake, they are my children, my… insurance…Snake. Do not fear, for they are not to be sacrificed. But their mother was and now so will you be!"

What was left of Snake's being, curled up inside itself, moaning in fear and agony while Kolonth marched the limp form across the room to the open window and tossed it out, where it landed far below in the protective fires which encircled the stronghold.

Kolonth bellowed to the guards he knew stood outside the room. "Bring me Snake's children! Now! I have need of them. We are going to have a family conference about their father."

Kolonth's hysterical laughter assuaged his anger and motivated the guards to act on his orders without delay. When Kolonth finally stopped laughing, he went back to the window, calmly and deliberately voicing his thoughts to the open air. "It is time to put an end to these three and silence my blathering soldiers before they spread any more fear-mongering rumours. I will tolerate their interference, their existence, no longer. They seek to confront me? They will soon know that I will do whatever it takes to end them and this so-called Prophecy. Lies!! My plans will come to fruition. All of T'varin will be mine and all will bow to me. That is the true prophecy and everything living in T'varin will soon know it! It is time now for Kolonth to act."

He looked over all he could see from his vantage point in the stronghold's tallest tower. He savoured the view of the devastated Rangdorrian Lands and smiled in satisfaction. He glanced at the flames below and then went to greet his guards and the children they offered him.

Kolonth cared not of the cost at which he would achieve his goal, he desired only to have all to himself, he would not hesitate to burn it all into nothingness if T'varin would not yield to him. For an immeasurably long time, he had battled against the Children of Light, the Children of T'var and longer would he still, until it was done.

While Kolonth brooded over his next steps, the three riders approached yet another scene of annihilation that Kolonth had left in his trail of wicked hatefulness.

*   *   *

"We have come a long way from my home of the Roaring Waters," said Barak as he surveyed the desolation of The Rangdorrian Lands before him.

"Yes, and yet much..." began Randak, cut short by the overwhelming squawking of birds flying away in terror as a dark silhouette filled the sky above them, blotting out the light. At the first sign of the shadow, the three slipped softly from their steeds and led them silently into the covering of what few trees grew along their path. The silhouette circled in the sky overhead, skirted over where the riders once were seconds before and then darted back towards the horizon, disappearing from view. The sudden chill upon them left but it was a short time before they dared move again.

"*Averi,*" whispered Wandarr. "Rumours say they are cursed by

Kolonth to live between substance and unbeing. Damned to follow the Evil One's will, lest it be unmade, dissolving into eternal nothingness."

"We should have called it out and fought, not cowered," Randak shook his fist at the sky.

"No, Randak," said Barak. "It is better Kolonth not know we are coming for as long as possible. We might use the element of surprise instead of him always holding the upper hand. Kolonth may suspect our whereabouts but not know them and it is unlikely that the Averi saw us. It looked to be searching for something else. Kolonth's spies are on the alert no doubt, and we must be cautious. Your homeland's Plains are level and wide open, so once on them, we are easily-seen targets."

"Yes, but if we cannot hide, neither can they and we will see as plainly as they do," Randak countered. "I must wonder too, if he established an outpost there near Kol, so close to the borders that he could watch Karnakon fall as he unleashed his army upon that land. It would not surprise me if that were the reason for his bold decision to show himself in that place, in our home! The…"

"Enough of this! If scouts are about, the sooner we reach our destination, the better." Wandarr drove her horse into the open, forcing the surprised Randak and Barak to catch up with her.

The thumping of hooves drowned out all else as the trio pushed on. A trip of three days at their present pace, would take only a day, perhaps a day and a half at most. Their steeds seemed tireless with the King's strength empowering them. They rode relentlessly, stopping only for short breaks, resting when needed.

Day finally broke as they neared their goal. The three had so far encountered no further resistance during their travel but from deep within the centre of the Plains arose a thick black cloud. It choked the air and the biting wind carried a putrid smell.

Unidentifiable groans and cries echoed from somewhere, permeating the air, making it feel like the land itself was constrained and bound in the grip of an indescribable horror. Even the land they travelled over seemed to groan beneath a great burden, though to the trio, it sounded akin to the noise of souls in terrible agony.

"This work must be of Kolonth's doing. This is what blocks the authority of T'var and blinds people to the reality and goodness of the King. This foul smoke born of Kolonth's deceitful dark magiks has them both bound and blinded," said Randak, choking back tears.

"You speak truthfully, my brother," replied Barak. "So, if it is battle Kolonth desires, it is battle Kolonth shall have."

That Kolonth had the audacity to establish an outpost right in Randak and Wandarr's homeland was an afront that caused Randak's anger to burn bright. Determinedly, he raised his Sonsword to the sky in challenge, moving Jip to full gallop toward where they guessed Kolonth maintained his temporary fortress, Barak and Wandarr on their horses thundering close behind. All three were intent on their destiny: bringing about the final reckoning of the most diabolical evil ever to plague T'varin, one even worse than its sire, Manglor.

*   *   *

When the final clash between T'var and Manglor had occurred, Kolonth had been studying more of the black arts in lands far off, territories unknown even to the most educated scholars of Glephas. Eventually Kolonth heard the tales of the confrontation from the accounts told through the generations by those faithful to T'var or T'vari as they were sometimes called. Though he doubted that all the details were accurate and much was likely now myth, grown in the telling over so many years, he believed there to be some core truths in the story.

In this way, he learned of the battle and how his father had been unexpectedly surrounded by adversaries from Astaria, Bjorqar and Vintar as Manglor sought some weapon in some accursed Castle of Crystal. He heard about the appearance of T'var, and the release of some extraordinary power from a weapon which vanquished Manglor and brought about the destruction of the Castle. He concluded, correctly, that the weapon was undoubtedly the very thing that his father sought. He also resolved not to make the same error as his father; he would not be taken by surprise.

From the day of Manglor's disappearance, in truth perhaps long before, Kolonth plotted. Since learning that Vintar, Astaria, and Bjorqar had been involved in the murder of his father, Kolonth held a deep hatred for those lands and determined each of them and their peoples would one day pay dearly for that affront.

His ultimate goal included the absolute rule of all T'varin and whatever lay beyond. Kolonth decided that one day, all his world, sky above, ground beneath and whatever other worlds there might be, would be under his heel. He would bide his time for thousands of years if necessary. For though his mother was mortal, as Manglor's offspring, Kolonth aged slowly, enjoying almost eternal longevity.

Kolonth interred himself in the shadowy recesses of the land of Mangloth. Occasionally he came out discreetly, disguised through his magiks to visit other lands. He would learn the weakness of their leaders and the vulnerabilities of their domains, formulating his tactics for their eventual conquest. On some of these forays, he would gain the trust of those to whom he pledged a reward. To a select few, he would share his true identity. He positioned his spies carefully and those who might chance to be disloyal, he dispatched without mercy.

Back in the safety of shadowy Mangloth, he concentrated his efforts on building his forces, drilling his recruits and perfecting his obscene magiks. The bulk of his soldiers were composed from some the youngest and strongest prisoners whom he ably bent to his will. Also kept in his ranks were darker, foul creations from Manglor's time. For long ages, they had remained buried in the silent subterranean spaces beneath Mangloth, fearing the light. Yet, they would heed Kolonth's call when it came. The creatures understood that the call signalled that the darkness they thrived in would begin to spread across all the lands, allowing them to finally roam freely above ground.

Of course, Kolonth believed that all peoples from the lands he would conquer, such as frozen T'barth's close neighbour Karnakon, would join his forces. They would take the brand of the circled hexagon and swear allegiance to Kolonth. Since so many had forsaken loyalty and love to T'var long ago, taking the mark would not hold the same meaning as it would have for their ancestors. To them, the brand was nothing more than a mark signifying they made the smartest decision and joined the side for which victory seemed inevitable.

These peoples would become totally enslaved husks of flesh, void of all but subservience to Kolonth desires, his will taking shape within them as a vicious bloodlust. It forced them to pursue an end to their internal pain by foisting the same on others for relief, a powerful motivation to drive them. The evil inside finding form, or more accurately, deformity outside. Building his army inside the ancient abode of Mangloth, Kolonth employed unholy strategies to recruit and enlarge his army and only his most trusted servants would he bring into his confidences. Gradually his lust for conquest reached its zenith and he prepared to unleash his designs on the unsuspecting world of T'varin.

Kolonth recognized that this could mean one day challenging T'var Himself. He would deal with that when the time came. He doubted T'var would ever show Himself. At least two millennia had passed now since the vanquishing of Manglor and no appearances from T'var had happened since. At least, none Kolonth was aware of. Stories persisted and there were always fools claiming visions or sometimes prophecies. Only deluded myths as far as Kolonth was concerned. Though there still lingered a slight doubt that T'var would let such iniquity as Kolonth proposed, sweep across all T'varin.

Kolonth's craving for more increased, as did his power. Each feeding the other in a never- ending cycle, finally securing its outlet in Kolonth's insatiable appetite for the lives of his foes. It drove him, making him more ravenous than Manglor. He imagined himself to be a god, never to be defeated. He would do more than take his rightful vengeance against the world that murdered his father. In memory of Manglor, Kolonth planned to make T'varin over into his own image and all of it would bear the imprint of the circled hexagon, the Mark of Manglor, now Kolonth's.

CHAPTER TWO
BALZERA

Kolonth viewed the scorched and smoke-encircled plains of Randak and Wandarr's homeland from his temporary stronghold. The fortress had been established during the invasion of The Rangdorrian Lands, strategically situated near the border town of Kol and within it, Kolonth now dedicated his time to meditating and brooding over how he would annihilate his foes and nullify the Prophecy.

Much as he was loathe to admit it, the Prophecy bothered him. He had not come so far, achieved so much, to risk all taken from his grasp by three of the so-called King's misguided fools.

"I will be supreme yet. I will rule over decimation and destruction, chaos and confusion, for my insatiable hunger sustains no limits and I must feed," he announced to the mindless servants around him, waiting to do his bidding.

"Four realms remain to be conquered now that my armies have conquered the first three. My emissaries did their preliminary work well; the fools were too blind to realize how badly they were deceived. The remaining lands will no doubt succumb to my iron hand quickly; their peoples carted off to my prisons, destinies they created for themselves by their deluded disbelief in T'var, ripe for the moulding, easily bent to my will."

He carried on with his ranting, his servants understanding nothing that he was saying.

"These, these so-called warriors *cannot* be tolerated. I will own this world in spite of the cursed meaningless Prophecy. This world…yes, of course!"

A malevolent but innovative thought crossed Kolonth's mind.

"The bothersome *Prophecy of Hope* is from this world and this world alone. What if…what if I open a gateway to another world and summon one from elsewhere? One who will destroy the troublesome threesome once and for all? A being such as that, bound to my will, may very well be the breaker of any fool Prophecy, bringing about the deaths of those three and the certainty of my ascension!

"Yes! Genius! Slaves, make haste! Bring me wood for a fire. Hurry! Much preparation is required before the midnight hour. The hour of doom for these three children of T'var comes."

*   *   *

The day moved on into evening with Barak, Randak and Wandarr galloping at a quickening pace deeper into the centre of The Rangdorrian Lands, the dense smoke encircling the landscape. It choked them, filling their nostrils with its foul odour, causing the horses to decrease their momentum and struggle against proceeding any significant distance. Kolonth had often employed spells to rapidly escape from his strongholds and they feared a similar tactic, wresting a head-on battle from them again.

"Do you think the monstrous coward may have already left the fortress we seek? We have been much delayed after all." Randak's impatience could be heard in his voice.

"The devastation he wrought in our homeland, T'barth and Karnakon have made them uninhabitable perhaps for him as well. Wherever he goes, the King will lead us to him. No place the horror may hide where we will not find him and bring about his demise." Wandarr's words were strong, her tone adamant.

"Maybe so, but these vapours choke the life out of everything, including us. Feel how the body weakens and senses dull. Now impossible to tell time of day, so veiled is the sky. My bones tell me we must be about the eleventh hour of the night, so long have we ridden."

"I agree, Barak. What good fortune is this? The fumes and fog are beginning to clear. Look! The night sky begins to be visible through the haze. Afar off, the path clears and see, there in the distance, vague outlines of the foothills leading to our enemy's fortification. The King's favour is indeed upon us."

"Are you sure, dear Brother? Are you certain this is the King's doing and not some new treachery of our foe designed to put us off our guard?"

"You are overcautious, Sister! What else but this be the King's doing? Surely Kolonth would not give us an unobstructed route to his own shelter."

"Perhaps, perhaps," said Wandarr. "But I, for one, will not throw caution to the winds."

"Nor shall any of us. Do you agree, Randak?"

"Yes, Barak, none of us. Onward."

"Your bones were right, Barak. The sky confirms it."

"Yes, we near the dark hour when Kolonth is rumoured to wield more power."

"A moonless sky tonight," added Wandarr, "This is not a good omen. I would be content with more light to guide our way. Kolonth relishes the deep darkness; it makes him strong. Many say that if he is not soon stopped, one day the stars themselves will fall into his black void and all will be an endless dark abyss."

"Quietly, Sister. Careful now! Our Sonswords flicker with the amber light of forewarning. Let us stop and pause here. Nothing appears yet, but these swords tell no falsehoods," said Randak.

"We detect nothing of import as of yet," complained Barak.

"You do not notice danger, child, because it is not yet upon you," an imposing voice spoke, shocking them all.

A Starborn Sentinel stood before them, outfitted for combat, tall and overpowering. For a moment they all stood speechless again in awe at the resplendent stature of this servant of their King.

Randak fell to one knee in respect, found his voice and asked, "What news, Herald of T'var?"

"Be vigilant, for your adversary seeks to bring about your end by breaking the *Prophecy of Hope*."

"Breaking the Prophecy? How can Kolonth accomplish such a feat?" Wandarr asked. "They are the unbreakable words of T'var, immoveable as the King Himself. And why speak this news to us, Sentinel?"

The Starborn Sentinel astonished them all by saying, "You three are the Prophecy he plots to fracture. *You* are the fulfillment of the Prophecy."

They looked to one another, uncertain of the accuracy of the Sentinel's words. Faithful T'vari, followers of T'var, they knew the Prophecy well but they had never before considered applying it to themselves.

The Sentinel acted oblivious to their reaction. "You must take heed."

"Does this mean at last we face Kolonth himself?" asked Barak.

"Understand only this: what Kolonth plans to unleash upon you, he does not fully understand himself. He schemes to bring about your undoing. There is no more time; the threat is nigh upon you. At Kolonth's hour of greatest empowerment, his plan will unfold."

The Sentinel continued, "These words granted to me, I now give you. Barak, look well to your left and remember, the only way out is through. Randak, be wary the venom of unworldly fangs. Wandarr, remember the jewel you hold, the one given to you long ago. Farewell and may the blessing of T'var be your strength."

When it finished speaking, the Starborn Sentinel began to shimmer with an unearthly luminescence, transforming into only light alone, until swallowed up into the shadows of the surrounding night.

"Wait," cried Randak. "What is this poison you warn of?"

"No use," sighed Barak. "Gone. Cryptic as usual. Do you think they have to take a course to learn how to be like that or are they just naturally that way?"

Randak tried to ignore the feeble effort at humour, an offering to lighten the mood, though Barak could see half a smile forming, before Randak's tone turned serious. "Be respectful of T'var's messenger, Barak. Though you are correct, for as usual, we were given only what was needful to know. We must consider his words. Barak, he told you to look well to the left, and his ominous portent to me was to beware the venom of unworldly fangs, whatever that means, and to you, Sister, the Sentinel spoke of the jewel in your belt: the Orbstar."

Wandarr did not respond for she was now deep in thought. The Orbstar was antiquated, much older than their foe; she remembered the odd day long ago when the Orbstar had come into her possession, or perhaps she in its.

Wandarr had been walking through the forest glade near the home she shared with Randak, singing songs to the King. She was young and her heart was light. Kolonth's reach had not yet extended far and even though her parents had gone missing a number of years ago, at the moment, all else seemed safe and peaceful in her world.

She paused at the sound of snapping branches and hurried running, but she saw no one. Before her eyes, a mist began to form, gradually solidifying into a man. The man was wizened and had long, silver, curly hair and wrinkled hands with oddly shaped fingers which ended in uneven dirty nails. He was dressed in a ragged grey robe which was dripping with dampness from the mist out of which he stepped. He had an air of fear, of someone who was being hunted. The man noticed Wandarr and hesitated, until she finally spoke.

"What trickery? Who are you? Where have you come from, Mist-Man? Why are you so frightened?"

"Hush, young maiden," he said. "Time is short. *It* follows me through the *tunnels of time*, seeking what no one should possess."

"What do you have which this *It* desires so greatly?" asked Wandarr. "Do you speak of a person?"

"No time, no time. Though you, yes, you are the one to keep it. I do not know why, but I am compelled to give the jewel to you. This is meant to be. It be true, I swear."

"Have what? What do you speak of, Mist-Man?" Wandarr asked, feeling uneasy at the thought of having something another desperately sought.

"The Orbstar. Some will outside of myself compels me to give it to you. By the Emperor, this is a certainty. To you this must befall. Safeguard the Orbstar well; the fate of worlds can be affected by its potency. The Orbstar is old. Not from my world, perhaps not from yours either, I would warrant, but perhaps… No, we have little time for explanations."

Wandarr was mesmerized.

"Listen well. This is no mere bauble. It is ageless, from the depths of time, beyond time. Ere many worlds were ever made, when the *Gates of Eternity* were being raised, is where its origins lie. It was later lost in a Great War, when a desperate unholy Rebel warred against his Emperor. It fell from the heavens, but enough of old histories, we must leave this place before I am discovered."

"Let us go to my dwelling," offered Wandarr, eager to find out more from this eccentric being. If only Randak were home and not away in T'barth, perhaps he could shed the light of truthfulness on this stranger's tale. "It is just a short walk down the path and yonder past, er ... I do not know your, name! What should I call you?"

"You may call me Balzera."

"Balzera," repeated Wandarr. "Such an unusual name."

They began walking away from the clearing, where Balzera had first appeared, when he suddenly stopped.

"No time to go much further. The Orb tells me my foe draws closer. It must have tracked me through the Orb's lingering afterglow. It's left a trail for the creature to follow. There is much yet to tell you, but my pursuer is too near."

"I don't understand how you sense these things, but we will find a hiding place through those rocks, on the other side of that small waterfall. I use it often for solitude and to speak to my King or when I need a respite from my elder brother," said Wandarr with a smile.

Running towards safety, Balzera shot Wandarr a puzzled glance.

"Speak to your King? Are you a princess?"

"No," laughed Wandarr. "But I am one of His children."

"This King you speak of is your father?"

"Yes, but not in the way you mean, but..."

"You speak in riddles, sweet child," interrupted Balzera. He thought for a moment, "Unless the King you speak of is-? Would this be possible?

By the Emperor's Throne...no these are too many thoughts to sift through and our time runs short. Enough of my curiosity, for we are at your rocks. No need for the cave yet. I must teach you of the Orbstar."

"Yes," said Wandarr, fascinated by this peculiar old man. She thought, *"He acts confused, and yet is totally in control."*

"You said the Orbstar was not from our world. I suppose neither are you."

"No, the Orbstar is one of three lost in the war I spoke of. The ancient tales say that one was recovered and dwells in the courts of the Emperor secure from harm, guarded by the *Warriors of Eternity*. Two went missing, this one came by various means into my hands. The third one is still missing, thought stolen by the Rebel himself, but this was never confirmed as truth or falsehood.

"The Orbstars are made of an imperishable glass substance, forged in the *Fires of Infinity*. They were made to reflect the glories of *The Eternal* and of *The Infinite*, but they would only do this work when kept in their proper place in the Emperor's domain. They gathered the light of stars from all the Emperor's creations and when triggered by touch or perhaps also thought, in sequence, they would spread their brilliance across all time and space, bringing music and harmony to the heavenly spheres. The intended outcome: all creations, would give glory to the Emperor for the immensity of his majestic works made manifest. Such was their original purpose and place."

Wandarr was enraptured by the stranger's tale.

"The Rebel became enamoured with their beauty. He grew jealous of all attention and adoration being given to the Emperor. He decided to take the Orbstars and twist them to his own design, believing that channelling their might would grant him the power to overthrow the Emperor.

"The Rebel convinced others to join him, through lies, deceit and promises of immense rewards. Believing his falsehoods, the others attacked the Emperor's loyal followers and sought to wrest the Orbstars from their keeping place.

"So swift and brutal was the attack, that two of the Orbstars were stolen. The might of three Orbstars together, if unleashed, would have shaken the foundations of The Eternal. This was not to be. The Emperor, seeing both the clash and the intent of the Rebel's heart, scattered his enemies and placed an impenetrable shield of his own making around the remaining Orbstar that none but Himself would be able to remove."

"Why did he not prevent the loss of the other two as wel,l if he was so powerful?" Wandarr wondered. "Perhaps your Emperor is not as formidable as our King?"

"Who may know the ways of the Emperor? Rest assured he had his reasons, including that this precious jewel would now be coming to you," replied Balzera.

"We have a similar story, of a Terror called Manglor who, ages past, rebelled against the King and was defeated by the King's own ..." began Wandarr.

"Perhaps young maiden, my Emperor and the King of which you speak are one and the same," interrupted Balzera.

"What do you..."

"No time to explain the foolish thoughts of an old man. Hear well and learn. Outside of their natural placement, the Orbstars do not work as originally intended, though they do have other uses. Each holds different powers, although I am acquainted with only this one. Watch as I hold the Orbstar in my hand."

He reached in the folds of his garment and Wandarr gasped, for Balzera had vanished from view. Only a small trace of the same mist she had seen when he first arrived floated in mid-air.

"I am here," Balzera said, appearing behind Wandarr. "Other applications exist as well, though I have uncovered only a few. One is the ability to travel between worlds and times and it is how I have come here. Another is the Orbstar's fire, which brings forth the ability to bring down..."

"How do you journey between times and locales? What will its fire do? What other functions do you speak of?" Wandarr asked, excited and unable to contain her questions.

Balzera had no time to respond as a flash of blinding light and a thunderous roar knocked Wandarr off her feet. The Orbstar fell from Balzera's hand and rolled towards the place where she lay. Wandarr saw it and driven by some instinct, reached out, grasped it and held it close to her, trying to conceal herself in the shadow of the trees. She was actually well hidden, for the moment she held the Orbstar she had become invisible to anyone else. Unaware that her own presence was undetectable by others, she viewed the terrifying event unfolding before her.

"Did you think to shroud yourself from me forever? You will not outrun me, reckless magus. Now I have you and my prize: its scent led me to you both."

There was a creature towering over Balzera by at least four feet. Its body made entirely of flame, except for eyes of deep black in what passed for a face and two long fangs hanging down from its mouth. The fangs shone white in the glow of the creature's fiery body, which was composed of red, white and blue fire.

Despite the intense heat and awful stench of burning flesh, Wandarr stayed perfectly still. She had not moved since the monstrosity had spoken.

"What should I do?" She could barely distinguish Balzera's voice above the monster's screeching laugh.

"Yes, demon, you have me," shouted Balzera. "Yet you do need me to tell you how to use the jewel. Employing it improperly will result in your own obliteration."

"Stupid mortal! I should fling you to your death, but I will keep you alive until you tell me that which I must know. Afterwards, I will slowly consume your remains in my flames."

"What is Balzera saying?" thought Wandarr. *"He knows he dropped the Orbstar...or did he purposely toss it in my direction? Is he trying to distract the demon long enough so I will be able to somehow use the Orbstar against it?"*

Wandarr felt the monster looking right at her, almost right through her. Awareness dawned. Of course, it was looking right through her because it could not see her. She finally realized that the Orbstar had made her vanish as Balzera had said it could do. *"What should she do now?"*

Wandarr had no chance to do anything. The demon shrieked a profane sound and a wind whipped up which engulfed both the demon and Balzera in a whirlwind of dust and leaves. It started at their feet and rose until both of them were caught up in the swirling maelstrom. Wandarr experienced the force of the vortex as it passed by her, so she clutched the Orbstar tightly with both hands and closed her eyes. When the sound of the wind had stopped, she opened them again.

All was calm, with no sign of Balzera or the creature of flame. In fact, as the only one who had witnessed this whole event, she wondered at first if perhaps it may have been naught but a daydream. Except that Wandarr held the proof in her hand: the Orbstar. With the strangers gone, she took time to examine it.

It appeared to be about the size of a nicely grown apple, although she swore that when Balzera first showed it to her it looked much larger in his hands, more like the size of a fully ripe grapefruit. It was round, smooth and warm to the touch, transparent much like glass, though it was not any type of glass Wandarr recognized. It was thick and solid and felt unbreakable. Yet Wandarr swore that when she peered into it, she could see a glowing fire in the shape of a star contained within.

"How odd," she thought. *"The Orbstar feels both heavy and light. It is at times smaller and sometimes larger in my hands too. How is that even possible?"*

Looking around to confirm that no one else was near, Wandarr sat down and studied the Orbstar longer. After a time, she gave up, as nothing new or illuminating came of it. Even its internal fire seemed to have dwindled with only a very small portion of red still visible if Wandarr looked intently enough. She carefully placed it inside the pocket of her tunic and began her walk home, her mind filled with a multitude of questions, to which she thought she would never have the answers.

Afterward, Wandarr carried the gem with her always. She confided in no one and never attempted to use it. At times, she kept it safely tucked in the pouch of her belt in a discreet pocket she had specially sewn and reinforced to hold this other-worldly gift.

When her brother Randak returned from his mining expedition in T'barth, she held her secret no longer. She told him of her bizarre experience and of the Orbstar. Randak had agreed that Wandarr had been wise not to use it and to keep it secret. After she told him of her extraordinary adventure, he said, "Be confident, my Sister, the King keeps a purpose for this which we may not divine now, but one He will reveal when the time comes. If the account Balzera told is true..."

"I believe so; he was sincere. He would not have risked his life as he did, if he wasn't."

"I do not mean to doubt him, Sister," Randak was thoughtful. "I merely mean, if the tale is true, though he did not hear it firsthand, this *Orbstar* may in time be of aid against the evil whispered to be now arising, determined to sweep across all lands of our world. Only time and the King will tell. I wonder though, is it possible our King and Balzera's Emperor are one? The Orbstar, could it be?"

"What, my brother? Could it be what?" asked Wandarr.

"'Tis nothing, my sister, nothing at all."

As much as Wandarr would press him, Randak would say no more.

CHAPTER THREE
QUAD RAZAK

Shrouded in the layers of his red and black hooded outer cloak, Kolonth stood inside the circled hexagon that had been drawn and painted on the floor of this particular room in his outpost. The fortress stood defiant, brazenly situated in The Rangdorrian Lands, not far from neighbouring Karnakon, Kolonth now master of both.

His thick and numerous robes, black upon black, were worn underneath his outer vestment. How many was difficult to say, as the garments themselves vainly attempted to give form and substance to a persona, already mostly shadow. The outermost robe did manage to give a defined shape to the form and it was emblazoned with the insignia of the circled hexagon. It also provided cover for its master's grim face – one that looked wizened, shrivelled and cracked as a result of delving too deep and too often in forbidden magiks and mysteries which had taken their unnatural toll. A face that was usually covered and only uncloaked for Kolonth's most favoured victims, the stubborn and strong-willed ones who struggled the most before giving in to his will. Notably and not unusually, these were often T'vari, the loyal followers of T'var.

Within the circle, the fiery-red lines of the six-sided hexagon intersected the circular ring of icy cold blue. An ancient symbol appeared, a ward designed to protect the one making an incantation and assure control over the entity summoned. Kolonth learned this black art long ago, only now he planned to use his knowledge as never before. The fire lit, burned rapidly, surrounding the diagram. To the fire he turned his attention, while his robes reflected the glow of the hungry flames.

Kolonth dismissed his lackeys. The window in the tower room opened to allow the smoke from the fire billow out and mix with the fog surrounding the fortress.

"The time is now," he said. "The incantation will take one minute of the midnight hour."

So saying, he raised his gnarled hands, bony fingers outstretched towards the fire. He began to wail in uneven, rhythmic tones, his voice rising with shouts and quieting to whispers, at times speaking in his own tongue and alternating to the languages of shadows, long forgotten, forsaken in obscurity.

"Depths of the deepest darkness,

Time beyond time,

Worlds afar,

Worlds both dark and darker,

Mangloth nir dolot tan engorgeflit.

By the power of the ancient wrath

And the evil between the voids,

Creatinsh vorleovt mekeole.

By the dark powers through and past the veils which separate and bind,

From netherworld dimensions,

Ajun bratnes telinwer.

I SUMMON THEE,

I SUMMON THEE, CHAOS AND CALAMITY ABIDING,

DEMON BIRTHED OF BLOOD AND FIRE

QUAD RAZAK, I CALL THEE NOW, I COMMAND AND THOU MUST OBEY.

SCUGOL MISHRAK INTONALEVARGATAON,

DEATH HERALD, YOU NOW MUST COME TO ME!"

From fire and smoke, an enormous form took shape in the centre of the circled hexagon. It emerged from the flames until its height reached almost to the ceiling of the room. Its eyes blazed black, the body all aflame. The mouth visible only by two gleaming white fangs jutting out from massive jaws. The reek of something unholy burning filled the room.

"Who summons I, Death Herald, Scourge of All, from The Else When?"

"I, Kolonth, have summoned thee from beyond. Kolonth, servant to the darkness of Manglor. I have imprinted my mark on you, the mark of the circled hexagon binds your will to mine, so that you must obey my commands. Go now I bid thee, go to the Plains of Rangdorr, to the place where the fog clears. You will find three warriors there. Destroy them and then return to the depths from whence I called you till I require your services again."

"I am compelled to comply, Kolonth of Manglor. Though you should know this: I am no mere servant, to come and go at your bidding. Though I will do your will, be mindful that there is always a cost, and you *will* provide recompense."

Kolonth smiled at the empty threat.

Without hesitation, Quad Razak sped from the chamber. Only Kolonth, his laughter echoing in the empty hall, remained. With a wave of his hand, the fire went out and Kolonth marched from the room with a victor's stride. He had not gone far when one of his misshapen servants approached and fearfully relayed an urgent message. Kolonth was both pleased and angry. Pleased at what he now learned, but furious as to why his Averi, carrying such vital information, was delayed on its way back to Mangloth.

Disgusted, he picked the trembling creature up with one hand, forcing it to stare into his eyes as he drained its life force out until only an empty shell remained. Though it was for all intents quite dead, for his own amusement, Kolonth snapped the creature's neck with a satisfying crunch, letting the body fall to the floor commenting, "It would have burned with the rest anyway."

Kolonth's hunger satisfied, he called for others to aid him in making the necessary preparations for his return to Mangloth. He expected that even before he reached his own domain, he would learn of Quad Razak's victory. The so-called *Prophecy of Hope* and its *Warriors Three* would trouble him no more.

As Kolonth rode his ebony horse at the fastest pace possible, staying in front of the forces marching back to Mangloth, he raged internally about his Averi. He had been so preoccupied with dispatching Quad Razak to eliminate the three pests, he had not even sensed his Averi's injury when it happened. Whoever was responsible would pay dearly for the harm done to his pet.

Even though Kolonth drove his steed at the fastest pace possible, Generals following just behind and Captains with whips to keep the troops moving quickly spread throughout the marching soldiers, his thoughts were preoccupied, thinking back to how his relationship with the Averi had developed. For there existed only one exception to Kolonth's hatred of all things: The Averi.

Creatures originally created by Manglor, or at least things he attempted to create. A mixture of magiks and unnatural breeding, Manglor's goal was to design an army of serpentine warrior creatures capable of flight and the breath of flame. His vision was to breed hundreds, even thousands of these to cover all of T'varin. They would be his sentinels and his advance force, ever ready to follow his commands.

Unfortunately, most did not survive past birth. A few lasted perhaps two or even five years but only a handful made it to adulthood. Only one, a smaller one, now quite old and weak, survived into the time of Kolonth. A paltry two others survived long enough to mate and have offspring; considered the last surviving Averi, the other older one dismissed from thought since no one believed it would live much longer.

Tired of the failures, Manglor forewent any future experiments, directing the young Kolonth, not yet fully into adulthood, to tend to the newly-born creature. It would give his progeny something to do while Manglor attended to his quest. After all, the creature would probably die early like all the rest; a fine method of hardening the boy's heart with loss.

For some inexplicable reason, the young Kolonth became attached to this creature. With Manglor detached, indifferent and departing so often, Kolonth felt as much of an orphan as the Averi. Their common loneliness forged a unique bond between them. Kolonth actually developed a tenderness for the creature, a pet he could call his own. The two became inseparable.

Kolonth believed the creature had at least a rudimentary intelligence, or perhaps a higher intellect. His belief was confirmed when one day the creature spoke his name. It spoke rarely, and when it did, its words were few, yet it caused the connection between them to grow even stronger. Sometimes Kolonth disregarded his father's commands and during Manglor's absences, secretly rode the Averi in flight, though never beyond the bounds of Mangloth.

As Kolonth aged, he truly did become more like his father, full of hate and loathing for all T'varin, yet the Averi remained that one thing in his life for which he always felt a deep connection. One observing them together might even dare to say love. Contrary to Manglor's expectations, under Kolonth's continued and affectionate ministrations, the creature did not die prematurely like the rest of its kind but thrived and lived on.

Surprisingly, so did the older Averi. It was if the new one surviving beyond all expectations caused the other to rally. The two Averi took to each other, the older one taking on the role of a protective caring mentor in some fashion. By no means did the older have the same bond with the Averi as Kolonth did, but the two were connected and could often be seen together in each other's lairs. Although Kolonth did not care and was relatively dismissive of it, the two had become friends.

It was only later in his adulthood, as Kolonth's heart turned darker, that the Averi matched him in turn. Earning his master's love and affection now meant the Averi must follow its master's lead. Its innocence lost, what was modelled for it became its way of life too; the way of destruction and death.

By having his Averi and occasionally the older one as well fly randomly across the skies of T'varin at various times, sometimes frequently, Kolonth wisely propagated the belief that there were multiple Averi patrolling the skies, seeking out prey; a way of instilling fear and worry in a land that would one day be his own.

*   *   *

Reaching their destination, Wandarr, Barak and Randak dismounted from their steeds. They waited in sombre silence.

Finally, Barak spoke, attempting to break the quiet. "The hour of darkness approaches. All is still, though it is an uneasy calm."

"Yes, even now, the warrior's star reaches its highest point," said Randak pointing to the sky. "Yet there is no sign of any foe. Maybe the messenger misspoke and our Enemy changed his…"

"I think not," interrupted Wandarr. "Both of you, look west to the foothills and witness the distant red glow moving fast and towards us."

"Yes, it is as though a fire is moving on a path to where we stand and coming with great speed. Look! The fire grows in size as it draws nearer. Let us mark well the warnings given us. Stand firm comrades, the battle is about to be joined! We shall-"

Barak never finished his sentence as Quad Razak's form fell upon them. So overwhelmed by the intense heat, they could barely breathe in its midst.

"What ho, creature of flame! Whom do you serve?" Randak said at last, finding his voice.

"Quad Razak is no one's lackey, impertinent one," bellowed the creature.

"I wonder what Kolonth would say to that, flame demon!" shouted Wandarr above the din of the creature's cackling. She thought for a moment that the voice sounded familiar but could not place it and instead focused on the impending fight.

"Kolonth may think what he pleases. He may use me as long as it serves my purposes. Who dares question Death Herald?"

The creature turned to face Wandarr. Until then, she had only glimpsed its side profile from where she stood, but as the creature turned to view her straight on, Randak thought a look of recognition crossed his sister's face. From her horrified expression he surmised he guessed right. She wore the shocked look of one reliving a nightmare from a time long past.

"Randak, it's Balz-" began Wandarr.

She had no time to complete her statement for Quad Razak raised an arm of flame and hurled a great fireball right into the centre of them. They scarcely were able to get out of its way, their horses bolting in all directions to avoid the searing heat.

Though all three were agile enough, the fireball's fierce heat still singed their clothing. Randak, somersaulting to the right of the flame, now stood firm, Sonsword drawn, gasping for breath. Mindful of the earlier warning, he eyed the creature's fangs, considering how best to deal with them; they appeared to be the only solid part of the creature.

Barak, not so fortunate, rolled in the opposite direction of Randak, only to find himself face down in the dirt, his foot caught underneath a tree root. He remained stuck there in spite of his best efforts to pull himself free. His Sonsword, which had tumbled from his hand as he fell, lay just beyond his reach.

If Barak could only stretch an arm far enough, he might be able to grasp the edge of the sword to bring it closer, then he could hack himself out of his dilemma. He knew he should attempt it before the creature discovered his predicament. The intensity of the heat caused him to perspire as if the sweat on his brow was on fire and he felt faint. Fighting it off, he struggled to turn his head to see what was happening with his comrades.

Wandarr, somewhat sickened from shock, was the farthest from the fireball, the heat affecting her the least. Out of all three, she kept her senses sharp in spite of the memory that the creature had brought up. When she saw the creature hurling the flame, she leapt aside and in the same moment, placed her hand on the Orbstar which was safely tucked in her belt. Wandarr vanished.

Barak could see none of this. He tried again to get a hold on the edge of his Sonsword.

"Is this all there is to my left?" he thought as he recalled the Sentinel's admonition. *"And what is the way out? I am a fool. This is not what I expected*

at all."

Barak found himself drifting in and out of consciousness. *"Left, look to your left...look well to your left..."* The words came from far away. *"What did they mean?"* He fought to clear his mind. He looked to his left.

Meantime, Quad Razak addressed Randak with contempt. "I will suffer you pitiful fools no more. Prepare to be consumed in my fires!"

Randak wondered if his Sonsword would do any harm to the fiery body of the creature. Even if able to withstand the heat to draw close enough to pass his weapon through, he wasn't sure that any damage would be done.

"Would the flames simply part and reform and the Sonsword, powerful as it might be, somehow survive? What about the fangs? They look solid enough. Perhaps they hold some secret to the creature's demise." All these thoughts raced through Randak's mind as he attempted to form an attack strategy. He glanced around to see no sign of Barak or Wandarr. Alone with this self-proclaimed Death Herald, he worried that its name would prove all too true.

Wandarr noticed Randak's and Barak's dilemmas the moment she touched the Orbstar. She did not know if she had enough time to go to the aid of them both and she felt her heart drop. Her instinct was to rescue her brother first, but when she saw what easy prey Barak was, the thought of him being injured, or worse, summoned up a cold dread in her spirit and she felt a terrible pang of fear. A trained warrior, she reluctantly ignored her feelings and refocused her thoughts. She wondered if by some chance, Quad Razak could detect her scent.

"Did he sense I held the Orbstar? Is this what lured him?"

She certainly recognized him; he was the same creature which had disappeared with Balzera those many years ago. Perhaps it wasn't her, but rather the presence of the Orbstar which attracted him. Wandarr remembered how the creature had spoken to Balzera of having sensed the jewel as he tracked him.

"Did the creature somehow detect the Orbstar again? More importantly, how do I use the Orbstar against this foul thing and save Randak and Barak? A distraction perhaps? Enough of standing still!"

Wandarr began to move towards Barak, but her attention shifted, pulled away by a scream of pain. She spun around to watch great drops of blistering hot venom shooting from Quad Razak's fangs, showering around Randak. He did his best to dodge them, but one hit his arm and another seared his pant leg.

Unable to stifle his cry of pain as the venom burned through, deeper and deeper into his arm, Randak felt the inside of his body ablaze and found himself immobile. He stayed still, waiting for Quad Razak to strike the killing blow. In spite of his unbearable pain, he rejoiced that he would be dining at the King's table in moments.

"Now, insignificant warrior, your time is at hand!" shouted Quad Razak, feeling victory within his grasp. "Death and you shall become acquainted."

Randak experienced severe pain, but also anger. Anger at being immobile and incensed at this turn of events. His pain-fuelled fury grew until he shouted back at Quad Razak, amazed at the strength of his own voice.

"Even be you the herald of my death, fiery one, understand this: the King I serve is Deathslayer. Death strove in vain to imprison Him and failed. I care not what your world calls you or from which domain you come; you pale in insignificance compared to He who stormed into its ancient corridors and slew Death itself. I fear you not."

"Strong words, little warrior! Let us see if you are as brave as you claim, or if you will scream some more in the torment of my flames," laughed Quad Razak.

"ENOUGH!" came a shout out of nowhere. "Your time is at hand, vile one and no one else's."

Randak smiled at the sound of his sister's voice.

"What sorcery is this? Who speaks to me so? I hear the voice but distinguish not its point of origin."

Quad Razak whirled around exasperated. Something tugged at its memory, an uncomfortable inkling of a possibility long dismissed.

"I possess something you desire, flaming one." Wandarr prayed she was not risking too much.

"Yes, you do. I sense the gem now. Though Kolonth's magiks' weavings rob me of full perception, I recognize the scent. I thought I detected something vaguely familiar amongst you. I had! The Orbstar! Give it to me!" it screamed. Then, more gently, "Give me the Orbstar and I will spare this comrade of yours."

"You lie!" Wandarr randomly moved about to throw it off of where she actually was and also to distract its attention from Randak.

"You deceive. For were I to give this to you, you would take it indeed, yes and undoubtedly slay us all anyway, without hesitation."

"You read me well mortal." Infuriated, Quad Razak tried to determine her whereabouts. "Now give me the Orbstar or I will pry it from your charred remains."

"How can you take what you cannot catch?" Wandarr prayed this was the case and that Quad Razak could not determine her location.

"I warn you, do not taunt me. I will make your death painful and long, rather than instantaneous like your friends. Enough! I will put an end to all of you now. Wait! Where is the third one?"

Between his lust for the Orbstar, his frustration at Wandarr's invisibility and not seeing the third warrior, who a moment ago had been visible and trapped in a tree root, Quad Razak's rage intensified. In his madness, he began to question if this other one owned an Orbstar too and used it to vanish as well.

Wandarr understood that time would be short before the creature reacted with greater violence. Randak seemed immobilized and what of Barak? Quad Razak was right. He was nowhere to be seen.

Barak had found their salvation to his left. Beside him, in the ground, a little pool of water bubbled. A pool that had no business being there. With one valiant last stretch Barak threw himself forward and grasped the hilt of the Sonsword with the tips of his fingers. He clawed it to himself, and while the sounds of the clash between Randak and Quad Razak carried on, he hacked himself free, and rolled over to the pool.

"What is this doing here?" he thought. "So out of place, but..."

He dunked his head in the icy waters to escape the extreme heat still being generated from Quad Razak. The moment he plunged his head in, unexpectedly, the rest of him followed. Barak fell right through the pool. He maintained sense enough to hold his breath but did not need to do so for long. He gained his balance, managing to land feet first on a small ledge next to an underground stream.

"By T'var's Hope! Just what we need to combat a creature of flame. How to use this against him? Perhaps this ledge runs far enough? Yes, I believe it does and the stream continues its course right underneath where the behemoth stands. Though what good will this do? How can I take all this water to the creature?"

Barak hesitated, for a scream of pain from the surface above resounded loud enough for him to hear.

"No time to waste!" Barak ran to where he estimated the flame demon would be right above him. There, a great heat poured through the rocks and soil overhead. Immediately he put his Sonsword to work loosening them.

Vague sounds flowed down from above while Barak worked. Wandarr's and Quad Razak's voices mixed, arguing. He heard the word *Orbstar* shouted erratically and guessed what was happening.

Wandarr kept her distance, evading the fireballs that Quad Razak now tossed in every direction that he thought she might be. Frenzied with fury and hunger at the thought of being close to possessing an Orbstar, he forgot all about the injured Randak and the missing Barak. Kolonth's directives were also forgotten - all his attention on Wandarr and one goal, obtaining the Orbstar from her.

Wandarr relentlessly taunted the demon to keep up the distraction. She moved with lightning swiftness, searching her memories, trying to remember all Balzera shared with her of the Orbstar.

"You cannot keep this up forever. Soon you will become weary and both you and your precious jewel will be mine. Time is on my side."

At that moment, two things came to Wandarr's attention. The word *time* took on a new meaning and she observed the unmistakable end of a Sonsword pierce the ground from below, near to one side of Quad Razak.

"Time!"

Balzera had said that the Orbstar's properties included the ability to travel in time.

"Maybe I could send this monster back through time, or lose him in it, but must I sacrifice the Orbstar to do this? How do I activate it to achieve this? And what in the name of T'var is Barak doing?"

Barak had found more than he expected underground. He encountered not only a stream, but fountains as well, spraying up like geysers, as the chill waters fed them. Some of the geysers forcefully sprayed directly under Quad Razak but without quite hitting the ceiling of earth above.

"This may be easier than I thought. But these fountains are not high enough to do me any good. I must get them to spray higher. How to do that in time?"

Still standing on the ledge, he absentmindedly jammed his Sonsword into the stream itself. In response to his wish, the geysers rose, spewing water in greater force upwards.

"I guess I broke up some blockage," he said. "Oh, I see now. The only way out is through!"

He used all his might, furiously driving his Sonsword through the softening earth overhead. He did so in an ever-widening arc right around where he determined Quad Razak must be standing.

The moment Wandarr thought of time, the Orbstar in her hand began to glow. She found herself revealed and facing the fiery demon before her, with only the jewel for protection.

"It's as though the Orbstar read my mind," she thought. *"But what will it do next?"*

"Now I have you! Ha! So much for your precious life! I will crush you as the worm you are. Wait - what are you - stop, stop I say," Quad Razak said, fear tinging his voice.

"Back to the darkness and to the abyss which spawned you, Herald of Nothingness. Back to the emptiness that bore you. Kolonth's summons now be broken! *Regor en nullpoth kotu mayne trival! Stalot Meri!*"

The last phrases came unbidden to her lips. Wandarr assumed they flowed into her from the Orbstar itself, expressing its will and power through her. Even afterwards she did not remember the strange words she spoke.

A small pinpoint of soft green light began emanating from the Orbstar, the light expanding in proportion and substance drawing closer to its target.

Quad Razak hesitated and said, "You will not succeed. A vortex of wind will easily reverse the Orbstar's ray and you will be taken up, not I. I will yet possess my prize."

Quad Razak raised a hand and a biting wind began to expand in ferocity. Two things happened at once: the green light of the Orbstar grew intensely bright and swallowed up Quad Razak's entire form, while simultaneously, Quad Razak lost balance as the ground underneath gave way and fountains of water shot up, immersing the fiery form. The water relentlessly pounded upwards, its pressure released to its fullness, heedless of Quad Razak's screams of agony, as the chill waters worked to douse his flame. For a moment the green glow around Quad Razak grew so bright that Wandarr had to shield her sight. She heard the creature give a faint cry, felt the light diminish and upon uncovering her eyes, saw that Quad Razak was gone. This enemy would trouble them no more.

Barak could not see what had transpired above, but removed himself from the loosened ground as far as he could when it had begun to give way. He gave one last great thrust of his Sonsword into the stream itself which caused the fountains to erupt upward yet more strongly. One massive gusher in particular responded by exploding into the ceiling and smashing right through it, causing all the ground above and around to cave in. Barak was prepared to be crushed by the falling form of the demon but thought it a small price to pay to give his companions safety.

He overheard the scream of pain from Quad Razak as the water hit the creature. Great clouds of cooling waters rose high as the fountains burst through the ground, reaching towards the sky. The ceiling above crumbled and Barak glimpsed a fiery clawed appendage, scrambling for balance, before plunging towards the river below. He thought too, that there seemed to be a strange green glow above him.

Barak braced himself for the imminent crashing of the creature with the stream. He knew if its great body did not crush him, he would be fatally scalded in the resulting explosion if Quad Razak still maintained his fiery form when it met the stream. Barak knelt down, squeezing as far back into the ledge as possible and closed his eyes, dreading the inevitable impact. He anticipated being enveloped in a death storm of earth, steam and water. Surprisingly, only silence endured.

He looked up to see nothing; no part of the creature was in sight,. The green glow dimmed and he heard a scream of, *"Nooo-ooooo-oooooo,"* coming from nearby.

"What? Did the brute regain a foothold?" Barak needed to find out. Cautiously, he crept to where he was underneath the opening in the ground created by the force of the water when it exploded upwards and looked up to see only sky. He found some footholds in the ledge's wall and began to climb. He reached the opening, lifted himself up by his hands and peered out. He witnessed no creature. No sign of Quad Razak at all, but Wandarr was running to an unmoving form stretched out on the ground. Barak did not need to obtain a better view through the spraying water of the geysers; he knew that form. He hoisted his now-soaked body the rest of the way through the hole, scrambled out and rushed to join Wandarr beside their fallen brother-friend.

"Randak, Randak," she cried. "Brother, Brother, awake. In the name of T'var, please be all right."

Sluggishly, Randak raised his pain-filled eyes.

"Sister," he said weakly. "The venom."

"What happened?" yelled Barak through his tears, running towards them. "What ill did this emissary of Kolonth perform and where be the flame demon now?"

Ignoring Barak's questions, Randak raised his head, speaking softly, "I managed to clean the venom from my pant leg. I thought the poison only brushed against my arm, but my arm is now numb. I could not wash the wretched stuff off in time. The water drove away the other burn and I think cleansed it. I lost consciousness before I could do anything. Look at the stain where it scorched and it has gone under the skin. There is little to no feeling in my arm."

Barak and Wandarr looked at the wound Randak spoke of. Small, with an ugly blue appearance, the gash gave off a foul odour. They looked closely and both drew sharp breaths. The scar exposed a distinct shape. The shape of a blue circle around a red hexagon - the mark of Kolonth. Even as they studied the image, it began shrinking, drilling into Randak's wounded limb. Randak shook, feverish, drenched in sweat, his eyes lolling in his head, trying to resist his body's attempts to succumb to the peace of unconsciousness again.

"Quickly, Wandarr, give me your dagger. We must cut this away before it vanishes completely."

Barak took the knife, and as gently as possible, cut away at what was left of the mark. Randak winced in pain but did not cry out, for the numbness had spread, dulling the sensations of the knife's work. Wandarr tore off a part of her tunic's sleeve and began to soak up the blood.

"We must sit him up so the poison will drain from his arm." Wandarr walked behind Randak, lifting him up, allowing his body to rest against her. More blood dripped from the incision.

"'Tis only blood," said Wandarr. "Perhaps there is no need to believe the worst."

"No, look. Black liquid has begun to pour out."

Venom oozed to the ground from Randak's arm, sizzling when it hit the ground, scorching the dirt.

"You are right, Barak." said Wandarr. "Smell its putrid odour. How will we confirm if all is drained?"

"Look," Barak sounded relieved. "It is slowing down. I think this is a good sign. We may have drained all away. On the ground, the unholy signature forms."

There in the dirt, the same emblem appeared which moments before had been on Randak's arm. Charring the ground was Kolonth's brand: the sign of the circled hexagon.

"Barak, we should bathe him now in the pool."

"Agreed, Wandarr, that pool must somehow be from T'var. It is out of place here, yet has been our salvation and now, too, a balm for Randak. A true unexpected blessing."

Randak had again passed out. They moved him carefully to the pool and first placed his arm in its soothing waters. With a start Randak opened his eyes and looked around. He squeezed the fist of his afflicted arm, extended it, examined it with his good arm, moved it about, and found the pain greatly diminished.

Randak smiled, "The feeling returns. Praise King! What of our fiery adversary?"

"Peace now, Brother. You must rest. There will be time for tales later," cautioned Wandarr.

"Yes, we must bind this cut as well." Barak ripped a piece of his tunic and tied it around the incision. He had just finished examining his handiwork when a sudden chill passed over them all. Far above, the piercing wail of an Averi rang out. Automatically they looked up and scanned the sky. A remote black speck flew towards the foothills, becoming smaller and smaller, until against the backdrop of mountainous peaks they could see it no more.

*   *   *

Once Kolonth's magiks breached the River Brandor and his schemes manifested openly in T'barth, he discerned the time would be short to attain conquest across the Rangdorrian Lands and in Karnakon; the very reason why his agents began their deceptive work long beforehand.

Almost simultaneous to the revelation of the betrayal in T'barth, Kolonth's legions, led by his Carnivores, savage beasts bred through his magiks, were to be unleashed on these other unprepared lands. From that point on, it would be a small matter for his forces to conquer Vintar and move back up along the River Brandor with continued devastation until his victorious hosts once again encamped in his own realm.

For the land of Glephas, the Centre of Learning for T'varin, Kolonth had a unique plan known only to himself and a faithful apprentice. No invasion force was required to conquer a place already ripe to be brought down from within. Plus, Kolonth did not wish to risk his hordes destroying any knowledge of significance which he might use to further his designs.

Great as his success might be, the lands on the other side of the River Brandor concerned him greatly. Astaria, the land of Warrior Women, was protected by the Brandor and Astarian rivers and the majestic Astarian Woods. It was rumoured that forest was rooted in a primordial strength and wards made of powerful magiks. Kolonth judged this land a formidable obstacle and it deserved special attention to ensure his inevitable triumph.

Bjorqar, gateway to the Island Land of Narxa, possessed a jagged and rocky coast which left only one way to approach; crossing the Great Bridge. The Bridge was so immense, three dozen horseman could ride abreast across its hundred leagues length to the Island. No one in this age, including Kolonth, remembered when or how the Bridge came into being.

Aside from his plans for taking over T'varin, this one other passion also steered him. Kolonth was determined to discover the object of his forebear's hunt, whatever the weapon might be. He searched long and hard, devoured all the archaic texts he found. He did everything possible to find it, discover how to use its power and then bring all of T'varin to its knees, avenging his father's defeat and ensuring his own final victory.

Kolonth studied the many legends that kept The Island Land Narxa veiled in obscurity. He recognized, somehow, his destiny and that of the three warriors he so vehemently despised, were bound up with as of yet an unknown prize buried in the isle's ageless ruins.

CHAPTER FOUR
FROZEN T'BARTH

The land of T'barth, once a thriving prosperous country admired by many in T'varin, now lay frozen in the bitter chill of the Enemy's grasp. Its vast mines, towns and villages were now deserted. No motion, no life. Of its inhabitants, most were merely frosty statues scattered throughout the sub-zero wasteland. Others had suffered a worse fate: inmates in Kolonth's dungeons. What few survivors had existed, had long fled to other lands. There too, they often found Kolonth's foul handiwork and soon fell with the rest of the populace under his profane spells.

The strangers appeared friendly when they first arrived in T'barth Proper, the heart of commerce and trade, capital of the land. They showed the people how to build stronger defenses against their as-yet-unnamed northern enemy. Of all the lands of T'varin, T'barth's position made it closest to the ancient kingdom of Mangloth.

Many opinions surfaced when the first freezing winds blew out of season from the north. The gales began to wreak havoc on the outlying parts of T'barth, closest to the River Brandor. The rumours slowly found their way into the city centre; whispers of Manglor himself returning to take his vengeance upon T'varin. Others said a new malevolence had come to take up residence in the old land. Oddly enough, the new visitors did not deny the existence of a possible foe northwards, nor did they acknowledge one. They simply pointed out that a robust defense was always appropriate since an adversary might come into being in the future. In this way, they became privy to the inner workings of T'barth's military and political systems, learning all of the country's strengths and weaknesses.

"This change in the weather is quite normal," Austly, one of the young men of the capital city who had become enamoured with the strangers, addressed the crowd gathered around him in the marketplace.

"But it's not normal," countered one of the women in the crowd.

"We have never seen such a change as this," agreed one of the elder men who had once been on the Ruling Council.

"Yes, that is in your lifetime, but do you think it not unusual after so many centuries for there to be some shift in nature take place?" Austly was skilled; both eloquently convincing and simultaneously mocking, a talent he had picked up from the strangers. "Surely you and many here no longer put their hope and belief in old fables and children's stories."

"If you speak of T'var, know that some of us still do," yelled one brave soul above the growing noise of the affirming crowd.

"I suppose that is both your right and your loss."

Austly left the people to their debating and made his way home. He had done as the strangers had asked, allayed fears and caused dissent.

The strangers, wearing bright blue hooded cloaks, were constantly helpful while consistently exuding cheerfulness, hearty laughs and an anxious desire to assist wherever and whenever aid was needed. They were skilled in so many different areas that the people of T'barth marvelled at the blessings they now enjoyed because of the strangers' expertise.

It was these traits that drew Austly and others to them. It was not just young people like Austly who were infatuated with these new visitors. Many of all ages appreciated how the strangers' assistance increased the production of the mines through their new methods and suggestions. Their ideas helped the farmers grow more food and richer crops. Trade and commerce grew and so did the prosperity of all T'barth.

"Catch it! Catch it!" Rekels yelled to his younger brother as they played in the town square.

Malakoff groaned, "Ah, sorry, I missed the ball again. Again!" He looked downcast.

"It's alright. Takes time to learn! You just don't have my coordination yet."

"Maybe I never will."

"Oh, don't say that! Plus, you need a haircut with that mop of red over your eyes half the time," Rekels teased. "Now throw it back to me! It's still light out, so we have some time yet."

'Well, if you weren't so tall already! Anyway, here goes!"

"What a throw! That was so good! Just a bit high! But hard and fast! See?" Rekels turned to see where the ball went and was horrified when he realized it landed on the nearby sidewalk in the midst of a group of people leaving the theatre.

"Whoa," another voice interrupted the boy, directing his comment to Malakoff. "Quite the throw, young man! You will be joining our team at school next year for sure if you keep that up." He smiled and so did the boys.

A couple leaving the theatre overheard the conversation, then engaged in their own discussion with their friends about the play they had just seen.

"Let's go to that dessert place; we can talk there. All those speeches about food in the play has given me a craving!"

While they walked off, a larger group of about a dozen people, slightly older and looking a little more tired, though laughing, walked past the boys. Malakoff and Rekels guessed that they were farmer and miner families. The boys could hear their discussion on the funny parts of the play and their comments about needing to be in the mines and out in the fields before sunrise.

The chatter they heard from that group encouraged the two brothers.

"Our new visitors have certainly improved things around here, don't you think?"

"Aye, my farm has been producing so much more! I am making far more money than before and the vendors in the marketplace buying my goods are too!"

"It is the same with the mines, Shevelek. They are much safer and we are finding so much more material and it is easier now to extract it, thanks to them."

"Yes, everything is so much better since they arrived. T'barth is definitely a much happier, safer and more prosperous place."

"Indeed, it is truly a wonderful and joyful environment for our children and will be for their children as well, as long as this prosperity continues," bragged one of the women in the group.

"Can't agree with you more, Lindy. We are truly blessed with no doubt more to come. Why. just look at those boys playing catch. What a great legacy we are leaving for our children and youth. They will be so lucky."

The boys grinned to hear such good news about their future. "Did you hear that?"

"I did and it sounds great!"

"You know what won't be great, though?

"What?"

"I didn't realize how late it is getting! If we don't get home before dark we're going to be in big trouble."

The brothers ran laughing and giggling and making fun of each other all the way home. Just before they opened the front door, Malakoff said to his older brother, "Those strangers really have made a great difference to T'barth haven't they?"

"Nothing but good, little brother, nothing but good."

All the while, these strangers kept the purposes of their Master close to their hearts. Some thought it curious they turned up as the frosty winds began to blow. Also unusual, that they never truly revealed their origins. Asked where they came from, the strangers would only say, *"From a land afar off, across the Great Sea."*

Not all believed the strangers' intentions were as good as they seemed. Some whispered amongst themselves that the messengers could be the ones responsible for bringing the growing glacial cold into the land and even into T'barth Proper itself. Those who spoke their mind seemed to drift away, mocked by those who placed their faith in the strangers. The people who cherished T'var underwent even more ridicule.

Should anyone ask about the disappearances of these foolish T'vari, the common response was that embarrassed and ashamed that they still believed in folk tales, they snuck away in the night and most likely travelled to warmer climes. Only the strangers and a number of T'barthians loyal to them understood the real reason behind their absence.

The day had finally arrived. It was bright and sunny as a great crowd gathered to witness the unveiling of the pinnacle of the strangers' efforts: a magnificent machine designed to protect T'barth for all time. The excitement was palatable among the many who had welcomed and supported the visitors and their great work on behalf of T'barth. The hum of multiple conversations filled the air as people shoved and jostled each other to get as close as possible to the machine, everyone wishing to have a first-hand look at the moment of the great reveal.

The cloaked strangers stood solemnly on the platform in front of their work, still hidden under tarps. A number of T'barthians assigned to pull the tarps off scurried around the platform in preparation. The assembly was surprised when the strangers threw their hooded garments to the ground, revealing the dark breastplates they wore and the swords they carried at their sides. Only people closest to the platform could see the insignia on the breastplates and they began to tremble.

By the time others realized the truth, it was much too late. The devilish engine built under the guidance of the visitors was unveiled. The giant machine was a mix of levers, mirrors, fans, hoses and gears, made to turn by horses beaten into submission, running steadily in circles. Its size dwarfed anything the populace had ever seen in their lifetimes. Much worse, it bore a large symbol in its centre, the insignia of ancient evil: the circled hexagon, the brand of Manglor.

"This is getting boring!" Malakoff complained to his older brother, for they were positioned far back in the waiting crowd.

Rekels agreed. "You know nobody is watching us. Mom and Dad's attention is on that big thing at the front and we can't even see it. Why don't we just sneak away to the park over there?"

"Sounds good to me! Did you bring your ball and glove too?"

"Of course I did! In case it got boring just like I knew would happen!"

"Great. Let's go!"

The game of catch was going well until Rekels overthrew his younger brother and the ball landed to the side of the now anxious crowd.

"Don't worry, I'll get it! Just don't throw so high. Wasn't my fault I didn't catch it!"

"I know. It was a bad throw. I'm sorry!" Rekels needed to raise his voice over a noise that continued to grow louder. He turned to look towards the front of the crowd where the sound seemed to be coming from.

His attention was diverted by his brother's shout. "Hey, the ball feels really cold! Isn't that strange? It's been so warm out, but now it's getting chilly!"

Malakoff was facing Rekels so he could not see what his older brother was looking at and only heard his sibling screaming, "Malakoff! Get out of there! Run! Don't look behind you!"

That was the wrong thing to say. Malakoff took a glance behind him as he simultaneously started to run towards his brother. It was too late. He made it only a short distance before he was caught up in a draft of cold that froze him over in mid-run.

Rekels' tears ran down his face as he sprinted away, knowing there was nothing he could do to help his brother. He desperately looked around and called out for his parents, but there was no response. From people behind him he heard terrified screams that stopped abruptly and could guess what had happened to them.

Once he looked behind as he ran, only to see people running and caught off balance as they froze falling to the ground shattering into pieces. The sight drove him to run faster. He made it as far as the town square before he felt the tears on his face turning to ice, and then he couldn't move. Before his eyes were frozen over, the last thing he saw told him he was not alone. He was surrounded by countless other frozen statues. The rest of his body frosted over as he succumbed to the work of Kolonth's machine.

With the turning of its massive lever, the machine had gone to work immediately drawing down more of the cold from Kolonth's land. Soon the cold became a bitter wind; the wind changed to snow; the snow to ice which spread from Mangloth to T'barth. In mere days, the deadly winter crossed the border and expanded across T'barth until the land was covered in a thick, white blanket. The strangers and the machine may have borne the ancient mark of Manglor but T'barth quickly learned that it was not Manglor they need fear, but rather his offspring, whose magiks now powered the vile contraption. The name of Kolonth was more abhorrent than any accounts ever told about his sire.

Kolonth. *Doom of Darkness,* they called him. *Ice Lord.* They gave him a thousand other names as they grasped the severity of his evil rule. Only the visitors and the small number of trusted T'barthians, promised wonderful rewards for their silence, grinned with satisfaction on the day of the weapon's reveal. Those faithful few T'barthians received their reward quickly; they perished first at the pointed end of the strangers' swords. Kolonth believed that people who would betray their own were not trustworthy. He would brook no betrayal of his own forces.

"Treachery! Treachery!" cried the T'barthians.

Next, came the Carnivores spreading their own brand of horror, followed by the Night Trackers. Those somehow able to escape the freezing cold were hunted down. Some attempted to hide in remote parts of T'barth where the cold had not yet fully reached, or even in the mines but Kolonth's hunters used their enhanced senses to catch even the most elusive prey. They found their victims and dragged them away, screaming in terror, some to face death, others doomed to slavery in Mangloth, the former preferred over the latter, for Mangloth harboured a terrible secret.

No one but Kolonth knew from whence he found them, the ones he called his Shadow Smythes. The smithies they worked were dark forges powered by a mix of their own sorceries and Kolonth's magiks. They endeavoured to please Kolonth by creating warriors of both shadow and substance forged together, experiencing some success but many more failures. The worst failings created creatures of such unpredictable power that even Kolonth found them so untenable that he banished these unruly ones to the deepest caverns within Mangloth, bound with unbreakable chains of his own making through his most potent magiks.

He then set the Smythes to a new work; using their gifts to enhance the size and fighting skills of his prisoners-turned-soldiers. Of the prisoners taken away to Kolonth's citadel, the youngest and most able-bodied captives were forced to take Kolonth's mark and participate in the Smythes' unspeakable experiments, designed to make them willing and powerful soldiers in Kolonth's army. Some were made extraordinarily strong through experiments infused with the Smythe's knowledge of the black arts and Kolonth's own magiks and alchemies.

In this task they had much more success, taking many of the captives and creating from them burly, muscular, though not always intelligent, beings with a bloodlust for fighting. Further experimentation on some resulted in increased height, creating giant-sized beings, terrifying at first sight. Unfortunately, these "successes" seemed to have short life spans.

However, thanks to the more successful experiments, the vast hordes of Kolonth's soldiers had great endurance and were now capable of marching great distances without tiring. This was a purposeful plan, for horses were sparse in Mangloth, the ones available mostly captured in random secretive raids. Thus, they were reserved only for Generals and Captains, that is, if the horses could tolerate them. The poor beasts were often mistreated and beaten into submission, until they yielded to their abusive masters. There was no love between horse and rider in the armies of Mangloth.

Likewise, only Generals and Captains were privy to the spells of fire and ice taught to them by Kolonth or his Shadow Smythes. This was valuable knowledge to have in a pinch, but even Generals and Captains could be easily distracted, forgetful, living only in the moment, unable to think too far into the future; a side effect of the experimentation that made them as they were and a serious deficit when planning battle strategy.

Kolonth was the true strategist though and his word was law, unless one wanted to face the consequences of disobedience. Since he trusted no one, Kolonth was always cautious about how much he shared and to whom, limiting knowledge of his plans through compartmentalization. A great advantage if done cautiously and wisely, a potential disaster if not.

Kolonth thought himself both cautious and wise, keeping much information from his soldiers and sharing just enough with his generals and captains. His goal was to have a military set up with ten generals overseeing ten battalions of five hundred soldiers each, with fifty captains in charge of one hundred soldiers within one of the ten battalions, creating a force of up to five thousand strong, more than enough to destroy all of T'varin and make it his.

Functioning outside of the battalions, were the Raiders, the products of experimental trials that did not go as planned, the poor souls suffering physical mutations and deformities, their intellect dimmed and though brutal, they were skittish. They were fine for raids when there was little opposition but it became clear through testing in the arena. that they lacked the ability to develop any skills for true warfare, quickly turning useless and cowardly in a genuine battle.

With no real leadership they were wild and untamed, assigned by Kolonth to randomly attack villages, secure horses, test the strength of some places to determine what level of threat they might pose and at times, randomly secure captives, more fodder with which to build Kolonth's military might. Unbeknownst to Randak and Wandarr, but suspected and unable to be proved, it was one of these raids that was responsible for the disappearance of their parents when they were children. Other prisoners were enlisted as lackeys, more slaves than servants, spread about to do Kolonth's bidding. Often women and children became forced labour: tasked with cooking, cleaning, sewing, and performing errands for their captors amongst other tasks too hideous and burdensome to describe. The stronger women and children were conscripted to work in the mines of T'barth, assigned to the heavy work of digging and excavating the elements and materials needed for armour and weapons.

The rest were made to toil, using Kolonth's own spell-infused fuel to feed the unquenchable fires of his breeding pits or to serve as food for his ravenous creatures. Occasionally when Kolonth's overseers needed entertainment, some prisoners experienced the misfortune of becoming fuel for the fires themselves.

There existed a worse fate too; only select privileged ones were chosen to endure that hideous end. Taken to his throne room, they were forced to look into Kolonth's vacant eyes. They viewed their reflection in that terrifying abyss, feeling their very souls being drained and sucked into his own emptiness, until nothing remained of their bodies but shrivelled shells. The more they resisted his power, the greater Kolonth's pleasure. His life force sustained and his power amplified. The people of T'barth were the first to suffer the extent of Kolonth's hunger and the land of T'barth was the first to feel his choking grip of wintry death. They were not the last.

*   *   *

In the distant Rangdorrian Lands, following the devastating battle with Quad Razak and the pass of the Averi, Wandarr asked her comrades in hushed tones, "Do you think the dark servant saw what transpired here?"

"It knows, Sister, it must," Randak spoke softly, but definitively.

"Kolonth won't know yet, if it leaves only now," said Barak. "Look!

The foul messenger returns. Maybe it's coming to attack us."

"Is it the same one we encountered in Glephas?"

"I cannot tell with any certainty from this distance Sister. Though I dare say it does appear somewhat smaller than the one that breached Glephas, nor suited to carry a rider, but I could be mistaken."

"Look," Barak pointed to the sky, "Right where it disappeared only moments ago, it now returns. It soars in ever widening circles as though it searches for something."

The mountain peaks were now clearly visible with the first rays of sunlight. The thick fog dissipated. The trio stared as the creature came swiftly in their direction. Suddenly stopping, it hung in space as though listening for some far away signal.

It hovered over the area northwest of them, where they believed Kolonth had made his temporary fortress on the western edge of The Rangdorrian Lands. They watched as the Averi circled downwards until it was out of sight. From that same spot, a sudden burst of flame erupted, spurting into the sky, followed by a tremor in the ground which they felt even at their distance. They saw the winged shape rise high in the sky once again. Abruptly Kolonth's servant turned northward and flew on in a blur, vanishing again.

"The Averi flies north! This can only mean one thing: Kolonth is removing himself from Rangdorr and must have destroyed all evidence of his doings there in flame. His fortress gone by his hand so, now they fly away from us!" exclaimed Barak, frustrated that their Enemy was on the move again before they could confront him.

"If Randak is correct and the Averi cannot carry a rider, then they will be marching to Mangloth, to his Home, the Dark Fortress," Wandarr shook her head in disgust.

"His lair, his own land, place of penultimate wickedness," added

Randak. "The land of

endless night and endless cold."

Just hearing the words made Barak visibly shiver.

"Our path is clear," said Randak, now feeling somewhat rested and stronger. "We must now journey through to T'barth and then onward to Mangloth."

"But T'barth is frozen," Wandarr reminded them. "And we possess no horses, no supplies and certainly no protection against any kind of inclement weather or the freezing cold of the T'barthian waste."

"No choice, I fear," Barak spoke slowly, almost reluctant to voice his thoughts. "Our foe seeks to evade us. He left his stronghold in the Plains and now draws us to his own territory. He conspires to face us on his own terms, in his place of supremacy."

"Are you certain that is the reason? Simply to confront us in his homeland where he has the advantage? We wondered why he has delayed going to Narxa and if the Averi ever reached him. Perhaps the news of the creature's catch finally caught his attention. Though why it would take so long to reach its destination is a mystery indeed."

"Spoken true, my Sister. You may be right after all. I wonder what could have delayed the foul beast?"

"It's all good to talk about travelling northwards, but how will we manage without our steeds and provisions?" Wandarr felt like she was lecturing her companions but carried on. "You two sound as though we can easily get up and walk all the way. Randak, you still need time to heal from your wounds. Let us not be unduly hasty in our decisions. We must take time, consult with the King and allow Him to chart our course."

"You are right, of course, Sister," agreed Randak, somewhat chastised by Wandarr's logic. "Even were they back, I doubt our mounts will endure a trek through the ice fields. T'barth is already lost from what we know. No point in us becoming fatalities of that frigid wasteland as well. Regardless, we will start towards T'barth on the morrow. T'var willing, we will think of something. I know not how, but we must breach Kolonth's domain, even if it means walking the entire way."

*   *   *

Mangloth; Kolonth's domain, the land the trio now owned as their goal, where they were determined to fight and end Kolonth's madness, right in his own home if that was what it would take to achieve victory.

Kolonth's home, a massive castle-like fortress in the land of Mangloth, rested beyond the frosty region, carved into the icy mountains, providing a safeguard to the west. On the westernmost side of these peaks, the Bay of Karabarth and farther past their northerly precipices, existed nothing but a sheer drop to the Ocean Sea's hungry depths. South of Kolonth's dark abode, steamed Lake Scugoll, a manmade hole fed by the mountainous streams. Mixed with Kolonth's conjurings, it bubbled in constant turmoil, fetid steam arising from its depths, wrapping the fortification in shadowy billows.

To the east of the fortress, just above the ice fields and in the central plain of the land, lived the fearsome training arena, the place where Kolonth's troops camped, practiced and honed their fighting skills. Unfortunate captives were often used for target practice here and so it earned its other name, *The Frohme*, meaning in an ancient tongue, *Arena of Death*.

Above the arena just to the north, was one of Kolonth's greatest accomplishments, and worst evils. For here also were the breeding pits, the home of Kolonth's Carnivores. An inferno nourished by his captured slaves, kept the beasts warm. These monstrosities Kolonth held back in preparation for the day when he would order the remainder of his invading armies across the lands. Fear would keep his enemies at bay until they would bow down before him or be damned.

In the far eastern corner of the land were hidden the immense underground prisons. Bound by the wide Ocean Sea, the high cliffs and the outpost above the cold expanse, this ensured no escape for Kolonth's weary captives. Not that they would ever see the world above anyway.

Amidst the numerous caverns and cavities, his prisoners existed, if it could be called that, in the underground mazes with the vilest and most unholy creatures of Kolonth's nightmarish imagination. The only escape offered to these poor souls was to be fodder for the Carnivores, casualties of the arena or sustenance for Kolonth himself. Fate was never pleasant for any captive in Mangloth and all prayed for an end to come soon, even those who long ago ceased to believe in prayer. Kolonth ruled Mangloth with an iron hand, his way of honouring his father Manglor, believing if Manglor were present, he would proudly approve of his son's works. Yet there were still things of which Kolonth was unaware; things his father had kept hidden from him.

CHAPTER FIVE
OLD FRIENDS

None of the stranded trio slept restfully the first night after the battle against Quad Razak. They spent the remainder of the day foraging for food and concocted a meagre mixture of herbs and leaves which they cooked into a sour stew. Unfortunately, there was not even a rabbit around to sweeten the meal; the animals had deserted the area in fear at the first hint of danger. Overcome by hunger and battle fatigue, they soon collapsed on the ground and attempted to find sleep.

Their slumber was fitful and not restful in the least. Each one found their sleep intermingled with strange and vivid dreams. In her dream, Wandarr found herself in a long, narrow passageway that twisted and turned endlessly. Every time she thought she had reached the end of the passage she would meet another twist or turn. Then, just when the passageway straightened out and it appeared as though she would see what lay beyond, Randak and Barak both stirred in their sleep and she awoke. Falling asleep once more, she attempted to find the place where her dream left off but she only found herself back in the same never-ending passages.

Randak's dreams were of being in complete blackness. Voices float-ed about but he could not recognize them. Gradually, a dim light revealed a shadowy outline of his surroundings but he could not see clearly. He tried taking a step forward, then found himself falling. At this, he awoke to his own cries of, "Noooo…" Looking up, he first saw a starry sky above, then was reassured by his sleeping comrades still beside him and realized it was only a dream. In no time, exhaustion from the day's battle and his wound overtook him and he fell into a dreamless sleep.

About the time Randak's dream ended, Barak shifted in his sleep as his own dream began. The heavy pelting rain permeated his dream. He rode on horseback, low in the saddle, crouched down as far as possible to protect himself from the downpour. A small crowd of soldiers on horseback galloped ahead of him. He tried to catch up with them but found no mat-ter how fast he urged his steed on, the distance between them remained constant. He thought he saw a figure on foot farther ahead, beyond the other riders, perhaps standing on a walkway over water, as he could hear the sound of rippling noise, perhaps rapids. He started calling those ahead to wait for him, when all of a sudden, he realized he stood before two im-mense towering figures and feared for his life, lest they reach out and crush him.

The dream was broken when he awoke to the sound of animals breathing heavy and the nuzzle of a horse's nose upon his neck. Praise King! Their steeds had returned. Barak discovered that their supplies had remained strapped to the horses' saddle bags. He then began to prepare a morning meal to satisfy their great hunger.

"Randak, Wandarr, awake comrades!" shouted Barak. "Look who returns to us."

"Evad! Nayr! Jip!" they each cried in turn.

Randak and Wandarr shook off their slumber and eagerly sat up to welcome their steeds back. They were grateful that Barak allowed them to sleep in while he prepared breakfast. However, they broke their fast in a sombre silence as each one reflected on the strange dreams the night had brought them.

The thought of travelling to T'barth also loomed over them. Not one of them wished to bring up the topic of the frozen waste which lay ahead until necessary. At this point, they owned little in the way of clothing that would protect them from a regular winter chill, never mind the bone-chilling, evil cold Kolonth inflicted upon the land.

They cleaned up and refreshed themselves in the pool, their salvation during the previous day. All secured and their camp clean, they mounted their horses, pointed them north and began to ride forward at a slow but steady pace. They had travelled for about thirty minutes when Wandarr, frustrated with the uneasy brooding silence, finally spoke up.

"Well, aren't we a cheery bunch? Praise King indeed! We have defeated a mighty enemy, experienced great victory, yet to look, one would think us conquered rather than conquerors. What think you, my brothers? What is this darkness stifling even our lightest conversation and chokes all joy from our victory? Could it be my strange dream last night has infected us all? I know not what to think of it."

"Strange dreams indeed," Barak and Randak agreed.

"You too?" Wandarr asked. "This must be of T'var, for all of us to experience it. I will tell you what I dreamt; perhaps one of you can make some meaning of it."

Wandarr related her dream of the night before and then Barak. They listened to each other with rapt attention, heedless of any danger which might be lurking nearby. They focused only on making sense out of what must be a message T'var wished to convey to them. Randak too related some of his dream but could not tell all of it. Wandarr thought he limited what he shared and made a mental note to ask him privately later to see if her suspicions were correct. She did not wish to press him in front of Barak for she knew from experience when Randak felt pushed, he became less inclined to share his thoughts.

Randak wondered if Wandarr realized that he had held back sharing. If so, he knew she would ask him privately. He could not predict whether he would tell her the depth of the dark feelings accompanying him. Reflecting upon the dream now, in the light of day, a heaviness rested on his spirit and his arm ached with what he hoped to be only the approaching T'barthian cold.

They travelled northwest towards the T'barthian River for three days. They thought to cross the river near the border of the land of T'barth. Already the air changed, for the nearer they drew towards T'barth, the more the chill grew. The lack of wildlife and the silent skies confirmed that the cold had either captured the birds and beasts in its grasp or driven the poor creatures from their homes, perhaps both. On a spur of a moment decision, they decided to change their direction slightly and travel in more a westerly direction. They planned to meet the river a little further south than the border, hoping to delay the utter chill of the devastation for as long as possible.

They came to the river on the fourth day and found it almost completely frozen. They spied some visibly open spots here and there along the bank which they might use to their advantage. The water was icy, but refreshing enough such that they splashed their faces with it and allowed their horses to drink. In spite of the water's brisk temperature, the horses happily drank, their masters pleased to see some fresh vigour return to their mounts.

The trio stopped for the night and lit a fire. The past three nights they cared not how high and hot the fire, nor what enemies it might attract;

warmth always stayed their main concern and tonight was no different. In fact, they shivered uncontrollably at times, now being so much closer to the chill of the river. The path of the river, now their route as well, led into a dismal and frigid wasteland.

These past nights, each took turns at watch but all remained uncomfortably peaceful. In spite of the crackling of their nightly fires, visible for leagues around, no signs of the enemy manifested. The trio determined amongst themselves not to be overconfident at this apparent lack of interest on Kolonth's part.

At least their conversation had picked up since they started towards T'barth on that first morning after their strange dreams. They began joking with one another again, laughing every once in a while and the sombre mood plaguing them earlier now dissipated.

"So how long have you two been such great friends?" Barak was curious for a few reasons. "I grew up as an only child with no siblings, though I hear sometimes brothers and sisters do not always get along."

Wandarr stirred the fire before she looked at Barak, "Well, we still do not always get along or, maybe better said, do not always agree. Isn't that right, Brother?"

Randak, who lay stretched out on the ground looking at the stars overhead and was too comfortable to move, teased, "Yes, true, but much better than as children. Especially younger, after all, I, being the eldest knew more, she just didn't always like that."

"Mnn...and who is the smarter one now?"

Randak chose not to answer, redirecting the conversation. "What of your youth, Barak? You have not told us much of that. What was it like growing up in Vintar? And how could your people even hear anything over the annoyingly loud noise of the Vintaran Falls? How could you even have conversations?"

"Well, see how our ears develop differently from childhood on?" Barak tugged at his ears forming them into an odd shape, while Wandarr and Randak tried to look more closely until they realized he was joking.

Barak laughed. "It wasn't that bad! You get used to it you know." He noticed Wandarr staring at him and returned her look with a heartfelt smile.

She turned away as soon as he did that, but it wasn't long before both sat close beside each other by the fire. Loud snoring indicated Randak had fallen asleep but the two kept their voices to a whisper as they talked long into the night. Realizing they best get some rest before another day of travel, they hugged each other, for both warmth and affection, prior to putting out the fire and finding their sleeping bags. They had just finished a midday meal, on this fourth day of travel, remounted and once again began following the river, when their conversation turned again to their dreams of three nights past. They debated the possible meaning of Wandarr's dream and Barak tried to make it connect to is own when they became aware of something off, a difference in their surroundings.

In spite of their determination to be cautious, they had been unaware of the almost imperceptible noise of the riders who had been following them at a distance for the past few leagues. Immediately, in unison, Randak, Barak and Wandarr brought their horses to a halt. Now they listened to the sounds of approaching hoof beats and knew their folly. By the time they their hands touched the hilts of their swords, they found themselves surrounded by six well-clad, masked warriors dressed in white clothing, all riding white horses of the same stature as their own. No wonder they had not see them in the white landscape; their white attire and steeds blended in, making them nigh on invisible. Not until they were almost upon them were they fully revealed.

The trio drew their swords, as six riders encircled them and rode round and round them in an ever-shrinking circle. The three needed no signal; all their past experiences of fighting together had made them into one cohesive unit. The silent communication that passed between them, not understood by their foes, won them victory after victory in the past. In one fluid motion, the three manoeuvred their swords and horses together in such a way they quickly knocked the six riders to the ground.

The riders slowly rose to their feet. Barak, Randak and Wandarr were still upon their horses watching carefully for the next move their opponents might attempt. To the astonishment of Barak, one of the riders laughed as she turned to face the trio and removed her mask, saying, "Well met, Wandarr."

"And that certainly explains why our swords did not glow with the amber of light of warning. These are friends, not foes, Barak."

"And I would recognize that lilting brogue anywhere," Wandarr returned the laugh.

Barak gasped, for as this tall warrior removed their mask, long, flowing, jet-black hair streaked with white blew in the frigid wind and he suddenly realized he had battled with a woman. Not just any woman but an Astarian Warrior Woman.

The rest of the contingent followed suit, removing their helms, revealing hair of varied colours. Some wore theirs long and flowing, while others' was cut short and tight to the head. The hair colours ranged from black to white to grey along with more exotic pastels like blue, orange, pink and even some deep reds. Barak tried to determine how many different colours but lost count. He was fascinated when he later learned that the varied hair colours served to identify the familial ties of each warrior.

"Well met indeed, Warrior Woman! Starry, what in the name of T'var are you doing in this frozen wilderness? Never mind, it is so good to find you!" Wandarr jumped from Nayr, running to embrace her friend of many years.

Randak began laughing as well, dismounted and ran over to share in the embrace of this joyful reunion. Barak could only stand and ponder at this strange turn of events. He really didn't know whether he should join his friends or stand guard over the rest of the fallen riders who hesitantly began to get up.

"Come Barak," Randak said, raising his voice above the laughter. "Leave our fallen friends and come meet the leader of the legendary Warriors of Astaria."

"Legendary indeed," replied Astar. "If there be any legends come to life this day it is the legend of the Warriors Three. Your exploits against the evil one have not gone unnoticed. They have been whispered afar off, even in my homeland."

"Come hither, Barak. Legend I may be, but I will not bite," Astar said, laughing as she motioned him closer.

Barak thought her voice of a unique quality, rich and deep, gentle yet powerful, with an almost melodic tone. He would not have been surprised if the woman broke out in song. Cautiously, Barak made his way toward his companions and this stranger with whom they were so at ease. Then, as he looked into her face, a new light of recognition dawned and he grinned in spite of himself.

"Starry, Starry. Of course! Greetings and I am honoured your majesty. Wandarr has told me stories of…oh, forgive me for my rudeness," Barak said and he kneeled before Astar and bowed his head.

"What kind of warrior is this? Both battle ready and polite!" said Astar. "First to call me a nickname known only to my closest friends and then to kneel and pay me homage. I see you have told Barak something of me then, since he knows the name you used to call me in childhood when we played together."

"Yes, we have shared much with each other," Wandarr said to Astar as much as to herself. Her eyes glanced from Barak to Astar, with a look that told of a deeper meaning, the hint of a growing love between the two.

"I see," said Astar. "You are King-Blessed indeed, dear friend."

Wandarr thought back to that strange day in the camp near the southeastern border of Rangdorr and T'barth where she and her brother were looked after by kind people after their parents had disappeared. They, like the other children with them, did not realize that their parents had been murdered. Victims of Kolonth's initial raids as he tested his strength, becoming bold enough to skirt into The Rangdorrian Lands with attacks conducted by raiders from his growing army.

They and the other children who lost parents, were collected and protected by kind women who organized and ran the camp, adopting the children as if they were their very own. There Wandarr and Randak learned about the rewards of continual faithfulness to T'var and how to protect themselves should evil seek to triumph. They learned the way of the warrior.

Only near the end of their stay in the camp, did they, Randak, then twenty-one and Wandarr, almost nineteen, learn that their teachers were Astarian Warrior Women from the land of Astaria. The Warrior Women mixed their own children with the other orphans to provide friendship as well as challenge.

A close bond of friendship formed between Wandarr and Starry before Wandarr ever grew aware of her friend's true origins. It was much later on, after they became close friends, when she learned Starry's significant heritage, being of the royal house of Astaria and a princess in her own right.

Wandarr and Randak continually proved themselves with the sword. Though not of Astaria, Wandarr and Randak certainly fought as those bred to be warriors, consistently demonstrating a natural ability, amazing their teachers.

Kolonth had heard rumours of a training camp raising warriors led by strange women but he searched in vain, for the Astarians used their own skills with wards to hide the camp from sight. Kolonth dismissed the tale as a falsehood and slew those who brought it to his attention.

"Praise King, it is good to find you," Wandarr said before her tone turned serious. "But tell us, what brings you so far from your homeland and who are your comrades? We apologize for any harm we inflicted on them but I am sure you understand our caution in these dark days."

"We understand it all too well," Astar replied with a nod. "Indeed, it is why we followed you at a distance for so long. We did not know who, aside from the Evil One's emissaries, would be foolhardy enough to ride into frozen T'barth. We did not realize that we tracked The Three Warriors of Prophecy until we were almost upon you. By that time, you had grown aware of us. Why are we so far from home, you ask? We ride to face the harbinger of these evil days, as I imagine so do you. We will tolerate the evil no longer. We go to battle Kolonth himself, on his own ground, if we must."

Randak, looking surprised, asked, "These few of you to face Kolonth? That is madness."

"Yet you three alone, strong as you might be, are you not aiming to do the same?"

Randak looked sheepish.

"We are not so foolish, friend Randak," replied Astar. "A way off from here is gathered most of the strength of two lands, our own Astaria and that of our neighbour, Bjorqar. We have left behind only a small contingent of warriors at home to defend our lands if need be. But we are well over five hundred strong and we are marching to fend off Kolonth on his own ground before he marshals his forces to invade our territories. It is clear he desires to move and conquer soon. We are determined to prevent his evil from spreading further."

"King's Praise!" exclaimed Barak. "Let us join you and if you will have us, your five hundred will be three stronger."

"More than three strong by all accounts and our experience of to-day," said one of the men of Bjorqar.

"No doubt, Captain Jorkan," agreed another rider named Belsharn. "From what we have seen here, six against three is little match for these ones."

"Aye!" said Astar. "More likely it will be as if we added be ten or even fifty more warriors to our host rather than just three."

"Now who makes legends," said Wandarr. "We do only as the King enables us. But you still have not really answered my question as to why you are here. I understand your desire to confront the Enemy, but why have you come this way? Surely your path would have been better chosen directly through Astaria to the north and then on to Mangloth from there?"

"Perhaps, but after much meditation and seeking after T'var's will, all agreed that was not the way the King was directing us." Astar continued. "Come, let us ride to meet our troops. They can be no more than twenty leagues distant now. But first, you need some warmth from the looks of you. Captain Jorkan, might Belsharn still have those extra cloaks of Bjorqar in your supplies?"

"Yes, Majesty. Here they are."

Belsharn, handed the white hooded cloaks to each of the grateful three, still amazed at this strange meeting. He felt his hands tremble as he looked into the faces of these warriors he previously knew of only in legend.

"Peace, Brother," Randak took Belsharn's hand as well as the cloak.

"We thank you for your kindness. We are honoured to ride with you all and there is no need to tremble. We are mortal like you. As the King we both serve enables you, so He enables us. Peace, my friend."

"Thank you," replied Belsharn. "I think we are the honoured ones but thank you for your kind words."

The three pulled the warm, pure white, hooded cloaks around them, mounted their steeds and faced Astar. They now found themselves well-insulated against the weather which continued to grow colder with the approach of evening.

"Come friends," said Astar. "Let us make haste to rejoin our armies before night overtakes us."

With that, they all fell into line. Wandarr, Astar, Randak and Barak were four abreast in the first line with the other five riders close behind. They had ridden for about ten minutes when Astar began to relate her story to her friends.

"Months ago," Astar said, "Emissaries came to Astaria and Bjorqar, friendly at first, adorned in bright blue, with long silver earrings, strange tattoos and an eagerness to offer us aid in the form of wisdom and what they referred to as *secret ways*. They said they came from lands very distant, lands with great wealth and knowledge that they wished to share with both our countries. As you know, the River Brandor keeps us separated from the outer lands. Except for rare occasions, our people seldom venture forth, because we prefer to keep to ourselves. Perhaps we secretly hoped our land would be overlooked as the stuff of myth by any would-be conquerors. After all, though we are warriors, we are still a peaceful people at heart; we fight only when we need to defend and not for battle alone."

Astar looked up to the sky before continuing, "But my thoughts wander. As I said, seldom do our people venture forth. Some brave the perilous journey along the coast of the Great Sea, around Narxa to the

Vintaran Falls and then take the ancient hidden passage into Vintar and the lands farther south, but that is not a frequent thing among our people. The King, it would appear, deemed it so after the last battle with Manglor when the lands shifted and the River Brandor became so much wider with few places to cross safely."

She spread her hands to illustrate her point.

"Thus, we have been separated for ages by both the River Brandor and our own choice, seldom having dealings with the outer lands. We are self-supporting and what we need we are able to take in trade with Bjorqar, as they do with us. Our two countries are still friends with an open border through these ages past. And too, Astaria and Bjorqar together, remain the joint guardians of the Bridge to the Island Land of Narxa."

No one noticed that at the mention of the Bridge, Barak started and leaned in more closely to hear Astar's words. He decided to say nothing for the moment, determined to see if Astar would say anything that might relate to the meaning of his strange dream from those many nights ago.

"So, we grew suspicious about the origins of these strangers, especially since they apparently did not come across the River Brandor, but rather first appeared in the northern part of our land. We could only surmise afterwards that they had sojourned in from cursed Mangloth, somehow crossed the waters of the Astarian River, eluding its defenses with Kolonth's magiks and entered Astaria unseen and unbidden through the shelter of the woods.

"As you are aware, our woods are not just legend, for their unique power, long ago placed within them by T'var, protects our land. Some dark spell must have let these intruders through and later we found parts of our forest weakened or dying, no doubt a result of their evil doings.

"In a short time, the emissaries revealed their true nature. Encouraging us with promises of wealth and more knowledge, they began to share their theories about the tales of T'var as only stories and fables, the stuff of myths. They soon urged us to ignore the King's laws and told us how well other lands fared who put aside such foolish notions. They spoke of progress, wealth and a new freedom that would come by throwing off the shackles of ancient superstitions. They encouraged us to give up loyalty to our mythical sovereign and said if we still insisted on worshipping a powerful leader, there now existed a new master to whom we could swear our unfailing devotion.

"A new master to swear allegiance to, but they would not reveal his name, saying he preferred to remain in the background, due to his humble nature. But we knew; either Manglor himself had somehow returned or Kolonth now worked the same evil his father once did. We did not yet comprehend the havoc he had wreaked upon other parts of T'varin or perhaps we would have acted sooner. But we cannot change that now.

"As soon as we realized the evil amongst us, we chased the emissaries out of our land. Some fled into Bjorqar to meet up with their other comrades there, all engaged in trying to stir up the same evil they attempted in Astaria. They found no support in Bjorqar any more than they did in Astaria once their true nature and true master revealed themselves.

"Perhaps our joint guardianship of the Island Land of Narxa helped us to avoid falling into the deceit that befell the other lands of T'varin. Indeed, we wondered if perhaps part of the mission of these strangers was not only to stir up dissent, but also to spy out the location of the Bridge to Narxa."

Barak spoke up, "Then this is not a myth. Twice you have spoken of Narxa now and this great Bridge. Is this a real place? Not the stuff of ancient legend?"

Astar looked at him surprised and said, "Real, Barak. So real, that it is the place where Manglor suffered defeat at the hands of T'var Himself. Your people were there too, Barak, a contingent from Vintar was present to witness as well. Some of our elders still remember the tales of their grandparent's grandparents' grandparents who witnessed the defeat of Manglor and the shifting of the lands which remain to this day. Indeed, my mother's great grandmother four times past that, enjoyed the honour as one of the warriors in the small troop that accompanied the Great Lord T'var across the bridge to Narxa. She heard T'var's orders and His final words to the stone guardians at the bridge. Those words have been passed down and never forgotten: *Call me when the Warriors Three are in their time of need."*

Astar thought she saw her three friends shiver with recognition that this Prophecy spoke of them but she continued anyway. "No, Narxa is real and still exists and though the palace continues to lie in ruins, Astaria and Bjorqar have still maintained their sacred trust of guardianship. To the rest of T'varin, Astaria may be legend, separated by the River Brandor, the Astarian Forest and Astarian River, but we and our friends in Bjorqar have not forgotten our duty.

"Apparently my people did," Barak lowered his head, embarrassed. "This is the first time I have heard of Vintar's part in this tale of so long ago."

"No need to lower your head in shame, Barak. It was not your doing that, over time, Vintar chose total neutrality in all matters of the lands of T'varin and withdrew from the original guardianship. Rest assured, we of Astaria and Bjorqar still guard Narxa and when all others have forgotten or given up hope, we keep the promise burning. We have never forgotten or doubted His words to the guardians that day and treasure them for we trust in His promise: He will return when the warriors three are in their utmost time of need."

Wandarr and Barak could hold back no longer but almost simultaneously plunged into the accounts of their dreams.

Barak said, "Then this is no coincidence either, that we have met you who may enlighten us about the visions that came in our dreams. This is T'var's doing, having us meet up with you, of that I am certain. The walkway over water must be the bridge, the ancient battle, the small troop that accompanied T'var, that was my dream but to what purpose I cannot yet discern."

As Barak and Wandarr related their dreams to Astar, Randak remained silent and fell somewhat behind their pace. As Astar listened to their accounts, Barak and Wandarr hoped Randak would now feel at ease to share his dream.

"And Randak, what of your dream that you were reluctant to share? Does it lend itself to interpretation too?" Wandarr asked, turning her attention to her brother, hoping he would say more of what seemed to be such a nightmarish vision to him.

She motioned him to ride alongside Astar, saying, "Come now, Brother. Relate your strange vision of the other night, for Astar may be able to give new meaning to what seems so bothersome."

After a moment of deep thought, Randak said, "I feel I still must keep this to myself for now, dear Sister, although I cannot explain why."

Astar further encouraged him, saying, "You are in the King's company; you may speak freely. All are trusted servants of T'var here."

"I doubt not your company, dear Starry, but rather all is unclear in my dream and I doubt it would be coherent enough for any type of interpretation, as well-meaning as the effort would be." Randak then grew silent and finally said, "I trust not myself in this matter."

Barak said, "Yourself? You jest. You are loyal beyond question. Don't be so foolish."

"Yes, yes, perhaps you are right," said Randak.

But as he spoke, a strange cold pain pierced his arm and he stopped his words short. He winced, struggling to force the pain out of his system, hoping no one else saw his expression. After a few moments the pain left and changing his mind about relating the dream, he reassured his friends.

"Perhaps I will tell you more later. For now, I must keep these thoughts to myself. Let us not spoil our happy reunion with strange dreams that come to weary soldiers in the dark of night."

"Very well, Brother," Wandarr said, giving up. "You are determined to keep it to yourself and I know it well that no amount of prodding will convince you otherwise. I will leave it then. Starry, look ahead! Would those be the fires of your troops you spoke of? Have we covered that much ground already?"

"Indeed, we have."

Astar gave a special call sounding like a bird, which Wandarr knew as a signal to the scouts alerting them to their approach.

"Let us go warm ourselves by the fires and have some food. I am sure we all could do with some refreshment and nourishment."

At that, they spurred their horses on and soon rode within site of the camp. Barak was amazed and silent as he took it all in. He hadn't been sure what he expected to see when they arrived, but certainly not such a massive, well-organized encampment. They trotted down a path through the middle of the camp and as they rode farther in, he noticed the smell of small fires burning throughout the camp and heard quiet conversations amongst those around them and from other soldiers they passed.

Barak expected he might see people running to and fro on errands, perhaps some disorganization and chaos. He was certain to be greeted by the smell of sweaty soldiers at their various tasks, whether it be sharpening blades or practicing their battle skills. So he was surprised to see complete order before him and a pristine set up that carried the unmistakable scent of a thorough spring cleaning everywhere. Barak couldn't help but wonder, *"They look organized now, but what happens when they have to take everything down when we move on? It seems like that could take days!"*

The soldiers he saw were in varying states of dress; most had some armour on, though not many currently wore swords or carried shields from what he could tell. Both men and women looked up as the trio rode by, formally acknowledging the group with a nod, salute or a hand moved over chest, depending on where they were from and their station.

Totally unsure of the proper response, Barak looked to Wandarr and Randak and followed their lead; a simple nod of the head to those saluting seemed to be their response, so Barak did likewise. He knew there were more formalities to come, but he was also anxious to speak to the soldiers themselves. He wished to learn more about Bjorqar and Astaria.

He knew he felt something special for Wandarr, but that did not mean he could not be curious and learn more from the Astarian Warrior Women. Wandarr had shared some details of their childhood encounters with the Astarians, but now, meeting them in person, they seemed larger than life. The Astarians had played such a significant role in Wandarr's early life, he felt it prudent, perhaps even honour-bound, to learn more about these people who had taken this girl under their wing, now a woman he was beginning to care for more deeply with each passing day.

As the group came closer to their destination, Barak realized the tents were not only of varying sizes, but also of varying designs. It became apparent that the designs were indicative of those either of Bjorqar or Astaria. Upon a closer look though, it appeared there were also different designs within the Astarian grouping, though he had yet to learn the reason for that.

He assumed, correctly, that the larger tents were for the commanders and it was towards two of these that their path led. The two largest tents stood beside each other and belonged to the commanders of Astaria and Bjorqar. Now the set up of the camp made sense. Those of Bjorqar on the same side as their leader's tent and similarly the Astarians aligned round about Starry's. The group finally reached Starry's tent and dismounted.

They entered her tent and saw that others had already gathered. They met Captain Qentif of Bjorqar and the commanders from both lands. Qentif introduced his men. "From our beloved Bjorqar, here meet Redan of the Left Hand, Donker Treetop, so named for his immense height, Sterling the One-armed, Wheetly of the Bridge Men and Captain Jorkan you have already met."

Astar bid them meet her Captains saying, "Our people name not in the way of Bjorqar for Astarian names by themselves carry a secret meaning in our own language. Meet here Hawthorne, Nerma, Lymos and Elmina."

Elmina spoke on behalf of the group. "We warmly welcome you." Then, staring at each of them, she spoke solemnly. "You three are the fulfillment of *The Prophecy* and it is truly the hope we need in these desperate, dark times."

The Captains nodded their head in assent and then followed a brief discussion of next steps in their strategy to which all agreed, before dispersing to see how fared their soldiers.

Introductions, welcomes and inspections complete, eventually the three comrades and Astar found themselves with a few of the other warriors not yet laid down to rest, around the fire, speaking of their futures. Barak being left-handed himself, desired to speak to Redan, to see if he could offer any fighting tips. He also wanted to speak to Belsharn again, to see what else he might learn. Speaking to one or some of the Astarians was also on his mental checklist.

Ever the knowledge-seeker, he hoped the journey would allow time for these conversations. He was mulling over which of the Astarians he had just met might be the best to start a conversation with, when he was distracted by a voice that always caught his attention. One that made him feel warm even in the midst of the biting cold.

Wandarr asked the question on her mind since Astar first informed them of the size of the troops.

"Starry, what if Kolonth moves his troops to invade Astaria and Bjorqar with the bulk of your troops here? How long could they survive?"

"Fear not, my friend," Astar replied. "Our defenses are sure and our own spies have informed us Kolonth has some new evil afoot preventing him from moving his forces to war too quickly."

"What new evil can the monster unleash, not yet devised by him already?" asked a warrior named Marsu.

"We wonder too, my comrade. As you all well know, some of our own spies paid with their lives to furnish us with this little, but valuable, news," replied Astar.

"Yes, and their lives will be avenged, for one of them was my kinswoman," said Marsu.

"Avenged indeed," said one of the other warriors.

Amidst the high emotion running throughout the camp, Astar continued to explain the plan to her friends.

"We plan to cross the T'barthian near to the city proper. We desire to check for signs of life and to see if we can find the evil machine which unleashed this bitter cold and destroy it. Our success at this may affect part of our plan, however, for we intend to cross the frozen River Brandor under the cover of darkness. But, if we are successful at destroying Kolonth's device, we may find the River Brandor thaws too soon. We do not know if the cold will end instantly or begin a gradual thaw. Our hope is, that after destroying the thing, that we will be quick enough to have all the time necessary to cross the River Brandor into Mangloth."

"But," Barak said, remembering his discovery of the underground stream, "Will not the thawing unleash a great flood? Why, all of T'barth proper, as well as the mines, would be flooded if both the Brandor and the T'barthian rivers overflow their banks at the same time as they are sure to do. Plus, if all the snow now on the lands melts as well…"

"Indeed," Randak finished Barak's thought. "Such a thaw would cause water to cover all The Rangdorrian Lands as well. But then flooding is a small price to pay if it will wash away the filth and stench of the Enemy once and for all."

"Once and for all!" roared Wandarr and Astar together.

Soon the phrase echoed through the whole camp reaching even the guards posted on lookout for the night.

When morning arrived, it found the troops assembling into formation, preparing to retrace the steps of some of its members as the assembly prepared to head into the chill of T'barth. Randak could not believe the camp was already disassembled, the site cleaned, leaving no trace that an encampment had been there at all. *I must ask how they accomplished that. Unless it is some kind of secret, I suppose…*

"Unusually quiet last night," said Belita, one of the Warrior Women from Astaria.

"Yes, indeed," Javed, a man of Bjorqar agreed, adding, "I would almost say too quiet, except that there is a sense of the protection of Lord T'var around us."

Randak, sitting on Jip not far away, happened to overhear their conversation, smiled. "I sense it, too."

He also thought to himself, although he did not say it, that his arm felt less painful when he sensed that comforting presence nearby.

"Make ready to move out," Astar said to the commanders of the different divisions of her troops and Captain Qentif likewise commanded his men, after which he turned to Astar. "Behold, the sun is obscured by mists and clouds and this is not a good omen with which to start our journey."

All eyes turned skyward and they saw a dark haze settled in the sky overhead, beginning to block out what little warmth of the sun could penetrate into the frozen wasteland that was their destination.

"Indeed, let us make haste," said one of the commanders of the Bjorqarn troops. "I feel danger is upon us and it is time we move on. May our journey prove to be the beginning of the end of Kolonth and all his evil schemes."

"Once and for all!" the cry resounded throughout the troops.

The company rode on; their horses and white robes merged into the landscape of white, becoming practically invisible to all eyes, including those of the Averi, circling far above, hidden in the mist.

"Tell me," Astar said as they rode. "How have the other lands fared? We surmised your homeland, The Rangdorrian Lands were laid waste as well and of course, we know now of T'barth's fate but what of Karnakon, Glephas and Vintar?"

Randak and Wandarr looked at one another sadly.

"What say you, Brother, shall we begin with the sad story of Karnakon, telling our tale up until we encountered Barak? If so, you may speak first."

"Indeed, Sister, so I shall and you may fill in any pieces I might leave out."

So, between them, the siblings began to recount their sad adventures in those lands when they had been but two, before there was even a thought or whisper of *The Prophecy of Hope*.

"Here begins our story…"

CHAPTER SIX
THE ROUT OF KARNAKON

The light of the setting sun reflected off the coastal islands and spread across the land of Karnakon as it rested peacefully in the evening twilight. Karnakon: bordering the Great Ocean, the land closest to the King's lands. The land of the Great Orchards which were the talk of all of T'varin. The orchards whose varied fruits supplied not only neighbouring Glephas, but the Rangdorrian Lands, T'barth and Vintar as well.

Karnakon was the land with the mountain path which was the only route to the massive learning centre of Glephas. Karnakon; the last outpost to the King's lands, which lay across the ocean and the rumoured location of T'var's return. Karnakon was a peaceful prosperous land, rich in people and produce and the envy of many in T'varin. Since Karnakon had experienced peace for so long, few would bear arms. In fact, many asserted that any defense was needless since they were the nearest land of T'varin to the King's lands. Even if the King still lived far across the vast waters, they believed that their proximity to His country should afford them all the protection they needed and deserved.

The Etrarian River flowed as the only waterway within the land itself. The River found its origin at the ice caps of the Glephoid Mountains. They melted regularly in the warmer seasons, thus feeding the Etrarian River. The River then wound its way gracefully through the countryside with a gentle flow, nourishing the Great Orchards, Karnakon's major industry and true pride, until it eventually emptied into the Great Ocean.

During more recent times, strangers who came from far away lands had assisted in the building of a series of dams and canals that pushed a portion of the Etrarian River to also flow north, first to large Sythm Lake which shared itself across the borders of both Karnakon and Rangdorr. From there, a lock system directed the waterway to wind around the capital of Etraria before one part of it branched off to the west and flowed into that part of The Great Ocean where Karnakon's Coastal Islands lay.

Additionally, a canal skillfully built by the strangers just above the northeastern part of the capital, moved another portion of the river further north, through a barren landscape, where eventually the waters emptied into the Bay of Karabarth. Though very few could understand how the strangers had accomplished these amazing feats, a huge portion of the population enjoyed their pleasure cruises now afforded by these wonderful additions to the waterways.

It was not unusual, particularly in spring and summer, to see multiple sizes and types of watercraft enjoying the circle tour of Etraria itself, or travelling south, following the winding Etrarian River's leisurely path for a tour through the Great Orchards. Very few had any appetite to pursue the waterway's course northwards, the colder climate and lack of anything special to see dampening any enjoyment that might be had.

For in the far north of Karnakon, lay the barren wilderness called Nomadia where the Bay of Karabarth bordered Mangloth. But Karnakon feared no evil from that ancient and desolate abandoned land. Their leaders repeatedly assured them no harm could befall a country so honoured by T'var himself. The people of Karnakon took immense pride in their commerce with other nations, sharing their wealth and bounty in trade for what goods their own domain could not provide. Still, they remained quite unaware of the events unfolding beyond their borders.

Not that calling on the King's protections would be futile; rather, most inhabitants of Karnakon had forgotten how to do so. Their haughtiness and assuredness became a deception that Kolonth could craftily use to his advantage. Time passed and Karnakon forgot the true teachings of the King, T'var now more a distant legend, than a tangible sovereign. Ceremonies to celebrate His victory as Deathslayer evolved to be more ritual and formality than actual ceremony. Most would have laughed to think of the story as a tale of a real battle. More often than not, in the thinking of most of the people of Karnakon, Mangloth and T'var were merely fables from a time long ago with no relevance.

Only a few of the elders still knew and truly believed in their hearts in T'var. Often mocked, their persistent warnings of an impending menace and pleas to prepare for it were ignored. The majority of the people felt overly brave in their smugness and relaxed in a false security. Their nearness to T'var's Land turned to pride, their pride to arrogance, from there to conceitedness and ultimately, to their undoing.

In the quiet town of Mondaumin, only a few leagues east of the capital, three elder priests of T'var sat quietly at an evening meal together, lamenting the current situation. The delicious taste of fresh fruit from the Great Orchards, the newly caught fish bought at the market that day and the enticing smell of a freshly baked apple pie, did nothing to allay their concerns or the sadness in their spirits. A question broke the silence.

"What say you, Brother Steadmont, can you remember when the

whispers first came?"

"Sister Verona, I have a vague recollection, but it feels long ago now. They were shadows at first, without source or substance, maintaining T'var's laws written down in ancient times, now irrelevant to the new age. Whispers that grew louder and said often enough began take on the semblance of truth."

"Indeed, Sister, slowly the rumours took form, and became more defined. People argued that T'var understood the changing times and His former commands should be moulded to fit the new ways. People reassured themselves the protection of the King would still avail, His blessings would continue to rest upon Karnakon, though in truth, they long ago abandoned the ways of T'var and the lessons of The Books."

"This has not happened overnight, my fellow elders. This has been a well thought out strategy that began long ago." Brother Derwent was animated as he spoke, waving his hands as though preaching to a large congregation. Finishing his address with, "Perhaps our order must bear some of the blame," he bowed his head and grew silent.

"'*We trust not in our own strength, as T'var's teachings say,*' was the people's boast. How can that be laid on all our kind, Brother? Our teachers constantly countered with, '*But now you know not the true giver of those laws which brought strength and truth to us.*'" Sister Verona was adamant the fault lay not with them.

Brother Shalomarn slammed his hand on the table, rattling the dishes and shocking the other two. "The fault lies with us as much as the people! How long did we hear, '*We have followed the ceremonies, fulfilled our obligations, performed the duties on the High Days.*'?

"Yet we knew! We knew that eventually they followed the ceremonies without meaning and we were loathe to say anything that would stop the crowds from coming. From filling our offering boxes with their karns.

Not just us, but all of our faith! And when the people asked, '*What more would you have us do? We obey T'var, we meet His requirements, and so T'var must fulfil His. Should Karnakon ever be threatened He must defend it as He is bound to do.*'

"For those few of us brave enough to say, '*But you do not truly know T'var or understand not His words. It is your hearts T'var desires, not your fulfilment of empty rituals. They are meaningless without first giving Him yourselves,*' but it was too late! The words fell on closed minds! Now all of us, priests, elders, teachers of the faith, are restricted in our duties. Even these ghastly-coloured robes are supplied by those who govern to keep us in line. We can no longer celebrate the holy days publicly. Remaining true believers must do so in secret, lest they be mocked, scorned or in some parts of Karnakon, even arrested."

Brother Steadfast stood up to speak, but Shalomarn ignored him and rising up, continued. "Yes, faith in T'var was clearly lost when whole generations began to say, '*Why should we do more when T'var is a children's story, a fairy tale from long ago, not worth its telling.*' By now his loud, agitated and rapid speech had the other two arguing back. They were not in total agreement with his words. The heated discussion carried on and dessert was long forgotten.

"One thing, perhaps, we all agree on: we have failed T'var and failed the people and the people have now failed T'var as well. I fear punishment is coming for all. There are rumours of an ill chill from the north, that may soon engulf us too." Brother Shalomarn's voice trembled as he spoke, clasping and unclasping his hands in an odd rhythm, his furrowed brow reflecting his anxiety and deep thoughts. "Though I have heard some believers who remain have recently started speaking of *The Prophecy of Hope* again."

Sister Verona placed her hand around Shalomarn's back in a friendly manner, saying with a weak laugh, "Now who is speaking of myths?"

Shalomarn turned to stare at her so intensely, she had to turn away.

All fell silent and sombre, when Brother Steadmount thoughtfully suggested, "Perhaps betrayal is a better word than failure."

The betrayal began during the one thousand and seventh generation of the ruling family Arkon, who were descended from the first settlers whose ancestors were said to have been placed in the land by T'var Himself. Festivals dedicated to celebrating T'var's triumph were abolished and the priests were regulated to performing only civil tasks so as not to offend anyone. The words of the elders were fine for older times but appropriate no more, as per the decree of the present ruler.

It was during this time that *The Karn* became the title of the ruler of all of Karnakon and *Arkon* became the title of those who served to rule over all of the smaller cities, towns and villages across the country and who were answerable to The Karn. The Karn continued to rule from the capital Etraria, situated in the northern part of the of Karnakon, that seat still held through the centuries by some of the true descendants of the Arkons. The titles were an homage to those many generations, but the original meaning and the gifting was now diminished and obscure.

The emissaries of Kolonth fared well; Karnakon succumbed to their deceptions much faster than anticipated. While the final plans for the end of T'barth took shape, Kolonth's agents continued to work themselves into positions of power with the current ruling family of Karnakon. They became counsellors and advisors not just to The Karn, but to all the Arkons in the smaller locales as well. All across the land of Karnakon, they were most respected and often sought out for their wise words. The emissaries patiently bided their time in these positions, waiting for the signal from their master afar off.

To this land, Randak and Wandarr now spurred their steeds on, having left The Rangdorrian Lands to their fate, after doing what they could to help, whether battling the foe or aiding many in their escape. The growing chill engulfing T'barth somehow amplified, so that it was now beginning to cover The Rangdorrian Lands, pursued them, and they knew not if it would cease at the mountain border or chase them past it and swallow Karnakon in its frozen clutches as well.

It seemed like only hours ago they had been fleeing their home in Ponsfort, a quaint town within the Rangdorrian Lands. Yet in reality, it had been at least four days, maybe five. They both had lost track of time. As they rode forward, Wandarr thought back to the moment that changed everything.

Randak had come rushing in the door about midday shouting, "Sister, you need to pack everything that is needful for a long journey. Food, clothing, provisions, keep it minimal, only necessities, but fill your pack and ready Nayr."

"Why, what is going on? You are out of breath. Where have you been all these weeks?"

"Warning and training our neighbours to the north and east. At least, training those who would listen. I fear for some it was too late, for they may have been taken before they had time to gain their skills. There are yet still more to warn and prepare for what is to come. I need your help now. Not everyone has listened but some have, perhaps if your voice is added to mine..."

"Warning them? Of what?"

"The day has come. T'barth has fallen, riders from the south of it rode into Rangdorr saying T'barth is frozen by Kolonth's doing and his Carnivores and troops have begun marching through that land."

"By T'var! What next?"

"Next is us! They have not stopped with T'barth proper, they are marching ever southwards towards our lands. I do not understand why they are not already here, but trust me, it will not be long. And I have heard that whatever freezing magiks Kolonth has unleashed, have flowed into the northern part of our Rangdorrian Lands and is beginning to spread in all directions."

"What would you have me do? How long before they arrive here?"

"No idea, but we will fight if we must. This is why I kept up our training from the camp, just in case this day should ever come. We will warn our neighbours towards the west as we travel that way."

"But where are we going?"

"To Karnakon. It, at least, is still free as far as I know. I go now to warn the neighbouring farms to the south in the towns of Ewald and Nolan.

"That is a great distance. I will pack up for both of us in the meantime."

"Perfect. If I am not back by dusk, leave here and make for Karnakon. T'var willing, I will meet you at the pass into it."

"But, Brother, should I not wait?"

"No, we must move fast. If you leave without me, you will be able to warn the towns to the west as you pass through. Tell them to head for Karnakon or as far south as they are able. Not west, for Astaria is not an option now, for I doubt any would make it there in time. They would more likely perish, or worse."

"Yes, Randak, I will do so but hopefully you will be back to ride with me."

"We shall see. And do you have it? Still hidden in your pouch?"

"You mean the Orbstar? Yes, of course, it is never far from me."

"Good. It may be a small piece of the only hope we have. Give me a moment."

Randak ran into his room, yanked up a floorboard and returned with a sword which he presented to his sister.

"I have not seen this before, Brother. Have you been hiding it for so long?"

"They are gifts." Randak pulled out his own and Wandarr saw his sword was almost identical to the one he had just given her.

"Where do these come from?"

"I brought them home from the mines, but there is no time to explain. It is a story for later. You will find the grip fits your hand as though made perfectly for it."

Wandarr grasped the sword and found it light and the grip exactly as Randak described.

Before she had time to ask him any more about it, Randak ran out to mount Jip. "I must go so you can prepare for our journey. T'var willing, I will see you before daybreak," and he was off.

Randak did make it back just before dawn and the two started off without incident. Ever the strategist, he had their route already planned out. "We must bring this dire warning to our neighbours to the west now. We can cover all of the villages on our way if we split up. I could take Biscay, Vallet, and Hazeldon to the north, if you go to warn Hartson and Cayley to the south. Then our path will bring us together as we cover the last two places, Flintlock and Chalfont, further northeast. It is kind of a circuitous route, but at the end it will bring us close to the pass into Karnakon. What do you think?"

"Honestly, Randak, I don't like the idea of splitting up, but I understand how it will help us save time."

"Indeed, brave Sister and time may be short, so let's do this."

"Agreed, but what if they don't believe us? I mean, there is no sign yet of Kolonth's army."

"Then that is their loss, Wandarr. We can't force them to believe, only tell them what we know. What they choose to do with that information is up to them. T'var help us, that some may believe before it is too late for them."

"I will join you in that prayer for every place along my path. Nayr, let's ride!"

The two provided their warnings as planned to communities north and south, with a mixture of success and failure. Some residents took heed, some laughed. Others panicked and began packing up things and abandoning their homes to head away as quickly as possible. Many of the younger people mocked at the ridiculous idea that an invasion was imminent. Kinder residents in both Hartson and Cayley provided Wandarr shelter and a meal for the nights she was there. Randak was not as fortunate, having to fend for himself and sleep under the stars at a safe distance between his destinations.

Wandarr left Cayley in the early morning, making for the pre-arranged meeting point with Randak. Nayr was galloping at a steady pace, the morning air still fresh, the day not yet too hot, when Wandarr noticed the sudden lack of sound. Abruptly the sword Randak had given her started to emanate a strong amber glow and she instinctively freed it from its sheath.

Just in time too, for a huge, fanged, yellowish-orange beast broke out from the bushes along the path; it stank of decay and death and with its hungry eyes focused on Wandarr's throat, it leapt at her. She was too fast for it, her years of training taking over and her glowing sword sliced the creature in half in mid-air, black blood spurting everywhere coating, both her and Nayr.

She was surprised at how easy she was able to use the sword and thought in her hand it became as ferocious as the thing that attacked her.

In fact, as she dwelled on what happened afterwards, she realized it had an undefinable power to it when she used it. Somewhat familiar, it harkened her back to that one time she had used the Orbstar. *"Alike, yet unlike,"* she thought. *"I must hurry though, for this is not a good sign and I hope Randak is still safe."*

"Nayr, we will find a place later to wash this stink off of us. For now, though, full speed, my faithful friend."

She was thankful to meet Randak as planned and related her brief encounter, which explained the awful smell Randak had noticed approaching even from a distance.

"A Carnivore no doubt, one of Kolonth's grossest creations. I am glad you are safe, Sister, The Sonsword came to your aid as I knew it would."

"Sonsword? That is what it is called? But…"

"Later, Sister," Randak continued to avoid the question. "I fared better than you with no attacks, but this does not bode well for Flintlock and Chalfont, for they are slightly more to the north, so may be right in the path of the enemy's approach. Did you notice if the sword gave off an amber glow?"

"Yes, it did, but why do you keep evading my questions about it?"

"A longer tale when there is time, I promise. That amber glow tells when danger is near."

"Ah, I see, well that is fortuitous indeed and I look forward to the tale."

"Thank you for your patience Sister. Now we must fly." The two brought Jip and Nayr side by side and rode like the wind towards Flintlock. As they drew closer to the town's outskirts, they could see smoke already rising in the distance and once nearer, they encountered people of all ages fleeing in terror, screaming that the end of the world was upon them. Randak's anger soared and Wandarr felt her ire grow as well.

"We can not let them get away with this, Brother. We must fight, perhaps give whoever is left a fighting chance." Both siblings pulled out their Sonswords simultaneously, raising them to the sky in defiance to those who had attacked the town.

"I am with you on this, Sister. Look, we are about to encounter the enemy, for our Sonswords glow amber." They rode ahead and the swords blazed even brighter, blinding the foes before them, immersing the siblings in impenetrable shields as they sliced through the attacking army until everyone of them lay dead. Some of the town's survivors stuck their heads out from their hiding places and thanked the strangers with the glowing swords, pleading for more help.

"We do not know if Karnakon is still safe, so we will go there soon to find out. Your best route is to go as far south as possible. Find refuge wherever you can, perhaps in Glephas or even the Soutvold if you must, as awful as that land is. No place may be safe for a long time yet. We wish we could stay to do more, but we must see how Chalfont fares, as they may need our aid too."

Some heeded their words immediately, others sat down and wept until they could pull themselves together again and begin a long trek south to nowhere.

Unfortunately, by the time Randak and Wandarr had reached Chalfont, they encountered the same conditions as they had in Flintlock, only somewhat worse, as there were more dead and from what they could tell, no survivors. They could hear the sounds of a troop not far out of Flintlock, rode in fury to catch up with them, surprised their foes and hacked them into oblivion as they had done with the others. A couple of the enemy hid securely, waited for the two to leave, and then stealthily made their way back to Mangloth to give their Master a report. That is how Kolonth came to know of two powerful warriors, a man and a woman with glowing swords, who by all accounts, if his soldiers' reports could be trusted, were well nigh invincible.

*   *   *

"We fared well in battle, Sister. You have obviously kept up your training in my absence. A warrior to be reckoned with, indeed."

"Thank you, Randak, but still, all those villagers dead and what hope will the survivors have?"

"Perhaps some will find safety to the south," panted Randak as he struggled along with his sister to guide their horses up the treacherous path. It was a route which would lead them far from ice-covered T'barth and their invaded homeland and into Karnakon.

"I know not, dear Brother, who is to say if Karnakon may not already be destroyed by another of our Enemy's devious plots?" Wandarr asked. "Easy, Nayr, easy, old friend."

Wandarr gently guided her steed carefully over the rocks and along the steep slope.

"I pray to T'var 'tis not so. Our homeland will soon be in complete ruin and T'barth is already frozen - is this the end of all T'varin? What hope do we two warriors have against an enemy so strong?" Randak found speaking difficult as the incline to the path became steeper.

"Come, let us concentrate now on outrunning Kolonth's desecrating winter. We must make our way to Karnakon no matter what awaits us. No doubt, it will be better than the devastation lying behind us."

Wandarr paused as Nayr momentarily missed his footing on the rocky trail.

"Steady, steady, Nayr," she gripped the reigns tightly as she helped her horse regain his balance.

"Are you well?" Randak, now further up, called behind him. "We are almost to the opening which will lead us to the descent and onto the land of the Great Orchards."

"Yes, Brother, I am fine," Wandarr replied as she came along side Randak where the pass widened. "I pray to T'var the Great Orchards do not become victims of his icy stranglehold as well."

Except for the happy sounds of some songbirds, who cheered them up along the way, Wandarr and Randak travelled downhill quietly.

Eventually Wandarr tired of the silence and decided to broach a subject she had been curious about since Randak's return. "By the way, Brother, you have not said much about your journey in the west of our land. Did any of it go well? You said you warned the people and took time to train some. Were you successful? Did many respond favourably?"

"So many questions, Sister. It was, it was in some ways heartbreaking, in others encouraging, but perhaps more so the first than the last. And it was also strange."

"How so? What do you mean?"

"You know that in the west of Rangdorr, homesteads and farmhouses are very spread out. Often neighbours not close at all. Much like where we..." Randak hesitated, so Wandarr finished for him. "Where we grew up. Our home. Yes, I know of which you speak. Only in the town centres, where people gather for worship, or to purchase food and clothing and other goods, might one see neighbours. Other than that, the homes are isolated."

"Which makes them the perfect spot for the Raiders, Kolonth's raiders. You wouldn't know the people from the closest farm to you had gone missing, maybe not for a week. Only if they were eventually missed in the town square."

"Oh, I see, oh no! Do you think, do you think that is what happened to our parents?" Wandarr slowed Nayr and Randak did the same with Jip.

"I wasn't there to help them, Wandarr. I was so far away, touring the mines in T'barth with our cousins. I wanted to see them so badly because of my dream of working in them one day. But if only…"

"I wasn't there either, remember. I was visiting our Aunt and Uncle at their home in Ponsfort, now our home thanks to their kindness, leaving it to us when they passed on. Listen, Brother, if there is any blame, it falls on both of us, but I don't think our parents would want that. Do you really think these Raiders responsible?"

They stared at each other, eyes watery and glistening. "Perhaps. I saw them, Wandarr and at times fought some of them. But there is something else. Something strange about them. They were grotesque, yet there was still some small semblance of humanity about them. The larger part buried or drowned. In my estimation, they were definitely not what they once were. It was like they were mindless soulless beings, dedicated only to performing Kolonth's bidding. I think he is turning them."

"Turning who? I don't understand what you mean."

"Kolonth. He is turning them, turning his prisoners into his soldiers. I don't know how other than by some dark foul magiks, but I think the captives are being turned, for the Raiders don't just steal horses, they take people prisoner too. That may be how he is growing his army. We may very well be fighting against our own countrymen."

"T'var help us!" Wandarr didn't want to say it, but at that moment all she could think of was what might have happened to her mother and father.

"There was something else too."

"I am not sure I wish to hear anymore but tell me anyway."

"At the last couple places I went to warn, I encountered the Raiders and gave chase, until they were gone. I had the feeling they and I were being watched, monitored if you will. One time, I thought I saw in the distance, someone on horseback.

"Kolonth?"

"No, I doubt that, but perhaps a Captain or a General by their stature. For even from a distance, it looked like a commander of some sort, sitting tall in the saddle. It was hard to make out his appearance but I think he was less deformed than the Raiders that I and some of the angry villagers encountered.

"In fact, often the Raiders seem totally unprepared, almost frightened when confronted. They would run rather than fight. Yet, I still had a sense during that last time, that even the Raiders were more organized, more in control and perhaps there was a larger organized contingent just watching and waiting. Maybe a troop or a battalion watching from a safe distance, where they could not be well seen. I am only guessing. I don't know for certain."

"How odd!"

"If this is how Kolonth is growing his army, it will eventually be a massive number of soldiers, too many for even a combined force of all the lands together."

"By T'var!" Wandarr pushed Nayr further ahead, now unable to speak, her emotions a mix of anger, fear and frustration.

Randak's observations and guesses were actually closer to the truth than he would have wished. Kolonth's plan was to have his forces set up with ten generals overseeing ten battalions of five hundred soldiers each, with fifty captains in charge of one hundred soldiers within one of the ten battalions: a force of five thousand strong. His goal had not been completely achieved yet, but with every land conquered, every prisoner taken, every captive turned, his objective drew closer to becoming reality.

Randak's assessment of the Raiders was also somewhat accurate. The Raiders functioned outside of the battalions. With no real leadership, they were wild and untamed, assigned by Kolonth to randomly attack villages, secure horses and test the strength of some places to determine what level of threat they might pose. They were fine for raids when there was little opposition, but it became clear through testing in Mangloth's arena that they lacked the ability to develop any skills for true warfare, quickly turning useless and cowardly in a genuine battle.

Both silent once again, Randak and Wandarr rode with utmost speed to the first village which they knew they would find to the south. Far away, to the north, lay the vast plain of Nomadia, named so for the wandering nomads who used to inhabit the region.

During their trek, Randak took his mind off their recent conversation by remembering all the tales told to him during childhood about these strangers who were now part of Karnakon and yet not part. He recalled learning how the people of Nomadia lived in uniquely-made tents in the warm seasons and then, when the cold season approached, began to move into caves carved into the mountains, caves said to have been formed by T'var's hands in a time before known time. Certainly, long before the citizens of Nomadia began dwelling in them as protection from the northern winters.

Randak thought he remembered how some of the descendants of this strange race settled in the harbour town of Karabarth. There they fished the icy waters year-round, sending their bounty to the inner cities of Karnakon and the other landlocked countries. If the stories held true, some of the race's descendants still lived in small, scattered villages beneath the shadows of the mountains. No one had dared venture there for a long time, so none could verify the stories. The stories expanded over time, telling how the people of Nomadia intermarried with settlers from Glephas and other realms and thus no true bloodline endured from those original peoples.

Randak knew from his studies that the majority of the populace of Karnakon, mixed bloodlines or not, settled and populated the capital of Karnakon, called Etraria, or in the second largest city known as Kol. The tenders of the Great Orchards actually functioned as the mainstays in the population of Karnakon and they kept the country alive through the trade of their produce. The Great Orchards earned fame throughout all of T'varin for the freshness and variety of their crops. The families who tended the Great Orchards had done so for generations, with each new generation improving on the farming skills from the past one. The farmers lived in small villages, dispersed throughout the Orchards, each with its own particular specialty of harvest. Randak's reverie was broken by Wandarr's question. "Did you go by it?"

"Pardon?"

"Our old home in eastern Rangdorr. Did you see it? Ride by it?"

"Oh, I see, yes, I did. I couldn't help myself. I'm sorry, there was really nothing left of our farmhouse. It was a shambles, just some burnt timbers left sprawled about. I'm afraid the Raiders, if it was them, torched everything. Other places I passed shared the same fate."

Wandarr had no response, other than Randak could hear some sniffling, perhaps a sign she was crying but she stayed slightly ahead of him, so he could not see her face.

He made a decision to catch up with her and trying to be encouraging suggested, "Perhaps we should stop for a break? We could have a quick bite, for I know you packed well and you and Nayr could wash off."

"I'm fine, Brother. I would rather we keep going. I know we must clear our minds, be vigilant and alert, for who knows what may await us." Her voice sounded firm, clear, almost cold, but Randak couldn't argue with what she said, for she was right.

Surprisingly as they passed by a small brook, Wandarr relented, quietly stopped Nayr, dismounted and said, "We do need to clean up. Nayr and I can't go into any town looking and smelling like this."

"Let us know when you two are ready to move on." Randak brought Jip to a halt, walked him a bit further away and sat down against a tree to eat some food from his pack. Wandarr and Nayr joined them about thirty minutes later. After eating some food as well, Wandarr seemed to be in a better mood.

"Let's carry on, Brother. Whatever awaits us, we will face it together. T'var be with us both."

Back on their horses, they raced towards their destination. Their path would now take them to the smaller town of Diakon a few leagues to the north of the Great Orchards and the last settlement before the region of the Orchards began in earnest. Unbeknownst to them, the Arkon, representative of the Karn in Diakon, had already been seduced by one of Kolonth's servants. Deemed to be old and wise by a people who now trusted no one but themselves and believed less in T'var than in their own prosperity, he blindly led the blind, being led himself by one who could see only all too well.

The sun had dipped below the horizon some time ago and dusk had already transformed into early evening, with a few lonely stars beginning to show. Thus, the people of Diakon were rightly surprised to hear the sound of thundering hoofbeats and a male and female voice crying out as they passed by, "Quickly! To arms! Defend yourselves! Doom approaches! Show us the Arkon, which way to his abode?"

Upon hearing the shouts, people began to leave their houses, some abandoning late evening meals and others their beds, to stand outside their doors to see what all the commotion was about. They watched two strangers ride by shouting at them and yelled back, "That way to the Arkon. What is this about? We see no signs. We hear no danger. The Arkon would know and tell us of anything wrong. You are mad with weariness! Fools! The only dangerous people we see are you."

Their cries fell away with the wind, as Randak and Wandarr only drove their horses more swiftly onward to the Arkon's home.

"How much further, Randak? I feel like this ride is taking longer than it should. I did not realize Diakon had grown to such a large size."

"Nor I. I always thought of it as a small town. Now it seems to have grown into a little city."

"Agreed. Surely, we must be getting closer. Even riding as fast as we are, it feels like it may be well towards the midnight hour before we reach the Arkon."

"I know but see here, the dusty path we have been on is becoming firmer. If my eyes don't deceive me in what little light there is, I think it turns into cobblestone streets and walkways farther ahead."

Similarly, the simple huts and straw homes they first came across as they entered the city gradually shifted into larger houses of stone and brick, some even two-storied, the further they rode.

"It appears shops and stores are lining the streets now. Some look to have living quarters above them. Perhaps these are the streets for commerce."

"Possibly, but it will all come to naught, if Kolonth has his way."

"Let us hope and pray that is not the case and that some will listen to us."

Ahead they could see a very large, gated estate, surrounded by gardens and a well-constructed home whose immense size dwarfed all around it.

"That building standing out above the others must be our goal," said Wandarr above the heavy breathing and thundering hooves of Nayr and Jip.

"There is a locked gate ahead, Sister. Shall we…"

"Well ahead of you, Randak," Wandarr laughed as Nayr leapt over the obstacle in their path and Randak had Jip follow suit, startling the guards at the gate. They rode right up to the entrance way, dismounted and ran towards the bewildered doorman who didn't quite know what to do.

At the sound of the din outside his windows, the Arkon stirred uneasily. Feeling the weight of years and still in his ratty nightshirt, bare feet padding along on the cold bedroom floor, he slowly made his way to the terrace overlooking the street and peered out to discover the cause of the ruckus. He scrunched his face to squint at the ground below where he could see two figures on horseback racing towards his residence, followed by a crowd of guards yelling behind them.

"Mara, Mara," called the greying Arkon, known as Knast, picking up his pace slightly as he strode to the door of his chamber, absentmindedly tugging on his beard. "What manner of ruckus is this? Who are these intruders raising such a clamour in Diakon?"

"Do not fear, my lord," Mara's tone was both calming and hypnotic. It soothed away any fears that the Arkon felt. "I shall deal with them directly."

With her long, black hair flowing over her shoulders, thin and pale, Mara appeared. As was her custom, she was fully dressed in purple and red robes as though already prepared for the next day. She met the Arkon at the door of his bedroom and urged him back to his rest.

"You know how you tire, my liege. As your court advisor, I must recommend that you stay still. Such activity is not good for you."

"Yes, but I thought I would…"

Mara rose to her unusually tall six-foot height, as though she somehow had stretched out from her sandalled feet. "No need for thinking," she cut him off. "Such is my task. Rest is the best thing for you. You have experienced a tiresome day and need no more to tax yourself."

Mara carried a hidden ability where not many could withstand the mesmerizing stare of her eyes and this included the Arkon.

"Yes, yes."

For a moment, Knast seemed to have his mind elsewhere as he heard the riders dismounting amidst the shouts of the townspeople.

"Now what was I saying?" he asked, somewhat distracted by the noises outside.

"You were saying how I should deal with our guests as you have endured such a long hard day and desire to go to bed and not be disturbed," Mara's voice was more compelling than ever.

"Oh yes, that was it, yes, yes indeed, I am weary. By T'var, it is time to retire."

Mara's face winced at the mention of T'var's name, but this went unnoticed by Knast. By the time Mara left the Arkon's chamber and made her way to the welcoming hall, Randak and Wandarr had already forced their way past the shocked doorman and prepared to demand a meeting with the leader of Diakon.

Spotting Mara, Randak said, "We request an audience with the Arkon of Diakon on a matter of the utmost urgency for all of Karnakon. We apologize for our appearance, but we have ridden far to bring warning." Randak's request was hurried and loud, spoken without taking a breath.

Wandarr wiped the sweat and dirt from her brow, adding in a firm yet calm voice, as if to make up for Randak's brashness, "If it please the Arkon, we must needs speak with him about a topic of dire urgency. Are you one of his attendants?"

"I am Chief Advisor to the Arkon of Diakon," Mara answered, in a voice so sweet it felt almost overpowering.

"We are on our way to the capital Etraria, but since Diakon was on the way, we chose to stop and warn you as well. Your people must prepare for what is coming their way so perhaps at least some might yet be saved." Randak added to Wandarr's words, "We do not mean to be rude, but haste is essential if Karnakon is to survive."

"Survive?" interrupted Mara. "Survive what? Karnakon has survived for generations. It is under the protection of the Great King. He would never allow harm to come to this land, land so close to His own lands."

Randak and Wandarr felt odd but could not tell why. Mara's voice tugged on their minds and blended with their thoughts. They began to feel comfortable and at ease, wanting to put down their weapons and relax, perhaps even sleep. Though her voice sounded appeasing in the way Mara referred to the King, it bothered them both, yet they could not yet explain why. The more Wandarr thought, she realized Mara only referred to T'var's title, and avoided using His name. She thought Mara's tone was almost mocking when she spoke of the King's safeguarding. Her speech lacked the reverent attitude one would have expected from a true follower of T'var. Wandarr shook herself and began to grasp for words to express the threat she inexplicably sensed all too near.

Mara continued, "Surely you do not wish to trouble the Arkon at this late hour. Please come back in the morning and you may have a meeting then."

"It sounds like a reasonable request, doesn't it, Sister? Where might we find lodging for the night?" asked Randak, still entranced by Mara's hypnotic voice.

"Hush, Brother," interrupted Wandarr.

During Mara's last comments, out of habit Wandarr unconsciously touched the hilt of her sword. It began to vibrate calling her attention to the soft amber glow it emanated, though it stayed sheathed. At this she shook off the remainder of Mara's deception and in a more commanding voice which took Randak by surprise, Wandarr demanded, "We must see the Arkon immediately."

"The Arkon has retired for the evening," said Mara, her voice now with a sharp edge to it.

"Best summon him, woman!" commanded Wandarr. Wandarr's gaze met Mara's and held her eyes fast. Randak watched the tense glares, unable to comprehend what passed between the two, until he noticed Wandarr's hand resting on the top part of her Sonsword.

"Strange," he thought. *"Does she think to slay this woman? She may be impertinent, but surely that's not reason enough for murdering the Chief Advisor of the Arkon, even if she does seem unwilling to aid us."*

Randak looked again from Mara to his sister as the battle of glares carried on in silence. Then he saw the amber glow of his sister's Sonsword and became aware of the danger all around. His hand went to his own sword and then looking at Mara once again, he took more accurate stock of her.

At first, she had appeared beautiful, but now with the Sonsword pulsating in his hand, Randak saw Mara in a different light. All of her outward beauty revealed itself as a projection which covered an inner evil, now visible through the power of the Sonsword. He understood that the covering had been Mara's voice. Enticing, charming, pleasant, it acted as a shield for Mara and a blinding camouflage to any who might try to see the truth underneath. Now Mara reminded him more of a serpentine creature than a beautiful woman. Seeing through the trickery of her voice, Randak recognized one of Kolonth's servants through her hollow eyes, empty of all but hate, mixed with Kolonth's contempt for T'var and His followers.

Randak gripped the hilt of his Sonsword and felt the same vibration which had alerted Wandarr to danger. He also knew without looking, that its blade glowed amber.

"Enough!" Randak's shout broke the eerie silence of the staring contest between Wandarr and Mara.

"Impertinent fool!" Mara screeched, her voice no longer carrying the same enticing spell of a few moments ago. "I know well why you have come, but you are far too late. My Master's plan is succeeding all too well to be waylaid by the likes of you. Now go! Or I will call the guards and have you killed where you stand."

Mara's voice carried the sound of anger but tempered with what Wandarr sensed as a bit of fright.

"Enough, disciple of Kolonth! Your deception is over. It is not our habit to slay a woman, but unless you stand aside, so will it be!" Randak's voice burned with fury.

"What nonsense is this? By T'var, this commotion is loud enough to rouse the dead. Mara, why do these intruders threaten you? Answer now strangers, or it is you who may die, not my loyal and trustworthy advisor."

Knast had entered the room. The old man was wizened not only with age, but with the secret charms and spells of Mara, for she was a deceitful but learned student of her Master. Mara had managed to keep Knast indoors and apart from his people for so long that he was aged beyond his years. Wandarr and Randak decided they had no more time to waste. Wandarr had been ready to use her Sonsword on Mara and make short work of her until Knast entered the scene.

Wandarr looked to Knast, addressing him by his title, "Arkon, your Chief Advisor is nothing more than an evil minion of Kolonth, scion of Manglor. She has deceived and bewitched you. As we talk, not only Dia-kon, but all of Karnakon lies at risk of being within Kolonth's control. T'barth has already fallen and lies frozen under Kolonth's winter of despair."

"And even now, armies are likely flooding through The Rangdor-rian Lands as our own homeland falls prey to their desecration," Randak tried to emphasize how serious the danger.

"T'barth fallen? T'barth has fallen, T'barth..." Knast muttered to himself, lost in thought.

"They lie, my master," Mara said, her voice taking on its enchantment once again. "My dear Arkon, these people come to us with false tales of T'barth's fate. They are mere frauds and need to be dispatched; they will destroy the tranquility our people have enjoyed for so long."

Speaking in her lulling tone, Knast quickly fell under her sway. After years of exposure, it did not take long for him to succumb to Mara's wiles. Even Randak felt himself once again slipping into the enchantment generated by her voice and loosened his grip on his Sonsword.

Wandarr however felt her hand move to the Orbstar tucked safely in her belt. The moment her fingers grazed the gem, Mara's voice held no sway with her. Wandarr held the Orbstar tightly. So absorbed was Mara in maintaining her deceit, she failed to notice Wandarr vanish.

Mara turned her attention from Knast to Randak. Wandarr, now invisible, stood behind Mara with her blade drawn, ready to drive it home at the first opportunity. From her position, Wandarr noticed a necklace on Mara that must have been hidden from view by her gown.

From her position, Wandarr could see the jewelry consisted of bone, each piece fashioned into the symbol of a circled hexagon. Whether due to some extra property of the Orbstar, or just because she stood so near, Wandarr saw clearly how the adornment around her neck gave off a sickening yellow colour and a rancid smell which reminded her of death and decay.

On impulse, Wandarr reached out grabbed the necklace and pulled with all her might, snapping it lose from Mara's neck. The moment the chain broke, Mara's voice drained of all its charm, and immediately Knast felt himself waking from what seemed a long, deep sleep.

Mara turned to see who dared perform this awful deed and only then did she become aware of Wandarr's absence. Randak and Knast, both now free from the charm, looked to see Mara beating at the air.

"Mara, what madness has come upon you?" asked Knast.

"The only madness is that which I have infected you with, old fool," cried Mara to the astounded Arkon.

Suddenly Mara appeared as though caught in an invisible vice, struggling for breath. Randak smiled as he heard a voice fill the air.

"Tell him, Witch. Tell him whose servant you really are. Explain to him what you have done to Diakon."

Knast and Randak watched as unseen hands picked Mara up and threw her across the room, where she hit the wall and then lay sprawled on the floor. For the first time in many years, Knast saw true when he gazed upon Mara. He saw a snake with hollow empty eyes in which burned the fires of Kolonth's hate for T'varin. Knast shrank in terror.

"Why so fearful, cretin?" Mara demanded; her voice absent of power. "Oh yes, they are right: the substance of my charms is gone, but the seeds I have planted here have grown too strong for any to be uprooted. Diakon is lost to you, Arkon! Slave! You have been a slave to Kolonth all along. We tricked you so easily and soon Diakon will fall, along with all of Karnakon. My counterparts have been doing the same work in so many towns and cities of your pitiful land, that soon everywhere will be prey to your true sovereign. Long live Kolonth, rightful Master of T'varin. He will conquer and the cold will live. T'varin is his."

"Never!" shouted Randak. "Never will T'varin fall as you say."

"Oh yes, child," said Mara. "It shall! And you too, will be his before long."

"Liar!" Randak's rage drove him to end this.

Wandarr and Knast could only stare as he flew across the room and hacked her body in two with his now drawn Sonsword. The room became engulfed in a thick black smoke. The three watched as black liquid, not blood, oozed from the slain thing that was once Mara, coated it and ate away at the body until it faded into nothingness, leaving only a deep stain on the floor, one which manifested as the symbol of a circled hexagon.

Randak, Wandarr and Knast all ran from the room to escape the stench and clear their lungs in the fresh night air.

"Unbelievable," thought Randak looking up at the sky. *"This treachery delayed us so long that dawn may soon be upon us."*

Randak's fury had abated when he slew Mara but Knast's was just beginning. And that fury, for the most part, he directed solely at himself.

"What have I done?" Knast started weeping. "My people, my land, I have betrayed them, failed them all. I have been blinded, a foolish lackey to the enemy of all T'varin. Duplicity and deceit. It cannot all be all blamed on her either. I would not listen. Now when we have said peace, destruction comes upon us."

In vain, Wandarr and Randak attempted to rouse Knast from his self pity. At length, when they felt they could wait no longer, Randak barked at Knast, "Arkon, we can spend no more time here. Please come to your senses; you *must* warn your people. We *must* ride on. The Orchards are at risk, as you now know. We must move on to warn Etraria."

"Do we, though? Ride to Etraria? It will be no surprise to find its eldership as fooled as Diakon," Wandarr expressed her uncertainty.

"I know it well, Sister," Randak turned to leave the Arkon to his grief. "What should we do then? Leave Etraria to its fate and ride to warn the Orchard Keepers?"

"It is an evil dilemma, Brother, a hard choice to be sure. Etraria is many leagues to the north and the Orchards much closer. But still, all those people in the capital who will perish without our help. Children and families…" Wandarr's words hung heavy, suspended in the air as expectant grief.

After some deep thought, Randak broke the silence, "I hear you Sister, but there is more chance of saving the Great Orchards than reaching Etraria in time. Right or wrong, I deem that be our path. Perhaps this once, we may be in time to prevent Kolonth's evil from taking hold."

"Let us be off then," said Wandarr. "There is nothing more we can do here. Even as we talk, I feel Kolonth's deadly grip stretching farther into this land like some many-armed monstrosity."

Leaving Knast in a crumpled sobbing heap, they departed the dwelling, mounted their steeds, turning Jip and Nayr south towards the Great Orchards and commanded the surprised palace guards, "Care for your Arkon," and galloped away.

The pounding of the horses' hooves was only a long-lost echo by the time the people of Diakon roused for the day. Remembering the visitors from the previous night, they began to ask what the strange tidings meant and quickly learned the tragic tale and of the danger looming over them.

*   *   *

The city of Etraria had slept fitfully; most of the inhabitants had spent an uneasy week of sleepless nights. Even so, they remained unaware of the imminent danger on their doorstep. The omen of sleeplessness meant nothing to a people overly concerned with the business of busyness. That busyness drowned out all else and gave no time for omens.

On the High Day of the week, a day set long ago to revere T'var, the Altar Houses stayed nearly empty. Most Etrarians, now lived either too exhausted from the week's activities to attend, or chased after what they considered more pleasurable diversions which required less thought than concentrating on the words of a Speaker of T'var. Though priorities can change instantaneously when the enemy is at the city gates, or at one's door.

Hidden in a harbour on the Bay of Karabarth, a third of Kolonth's forces awaited their Master's signal. Once the onslaught of cold began to expand across T'barth's border and then covered The Rangdorrian Lands, this third started their attack on Karnakon. The Carnivores led the first wave, surging across the land in a terrifying rampage, bringing death to the screaming inhabitants, clawing, shredding and devouring anything in their path that had breath.

Next came Kolonth's soldiers, relentlessly moving through the northern part of Karnakon, trampling, killing and destroying whatever and whoever they came across. This was followed by ships full of more soldiers entering the Bay of Karabarth. Propelled by Kolonth's machinations, these vessels were empowered to sail against the current through the canal system using the waterways as a launch pad for their growing invasion, the troops jumping from the ships into whatever populated places they sailed through.

Many from Etraria ran from the Carnivores and the soldiers seeking safety in the waters that surrounded the capital, only to find themselves hauled up on to the ships as prisoners destined to travel north, where they would be forced into the service of Mangloth.

One of Kolonth's generals oversaw the remaining ships, which were driven past Etraria.

"You know the Master's orders. We are going to travel this water route to Lake Sythm and you will abandon your ships along the way, setting them aflame before you jump to shore."

A Captain, confused by the strategy, spoke up above the crackling timbers of the ships as the flames engulfed and consumed them, the smoke rising in billows carried away by the wind, the trail of wreckage floating towards the Lake. "Seems like a waste of good ships and means more walking for our soldiers, General. Why does the Master want them burned?"

"Not wasted at all and it's a good thing he can't hear you. I don't owe you any explanation but listen, he's wise, our Master is and trust his plan. You see all that cargo we loaded on the bottom of the ships? It's Kolonth's potions and poisons. The Lake will be the ships' graveyard but all that deadly poison is going leak out into the waters, spreading and infecting the ground, leaving the soil corrupted and desolate, unable to produce anything but death and decay. So much for the Great Orchards too, once they get a taste of it!"

In response to the explanation, the soldiers' gruff bellowing voices filled the air. "Victory! Praise Kolonth! Praise the wise Master!"

When they were done yelling, their General gave the order for the soldiers to continue their deadly march south.

No city, town or village, regardless how large or small, escaped Kolonth's wrath.

Shouting, *"Fire and Ice, Fire and Ice!"* as the soldiers attacked each new place, they set fire to everything before them and the cold from T'barth, somehow boosted to extend its reach, now swept down to solidify Kolonth's chill across the countryside. Even amplified, the cold did not have the power to freeze people solid as it had done in T'barth, but the chill was still strong enough to bring misery to the land. For as per Kolonth's directive, anything that could not be burned would be frozen and whatever could not be frozen was to be burned.

*   *   *

When the Arkon of Diakon finally regained enough composure

to address his people, he did it far too late. Destruction fell on Diakon in the shape of Kolonth's troops and all turned to rubble. The captains of Kolonth's army spared no time in their unrelenting march, for they possessed one dark goal to achieve for their leader: the devastation of the Great Orchards of Karnakon. Once the Orchards ceased to be, all the lands would suffer from the lack of crops and trade and in their suffering, they would turn to Mangloth for assistance and mercy. Or so Kolonth planned. He would then hold the keys to the health of all of T'varin, for without the Etrarian blessed fruit, the economy would fal, and famine be rampant.

The Rangdorrian Lands were already in such a state that farming was impossible. The destruction of the Orchards would guarantee Kolonth's complete control over the food systems of T'varin.

Kolonth's instructions to his armies always insidiously clear. The moment his soldiers reached the northern border of the Great Orchards, they were to burn the land. A fire inspired by Kolonth's mystical incantations which were rooted in deep and ancient magiks. A fire quickly spreading, set by his army, burning everything in its way. On the heels of the fire would come the cold of Kolonth. The two things which the Keepers of the Great Orchards feared the most: fire and ice. Kolonth had determined long ago that these two elements would be the instruments of his complete conquest over Karnakon.

Kolonth decided that once his ships had served their purpose, even the Etrarian River would be aflame, its banks burning bright red, while its waters dried up to a trickle before finally being frozen over. After fire and ice ran rampant through the countryside, on would come the rest of his soldiers destroying whatever remained in their way.

Kolonth's troops marched southward, through devastated Diakon, drawing ever closer to the Great Orchards. Randak and Wandarr travelled on, not daring to yet look behind them, sensing in their spirits that the land already suffered under siege. South of the Great Orchards, the rest of Karnakon lay silent and unsuspecting.

Quicker than they thought possible, Randak and Wandarr reached the northern border of the Great Orchards. Riding the gradually sloping path, they did not realize how high they had climbed until they halted and turned, finally looking towards Etraria. From their vantage point, far away to the north, what they saw made them turn cold.

"See, Sister," cried Randak. "Kolonth's devastation of Karnakon has begun. We are too late."

"I see it all too well. There is a black mass moving towards our direction. What is the red hue going before it, colouring the landscape?" asked Wandarr. "Behind it there looks like a massive white blanket, a sheet of, of..."

"Of snow and ice," finished Randak. "We have seen it before. It is alike to T'barth, but of the red I..."

"It is fire, fire for sure. See the dark smoke now rising and the sky full of birds fleeing as fast as their wings will take them? I think I can even hear them calling in fear." Wandarr pointed to the sky. "Fire and ice, fire and ice. I feel it, even as we see it afar off. Our Enemy is using not only ice alone, but fire as well, to decimate Karnakon."

"Yes, yes, of course," said Randak. "He means to ruin the livelihood of the land. Karnakon will soon be as immobile as T'barth, frozen in ice and all lands will be deprived of its Etrarian-fed fruit."

"There will be a famine of Kolonth's making before long," said Wandarr with frustration.

"Enough," said Randak. "We will have to wait to aid Etraria and hope it does not fall quickly, though that black mass moves too fast for my liking. Warning the Keepers that the Great Orchards are in peril must be our priority. We need to quickly descend into the valley. We will soon meet the winding pathway that meanders through the Orchards and the villages of the Keepers. We must warn them as we pass."

"Will they heed us or be as blind as the Arkon of Diakon?" Wandarr wondered aloud.

"Does it matter? Whether they choose to heed us or not, we must still warn them. Kolonth's deceivers may have been at work amongst them as well but let us trust they concentrated more of their efforts in the capital than in the Orchard lands. For T'var and T'varin, we must alert them," Randak pushed Jip onward.

"Agreed." Wandarr followed with Nayr.

As they rode, they drew their swords from their sheaths and declared, "*T'var, T'vari, T'varin.*"

"King's Praise!" proclaimed Randak. "On to the Orchard Keepers, friends or foes, we go in T'var's name."

Soon they were no more than a blur on the countryside, rushing headlong down into the Etrarian valley, fire and ice marching steadily onwards behind them.

CHAPTER SEVEN
THE CIRCLE OF ANDIVAR

At full gallop, Wandarr and Randak crossed into the region of the Great Orchards at its northern border, shouting their warnings to all within hearing.

"Fire and ice! Destruction is coming! Alarm! To arms! Orchard Keepers, arise and defend your flock! Kolonth's forces are bringing destruction in their wake! Fire and ice! Awake! Awake, caretakers of the Great Orchards of Karnakon. Your groves require protection!"

The shouts of Randak and Wandarr echoed as they sought to waken the sleeping villagers, travelling the winding path through the orchard valley. *Andini,* they had been called of old. Now it was a name long forgotten, except to the Keepers themselves, whose memories spanned many ages through which they faithfully passed on their knowledge to each new generation.

Even Randak and Wandarr knew them only as Orchard Keepers. Old histories told tales how in the early dawn of T'varin, T'var had assigned the ancestors of the present Orchard Keepers the task of nurturing, protecting and harvesting the Great Orchards of Karnakon. Long before Etraria grew into the bustling centre of activity it became, legends told how T'var called the Andini from another land or perhaps from another world.

Back in this early time, T'var Himself gave the Great Orchards to the Andini to care for and harvest and thus provide sustenance for all of T'varin. The legends told of T'var performing a miracle on the Etrarian River which caused it to flow through the Orchards and feed them with water unlike any other in T'varin.

Whether it was a by-product of that miracle or a more direct gift from T'var, since the beginning, through all generations, the Andini lived in a symbiotic relationship with the land. They tended it and the orchards that grew from it, always with a keen sense and awareness of not just its existence, but of its needs, desires and its state of being. Similarly, the land attuned itself to those of the Andini; a mutually-exclusive joining that benefited and blessed both.

Lately, their honed senses, powered by this connection, informed them something was not right in the land, though for some reason, its identity remained a mystery. They suspected it might be a threat to the Great Orchards themselves, and if so, these protectors were prepared to wage a battle most believed inevitable.

Along the winding path of the Etrarian River the riders flew, shouting their alarms each time to any Keepers and villagers who appeared. At the second village they entered, the two slowed their pace as children, field labourers and some mothers with toddlers and infants gathered about to see who these strange visitors were and why they were yelling.

"Your horses look so nice," said one of the little girls. Her blond curls and wide eyes accentuated her facial features. Her bright yellow top, matching blue trousers and bare feet, all covered in dust from playing, spoke to a childhood innocence that broke Wandarr's heart when she thought of this little one becoming a victim of Kolonth's nightmarish designs.

"Yes, please could my sister and I have a ride?" Her older brother was brave enough to approach Jip, but hesitant to get too close. The site of the boy's straggly hair, curious bright eyes and bold approach couldn't help but remind Randak of himself and his sister in younger, happier days.

"I'm sorry young ones, but maybe another time. Right now, we have important news to share, a dire warning of danger to come, I am afraid."

"Shhh," one of the mothers stepped up closer. "We have sensed something not right, but best not to scare the children, don't you think?"

"We are sorry," Wandarr apologized. "But soon, even that may not matter. We would stop and speak in detail with all of you in every village, if we had the time, but know this, The Rangdorrian Lands have been decimated, T'barth is frozen and Karnakon is under attack even as we speak. All by Kolonth's hand."

The shock on people's faces was followed by exclamations of disbelief and tears, while mothers shielded their children's ears, lest more horrific news be spoken. Some quickly removed themselves with their children, running back to the log cabins they called home, as the reality of the duo's words set in.

"You speak true then?" One of the older men who had just come in from the orchards tried to grasp the meaning of this news.

"Very true," Randak was losing patience. "We must warn the rest of your people. The Great Orchards are at risk of being no more."

"Continue on this path then. It will take you to The Circle. That is where you need to be."

"What is meant by The Circle?" But the man was already on his way home to gather his family together and make preparations. For exactly what, he was uncertain.

"He is gone, Brother, but let's do as he says. Follow this path wherever it takes us and whatever this Circle is."

These conversations were repeated at each village as people ran out to see what the riders' warnings were about. Randak and Wandarr's words often leaving behind frightened but courageous Orchard Keepers who took the warriors' words to heart.

Eventually the two ran out of patience, as slowing at each village was consuming an inordinate amount of time and they felt a growing sense of urgency within their spirits. Moving Jip and Nayr to a faster speed, they raced through the remaining villages saying little. Many still ran forth from their log homes or their work to discover why such a commotion occurred, only to see the backs of these swift and determined riders and the clouds of dust left by Jip and Nayr.

As word began to spread of the strangers and their warnings, the elder Andini, currently led by a man named Sargon, began to gather together in the Circle of Andivar. The Circle, an open place in the midst of the Great Orchards was used for ceremonies, worship, meetings and other sacred events. With Etraria too far to travel to on the High Days, the Circle served the Orchard Keepers through the years as a sacred ground and meeting place. Perhaps because they lived so far removed from the capital, the Andini escaped much of the deceptions and illusions which befell the rest of Karnakon.

Over time, the Andini had developed a method of using the Orchard's massive irrigation system to send a variety of types of messages, sometimes localized and other times sent throughout all the villages of the Orchard Keepers. It had started simply, colouring the water to indicate the status of things such as weather warnings and calls for meetings. Eventually the system evolved to be more complex, with a larger number of colours, the water's rhythm, height and duration, representing symbols that acted as an alphabet.

It was due to this unique system of messaging, that many of the Andini were already aware of Randak and Wandarr and the warning they brought. Since the messages were also sent to those south of the Circle where Randak and Wandarr would not have passed by, all Keepers would soon be present at the meeting place.

The elder Andini, already aware of an imbalance, something not quite right, took the warnings as confirmation of what they had already been feeling, but unable to name. Believing these riders spoke true and that the Great Orchards of Karnakon now lie in terrible danger, the Andini hoped their visitors would be able to enlighten their quandary. They knew that the strangers would be challenged to speak to their cause at the Circle of Andivar. The riders could not pass through the Orchards much further without coming to the Circle and there the elders would demand more information. All Keepers who were able began to press on toward the Circle.

Though not ancient by T'varin standards, the people still considered the Circle of Andivar to be old. Its unique properties had served the Andini, the Orchard Keepers, well over the years. Legends still declared in this spot, that T'var Himself commissioned their ancestor Andivar to begin the tending of the Great Orchards; a task that was handed down from generation to generation, eldest to the youngest, until the *time of change* should come. What T'var meant by the *time of change* remained unclear to all.

Randak and Wandarr reached the Circle of Andivar and found a host of Orchard Keepers surrounding them on all sides. Randak felt only slightly nervous at the sight of all the faces and commented to Wandarr, "They appear friendly enough."

"Perhaps, but caution is still prudent. We have been deceived before," Wandarr said, thinking of Mara and Diakon. "Though the sweet and musky scent of this place is somehow welcoming."

"Behold, Sister," said Randak and pointed. "They are clearing a path for us."

The Circle gave way as the riders slowed their mounts to a steady walk and made for the large, raised mound they could now see in the centre of the Circle, although the din from all the voices continued.

The moment Randak and Wandarr reached the raised mound, they could more clearly see the size of the throng surrounding them. Randak estimated at least five hundred people were in the crowd, if not more. Most were dressed as one would expect of farmers. Brown and green shirts, dark-coloured or matching trousers made of sturdy material, some wore hats. Looking at the massive crowd surrounding them, Wandarr thought to herself, *"It's like standing in the middle of a sea of green and brown, leaves and trees I reckon. Camouflage!"*

Randak and Wandarr stopped on the mound to survey the sight before them and caught sight of four Andini step out toward them, positioning themselves in each direction, north, east, south and west and then turn to face the crowd. These elders were dressed in what might be considered more formal wear. They wore billowing black pants and white shirts open at the neck, revealing silver chain necklaces. Simultaneously, the four raised their hands in a gesture causing almost immediate silence from the crowd.

Randak raised his own hand signifying his readiness to speak, but before he could, one of the Andini who stood apart from the crowd turned to him saying, "Hush, warrior. You are now in the circle of Andivar and no meeting of this host may commence until allegiance is first paid to T'var, Lord of all T'varin. Heed our elder Sargon first, young warrior."

Sargon's hand went to his side and then Randak and Wandarr became aware that the Andini were armed, with swords or axes in their belts. The weapons did not stay at their sides, for as Sargon spoke, the crowd raised their weapons towards the sky.

A brief wave of panic came over Wandarr as she saw all these swords and axes unsheathed until she realized these were faithful and loyal followers of T'var. Randak was ahead of her, but she was not far behind, as they raised their own Sonswords in unison with the Andini. They both joined in loud shouts of, *"T'var, T'vari, T'varin."* The cry soon echoed throughout the Orchards, from one end to the other. The chorus lasted only a few moments, piercing through the branches of the Orchard Trees overhead and ascending into the sky.

As quickly as it began, the sound of T'vari praises reached their crescendo and then softened to a whisper. Randak and Wandarr thought they could still hear the melody lingering, along with the echo of the Andini's voices hanging in the air all about them, though the crowd grew silent once again.

Sargon, as if on cue, sword now sheathed, raised his hands and cried out, "Great Lord T'var, we who gather once again in the Circle of Andivar, beseech You. King's Praise, give us ears to listen and hearts to do. Master of Masters, Deathslayer, Creator and Giver of the Great Orchards, our flock, Dayspring of the Etrarian, bring us light." His voice raised to full volume, Sargon spoke a command, "Circle of Andivar of T'var-T'var *Andivar Spaeshium Tempomora."*

At those words, Randak and Wandarr closed their eyes, for without warning the entire grove was flooded in brilliant white light. They finally opened their them but could see nothing around them except the Circle of the Andini. To their amazement they saw no branches, no leaves, no trees. Everything outside of the Circle and its occupants had vanished.

Randak used his hands to shield his eyes and said, "Forgive our ignorance, elder Sargon, we have heard of the Circle of Andivar before, but I do not even think we are in Karnakon anymore, almost as though we have been...have been...I guess, *removed* is how I perceive it, removed to somewhere else?"

"Indeed," interrupted one of the other elders who earlier helped to quiet the crowd. "That may well be. We ourselves have never been certain of how the protection of the Circle works, we only know that it does."

"Yes, and it is a rare privilege for ones not of Andini to be privy to this long-hidden secret. We recognize you as servants, and more than that, warriors of T'var. It explains why the Circle is open to you as well."

"And we are most honoured for the privilege," replied Wandarr. "But as my brother says, we feel terribly displaced."

"Displaced, yes," Sargon nodded. "As good a description as any. You are indeed displaced. We understand it as being outside of time and space. At least outside of the time and space which flows through T'varin. We are not on T'varin, although we still are. Anyone looking on will not detect us and simply pass through, unaware of the gathering in their midst and neither will we see them. This is the protection the Circle affords."

Another elder added, "No evil thing, nothing not of T'var, may enter here. None of His enemies, or things not of T'var's devising, can enter once the Circle of Andivar is brought to life. Any enemies who might have been among us, would not have been able to come here; they would be back where we left from, but unaware of what transpired, frozen in time."

"As you know, I am Sargon, this is my second, Mathiatar, and also before you, stand elders Rymol, and Amulret. We are all friends here, servants of T'var and you may now speak without fear."

"And speak we must, for time grows short," said Wandarr, looking to her brother.

Sargon and the other elders, smiled at her comment, explaining to a confused Randak and Wandarr, "We have learned time is of no consequence in this place. You may take as long as you like. You will find that we will all return to the exact same moment in time from when we left."

On that note, Randak began, "Thank you elders and all Andini gathered here for this chance to address you. I am Randak and this is my sister, Wandarr. We hail from The Rangdorrian Lands, or at least what used to be them." Before he could elaborate, his last comment was immediately followed by some exclamations of concern and fear from many in the crowd.

"Oh no, what do you mean?"

"Yes, please tell us more!"

"Your homeland is destroyed?"

"Do you bring only dire and bad news?"

"Is there anything good to say?"

Sargon finally raised his hand, commanding silence, allowing Randak to continue his account with Wandarr filling in the gaps. He spoke of their homeland and its devastation, of the fall of T'barth and the machine's devastating frigid work. He described all of the evil machinations across the other lands and their source finally revealed as Kolonth. The Andini listened with rapt attention, sometimes shaking their heads in a mixture of horror, disbelief, sadness and anger. When Randak began to describe what had just happened in Diakon, many of the Andini began to weep, while others fell prostrate, burying their faces in the Circle's sacred ground. Occasional cries could be heard from amongst the crowd beseeching T'var for aid.

Randak finished, describing how they had left Diakon and Sargon spoke up once again, saying, "Thus you have come to forewarn us, riding as it were, with Mangloth's forces bearing down on us."

"This is what we have been sensing," one of the Andini from the crowd said. "We believed something amiss in the land."

"Yes," added another. "But we could never identify the source of this nameless fear."

"It is not nameless," responded Wandarr. "It owns a name. Its name is *Kolonth*."

Sargon spoke again. "Yes, Kolonth, Manglor's heir. It may well be that *The Time of Change* spoken of to our ancestor Andivar by T'var Himself, may now be upon us."

"I know not what is meant by *Time of Change*," said Randak. "But I know fire and ice are on the way. Devastation will come to the Great Orchards and to all of Karnakon, unless something is done to stop the approaching horde. Whichever course of action is to be taken, it must be done with haste."

One of the Andini standing close to them looked at Randak and Wandarr and then to Sargon, his voice rising in panic, "But what can we do?"

"Fire and ice!" shouted another from farther away. "It will be our downfall and the destruction of The Orchards. This must not be."

The second elder said, "From your tale, Kolonth's forces will soon be at the borders of the Great Orchards, if they are not already there. Some of our countrymen remained behind to continue tending our charge. We cannot let them become victims of Kolonth's madness. They are defenceless and would be slaughtered without mercy or taken prisoner. We cannot let this happen when we are afforded the protection of the Circle and they are not."

A large amount of discussion among all the Andini began. To Randak, the discussion lasted an unbearably long amount of time. He kept trying to remind himself that time did not matter in this place, but he still found it hard to accept and wished they could do something more than stand and talk.

At length, Sargon again raised his hands and motioned for silence. "Enough, faithful Andini, enough. We know the danger; we know the protection of the Circle of Andivar. We need not to discuss the problem but come up with a solution to it."

"Yes, yes," said Wandarr. "By all means, if you know of a solution to defeat Kolonth, then please, let's have it."

Mathiatar, the second elder, fingering his silver necklace, said to Randak and Wandarr, "You must realize, we are not so concerned with the defeat of Kolonth, as with the protection of the Great Orchards of Karnakon. T'var never charged us to defeat the evil one, but He did commission our people to protect the Great Orchards and that is what we must do above all else."

"To Kolonth, even that would be a defeat," said Randak.

"Yes," agreed Wandarr. "No doubt the Great Orchards are a treasure Kolonth has long lusted after, desiring their complete destruction."

"How can you hope to protect the entire area with all the homes, people and families, as well as all the Orchard within?" asked Randak. "They mean to trample it, burn it and then freeze it, along with everything else in their way. You would have to move it right out of the army's path to keep it safe!"

"Indeed," Sargon said.

"Yes," Mathiatar said and looked at Sargon with a smile.

"Of course," another of the four elders said, stepping closer to the other two.

"Indeed what?" Wandarr asked rather impatiently.

She looked around as she spoke and realized she was the only one who did not understand what everyone else did. The Andini nodded their heads in silent agreement. Even her brother seemed to understand what the Andini spoke about.

Randak turned to Wandarr and seeing the puzzled expression on her face, said, "Do you not see? If they can somehow enlarge the Circle of Andivar, extend it to encompass the Great Orchards themselves, the protection will extend to the whole area and everyone within that radius; both Orchards and Andini will be moved out of the way, at least out of the path of the enemy's forces. The Orchards will still be on T'varin, but in the same invisible state as we are currently, and when Kolonth's forces start to march into it determined to burn and freeze it..."

"It will not be there," finished Wandarr.

"They will be so surprised that they will no doubt turn back in dismay," one of the Andini from the crowd said with a smile.

"Unlikely, my son," replied Sargon. "I do not doubt that they will continue on through the land to attack whatever towns and villages remain. It is likely that Kolonth's forces may have already stormed and taken the capital. We can do naught for them and we must consider our own plight now."

"Yes," said Mathiatar. "We must determine how to extend the Circle. Andivar's descendants will fulfil T'var's commission. The Great Orchards shall be protected. We shall be true to our duty. But how?"

Sargon said, "We must return to T'varin and somehow encircle all of the Great Orchards so all is removed. Perhaps if we all spread out in a chain around the entire Orchard?"

"I am afraid you would not have time," Randak said. "Based on what we observed, it is certain that Kolonth's forces already draw near the border of the Great Orchards, if they are not already at it. Before you would be able to complete any kind of chain as you describe, they will have struck many of you down."

"There must be a way to extend the protection of the Circle of Andivar," argued Sargon, "This would need to be done by T'var's might, as the Circle is a thing of T'var's power. If only we possessed another instrument to give us more of T'var's power, we must think…"

"Wait."

Wandarr now understood what she must do. She reached into the pouch hidden in her belt and felt the Orbstar. She placed her hands around it and felt it quiver, responding to her touch. By the time she removed it and held it forth, the blue glow manifested, humming in rhythm, as though already anticipating her thought.

"This should be of assistance in extending the protection of the Circle of Andivar, for it is of T'var's power."

The Andini looked on in astonishment. They all saw what few of this age had ever earned the privilege to see. There before them, held in the open palm of this warrior, an Orbstar of T'varin. It glowed and hummed with life-energy, anxious to be put to use.

"King's Praise!" exclaimed Sargon, the cry copied and shouted by many of the other Andini.

"How can this be?" Mathiatar asked, not sure he believed what he saw. "Do our eyes deceive us?"

"No indeed," Wandarr reassured him. "It truly is what you see before you, an Orbstar of T'varin."

"Timely now to reveal it," Randak looked at his sister with pride.

"How came you by such a treasure? Legends spring to life before us!" another of the elders said.

"It is a long tale and I think now is not the time. This place, the Circle of Andivar, is as much legend to us, as this Orbstar to you, yet here we are together."

"Well spoken, Wandarr and here we are together for good purpose," Sargon spoke thoughtfully. "If the stories of the Orbstar be true at all, distorted though they may have been through the centuries..."

"The stories are true."

"Then time and space flow from the Orbstar and its power will affect them both," Mathiatar excited everyone with his words.

"Yes. Enough to mix with the power of the Circle of Andivar and extend its protection around the Great Orchards and remove all from imminent danger," agreed Sargon.

"Thus, we will fulfil our pledge to T'var of protection and preservation of the Great Orchards. This too may be part of *the time of change* which T'var prophesied when He gave the charge to our forefather so long ago." Sargon turned to Wandarr, pointed towards her and declared, "It is time. Wandarr, can you communicate our desire to the Orbstar so it will do what must be done if we and the Great Orchards are to survive?"

"T'var alone knows for a certainty. But with His help, I shall try." Wandarr answered solemnly, for she felt the immensity of the task she was now called upon to perform and the grave consequences of her success, or her failure.

"Very well then." Once again Sargon turned to address the assembled crowd. "Fellow Andini, our plan is laid. We know we would all give our lives without hesitation in defense of our flock, but wisdom dictates otherwise. Our actions may change the face of Karnakon, of T'varin forever, but it means the fulfilment of our charge and the frustration of Kolonth."

Sargon looked to Wandarr and nodded his head. "For the honour of T'var and the protection of the Great Orchards, let the Circle of Andivar now grow through the power of the Orbstar of T'varin."

Wandarr held the Orbstar high. Its glow and hum grew in brilliance and intensity. Wandarr concentrated and focused her thoughts so that she imagined all of the Great Orchards from one end to the other.

Her thoughts and being spread out from the Circle and back onto T'varin itself. She pictured the Circle growing until it took in all of the huge area including the Orchards and all of the people of the Andini who had been left behind. She could see the Orbstar at the centre of the Circle begin to spread its power outward until it reached the borders of the Great Orchard on all sides, enveloping everything and everyone within its glow.

The Orbstar pulsated through her entire being with powers so much greater than herself or the Circle of Andivar, it reminded her of T'var and a far-off place of serenity. The feeling slowly left and it took Wandarr a moment to realize that the Orbstar's humming and glowing had ended. It took another moment for her to understand that she and Randak stood alone with their steeds; all around them there was only empty space. But for the ground they stood on, nothing within sight. No Andini, no Circle of Andivar, no trees, no forest, no Great Orchards.

"We are back then," Randak was both surprised and relieved.

"It appears so," Wandarr was still shaking from the vast power that only moments ago had flooded her being. "I guess it must have worked!"

Wandarr looked at the Orbstar lying quiet in her hand. Carefully she tucked it back into the secret pouch saying, "We are back on T'varin, in Karnakon I would say, and I do believe standing where the Andini host were assembled at the Circle of Andivar."

"And now it is all gone. Circle, Orchards, people, and all."

"Praise King! At least Kolonth won't obtain this treasure. I would love to see the expression on the faces of those he sent to destroy the Great Orchards when they reach the border," Randak laughed.

*   *   *

Gruntlurch, Captain of the advancing host, led his troops stalwartly forward to the borders of the Great Orchards. Villages lay in trampled ruins behind them. Craving real battle instead of the weaklings already slaughtered, they pushed on with their hunger growing for more blood. They looked forward to the battle with the Andini, even if short-lived.

The black standard of Mangloth blew proudly before them. Carnivores, ogres, damaged, broken and bent humans, corruptions of beings in forms only Kolonth could imagine, marched in their number. All hungry for battle, all hungry for blood. Under orders to march through the Great Orchards, bringing about their destruction through fire and ice and then march on to where they would meet their comrades, to complete the utter rout and fall of Karnakon.

Blood dripped off swords, armour and the lips of some. Gore was no stranger to this horde of Kolonth's. Murder their intent, devastation their life blood and carnage their mark. Whatever lay in their path, they destroyed with sword and fire and rejoiced in the screams of their victims.

T'barth had not fallen prey to this group; Kolonth had reserved an icy fate for that land. Whatever his reason they cared not, for Karnakon would be theirs to devour and they intended to do it with a passion. What they missed at not being let loose on T'barth, they more than made up for as they vented their rage upon every inhabited place of Karnakon to which they laid waste.

Once the host had crossed the northern border into Nomadia and began southward, everyone fell prey to their swords. Now they were about to come to their major goal: the Great Orchards of Karnakon. They would soon be at its border and able to begin the fires of destruction. Karnakon, and eventually all of T'varin, to be brought down through fiery ruin.

Gruntlurch, ogre-like, with a deformed face, yellowing teeth, semi-pointed ears and black eyes so dark most could not withstand them, waited impatiently for his advance scouts to return. He stuck out his abnormally long tongue, licking the rest of his meal off of his bloated cheeks but even swallowing the leftover portions of dinner did nothing to relieve his sense of uneasiness. He tried to dismiss it, convincing himself nothing could prevent Kolonth's plan from meeting fruition, but still worry nagged at him. The rest of the troops also seemed uneasy, provoking their Captain's already ugly mood.

"Tell those *mudwumps* to settle down. If they haven't had enough killing yet, they will more than soon be satisfied once we meet those wretched Andini. Now where are those miserable scouts? Rathnox, what do you see? Where are those flying spies of Kolonth's when you need them?" he roared to no one in particular. Profane and unintelligible answers from his troops carried through the dead air hanging around them.

Rathnox bellowed, "They come with haste, driving their steeds like a madness has fallen upon them."

"Humph," grumbled Gruntlurch. "They probably helped themselves to the first killings and that's why they took so long. Selfish pigs! I never should have allowed them horses!"

Rathnox grunted, demonstrating his disgust.

"Well, let's find out how they excuse themselves with my sword at their throats. How long before they meet up with us, Rathnox? The rest of you move into formation. When the scouts have briefed us, be prepared to move out. This day the Great Orchards of Karnakon meets their end. Kolonth will be pleased."

"Lord Gruntlurch! Lord Gruntlurch! Magiks and sorcery, sorcery most awful and powerful."

Gruntlurch could hear the scouts shouting from afar off.

"What is wrong with those crazed fools?" Gruntlurch stared at Rathnox. "What are those maggots babbling about? Rathnox, can you make out what they are saying?"

"*Haste, make haste!* They are shouting something about sorcery and disappearance."

"I can hear, fool! What does it mean?" demanded Gruntlurch, his frustration rising as the uneasy sensation visited him once again.

"We will soon have blood one way or another."

Gruntlurch drew his sword, smacking his lips together, curling his long tongue around his bared fangs in a way that made Rathnox back away just enough to be out of his Captain's sword's reach.

The scouts approached, helms intact, their Kolonth-given black armour and long swords showing no signs of battle, yet they were breathing heavily with looks of terror and confusion on their faces. Gruntlurch threatened, "If they look terrified now, wait until I am through with them."

The scouts reached their Captain and paused a moment to catch their breath. They seemed to be speechless, trying to determine how to explain their behaviour.

"Maggots! Speak up!" Gruntlurch shouted at the scouts as they approached. "What are you idiots blabbering about? Make it quick! We have a job to do for the Master. Speak before my sword loosens your tongue and maybe your heads as well."

Shaken, one scout began to stutter, "C-C-Cap-Cap you- you don't...don't under-"

Gruntlurch had reached the limit of his patience. His sword moved swift as lightning and one scout's head lay on the ground, severed from his body with a single, swift stroke, the look of terror still on his face.

"Now before you join your comrade, SPEAK, FOOL!" Gruntlurch commanded the remaining scout.

"Yes, my Captain," said the scout. "Captain, we are defeated before we have begun. There can be no battle. No battle to fight. Gone! Gone! It's gone. All gone."

"What is this gibberish he is speaking, Captain?" Rathnox asked, eager to see if this scout too, would join his comrade.

"I don't know yet but I will find out. Rathnox, confirm everyone is in formation and if not, assemble them now. We move in ten." Gruntlurch's orders were clear.

"Let me loosen his tongue," begged Rathnox.

"NOW! I SAID, ASSEMBLE THEM, SCUM!" Gruntlurch screamed in such fury that his own horse shuddered. "MOVE THE TROOPS! *I* will deal with this fool. UNDERSTAND?"

Rathnox went off obediently without saying a word; he knew better than to cross his Captain when in this mood.

"Now, Jnstiv," Gruntlurch suddenly remembered the scout's name.

He sheathed his sword, dismounted and with fists clenched, walked up to the scout who was still seated on his horse. Gruntlurch's height was enough for him to be level with Jnstiv's face.

"Now, Jnstiv, time is short. Must I pound the answers out of your thick skull or will you tell me what in Kolonth's name happened?"

"The Orchard is no more, Gruntlurch," Jnstiv said. He had regained some of his composure, but forgot to address his superior by the proper rank.

Gruntlurch overlooked the breach of protocol and asked, "What do you mean exactly by gone?"

"Just that, my Lord," the terrified scout said. "The Great Orchards of Karnakon are no more. They are gone. Vanished off the face of T'varin."

"This is some illusion, some trick of the Orchard Keepers. The scum!"

"No, my Lord. It appeared to be no trick, which is why we took so long. We kept expecting to reach the Orchards' border but there was no border because there was no Orchard. No trees, no people, no villages, nothing. Absolutely nothing."

"What nonsense are you spouting, Jnstiv?" growled Gruntlurch.

"Massive orchard groves do not just up and disappear, much less the Great Orchards of Karnakon."

"Yet it is so. It is so!" Jnstiv said with a high-pitched whine. "Nothing there, not destroyed, not barren, nor laid waste, just gone."

"Well then what is in its place, fool?" Gruntlurch screeched, bringing Jnstiv back to his senses.

"Just empty space my lord. Empty land, as though nothing ever existed there!"

"At least you have found your tongue," Gruntlurch muttered, "So I will let you live. You have fared better than your comrade." Gruntlurch smiled, looking at the headless heap of flesh on the ground. "I would see this emptiness for myself. If it is true, it is our enemy's doing. Curse His power! If it is not true...well, you will ride beside your Captain. At the first hint of falsehood, you will lose more than your head and more swiftly than your comrade's. Do I make myself clear?"

Gruntlurch's glare was so harsh that the scout feared he might faint and fall off his horse. Finally, Gruntlurch turned away, marched back to his steed and mounted.

"Rathnox, are we ready?"

"Yes, Captain." Rathnox emerged from the dark horde. "Very well, then. We ride day and night, orchard or no orchard."

Gruntlurch directed his stern glare at Jnstiv as he spoke and motioned him to come alongside so he would be riding right between Gruntlurch and Rathnox.

"NOW, ONWARD!"

The troops once again began their evil advance towards the Great Orchards of Karnakon. Except through the power of the Orbstar and the Circle of Andivar, the Great Orchards lay well beyond their reach.

*   *   *

In truth, disaster lay behind them, though not the total destruction that might have been, but for the power of the Orbstar and the Circle of Andivar. Unknown, even to Kolonth, through the unleashing of those powers, T'varin itself was now on the cusp, in the beginning stages of deep change.

Meanwhile, the astounded host of Kolonth, led by the now-silent Gruntlurch, walked an empty land. Captain Gruntlurch kept his thoughts to himself, but his scowling frown betrayed his fears of what Kolonth would do when he discovered the strange disappearance of the prize he so ravenously desired to eradicate. Gruntlurch was not sure how, but he knew as Captain of the invading force, he would be held responsible for this failure.

The Captain gazed to the skies every now and then. He searched the dark, smoke-filled horizon on the lookout for Kolonth's Averi. It would be the one to deliver the news to his Master, which would be announced long before Gruntlurch stood before Kolonth and attempted to explain things. Gruntlurch shuddered at the memories of those who failed Kolonth in the past. He knew only too well their hideous fates.

*   *   *

Alone in the Circle of Andivar, Randak and Wandarr looked northwards towards Etraria. Their Sonswords began to glow with the bright amber light of warning. Wandarr could feel the Orbstar, safely tucked away, throb with unusual intensity. A thick choking smoke carried on the wind brought with it the smouldering odour of death. It drew closer, beginning to sting their eyes.

Wandarr lamented, "There is no help to be given to Etraria. Karnakon has fallen. Their trust in a T'var they had ceased to believe in, proved to be of no help at the onslaught of Kolonth's hordes."

"They must have attacked from the Etrarian River." Randak's tone did not reflect the anger he felt welling up. "Even the Etrarian guard would be no match for that, being so long out of practice of any real fighting."

They had seen this too many times.

"The story continues to repeat itself and it grows tiresome. When will the people of T'varin learn that empty ceremonies do not invoke the protection or blessing of T'var when all is ritual and nothing is from the heart?"

"But the people of Karnakon, if any survived, will be suffering and in anguish, even if they have discovered the truth too late. Is there nothing we can do to aid them? We could give those hordes a battle they will not soon forget."

"We could indeed, Brother, but to what purpose? Should we not warn neighbouring Glephas? There is a land that we may yet help."

"The dry, desert land?" Randak looked towards the mountains and expressed his dislike at the idea, "Travel through the Glephoids? Those mountain paths are treacherous. The Glephoid Pass is the only way to get through from here and is said to be fraught with unknown dangers. If we exit the pass at the wrong time of day, we risk being roasted in Glephas' desert sands! What interest might Kolonth have there?"

"Kolonth has interest in all. He may desire Glephas, if for nothing else than for the ancient wisdom found in the Centre of Learning. Who can predict what new evils he might be able to concoct with what he could find there?" Wandarr abruptly stopped speaking, causing Randak to look at the startled expression on her face. "What is wrong, Sister? You look distracted or perplexed, I am not sure which."

He was surprised to see she now held the Orbstar in her hand, raising it up so he could see it clearly.

"Brother, listen! Speaking of going to Glephas causes the Orbstar to again pulsate, as though urging us in that direction. If I think of going to Etraria, it stays silent."

"Glephas it is then," Randak grudgingly assented.

Without looking back towards the devastation behind them, they aimed Jip and Nayr in the direction of the mountain chain named the Glephoids and began their dash to the Glephoid Pass.

Meantime, Vintar, soon to be like frozen T'barth and scorched Karnakon, unknowingly awaited its fate. Vintar, known across T'varin as the Land of the Roaring Waters, was the next target in Kolonth's rampage of destruction; a conquering by fire and ice. So far, only the Great Orchards had escaped that cruel fate.

CHAPTER EIGHT
THE GLEPHOID PASS

While they rode, Randak and Wandarr talked about the Centre of Learning in Glephas.

"Books and knowledge exist there, which it would be best that Kolonth not have," said Randak.

"Yes," agreed Wandarr. "The histories of all the ages of T'varin and prophecies of the ages yet to come, are hidden deep within the cavernous halls of Learning, or so I am given to understand."

"I visited it once with our parents before you were born," Randak surprised Wandarr with this revelation. "I was so young then; I only remember being overwhelmed by the immensity and solemnity of the huge building."

"If histories of T'varin can be found there, perhaps there will also be some information to help us defeat Kolonth."

"True, Sister. I must wonder if the ancient texts do not also reveal what happened to the Orbstar which disappeared during the conflict between T'var and Mangloth."

"And if Kolonth should find such information..." Wandarr started to say.

"We would all be in greater jeopardy than we are now," Randak finished. "We have now reached the Glephoid Pass. It is cut deep into the mountainside and will lead us down into the desert land which we must cross before we can reach the Centre of Learning. Supposedly the path was made by the ancestors of those in Glephas."

"Let us hope their descendants are as sage," Randak said above the neighing of the horses, who were stubbornly reluctant to enter the pass. "Hopefully wise enough to heed our warnings about Kolonth. I wonder if true wisdom and the wisdom of men of learning, might be two totally different things." Randak's comments were lost on Wandarr, who only heard the word *wise* as she struggled to convince Nayr to follow Randak and Jip into the pass. Wandarr paused for a moment, glancing behind her at the smoke now rising all across Karnakon. With tears in her eyes, she urged Nayr into the opening of the trail which led down into the land of Glephas.

It was the same entryway Randak and Jip had ridden through only a moment before, so Wandarr was quite shocked when she did not see them directly ahead. A thick soaking mist, which suddenly appeared out of nowhere, now surrounded her. She almost called out but thought better of it. Wandarr's battle-honed instincts alerted her that something was amiss, so she reached for her Sonsword but to her horror, grasped at nothing.

Randak suddenly became aware that Wandarr was not behind him, and slowed Jip until she could catch up. He thought he would hear Nayr's hoofbeats at any moment, but time dragged on and still she did not appear.

Wandarr was confused. Her Sonsword was missing and now a childlike voice spoke out of the mist.

"Cheat, bad boy! That is not yours. Now give it back."

Again, Wandarr distinctly heard the voice of a little girl. This time speaking directly to her.

"I am so sorry. Cheat must like you. He only steals from people he likes."

Wandarr did not know yet whether to laugh or be furious. There before her in the mist, were two forms struggling over what was obviously her Sonsword. The little girl had a round face and appeared to be all of eight years old, dressed in the manner of children, with a short sleeve blouse and short pants, although it was difficult to determine the colours, only outlines of the shapes were clear enough. The other form looked like it must be some kind of animal; it stood on all fours, but Wandarr thought she had never seen such a creature before. It resembled a mix of a dog and an animal she once saw in a book called a monkey, yet this animal had wings coming out of its back, though it didn't look capable of flight and hopped rather than walked.

"Here's your sword, Ma'am," the little girl's voice startled Wandarr, still fascinated with the animal and now also by the little girl, apparently lifting the Sonsword without any effort. The Sonsword did not glow, so Wandarr thought she must not be in any immediate danger.

"Please don't be mad at Cheat," the little girl pleaded. "He means no harm. What's your name? Mine's *Hodie*."

"Mine is Wandarr. Hodie, what place is this? Have you seen my brother? He was riding just ahead of me."

"Gee, you sure ask a lot of questions. Yes, a man rode on ahead. He frightened Cheat, so we did not bother him."

"I see." Wandarr did not wish to frighten this young child, though a safe question she could ask occurred to her, "Hodie, where are your parents?"

"In the mist," Hodie replied matter-of-factly.

"In the mist? I do not understand. What do you mean by *in the mist?"*

"That is where my people, I mean, we are," Hodie's explanation still confusing.

"Of what people are you?" asked Wandarr, trying a different aproach.

"Oh, I see. We are the People of the Pass. At least so our elders tell us."

"You mean The Glephoid Pass, I would think. Do you live here in the mists of the pass, Hodie?"

"We *are* the mist," the little girl's response was mystifying.

"I do not understand what you mean."

"It is not important," Hodie now spoke very softly, in almost a whisper. "Can I tell you a secret? You mustn't tell anyone I told you or I will be in trouble. Cheat, be quiet," Hodie ordered the peculiar beast, now scampering in circles all about Nayr, who was keeping strangely silent throughout this whole episode.

"Certainly, Hodie of the People of the Pass. Your secret is safe with me," Wandarr spoke in a very formal tone thinking it might help the child trust her.

"The secret is," Hodie actually whispered now, "People like you get lost in the Pass unless they know the right way out. If they find themselves horribly lost, I mean lost real good, they end up becoming part of the mist too!"

"Is that what happened to you, Hodie?" Wandarr asked, now acutely mindful of the enormous threat both she and Randak faced if they did not find their way out soon. "Do you know the way through, Hodie? It is important I find my brother and we leave the pass as quickly as possible."

"Yes, I know the way," Hodie said. "But can we play first? It can be lonely in here and Cheat doesn't always play the way I want."

"This is no time to play, girl," exclaimed Wandarr. "All of T'varin is in dire peril and we must travel to the Centre of Learning in Glephas with all haste."

Wandarr did not mean to, but she had raised her voice in frustration at this unforeseen delay. Hodie interpreted her tone as anger and in response she sat down on the ground and began to weep uncontrollably.

"Oh no! Now I've caused the child to blubber and we will be further delayed. T'var help me now! What shall I do?" Wandarr asked herself, not expecting an answer but almost immediately a new thought came to mind.

"Hodie, of course we can play! We can play a game while you lead me to where my brother Randak is. What do you think of that? Let's play a game of questions, or better yet, what about follow the leader? You lead and I will try to follow and if I can't find you right away, I will call out, *"Hodie where are you?"* and you will answer, *"Over here Wandarr, come and find me,"* and I will follow the sound of your voice. What do you think?"

"Oh, sounds like wonderful fun!" Hodie said and wiped away her tears. "Come on, Cheat! Let's play follow the leader with Wandarr."

Randak's concern at Wandarr's absence escalated. He did not want to go on forward without her, although he did worry that somehow, she might have passed him in the thick haze, yet he did not want to push on if something had happened to her and she was still behind him. He debated his choices, hoping Wandarr would reappear from somewhere before he had to make up his mind on which way to go. The mist also bothered him more than he cared to admit and it had an odd, somewhat familiar, clammy feeling that he couldn't place. He was suspicious as the mist behaved more like an impenetrable fog limiting visibility and wondered for what nefarious purpose that might be.

Unbeknownst to Randak, as Hodie steered the way through the

game of follow the leader, Wandarr moved closer to his position. As they played, Wandarr asked Hodie more things about the People of the Pass. From Hodie's responses, Wandarr began to wonder if her people were actually the true remnant of the original settlers of Nomadia. Perhaps the Nomadian survivors had somehow found their way down into the Glephoids following the first incursion of Manglor into T'varin so long ago.

Indeed, Hodie was right when she said they were part of the mist, for their being was now tied to it and they could not leave the pass without disappearing into the same nothingness the mist became once clear of the pass. Wandarr heard Cheat began squeaking and making odd noises and tried to guess what had upset the creature. She lowered her hand to her Sonsword ready to unsheathe it.

For while Wandarr trusted Hodie to a point, she remained uncertain about what kind of threat any other People of the Pass might pose. She also remembered Hodie's warning not to tell her secret, lest Hodie be in trouble. She wondered exactly what kind of trouble that might be, so she was determined to escape this place with herself and Randak intact.

Wandarr breathed a sigh of relief when Hodie commanded Cheat, "Settle down, silly. I bet he is as friendly as Wandarr. She said he was her brother."

Upon hearing Hodie's words, Wandarr immediately called out, "Randak! Randak! I am here!"

Randak heard voices, his sister's among them, but he could not yet see any figures in the midst of the obscuring haze.

"Wandarr, Wandarr! By T'var, I can hear you, but I do not see you. Where are you?"

Randak was astonished to hear a little girl's voice.

"He is just beyond us, Wandarr. Mister, stay where you are and we will be right over. We are playing follow the leader. Cheat, don't you dare take his sword. Hurry, Wandarr. Can you still follow my voice? Can you hear me?"

"I am right behind you, Hodie. Randak, this is Hodie of the People of the Pass. We have been playing a game of follow the leader because Hodie is being kind enough to show us the way out of the Pass so that we do not become stuck and become part of the mist."

Wandarr tried to say the last part in a way that would not alarm Randak but make him aware that they were in danger. However, Randak did not understand what Wandarr meant by *becoming part of the mist*. Hodie did though, and she did not appreciate Wandarr revealing her secret to another person. Not at all.

"Now you've done it!" she screeched at Wandarr. "Now you have told him our secret! You promised you would not tell anyone else! Now I will be in trouble again."

Hodie started crying once more. Randak and Wandarr were unnerved when they distinguished a number of voices muttering and surrounding them, though they were unable to make out any distinct words; there seemed to be a number of conversations going on at once.

Hodie sobbed, and from what Wandarr could tell, the expression on her face showed both fright and anger. This was confirmed by Hodie's outburst, "Now they will make me go and leave you. I will not have any friends again. Not like you. You were fun to play with and now you have gone and ruined it. You will be on your own and it is your fault. Oh no! They are coming. They are going to make me leave you. No, I don't want to go. Stop it! Stop it! Let me go! Cheat, where are you? Come along, we have to go back now. Back into the mist."

Hodie's voice faded away, as did the image Randak and Wandarr had been able to make of her. Eventually they could no longer see the outline of the little girl or of her pet. Hodie and Cheat mixed into the mist from which they had come, leaving the two warriors uncomfortably alone.

Randak and Wandarr looked at each other dolefully. They were relieved to be together once again, but apprehensive about their present plight. Hodie had vanished with the voices and Wandarr worried that she and Randak might soon join them as mist if they did not find a way out of the pass.

"Well, maybe our Sonswords will show us the way." Randak unsheathed his sword and held it high. There was no radiance from it at all.

"This is odd. We sense endangerment, yet the sword, faithful as always, now betrays us with a false sense of security," said Wandarr.

"I don't know if that is really the case," Randak frowned. "Perhaps it is more that some property of the mist interferes with the Sonsword's power, or else this murkiness is just so heavy the sword is glowing and we cannot see it. What of the Orbstar sister? Could it be of any use in this dilemma?"

"I don't know," answered Wandarr, hesitantly.

She had tried not to think about the Orbstar since the Circle of Andivar. The power coursing through her being had been overwhelming and extremely draining. Uncertainty about her readiness to deal with the Orbstar again so soon weighed on her.

Besides, she thought, the Orbstar is said to be more related to time and space. Not much use it would be here in this place.

Though reluctant to use the Orbstar, her hand moved unbidden to the secret pouch in her tunic where the gem lay concealed.

"All we need is some light," Randak surveyed the now thickening mist.

"By T'var, what is that glow coming from Nayr?"

"It is not Nayr," Wandarr corrected, "It is coming from my pocket."

"You mean..."

"Yes, it is and it is doing it unbidden. I began to reach for it, but it shimmered before I touched it. When you said *By T'var* it was almost if it reacted on its own."

"Look!" Randak pointed excitedly. His finger aimed at a fine white beam of light shining through the pass bidding them follow its direction. Eagerly, they pushed Nayr and Jip along the illuminated pathway, anxious lest the beacon the Orbstar provided vanish before they reached its end.

They followed the light through narrow passages, around crevices, over rocks and hollowed out caves, ever descending farther down into what they assumed must be the country of Glephas. All the while, they sensed that they were not without company. Every once in a while, they thought they saw shadows and outlines of figures, partially illuminated by the light from the Orbstar.

Sometimes Wandarr could hear voices whispering and see eyes glaring at them from the dark. Yet none approached or threatened them. She tried ignoring them, concentrating only on pursuing the beam of light generated from the Orbstar but every now and then she would feel a need to stop and listen.

Randak heard them too. Invisible presences wanting to reach out, grab him and crush him into the sides of the mountains until he too transformed, becoming as insubstantial as they were. He found it unnerving. He thought they called his name, beckoning him to turn aside from the light and follow them to safety. It was only as he focused on the Orbstar's ray that these distractions gave way to his renewed sense of purpose.

"*We must get to Glephas,*" he reminded himself. "*We must reach the Centre of Learning, the Great Library and warn them of the dangers that Kolonth brings.*" He repeated these phrases in his mind as he pushed all else aside and directed Jip on to where the light guided.

Wandarr and Randak rounded a bend and found themselves on

level ground. Jip and Nayr stepped out of the Glephoid Pass into the bright sunlight of mid-afternoon. They gulped fresh air into their lungs, now free from the dank, misty smell that had haunted them all through the pass.

The light from the Orbstar diminished, waning in the bright sunshine. The shadows and voices pursuing them were now only an unpleasant memory, vanished in the light of day. Yet Wandarr believed that, as they rounded the last bend, a little girl's voice called to her, *"Don't go! Don't leave us again! Please come back!"* Perhaps it was only her imagination, but she did not wish to dwell on the thought, for it brought an empty hollow feeling that she could not bear overly long.

"At last," said Randak with relief. "We are free. Let us continue our journey now. On to the Great Library of Glephas."

"Which way?" asked Wandarr. "We will soon arrive at the desert that makes up most of this land where none live with no water and no villages. It will be one long dreary ride; can we make it? Notice how Nayr and Jip grow uncomfortable with the heat of the sand below us. You said you came here with our parents when you were younger, but surely you took a different route than this."

"Of course," Randak said, not appreciating Wandarr's doubts. "I remember asking Father about that trip when I was older and he pulled out a map and showed me how we came from the east and travelled most of the journey along the Univer River. Now we do not have that option. The Forest Barizon is halfway between here and the Centre of Learning. The Pass brings us out farther to the south, so we need only travel as far as the forest and then rest before we proceed the remainder of the way."

A unique land, Glephas existed as a contrast of contradictions, cold as its mountain boundaries, hot as its desert sands. Bordered from Karnakon by the Glephoids, this odd mountain chain continued in a broken manner around most of Glephas' borders. It began to dwindle into small hills where the Univer River ventured into the land, cutting off from the River Brandor and finding its way alongside the Forest Barizon, finally dumping its flow into the Bay of Glephas to the southwest.

Travellers only had one easy way to enter the land, unless they wished to brave the Glephoid Pass. Since the only populated part of Glephas, the Centre of Learning, was the destination of all who came to this land, no one usually bothered to seek out any other route of entry. Everything else, but for the Forest Barizon, consisted of desert sands. The bulk of the country stayed too hot for travel during the day and too frigid during the night as chill winds blew down from the mountains on almost every side. It might be feasible, for one truly in earnest, to approach from the south, but that meant crossing the Univer River before entering the Barizon Forest and that waterway bore too mean of a spirit for most to ever consider attempting that feat.

To the Barizon Forest Randak and Wandarr now raced, heedless of the dwindling warmth of the day. They were anxious and desperate to find shelter in the Forest that would provide them with shade, refreshment and rest. During the cold nights in Glephas, the bulk of the forest trees offered warmth for visitors, just as they provided protection from the sweltering heat of the day.

The sun began its descent below the horizon, allowing Nayr and Jip to gain some reprieve from the hot sand beneath their hooves. Randak thought he could make out the silhouette of the Forest Barizon in the distance.

"Wandarr! Look!" Randak smiled. "Our destination is at hand."

"King's Praise," said Wandarr wearily. "How far?"

"I do not know. The distance is deceptive in this fading light. Let us not tarry here; the safety of the forest may be nearer than we think."

They made the trip without any difficulties and crossed the forest border as the dark of night lay over all Glephas. In fact, night always came early to the land, with the disappearance of the sun behind the Glephoids. They rode a short way into the forest and then made camp for the night.

Wandarr and Randak were relieved to be free from the scorching temperature and their horses, but perhaps not as much as Jip and Nayr were happy to be rid of them. It had been a long, hard and hot trip for the two steeds. They welcomed the cooling balm of the forest, the cessation of the hectic pace and the possibility of some fresh food and water.

Horses and humans all slept soundly in the forest that night. This was not a forest like those of the Great Orchards, neither was it like the mystical woods of Astaria, though of the two, it would have been more akin to the latter. Indeed, the forest existed as part of the contrasts of the land. Amidst a desert of intense heat, the Forest Barizon sat as an oasis in the corner of a peculiar geography. Where and how it sprang into being, no one, not even the wisest of Glephas, knew for sure.

Explorers learned of it early and found their solace and protection from the unwelcome nature of the rest of Glephas. It was in some way fed by the Univer River, which kept it alive in the midst of the desert sands. The only grass in Glephas grew on the floor of the forest. Unlike many other forests, its limits were distinct. The trees did not dwindle until they were no more, but instead the desert sands reached right up to the trees on all sides and ended where the two met. It was as though trees and sand were forbidden to trespass beyond each other's territory through some curious agreement made long ago. If there were animals who made their home in the forest, they remained invisible and inaudible to visitors, including these two new strangers and their horses, who sought shelter and rest in Forest Barizon.

The first rays of morning sunlight eventually penetrated their way into the forest, waking Randak and Wandarr from a restful sleep. They awoke to see Jip and Nayr grazing happily on the lush greenery of the forest floor. With what meagre supplies they had left, Wandarr and Randak ate slowly, trying to savour every bite. They knew the only chance for replenishment of their supplies was to reach the Centre of Learning by the next day.

"The forest is overwhelming, stifling even, in its denseness," complained Wandarr.

"Yes, I did not realize it was so compacted," responded Randak. "We will have to walk Jip and Nayr as there is little room to manoeuvre here."

They began their trek but after about thirty minutes of walking in silence, Randak protested, "The bushes are thick and growth is tangled in numerous places. It seems like we find a workable path but then something shifts and we start down another anew, as though we are being directed, though I am certain that is only because we are overtired."

"Imagination or not, if this continues, it will slow us down considerably," said Wandarr.

"Yes, but I think it will work for the best. It is impossible to travel across the desert in daytime anyway, so we must spend the day walking at a steady pace and thus should reach the opposite end of the forest by nightfall. Nayr and Jip will be well rested from our slow pace, the desert sands will have cooled off and we can then ride swiftly all through the night until we reach our goal."

"Well, at least the horses can take it easy at this slow pace," said Wandarr thinking that it was not the most appealing idea for her and Randak to be up all day and all night, though she saw the wisdom in Randak's words. "Your plan is sound, Brother, but we must be cautious. No doubt we will be overtired when we reach the Centre of Learning by charting this course; we must not let our guard down for an instant."

"You are correct. Weariness is an enemy we can ill-afford, especially if Kolonth has already had his spies at work as he did in Karnakon. We must be alert in spite of how spent we may feel."

Their conversation continued as they walked. Randak reminisced of his visit to Glephas with their parents and tried to impress upon Wandarr the grandeur of the Centre of Learning. Mention of their parents forced them both to stop talking for a while, each awash in thoughts of their childhood; a time before the menacing shadow of Kolonth darkened their homeland.

They continued walking in silence. Occasionally one of them would mount their horse and attempt to ride when there was a larger clearing. That was always short lived, as the trees soon hemmed them in again; walking consistently gave way as the better choice.

Wandarr decided she needed to stay awake and began speaking again. "Well, Randak, at least we do not have to travel near the Soutvold. Though I am surprised when still in Rangdorr you told some of our people to flee to that accursed place for safety. Do you remember telling them that?"

"I do. It was certainly a spur of the moment, but in that moment, it felt like no land would be safe from Kolonth's forces regardless of its reputation, good or bad. We did not yet know the state of Karnakon and as it turns out it is good they did not go farther west. East to Astaria would take them right into Kolonth's army within the Rangdorrian Lands and Glephas would be a long way around. I guess I thought if it is as bad as people say, maybe even Kolonth's soldiers would want to avoid it."

"I can see that. But what have you heard of that place? It is such a small pocket of land, stuck between Glephas and Vintar, yet no one speaks of it without trepidation."

"I have heard some things Sister, but as to their veracity, I cannot speak." Randak brushed the obstinate branches of trees away from his face, as he continued the conversation, he and Jip still walking at an annoyingly slow pace. "Whether it is true or not, people speak of it as an impassable terrain, pockmarked with craters, riddled with unpredictable geysers of both scalding water and randomly erupting poisonous gases from deep underground. Apparently, it is void of any life whatsoever, the air barely breathable, if at all."

"Sounds to be a horrible place; do any know how it came to be that way?"

"I think I remember reading some theories about it in the Library of Glephas, actually."

"Coincidentally our destination! What did these theories say?"

"Let me think back. Ah yes, one theory thought the land was as it is as the result of some great ancient battle or perhaps a cosmic conflict from on high. No one really knows, for neither the recorded histories nor the oral pre-histories of T'varin contain any reference to the Soutvold at all, if that was even its name in times past."

Randak sounded very scholarly as he spoke, something unusual for him, though Wandarr thought it was impressive and liked this change of tone in her brother. "You said theories, plural. Are there others?"

"Yes, there is one other that is more interesting and timely, considering the current state of T'varin, though of the two, I have no idea which is more likely true."

Wandarr's curiosity was piqued, and she also noticed they were making more progress on their walk as they conversed. "Do tell, perhaps I can decide which one holds more truth."

"Very well. By the way, have you noticed that we have moved much farther ahead as we have talked?"

Wandarr laughed, "Yes, I have noticed. But come now, *teacher,* let us hear your other theory."

"Well not mine, this idea belongs to others but as I said, it is timely and this is why. Some theorized that the beings who followed Manglor to T'varin in his self-imposed exile had originally populated Mangloth with their leader. But after Manglor's fall, they all abandoned Mangloth and sought refuge elsewhere.

But separated from T'var's Land over so long a time, eventually they drifted into unbeing; their essence becoming a mixture of shadow and light, never finding true form and as the centuries passed, they faded into myth as much as they became more shadow than light. They blamed T'var for this deterioration, believing it their punishment, as was the lack of access to return to His lands, for that doorway was forever closed to them.

"Stuck in a state of eternal unbeing, they found they were most comfortable hiding in the deepest and darkest places of the world. Over time, myths and legends grew out of their random appearances, the stuff of mortal's dreams and nightmares. These shadowy beings were often mistaken for ghosts responsible for hauntings, sometimes named as blood suckers or shape shifters and the theory proposes that eventually, drawn as moths to a flame, they all found their way to the Soutvold and made it their home, if anything could be a home to such beings."

"That is quite the lecture, Brother-Teacher! I think you have me believing in that last theory you just spoke of; very convincingly I must say. You were quite animated giving your explanation, much like a speaker of T'var."

"Why thank you, you are a kind student," laughed Randak.

"Is The Centre of Learning not still the main place of training for those who would study to be speakers and priests of T'var?"

"I do believe it is, though I fear there are few these days who choose to follow that noble calling. I certainly do not think *I* am fit for that role."

"Seriously though, you speak well. Perhaps when all this is over and the war won, you should enlist as a student in Glephas. You should ask about that when we arrive there."

"You jest. And the war is not yet won. We will see the state of things are after that."

"Fair, but I do not jest, Brother. I think you would excel in the Halls of Learning. One last question though, if I may. Does that last theory maintain that the Soutvold is now in such terrible conditions due to those beings who followed Manglor settling there, or does it purport that the land has always been in such a corrupted state?"

"A true student, always asking questions. And good ones too. I am afraid I don't remember the answer to either. But look, we have finally moved enough branches out of our way on this walk and our good conversation that passed the time now rewards us. Dusk has arrived, soon to transform into the night we need."

By the time light had begun to fade overhead, signalling the coming of nightfall, they had reached the eastern border of the Forest Barizon. They stopped momentarily and took stock of their surroundings one last time. They noticed a small stream nearby that meandered carelessly through the maze of trees. Randak and Wandarr filled their water bottles to the brim and splashed the icy-cold water on their tired faces and limbs to refresh themselves. Jip and Nayr drank eagerly and long, as though anticipating the intense heat which would pursue them on this last leg of their journey.

"Now, we must race with a fury if we hope to make the Centre before daybreak returns with its stifling heat. Should we be caught too far away from the city, the sun, winds and sand may very well be our end," cautioned Randak.

"I do not intend to give Kolonth victory that easily," declared Wandarr.

"Nor do I," said Randak. "Nor do I."

*   *   *

The young scholar of Glephas sat at the study table, hunched over, delicately examining an ancient scroll, the joy on his face such that one would have thought he had found the treasure of a lifetime. Indeed, as he began to read the flowing script, he believed he very well may have. Whatever the source, perhaps from the Oldentime, the account was fascinating and in the young scholar's assessment, completely true.

"In ages long past, Manglor had secretly recruited allies as he planned his rebellion in T'var's Land. When Manglor believed that his time was at hand, he reached out to claim the Orbstars, but had to stop and defend himself against those loyal to T'var.

"The intensity of that ancient battle escalated, heedless of the place in which they fought. The war of these titans grew so intense that the Sanctum of Reflected Glory, the holding place of the Orbstars, broke apart. The Sanctum shook and ultimately shattered as a result of the horrific conflict, causing the Orbstars to be knocked loose. As Manglor watched the Orbstars fall from their place into the empty sky, he started to chase after them, but Micahal, chieftain of T'var, rose up in a righteous anger at seeing the beloved Orbstars lost and possibly destroyed. He took to battling Manglor with such fury that the Evil One feared for his very existence.

"Manglor believed with a certainty though, that at least one of the Orbstars fell towards the new world called T'varin. He knew that even just one Orbstar in his possession might be sufficient to exact his revenge. Therefore, he forsook the battle and calling all those who took his side, he and his allies cast themselves out of T'var's Land and so came to the new world of T'varin. He immediately and wisely concealed himself and those who came with him in the subterranean places. When Manglor judged that sufficient time had passed, he cloaked himself in what little splendor of T'var's Land he still possessed, using its beauty to parade himself amongst mortals as something he was not.

"These early years in the world of T'varin were known as The Golden Time, during which a beautiful land arose, lush with vegetation, alive with colour and warmth. The pre-histories verbally passed down through the centuries, told the story of how during this time, King T'var appointed twins, a brother and sister, to rule over T'varin as Prince and Princess, from a kingdom which he bequeathed to them in the northern part of the world. It was they who named their northern kingdom.

"Thanks to Manglor, that name, part of the ancient language that was spoken back then, is now long dead, as it was forever lost during what became known as The Deceitful Time. For in this early dawn of the world, Manglor came full of promises of enhanced knowledge and wealth, and of a richer life for all. He asked only for the leaders to follow him and his counsel. So persuasive and impressive was he, that those who had first mistrusted him capitulated to follow his ways.

"Soon the Prince, Princess and all under their reign entrusted their loyalty and confidence in Manglor, choosing to ignore what the Great King had taught them. With this feat accomplished, Manglor bided his time until he saw his opportunity to thwart and twist his enemy's wishes.

"Cloaked in the deepest night, he and his accomplices slew all those in the palace including the Prince but not his sister. She, he took to himself as his bride and through his black arts, made her forgetful of herself and all her previous life. From this corrupt union many of the creatures which roamed the now despoiled land, renamed Mangloth, were spawned, yet none so malevolent, so like their father, as his child, who came to be known as Kolonth.

"With the murder of the Prince and the kidnapping of the Princess, the formerly lush and beautiful land, vibrant with colour took on the dark persona of its master Manglor, formed and shaped by his malevolent will and his hatred of T'var, into a symbol of proud and utter defiance.

"Similarly, the root of pride and evil within Manglor began to manifest outwardly so that eventually he was unable to walk freely among the people of T'varin without his true nature being revealed. For uncloaked, his face was battle-scarred and gruesome to gaze upon. He also bore a strange mark on his forehead; the shape of a circled hexagon that most took as a symbol of warning; a sign that screamed to their hearts and minds, "Beware this One!"

"Manglor was crafty, though and found a way to hide the mark from view. He was also subtle with his deceit and continually sought to draw away T'var's followers from the King's ways by methods and means obscured beneath niceties.

Manglor declined to marshal a conquering army as he was still smarting from the loss and the battle he had abandoned. Manglor was confident that if he controlled even one Orbstar, he would need no army, for the jewel would give him all the power he required to enslave all T'varin and overthrow the King Himself.

"Although Manglor could no longer roam openly, his disciples and the other T'vari he deceived and drew away to his cause, acted as his eyes and ears throughout the lands. Uncertain which spies and which route the information took to reach his throne, he was summarily pleased to learn that at least one Orbstar might be found on the Island Land of Narxa.

"Based on the spies' descriptions of a magnificent Castle of Crystal on the Island Land, Manglor now suspected that an Orbstar had fallen into this Castle which was once supposedly legend. He surmised that the Castle of Crystal may even have been birthed by the fallen Orbstar, for removed from its proper place in T'var's Land, it might very well function in unexpected ways; perhaps trying to mimic something of the eternal realm that Manglor once called home before his self-imposed exile.

"Either that or it was some creation of T'var whom Manglor was convinced was so self-absorbed, he would do just such a thing to reflect his own glory. Or perhaps T'var had erected it as some kind of challenge to Manglor or in mockery of him. To Manglor, T'var was a self-righteous fool. Whether the Castle of Crystal was a product of the Orbstar or of T'var, it mattered not, for Manglor's instincts told him that is where he would find the fallen jewel. If T'var was there or tried to interfere, he would deal with his former liege appropriately should that time come; a simple task once he possessed the Orbstar.

"Shrouded in shadow, he journeyed to the Island Land of Narxa to acquire the Orbstar for himself. Manglor planned to return and demonstrate the unfettered power of the Orbstar to his son Kolonth, but that day never came, for Manglor experienced ultimate defeat at the hands of T'var."

The young scholar turned to the next page and found it blank. "What is this? There must be more. Impossible! It cannot just end here. What does it mean by ultimate defeat? And what happened to the Orbstar? I must find out. There must be another scroll somewhere. It may be my life's work to discover it!"

He stared at the blank page, his thoughts awash in history and future possibilities.

CHAPTER NINE
THE BARIZONS OF GLEPHAS

Barizon of Glephas pondered the words of the ancient tome before him, delighting in the unique smell that came from being surrounded by piles of old books. He wiped wisps of his thick, black hair out of his eyes; his brow furrowed in such deep concentration that he failed to hear the approaching footsteps of Trackas. Not until Trackas' shadow began to loom over him did he realize that he was not alone. Barizon thought of reprimanding Trackas for not announcing himself and then thought better of it. He had ceased being tolerant with Trackas, although he could never pinpoint exactly when the rift between them developed and now his gentle spirit sought to avoid needless conflict.

Trackas interrupted Barizon's thoughts and broke the silence asking, "What is so absorbing, my young scholar?"

Trackas leaned over to see what Barizon was so engrossed in reading. Trackas was roughly the same five-foot-nine in height as Barizon, though standing over him, as he often annoyingly did, always made Barizon inexplicably feel much shorter.

He answered Trackas without looking up, "Oh, I was just reading this ancient scroll about the origin of T'varin and of the founding of Glephas by T'var."

Barizon detested the patronizing tone that appeared in Trackas' voice lately. He was confident his statement would draw a response. Trackas had become one of the more outspoken scholars of Glephas who regarded T'var and all associated with Him as myth and folklore. Trackas snorted, causing Barizon to look up, which reminded him how annoying he also found Trackas' good looks, strong jawline, athletic build, perfectly shaped and well-kept long blond hair and deep blue eyes, perhaps even to the point of jealousy at times, though Barizon would be loath to admit that.

Trackas' attractive physical characteristics were certainly a contrast to Barizon's leaner frame, roundish face, green eyes and bristly black hair that seemed to fight back every attempt to force it into any semblance of order. Trackas smiled as if reading Barizon's thoughts and continued, "Surely you are not on about this topic again?"

"We have discussed this before, Trackas," Barizon replied with just an edge to his voice. "You are entitled to your opinion, as I am entitled to mine."

"All scholars of Glephas have long since ceased to believe in these childhood tales, Barizon the Younger, perhaps it's time you grow out of them as well. You must understand that you will never take your father's place as Prime Lectern unless you do."

"Trackas, that is between my father and myself. I do not wish to discuss the matter any further. Please leave me."

His last comment stung and Trackas knew it. Aside from being called Barizon the Younger, a name which he detested, preferring simply Barizon, the role of Prime Lectern of Glephas was not a thing to be trifled with.

The role carried the responsibility for everything which happened in the Centre of Learning, including spreading the latest information, new discoveries and the Centre's wealth of knowledge throughout all of T'varin. The position currently belonged to his father, who did not seem to mind being called Barizon the Elder or Barizon The Senior One, though more often than not, he was referred to by his title, Prime Lectern.

To some scholars in Glephas, knowledge, or at least the pursuit of it, overtook the place of even T'var. Many no longer worshipped the Lord T'var, but rather knowledge itself. In fact, many, Trackas included, believed that knowledge alone would make a difference on T'varin and soon bring peace and prosperity to all.

Even so, the scholars were nothing if not dedicated. Whether it was a scroll or ancient parchment from ages past that spoke of T'var and His teachings or more recent writings, the scribes of Glephas were diligent in their precise copying of each piece of history for future generations and those who would become knowledge keepers.

It was a tedious and gruelling process, passing through many eyes to ensure accuracy, a science unto itself, and those who were most passionate and believed in the importance of this work, did not see it as a chore, but rather a privilege; their work would last for centuries, perhaps even millennia. A legacy created to help future generations.

Unlike his father's passion for geography, Barizon's interests lay in things past, not the present or the future. Something inside him kept convincing him the answer to whatever might ail T'varin would be found not in the future, but in the ancient past. He had spent many hours in the older, dusty sections of the massive library. Some even joked that he was beginning to smell just like the aged scrolls, letters, archaic manuscripts and older books with which he spent most of his time.

"I am searching for the origin of the name of the forest and whether my ancestors might be named from it. This information on T'var is help-ful. Now please leave me to my pursuit, thank you." Barizon put his head down to continue reading, not caring if Trackas remained or departed.

Barizon's tone, however, did not hide the hurt Trackas just inflicted regarding the position of Prime Lectern. Trackas knew that too and in-wardly he smiled, thinking to himself, *"Kolonth was right. A little dissent and disbelief go a long way in bringing down a kingdom without a battle."*

Inside, Barizon seethed as Trackas left the room. Trackas always knew just what to say to bring the most hurt or humiliation. He wondered if Trackas used the same tone when he spoke to Barizon's father. Barizon the Elder possessed great wisdom, wiser than all in Glephas, by virtue of his age, his experience and his station as Prime Lectern. Wise enough not to be hurt by Trackas' mean-spirited words about his son and heir appar-ent. The younger Barizon suspected that Trackas told tales about how the younger Barizon stubbornly held to his belief in T'var which, no doubt, did more harm than good, though they might appear to be in jest.

Indeed, of late, his father seemed more distant than usual. Barizon did not know if this was his doing or Trackas' handiwork. He and his father had agreed on at least one thing from their studies: T'varin lived on the brink of some changes of ultimate importance. Trackas even believed this to some degree.

"Trackas. Trackas."

Barizon stared at the book, but his mind wandered elsewhere, trav-elling back to the time when Trackas first became part of the household of The Barizons of Glephas. It had rained all of the night before Trackas' ar-rival and appeared determined to continue all of the next day. The down-pour slowed to a steady beat against the windows in the immense library of Glephas and finally ceased around midday.

Trackas appeared out of that storm a year, or perhaps now, a couple years ago. Barizon thought hard for a moment. Only a year ago. Sopping wet and with a tale of woe fit to move even the coldest heart to compassion, Trackas presented himself to the Prime Lectern of Glephas. He made it known that he, an orphan for the greater part of his life, came only as a simple man seeking after knowledge. An eager student who desired to learn all he could from the vast resources of the Centre of Learning, Trackas convinced the elder Barizon to take him in.

Since his mother had passed away three years ago, Barizon had been lonely for other companionship outside of the books he continued to study. His father was often busy with duties associated with the position of Prime Lectern and so the younger Barizon on many occasions found himself alone. At first, since Trackas was close to his own twenty-five years, he thought he had found a kindred spirit.

Now, a year later, they had developed irreconcilable differences of opinion. Barizon had possessed no jealousy, only pity, when this stranger was welcomed into his home but now Barizon found his pity for Trackas long gone to the point of non-existence. His feelings had transformed into a strong dislike for this man whom he found most annoying. Especially when Trackas minded everyone's business but his own, including involving himself in the affairs between Barizon and his father.

"Peculiar," thought Barizon. *"I can't recall the doings of Trackas over the last months at all, more of a blur than anything. But I do remember the sopping wet, pitiful stranger who came to our door those many months ago. I was reading something important then."*

"What was it? Ironic, how his habit of interrupting has not changed from the day he arrived! Oh yes, a history of T'varin. Which book? I committed something from it to memory. Ah yes. It said, *"And so it was in the early mists of the dawn of time that Manglor brought dusk to the infant world of T'varin."* And then Trackas appeared. Perhaps just a coincidence, then again…"

"You are correct, my son. The wise of Glephas do not dismiss any-thing as mere coincidence."

Not until his father spoke did the younger Barizon realize he had been thinking out loud. He did not remember when it started and won-dered how much his father heard.

"Was I voicing my thoughts aloud again, Father?"

Slightly embarrassed, he could think of nothing else to say. In spite of any distance that might currently exist between them, Barizon still re-spected and adored his father. He looked up to see the familiar sight of deep, penetrating grey eyes, peering out from his father's custom-made, uniquely-shaped glasses. At times, he wished he possessed his father's well-over-six-foot height, if for nothing else than to tower over Trackas.

"Yes, and you are asking a question to which you know the answer. Do not waste words, my son; they are precious. When in better times it may have been acceptable to think out loud, it may not be prudent to do so now. The walls listen, my son."

"What do you mean by better times, Father?" asked Barizon, not knowing the answer this time.

He studied his father's expression further, though with the greying beard covering a good portion of the elder Barizon's face, interpretation was a challenge. He looked at the grey robe his father wore; it was not just to complement the elder's eyes, but rather carried the markings of his position, Prime Lectern over all of the Centre of Learning, responsible for staff, visitors, new and old volumes and manuscripts. His charge was over all that was done in the Centre, including the comings and goings of all who sought knowledge within its hallowed walls.

Inside the Centre of Learning of Glephas, Barizon the Younger and Barizon the Elder continued their conversation, unaware of the listening ears just outside the chamber door. The younger Barizon began shar-ing some more details from the book he had been studying when Trackas first arrived those many months ago.

"It was quite a unique manuscript, Father, multiple pages from the Oldentime, now bound together to make them into a book. Following that portion, which I committed to memory, it also described the defeat of Manglor and of something else, the Orbstar. Or, one of the Orbstars. The records indicate that after the battle, T'var tossed the Orbstar back into the ruins of the Castle of Crystal on the Island Land of Narxa! Can that be right, Father? Why would He do such a thing?"

The young man then added, "The account notes some soldiers looked for the Orbstar but could not find it! Imagine if it is still there after all these centuries. One of the most powerful things in the world, buried amid tons of rubble on an Island few believe even exists anymore. I think part of it talked about the location of the chamber where the Orbstar may be, but Trackas' appearance interrupted my study then and for some rea-son I have not thought about that history until now."

"Indeed," Trackas' thoughts raced at hearing Barizon's words as he listened just outside the door. *"I must find this volume the young fool speaks of and relay the information to Kolonth with all speed. Rewards shall be mine!"* He slipped away.

"The Orbstar, you say," the elder Barizon spoke honestly of his doubts, "I am afraid these days there are times I myself know not what to believe my son. Orbstars, Narxa, T'var…sometimes they all are more like shadows of old legends than the reality I once was so convinced of."

It pained Barizon to listen to his father speak this way and he re-torted, "But T'var is real, Father. You of all the learned must believe in Him. You know for a fact, T'var is more real than us, or Glephas, or even Orbstars. He is All. I remember you teaching me of Him as a child and you spoke of these truths as one who believed them without a doubt in your mind or heart."

"Aye, then, 'twas so much simpler, but now all the learning, all the new thoughts and theories seek to replace the old. Men of wisdom, after all, have many new ways of explaining things and the older we become, the wiser we become, or so it is said to be."

"Is it, Father? Is it really? You always said, the way to remain true to belief in T'var meant maintaining a quality of childlike faith and trust beyond the understanding of the wisest or the most aged. Maybe age doesn't always bring wisdom. I remember too, you once lectured on how the wisdom of T'var is different from the wisdom of men. Do you remember, Father?"

"Yes, my son, I do. Strange how old words return to haunt us when we least expect it. I must think on what you have said; there is some wisdom in you after all. Young, foolish and trusting in what some would call fables though you be, you have a wisdom within which demands some attention."

At this the young Barizon smiled; such a compliment from his father made him glow with pride. He could not remember the last time such encouraging words came from his father and this was reassuring indeed.

"Father, what do you suggest I do now? If the rumours of the battles outside our boundaries are true, and some new evil returns to T'varin, perhaps I should learn more of the past to avoid having it repeated. I must seek out the book I was reading before, the one describing the battle of T'var and Manglor and the hiding of the Orbstar."

"Sounds a solid path as any, my son. May your pursuit be fruitful."

With that, the elder Barizon left the chamber to think on his son's words, while the younger Barizon sat down for a few moments and considered those of his father.

Trackas raced to the hall where he thought he would find the book Barizon had spoken about. He had no idea where in the countless shelves of books he should begin looking, but he thought he remembered which room the book would most likely be found.

Every chamber in the Centre of Learning was divided according to the books contained within. Each hall or chamber boasted countless volumes, as well as study areas for the scribes and scholars to pore over their research. Some students of Glephas copied old works, while others wrote new works of their own. "Always learning, ever increasing in knowledge," became the motto of every student of the Centre.

The Centre was the life of Glephas; massive, immense and old were poor words to describe this monument to wisdom. It started out long ago as a small centre founded by some faithful followers of T'var who wished to offer the adherents of the faith a secluded place for quiet meditation and study. In the beginning, only the histories of Oldentime, as well as some current chronicles were kept at the Library.

The country of Glephas seemed to be the ideal location for such a place; only those dedicated to true learning would dare to pursue entry to this strange land with its hazardous climates. Over time, the number of T'vari with a desire to learn outstripped the original vision and the Centre of Learning grew. From a small stone building housing a modest number of books and a study area, the Centre expanded and continued to grow beyond anyone's expectations.

Books were regularly added to the collection with each new topic that became popular. Soon every chamber was designated with its own specific subject. The building continued to expand and became massive. By the time young Randak visited with his parents, the Centre of Learning had become the undisputed centre of higher learning for all of T'varin.

Unlike the early days, students lived at the Centre for as long as they felt necessary with no short term stays for most. For some, they remained for their entire lifetimes. As the number of students grew, so did the population around the Centre. Many settled in the shadow of the huge library, seeing an opportunity for commerce. The students after all, would need food, supplies and other provisions so that they could continue their work and studies unhindered.

Eventually, the position of Prime Lectern developed as a system of government for both the Centre and the general population. The continuing expansion of the Centre grew so vast over time that eventually the homes and non-scholar population were considered to be a part of the Centre itself. No one minded this arrangement though, as everyone was caught up in one central thing: the pursuit and advancement of knowledge or supporting those who sought it. Knowledge above all else, even above T'var. Knowledge, and chasing after it, had taken T'var's place, and for many, knowledge became their god.

Toward this monolith of pride and learning, Randak and Wandarr rode as fast as Jip and Nayr could carry them. Already night was beginning to give way to the early dawn. The sand beneath them began to warm in the first rays of sunlight.

Barizon walked to the chamber containing the histories of Oldentime, still reflecting on the recent conversation with his father. So focused, he did not sense the presence of another as he stepped through the archway into the room, but Trackas noticed Barizon. Trackas watched in silence as Barizon went to a specific section of the chamber and began searching the shelves.

"Now where did I find that book?" Barizon asked aloud to no one in particular. "I am sure it was in this area. I remember it being in histories... Strange, come to think of it, I do not remember putting it back but the librarians would have done so, unless they have become slack with their work. Of course, since few study history anymore, they have seldom bothered to attend to this chamber." Barizon paused for a moment, thinking he heard something. He listened carefully, but hearing nothing, continued, "Pity, I still think we can learn much about the future from the study of the past."

Barizon studiously peered through the titles on the shelves, not noticing Trackas, who had slipped over to one of the study tables. Only when Trackas teased, "Could this be what you seek, young scholar?" did Barizon spin around to view this nuisance once again before him.

"What do you know of what I seek?" Barizon demanded.

"Oh well, hard not to eavesdrop when one thinks out loud as much as you do, *Young Barizon of Glephas.*"

Trackas' tone took on an unpleasant quality that Barizon found disturbing.

"What do you have there, Trackas?" asked Barizon both impatient and suspicious.

"Well, let us see," taunted Trackas. "This looks like it is called *Ancient Histories of the Old World.* Why, look!" Trackas flipped carelessly through the pages of the manuscript. "It even speaks of your precious T'var and the battle of long ago and of some silly gem called the *Orbstar.* More fairy tales for the young master to meditate upon. Now why would you be looking for such a book of fables anyway?"

Barizon had lost all patience. "Trackas, this be none of your concern. Now, by T'var, give me the book. Why are you so interested in it all of a sudden anyway? You do not fool me, Trackas. In spite of all your teasing and mocking, I surmise that there is something in those so-called fables which you want information about. Now tell me what it is!"

The tone of Barizon's voice rose and he found himself shouting. The noise did not go unheard either, with the echo of their voices reverberating throughout the chamber and finding its way out into the hallways and   beyond.

Trackas grew more than a little concerned. He realized that he had been foolish. So anxious to gloat over finding the book before Barizon, that he forgot he needed time to investigate its contents.

The urgency and sound of impatient desire in Trackas' voice made Barizon think that Trackas wanted the book more than he let on. Trackas thought killing the fool might be the best course of action. No need to draw unwarranted attention though and he worried young Barizon's shouts may already have done so. He resisted the impulse to glance towards the door, not wishing to lose his focus on Barizon. The last thing he needed right now was a crowd gathering. He flipped through the pages while he taunted Barizon and was sure he spotted more references to the Orbstar. A thought occurred to him.

Taking on the most apologetic and softest tone possible, he offered a truce. "Barizon, I am so sorry, I do not know what possessed me. I admit, I am more than a little curious to see what you find so interesting in these histories. You are quite a scholar in your own right. Someone of your stature of learning would not research these histories unless they held some kind of significance. Let us study the volume together, my friend. You may show me why you find this so absorbing."

"You can dispense with the false compliments." Barizon's anger was palpable. "If you want to review the book with me, fine, but please keep your own thoughts private. I have no intention of discussing what I learn from the writings with the likes of you. Now put the book back down on the table and let me get to work."

Trackas hesitated to let go of the book, so Barizon marched over to where Trackas stood and grabbed the bound manuscript from him. He placed it on the study table, gently opened it and began scanning its pages.

Now it was Trackas' turn to be startled. He had not seen Barizon like this before and it worried him. This was a new, authoritative side to the young man he had not witnessed before but befitting one destined to be Prime Lectern of Glephas. Trackas was also not the only one to be surprised, for the earlier shouting attracted the attention of many, including the Prime Lectern.

The elder Barizon smiled in pride at this demonstration of authority by his son. He signalled for the rest of the crowd to depart. So engrossed in their conflict, Trackas and Barizon remained oblivious to all else. The elder Barizon stood statue-like at the chamber entranceway to see how these two students of Glephas would resolve their differences. He was engrossed in watching the scene before him when a fellow Lectern caught his attention, motioning that he needed to speak to him.

"Excuse the interruption, Prime Lectern," he said. "I am told your presence is needed at the gates. Two strangers have arrived, soldiers or warriors I believe. They say they must speak with you on an urgent matter and refuse to discuss it with anyone but the Prime Lectern of Glephas."

"Very well," the elder Barizon sighed, looking back towards the room. "I would have preferred to observe how Barizon and Trackas worked out their problems, but duty calls. Let us see what is so urgent that it disturbs my eavesdropping."

Curious at the comment, the Lectern stared at him until realization dawned that the Prime Lectern spoke in jest to hide his embarrassment at what some would consider spying. Both men smiled as they walked at a brisk pace to meet the strangers.

The intrusion had not gone entirely unnoticed. Both Barizon and Trackas looked up to see someone addressing the Prime Lectern. They had no idea how long they had been monitored. Barizon thought it was amusing but Trackas seethed. If the Prime Lectern had seen him in action and caught any of the truth of Barizon's words and challenge, his web of deceit, spun over the past year, might unravel.

Barizon and Trackas returned to the passage in the book which Barizon had been scanning when they first overheard the voices outside the chamber. Barizon's finger followed the flowing script until he came to two lines at which point, he retraced them again. This repetitive action caused the distracted Trackas to pay more attention and then something caught his eye.

The words *Island Land of Narxa* and *Chamber of the Orbstar* leapt out of the page at him. Trackas understood their value immediately.

"Kolonth needs this," he said without a hint of emotion. He grabbed the book from the table, held it close and ran from the room before Barizon had time to react.

Shocked and angry, Barizon yelled, "Trackas, what are you doing? Come back here this instant! Have you gone mad?"

Trackas did not bother to look behind in his race to leave the Centre. He did not care whether Barizon followed him or not. If he interfered, he would kill him. He would be merciful and quick. Well, perhaps not merciful; he tired of this nuisance and of all the games he had been playing to conceal his true motives. He simply wanted to be himself: Trackas, a faithful servant of Kolonth, the one who would soon be the new master of T'varin.

Trackas now possessed something Kolonth would very much desire: information on the lost location of the Orbstar. He just needed to leave Glephas and travel back to Mangloth. Greed overcame him and smiling, he ran toward the front exit of the building. He could not help but think of the wonderful position he would occupy in the new order when Kolonth ruled all.

As he ran, he pulled a small whistle tied to the chain he wore around his neck. When he had first arrived, Trackas had told the Elder Barizon that the whistle had been a memento from his childhood, a gift from his parents before he was orphaned. The tale was certainly believable, so no one had bothered to examine the tiny whistle more closely. If anyone had done so, they would have noticed that there was a small emblem carved into the whistle: a circled hexagon. Trackas paused for a brief moment and blew the whistle. Though no audible sound emanated from it, the deed was done. Trackas then ran for the doors, knowing his exit from the cursed Centre was at hand.

Trackas' mission was almost short-lived; he nearly ran right into Randak and Wandarr as they walked beside the Prime Lectern towards the gilded doors that formed the front entrance of the Centre building.

"Trackas, where do you go with so much haste?" asked a surprised Prime Lectern.

"I must go. I have a sudden…a family emergency," blathered Trackas, at loss for words.

Without further explanation, he continued running, past the well-kept gardens and onto the wide stone walkway that formed the path to the city's outside gates. He finally came to a halt, and standing perfectly still, turned his eyes skyward.

"Odd," the Prime Lectern said, turning to Randak and Wandarr. "I thought he had no family. I wonder what possesses him to act so strangely. And he carries a book with him. He must be aware that by rule of law, books are not to leave the chambers. His distress must have made him take leave of his senses."

But when Trackas passed by, Randak and Wandarr both had felt the vibration of their Sonswords warning them of danger, the type of danger that meant Kolonth's evil was at work.

"He is an emissary of Kolonth," stated Randak.

"Nonsense," said the Prime Lectern. "Trackas is one of our most learned and eager students. He knows nothing of Kolonth or the evil of which you speak."

"The Sonswords do not lie, Prime Lectern," Wandarr challenged the Prime Lectern's assessment. She finished her sentence as the younger Barizon came running through the front entrance of the Centre, breathless and struggling to speak.

"Father, Father, you must stop Trackas! He has gone mad. He is muttering things about Kolonth and stole the book which speaks of the chamber of the Orbstar and the Island Land of Narxa. We must stop him. Have you seen him?"

The Prime Lectern pointed and Barizon turned in the direction of the city gates, as did Wandarr and Barak, in time to witness an unexpected sight. Trackas stood waving his arms at the sky. He abruptly stopped doing that and then began racing toward the gates again.

He had not gained much distance when suddenly a shadowy figure of an unusually large, fully-armoured Averi dropped from the sky right in front of Trackas and enveloped him in a thick black cloud. Of the people who milled about, some fled, but most froze in place, their hearts filled with an unspeakable fear as they gazed helpless at this sinister legend come to life before their eyes.

"Averi!" cried Randak and drew his sword in anticipation of battle. "Quickly, let's slay the beast." He started to run towards the thick dark cloud before him.

Wandarr did likewise, exclaiming, "This one is large enough to carry a rider! Perhaps two!"

Both Sonswords glowed with amber fury in the presence of this messenger of Kolonth.

The Barizons stood immobile, stunned at the site. "Incredible!"

"Yes. No mere fable is this abomination, Father, stretching its dark shadow over Glephas today," said the young Barizon. "And its foul stench is most distasteful to the point of nausea!"

"What does it wish with Trackas?" the Prime Lectern, ignoring the subtle chastisement from his son.

"They must stop him, Father. Stop Trackas. There is knowledge in the book which must not leave Glephas, much less reach the Master of Mangloth," shouted Barizon. He stared in wonder at the racing Randak and Wandarr, their shining Sonswords held at the ready. Randak overheard the younger Barizon's words and responded back with a shout of his own. "Then he must be stopped before that beast can carry him off to his master. Come, Wandarr, let us not tarry. Behold! Our Sonswords glow, hungry for battle."

The swords' glow now dispelled enough of the darkness for them to see vague shadows ahead.

"Yes, let us... Behold! Something transpires between the creature and this one called Trackas," cried Wandarr. "What is this? Magiks? Our pace slows!"

"Aye," Randak grimaced in frustration. "The closer we try to move towards the creature, the harder it is to proceed."

Wandarr felt them losing their chance, "It's like walking through thick mud, stuck deeper and we grow slower with every step. We will not reach our goal in time."

"We must try! This thick veil of darkness created by the Averi holds us back and I see only shadows inside the cloud. We can't really tell what evil transpires therein!"

Within the murky cloud, Trackas' eyes showed his relief at the arrival of his Master's messenger of darkness. Trackas stared into the creature's daunting yellow-black eyes without fear. "Fly me with all haste to

Kolonth. I have a great gift for him. A prize he will be pleased with." Trackas held the book before the creature. "The information in this book is essential to assuring Kolonth's victory over all of T'varin."

Trackas saw the glint in the creature's eyes and mistook the grin it displayed as its acceptance of his command. Awareness dawned too late that the Averi only mocked him.

"Wait, what are you doing? STOP!" Trackas yelled louder, as the creature's slimy, muscular tail began to wrap itself around his neck. Trackas tried to speak again, but panic and fear overwhelmed him. He was unable to utter any words as he felt the Averi begin to squeeze his throat, ever so slightly at first, as if teasing him. Tears began to run down his face

Trackas knew he was now helpless prey and waved his hands in protest. The creature paid him no heed. With great effort, he managed to mumble something that remotely sounded like, "But I serve Kolon… you must take me to… stop no…"

The Averi was enjoying itself too much to care, slowly tightening its grip until Trackas' eyes bulged and he struggled for what he assumed would soon be his last breath. He submitted in silent horror as the Averi used its tail to bring him forward towards its gaping mouth. Immobile, Trackas hung in the air, suspended directly in front of the creature's jagged teeth. The Averi moved him nearer, providing a close-up view of yellowing, venomous fangs. Unable to accept what was happening to him, Trackas' mind shut down.

He was now a detached observer watching an Averi's toxin-filled daggers of death sink deep into the neck of a person that looked like him. Hovering in the liminal space between life and death, Trackas' mind reconnected to his body. He felt the rush of intense physical pain and mental anguish flooding him to his core. Then he was gone.

The Averi carefully used its claws to remove the *Ancient Histories of the Old World* from Trackas' now-lifeless body. It stared at the empty shell with contempt, pronouncing, "No one, no one but Kolonth may command my kind." Then it lifted itself into the sky, taking the book and the darkness with it.

"The light of day returns to Glephas," announced the Prime Lectern to all those within earshot. He sounded relieved, but the younger Barizon knew him too well to not pick up on the worry in his father's voice.

"Yes, our Sonswords no longer indicate danger about."

Wandarr could tell by Randak's tone he was fuming at being cheated of the chance to battle Kolonth's misbegotten creature. She was secretly glad he had not had the opportunity, unsure if even her brother could survive an encounter with so challenging a foe.

She pointed ahead, "Look there! The darkness may have gone, but it has left a sacrifice in its wake."

Randak took the lead, running towards the lifeless body that lay face down on the ground. Wandarr, Barizon and his father followed close behind. They stood around the fallen body of Trackas while a crowd began to gather.

"What is that awful stench?" the younger Barizon held his nose, "Surely not from the body. It is too soon."

"I suspect it is from the Averi. Perhaps something to do with how it killed its victim," Wandarr guessed.

"Though why kill a fellow servant of Kolonth? That is a mystery." Randak stared at the corpse before them.

"Oh, Trackas, what have you done?" In spite of the enmity between them, the younger Barizon grieved deeply.

The elder Barizon spoke thoughtfully, "All Glephas will be stunned by this evil turn of events. This will shake everyone's sense of safety and security in the halls of learning and beyond." He turned to Randak and

Wandarr. "What shall we do? What advice do you bring now that mayhap the warning you were going to give came too late?"

"We are no strangers to arriving too late, Prime Lectern. Other than just recently with the Keepers of the Great Orchards, our journeys have not been…the most timely."

"The Keepers? You will have to tell us of that adventure."

"In good time, Prime Lectern, but first things first. Perhaps there are still clues we might learn from this Trackas, though even here, we came too late. Perhaps you could dismiss the crowds, so we are not disturbed?"

"Of course, forgive me." The Prime Lectern looked away from Trackas and towards the growing crowd, surprised at the number of people who were still gathering.

"Please, everyone, return to your duties, be it in the Halls of Learning or to your shops or your homes. All is well and safe for now. We will keep you apprised of anything of import should the need arise. Please go now and let us tend to our fallen friend."

Grudgingly, the crowd slowly dispersed, following the elder Barizon's directive, many having quiet conversations amongst themselves as they walked away. The four quietly waited to speak until everyone else had moved on.

Wandarr broke the silence. "With your permission, Prime Lectern, I will use my Sonsword to turn the corpse over. Perhaps he still holds the book in some final grip of death." The elder Barizon nodded his assent.

"Oh my!" Wandarr stepped back in shock. It was not the sight of Trackas' face, bruised and still blue from its final ordeal with death that caused both Barizons to gasp in horror and look away while Randak and Wandarr stared in silent recognition. Emblazoned on Trackas' forehead like some evil brand of doom, was a circled hexagon.

All four remained quiet until Wandarr finally spoke. "The book is not here." She was not surprised.

"We must talk," Randak glanced from Barizon to the Prime Lectern.

"Yes, we must," the elder Barizon motioned them to walk with him and his son, his face betraying his sadness. Once again, they directed their steps towards the Great Library of Glephas.

*   *   *

The Averi, believing its Master already back at home, finally reached Mangloth with its prize, though it had been significantly delayed on the journey due to an unexpected injury. Once home in its lair, the wounded Averi was helped by the older one. Its elderly companion knew enough where to find different kinds of herbs and plants that would assist its companion's healing process and it took numerous flights to do so, searching for the needed medicines until successful.

Kolonth was unaware that the creature had brought him a gift from Glephas until he received word at his outpost in The Rangdorrian Lands, not too distant from Karnakon's second major city Kol, which sat on the eastern borders of Lake Sythm. A choice place from which to enjoy the sights of fallen T'barth and The Rangdorrian Lands as well as to watch the progress of his invading forces within Karnakon.

Although Kolonth did not know the nature of the gift, his instincts told him it was something he needed to see as soon as possible. It was not long after receiving the message that his military escort began the three-week trek to bring their Master safely back to Mangloth. Marching tirelessly under the whips of their generals, the horde was driven without mercy and reached their destination in better time than anticipated.

Upon his return, Kolonth immediately rode to the Shedden, the lair of the Averi, to welcome his pet home and examine the injury to its leg. The wound was healing nicely and he sped up the process with some of his magiks, for he anticipated another flight would be required soon. Once the Averi's leg received his ministrations, he communicated his concern and his thanks to it and then examined the treasure Trackas had provided. Kolonth did not mourn the loss of that servant at all, even though it was Trackas' effort that had brought the plan to fruition, it was Kolonth who had set the plot in motion to begin with.

He sat down with the book, his back resting against the Averi. He began to read and eventually found the knowledge that awaited him. Finally, his patience was rewarded; he discovered the secret. So obvious; the weapon of power that Kolonth sought, was that which had brought about his father Manglor's demise: An Orbstar. Upon this discovery, Kolonth's vision shifted from creating only chaos and destruction to a higher purpose. The object of his father's quest now became Kolonth's overwhelming desire.

He raised his defiant voice to the air, "This is the answer and source to satisfy this ache for ultimate power. Once in my hands, I will be powerful enough to remake T'varin, to make it as it should be, in my image."

Kolonth looked up to the sky, his declarations growing more intense. "Hear me, Father, I curse you for hiding the truth from me. But I will avenge you, for now I know what I need do and where I need go. Hear me, Manglor! I will succeed where you failed, for my desire and my determination are unwavering and I will not be deterred. I will find this Orbstar in its hiding place on the Island Land of Narxa where you met your inglorious defeat."

Kolonth experienced an overwhelming desire consuming him. His eyes blazed with lust, for he felt need as he had never felt need before. It drove him to express one final pronouncement to his unseen audience. "Hear me! I will do more! More than my father Manglor who abandoned me. Who failed me. For I swear that one day I will possess not just one, but all of them. All the Orbstars of T'varin."

CHAPTER TEN
THE NEUTRALITY OF VINTAR

Vintar was known as a place of lush rolling meadows, idyllic pastures and friendly inhabitants. The Vintarans were a people dedicated to their flocks, herds and farmlands. A people who prided themselves on their neutrality. Long ago, the leaders of Vintar determined in any wars which might take place on T'varin, they would take no sides.

As the years passed following Manglor's defeat, newer generations forgot or doubted the havoc he had caused and the role Vintar played on the Island Land of Narxa centuries before. That account was long given up as more fable than truth. With Manglor's horrors and atrocities long out of mind, the Vintarans determined that during any conflict of T'varin, their country would remain neutral. They would not interfere in the battles of others, although they would defend their homeland if the need arose. By the days of Randak and Wandarr, that determination had ebbed and the Vintarans operated on one philosophy: if they did not bother anyone else, no one would disturb them.

For this reason, the nation possessed little in the way of defense when Kolonth's forces began sweeping down from The Rangdorrian Lands to attack Vintar. The leaders' protests of non-involvement were unheeded as Kolonth's soldiers began their march of devastation. The Vintarans discovered a Kolonth who did not respect their non-alignment. The response from his Captains, simply, *"Swear fealty to Kolonth or die."* There existed no in-between with Kolonth and the people of Vintar confronted this truth swiftly, at the end of bloodied swords.

During the time Randak and Wandarr were trying to find their way through the Glephoid Pass, Kolonth's troops were moving out of Karnakon and heading in different directions as ordered by their Generals; Kolonth's commands were followed by most, wondered about by others, but never questioned. Most battalions recrossed the border into Rangdorr, trampling back over what was left of The Rangdorrian Lands as they passed through on their way further south to Vintar, amusing themselves by causing whatever additional damage they could do a land already bereft of life and hope.

One of the Captains was assigned the task of taking fifty soldiers through the Glephoid Pass. Kolonth was curious to see if there might be anything of strategic value in that route, for he had heard vague rumours of strange magiks there. Magiks that perhaps he might make his own.

They were to exit the pass, march to the southernmost part of Glephas, well below the Forest Barizon, follow the Univer River to its bend and then cross straight east into Vintar where they would meet up with the rest of the battalions and continue their mission of destruction. That did not occur, for the soldiers never exited the pass. The loss of fifty was inconsequential to Kolonth, for there were always more prisoners who could easily be used as replacements. Whether those missing had deserted, or become lost, no one knew for certain, nor did Kolonth care. The mist knew though, as did the People of the Pass.

While Randak and Wandarr were struggling to find their way through the Forest Barizon, the hordes of the enemy, much to their dislike, were trekking through the Soutvold. It was not their preference, but Generals and Captains drove them on, whipping them when motivation was needed, for this was the shortest route to cross the Univer River and arrive at the borders of Vintar.

Taking this way also avoided having to endure the scorching desert sands of Glephas, and in spite of the challenges of a march through the chaotic and cataclysmic nature of the Soutvold, the troops did discover what was to them, a pleasant surprise.

For Randak and Wandarr had no way of knowing that some from the Rangdorrian Lands had taken Randak's advice and along with others they met along the way, did make their way to the Soutvold. It had always been considered completely uninhabitable, not passable by any route, and avoided by all, but that was until Kolonth's troops began their rampage across the lands.

Escapees, refugees, whatever name one might give to those fleeing their homelands from Kolonth's terrors, ignored the dangers the Soutvold contained and set up encampments wherever they could find even a small safe space in that unforgiving land. They were not always successful, many perished, but for them it was worth the effort. Even death in the Soutvold was counted as gain, compared to having to endure the horrors of Mangloth. It was a terrible plight, but at least some lived.

The refugees wondered if the land was truly uninhabited, for many swore they sometimes saw noiseless shadows of strangely shaped beings lingering in the fading light or hovering about some of the craters or geysers before fading into nothingness. These sightings did not bring fear, but rather an absence of joy, a loss of light, even of hope, a feeling akin to being betwixt and between something, although not entirely sure what that something might be.

It is doubtful that Kolonth knew some who had escaped his invasion forces were hiding out in the deadly terrain, but it didn't matter. His troops had detested those who dared, even complained about, the idea of going through the Soutvold at all, that is until they began marching through and started coming across the refugees. Nobody hiding out in the Soutvold was left alive after they were done. It was too much effort to bring captives back to Mangloth over so great a distance, so they simply slaughtered everyone they came across, sometimes in creative and to the soldiers, amusing ways, dropping them into bottomless craters or tossing them into active, deadly, gaseous or flesh-burning geysers. A number of soldiers also perished along the way; the deadly and unpredictable geysers were no respecters of sides, but the numbers lost were not of significant concern, certainly not worth reporting to their Master.

Once the majority of the forces made it through to Vintar's border, they began their invasion, so by the time brother and sister met with the Prime Lectern in the Great Library of Glephas, Kolonth's army had started to implement his plan that would ensure by the time they were done, Vintar would be laid waste from its boundaries all the way to the Vintaran Falls and back again. Ignorant of Vintar's ruin, Randak and Wandarr discussed their next course of action with the younger Barizon and his father, while Kolonth's forces took their time before beginning their slow withdrawal from ravaged Vintar. Many were in no hurry to march back to Mangloth.

"Prime Lectern," said Randak. "What you have seen here today is nothing compared to what has befallen T'barth, our homeland The Rangdorrian Lands and Karnakon. They have already fallen to the hordes of Mangloth through Kolonth's icy hand and there is more disaster awaiting all of T'varin. Now you understand, even this place of learning is not immune to Kolonth's foul touch."

"Indeed," Wandarr emphasized. "Now we may have a worse fate in store; Kolonth will soon have the book with the information about the Orbstar."

"If he does not have it already," said the younger Barizon. "How fast does that creature fly?"

"Too fast," Randak shook his head, saying with a look of disgust, "No point worrying about what we cannot change. The urgency of the moment is to determine our next move. Are either of you able to tell us what the book said about the Orbstar?"

"I remember," the younger Barizon grew excited, gesturing for emphasis as he spoke, "For it provided more details than what is normally spoken in the tales of the battle that have been handed down or how the priests of T'var have sometimes told it. It spoke of the fight between T'var and Manglor long ago on the Island Land of Narxa. It told of T'var winning but described how, at the end of the battle, T'var threw the Orbstar back into the ruins of the Castle of Crystal. It tells of how some soldiers looked for it but did not find it. It also described a chamber below the ground where the Orbstar may now lie. I think it may have provided instructions of how to find the room amongst the wreckage. This is all I remember from the book for Trackas seized it and ran off before I was able to read more."

"That may be enough," said Wandarr. "It is clear Kolonth will seek out the Orbstar. It is the same one his sire lusted after..."

"...and he will pursue it on Narxa," finished Randak. "That is where our path will lead us, to the Island Land of Narxa. We will have to cross the Univer River to traverse Vintar and find a passage across the River Brandor."

"There may be a shorter way," the Prime Lectern said causing them to stare at him questionably.

"How do you come by this knowledge father?" the younger Barizon asked with surprise.

"Well, my son, The Old Histories may be your specialty, but do not forget, my love for geography is at least as strong. I know from my studies where you will find the hidden gateway from the Vintaran Falls up to the Great Bridge connecting Bjorqar to the Island Land of Narxa."

"Excellent," Randak said, feeling more hope than he had in a long time. "By T'var, it is possible we may reach Narxa before Kolonth."

"We can only pray it is so," Wandarr was also hopeful.

"Come," the Prime Lectern waved them to follow. "I will provide you with maps to guide your way. I am sure you are famished as well. When is the last time you ate a good meal?"

Wandarr and Randak looked at each other, wondering who would speak first.

"Well, a long time since a good meal for certain. The pickings of the Barizon Forest were meagre at best."

The two Barizons laughed.

"My son, would you go to the kitchen, explain the matter to our cooks and see if they can create a bit of a feast for our honoured guests here. Perhaps some of the delicious roast hens left over from last night and those fresh vegetables. Whatever they did to season them was outstanding! The small potatoes as well. The chefs are becoming quite adept at experimenting with new cooking techniques – a true benefit of being a chef in the halls of learning: one is surrounded by multiple books of recipes as well!"

To everyone's amusement, the Prime Lectern rubbed his stomach in a gesture that indicated his great pleasure at the previous night's evening meal.

"We shall meet and dine in my quarters and review the maps afterwards. Oh yes, while my son speaks to the kitchen staff, I will send our young scholar, Francis, to the geographical library to fetch the maps I mentioned. The ones of Vintar, particularly the detailed one of the Vintaran Falls, along with maps of Bjorqar and The Island Land of Narxa."

"Of course, Father. And might I make a suggestion?"

"What is it son?"

"Well, not to offend, but perhaps while the meal and maps are being prepared, we might… perhaps we could… we could offer our guests hot baths and…" the younger Barizon looked from Wandarr to Randak trying to read their facial expressions.

"And?" Randak was curious what else the younger man wanted to say but was obviously hesitant to do so.

"Well, I think some new clothes are in order as well. And we could launder the clothes they currently wear while they bathe before they dine. They are a bit, a bit, how shall I say it? They have kind of a strong...."

"Odour?" Wandarr finished the sentence for him, laughing lightly.

"Are you saying we stink and need baths and that our clothes smell so bad that we need new ones?" Randak could not keep from smiling and burst out laughing. "Oh my! We cannot disagree with you there! We would be pleased and honoured to be looked after so well. And the thought of soaking in a hot bath is very enticing! Would you agree, my Sister?"

"Very much, I would. Most definitely!"

"Good thinking!" the elder Barizon chuckled. "Thinking fit for an aspiring Prime Lectern indeed. You look after arranging the meal and I will arrange the baths and new clothes for our guests. We shall also see if we can do something with what you currently wear. Once in your baths, we will have your clothing taken away to see if it can be well-laundered. In the meantime, we will provide you with the robes our scholars wear to keep you warm. If you don't mind, we will take a moment to measure you for some new clothes before you retire to your baths."

The elder Barizon reached into what was obviously a deep pocket in his robe, searching for something, and eventually pulled out a measuring tape. He motioned Randak to stand before him and went to work measuring his height, neck and waist size, arm, leg length and inseam while he called out the numbers to his son who jotted them down on a parchment.

Randak shook his head in amazement, "Do you carry many such things in the pockets of your robe and if I may ask, why a measure? Surely you don't measure people for clothes that often, especially since most of you wear these robes that seem suited to fit just about every body shape."

"Ah, yes," the Prime Lectern said. "It is to assist with shelving our many books, tomes and manuscripts."

Wandarr didn't quite understand the explanation as she now stood still to have her measurements taken.

"This measuring tape assist with books?"

"Yes, yes, oh I see your confusion," the younger Barizon enlightened them. "We often have books and volumes of different shapes and sizes that come to us, so we must measure where and how they will fit best and still keep them in their proper sections."

His father continued, "Some may stand up, but others are too big and need to lie flat, and so on."

"Now that we have both of you measured for some new clothes, I will send for two of our students to go into town and see if the tailor's shop might have something befitting two warriors of your stature. No promises though, for it is past midday already, and the tailor may not wish to work through the night."

The elder Barizon rang a bell, and within minutes, a male and female arrived at the door, were given the measurements, assigned their tasks and sent on their way.

"You are most gracious, Sir."

Randak and Wandarr bowed before the Prime Lectern to express their thanks.

It wasn't long after that, when a young male attendant appeared ready to escort Randak to a private room in the men's residence where he could clean up and refresh himself. Similarly, a female attendant, not much older than Wandarr herself, escorted her to the women's residence of the Centre where she could also enjoy the luxury of soaking in a hot bath. Like Randak's, Wandarr's soak and wash helped shed the dirt, grime and sweat from many battles and travels.

Once in their respective baths, the attendants removed their soiled clothes and replaced them with the scholar's robes the Prime Lectern had promised. Knowing this was about to occur, Wandarr had removed the Orbstar from the hidden pocket in her belt and placed it in the wardrobe in the room, carefully leaning her Sonsword up against its doors while she bathed. When done with her bath she was very pleased to find that the robe also had deep pockets, and conveniently enough, an inside pocket as well, into which she tucked the Orbstar.

As previously instructed, when finished with their baths and now outfitted with their robes, they rang the small bell that was in each of their rooms and the attendants returned to escort them to the Prime Lectern's quarters. There they found a feast laid out for them, at least what they considered to be a feast, for they had not had such a full and well-cooked meal in what felt like an interminably long time.

As promised, there was roasted chicken, actually four small hens, one for each of them, along with the tasty vegetables and potatoes, both seasoned with *Millmarx* from Vintar. Besides this, the kitchen staff had taken the liberty of adding two different kinds of salads, a variety of pickles, red beets and other dishes neither Wandarr nor Randak had seen before but were quite willing to sample.

Randak sputtered at the intensely hot spices in of one of those dish-es which set his mouth on fire, or so it felt. He discreetly spit the rest of that delicacy into his napkin, quietly asking for more cold water, downing two glasses in a row. Wandarr and the Barizons laughed, in spite of Randak's effort to hide his discomfort. Besides the water, the food was complemented with a very flavourful drink, a concoction made of wild berries and other exotic fruits from the Centre's storehouses. The meal was concluded with a tasteful warm dessert; a mixture of cream and some other ingredients that the siblings did not recognize, but enjoyed, nonetheless.

Since they were still waiting on the delivery of the maps from Fran-cis, the conversation turned to the library itself. Although Randak was a bit bored at first, Wandarr enjoyed the Barizons explanations about how the library was segmented as they described its vastness. Even Randak had to admit, it was fascinating to hear about the copying process of ancient scrolls that ensured their accuracy.

They also learned how the knowledge keeper's exactness, when fi-nally confirmed, turned series of scrolls on the same topic, or longer works, into actual books with leather bindings. This was something of which they were unaware and both Barizons fielded their multiple questions with ease, pleased at their inquiring minds and attention on a topic that would thoroughly bore many others.

As they were finishing their desserts, the scholar Francis arrived with the maps that had been requested.

"I am so sorry, Prime Lectern and beg your forgiveness for my delay," Francis' cheeks reddened. "I ended up in the wrong part of the geography section and it took me some time to find my way to the correct one on the fifth level of that particular room."

"I told you this place was massive Wandarr," Randak sympathized with the young scholar's dilemma.

"No harm done, Francis. Thank you for these. You may take your leave of us now but please take a dessert or two back to your quarters with you if you like. A reward for your diligence in finally finding these for us."

The Prime Lectern took the maps from the young man who quickly picked up two desserts and still somewhat embarrassed at how long he took, muttered a low, "Thank you very much," under his breath and left.

Once he was gone, the Prime Lectern spread the maps out at the far end of the table, away from the dishes and remnants of their meal.

"Now, let us begin."

Unbeknownst to Randak and Wandarr, at the same time that the elder Barizon began explaining the maps and routes from Vintar to Narxa, in Vintar itself, Barak's village had already been decimated by Kolonth's hordes. The threads of destiny skillfully weaving a prophetic tapestry, drawing the three together and thus beginning the process for the fulfilment of the *Prophecy of Hope*. In both Glephas and Vintar, each of the three remained ignorant of this interlacing of destinies; one lost in deep grief, in contrast, the other two, deeply concentrating on maps, routes and secret paths, so as not to become lost.

After one of the most peaceful and comfortable sleeps the siblings had experienced in a long time, they awoke to a hearty breakfast. Now with Nayr and Jip also refreshed, fed and properly groomed, Randak and Wandarr made preparations to leave Glephas and start their journey to Narxa. Both were now rejuvenated and had replenished provisions packed in their saddle bags, including their previous clothes which were now clean again and useable should the need for a change arise.

"I wish we met at better times," said Randak to both Barizons. They had come out in the fresh morning air to wish the two their farewells and the blessing of T'var. "There is much we might have learned from you and this place, Prime Lectern."

"That is gracious of you Randak but I think we may have more to learn from you than you from us. Better times will come. May the coming battles not prevent you from one day returning to enjoy our hospitality."

Both father and son bowed to Wandarr and Randak.

"Farewell," the siblings bowed in return, then waved as they moved Jip and Nayr out into the open air, preparing them to rush on.

The Barizons raised their hands, blessing the travellers on their journey.

"Farewell, warriors. May the power and grace of T'var keep you safe and guide your paths wherever He may lead you."

Jip and Nayr began with a trot that quickly turned into a gallop and the two warriors were soon almost out of sight.

Father and son met each other's gaze and smiled. The elder Barizon finally said, "Come, I have much to discuss with the next Prime Lectern of Glephas and, I might add, much to learn from him."

With a final wave to the departing duo, the Barizons walked back into the halls of books, arms around each other's shoulders, not only as father and son, but as friends and colleagues.

*   *   *

The route the elder Barizon gave to Randak and Wandarr was not complicated, though the first part of the trip appeared long. They would have to travel alongside the Univer River until its bend. From that point they would continue straight east on to the border of Vintar near Lake Vintara.

This to be followed by a race to the Vintaran Falls to complete their trek and thus enter Narxa, for behind the Falls was marked, *Rapid Pathway to Narxa,* or at least so the map indicated. What rapid meant was unclear and the Barizons knew of none living who could verify this. Yet the Elder

Barizon was confident of the map's accuracy, surprising all of them, including his son, with the simple admonishment, *"Have faith."*

It all seemed straightforward as they planned their journey, but they could not know of the terrors already falling upon Vintar while they busied themselves determining their route. However, it did not take long before they realized Kolonth's battalions journeyed well ahead of them.

They travelled along the Univer River up to its bend in two days' time. They rode eastward, noticing by the end of each day the horizon progressively took on a different look. Soon, even the ground they traversed had a familiar feel. They did not place the familiarity immediately, until it occurred to them that they had seen and sensed this before, only then they had been much closer. A grim awareness that Kolonth's handiwork now extended all the way to Vintar burdened their minds and hearts.

The stench of death permeated the air before they ever reached the periphery of the country. No birds sang and the scarcity of animal life was unmistakable. The sky grew darker as they approached Vintar. They expected their two-day ride from Lake Vintara would reveal the absence of rich pastures and succulent green valleys. Their expectations were correct, as only a burning wasteland greeted them.

The sickness in their hearts bolstered their wills to go past Vintar to Narxa, in spite of the temptation to turn back and retrace their steps. The closer they came to their destination, the more tense Jip and Nayr became. They too were overcome by the awful scenes which met them in this once verdant land.

Another three days since leaving Glephas flew by, before they reached the shores of Lake Vintara on the eastern boundary of the realm. The smell coming from the once pure waters confirmed their worst fears. The place had been under a ruthless siege. The lake, once mirror-like, sparkling with the beauty of reflected sunlight, was now stagnant, nothing more than a polluted cesspool. Kolonth's lackeys had spread his malignant potions to kill whatever life it may have had. Dead fish floated all over its surface and, as thirsty as Jip and Nayr were, they turned their heads away, as did Randak and Wandarr, for the odour of rotting flesh and the putrid stench of death overwhelmed them.

"How far in do you think the enemy is?" Wandarr asked. She couldn't tell if the enemy had finished their work or if she and Randak might accidentally come upon them.

"And which direction have they gone?" Randak asked, his frustration evident.

They needed to get to Narxa and also avoid Kolonth's fighters. They did not want their presence known. Conversely, they also felt a duty to warn the villages not yet attacked. Choosing a course where Kolonth's army had not been, might allow them to encourage the people to protect themselves, or find refuge and in so doing, at least save some lives.

It was an honourable thought, though the rejection of their message in other places weighed heavily on them. They did not wish to relive the experience of Diakon again or see the same deception that destroyed T'barth. Brother and sister looked at each other, balancing their options. They nodded. No words were spoken between them, yet they knew what each other perceived to be their duty. Regardless of the potential reaction to their warnings, they must alert the remaining, so-far-untouched towns of the imminent danger approaching. This duty called to them as they viewed the desolation of the countryside.

"Perhaps they intend to work their way along the southeastern edge of Vintar, then maybe split up, heading west and north, eventually meeting up somewhere in Vintar's north to begin their march back to Mangloth. That way they will have covered most of the territory in their destructive wake," suggested Randak.

"It sounds very much like what they might do," Wandarr concurred. "This means we must rush ahead of them, to the northeastern towns and inform all the places we come to along the way of this imminent danger."

"Let us be off with haste. By T'var, we may be able to save at least a few lives. Nayr! Jip! Now it is time to speed as the wind once again!"

On they went, a whirlwind of warning, but the answer from most citizens was as predictable as the siblings had feared. Even with the legions of Kolonth already in the country's southern region, the majority of northern villagers insisted that the impartiality Vintar committed itself to through the years would be their salvation. They believed they had nothing to fear from Kolonth once they explained they were not a people who would join any external warring. Most chose not to arm or protect themselves in any fashion.

"You speak falsely," challenged one of the young men from Salway, the fifth town they encountered. "We have sworn to be neutral. We have nothing to fear from this Kolonth you speak of. A child of Manglor you say? How utterly ridiculous. Both nonsensical fables from afar."

"Yes," agreed Tamarakle, one of the town elders. She started a moving speech to the small group that had assembled to hear Wandarr and Randak. "These strangers know not of what they speak. They are only here to spread false rumours so that they can offer us protection, no doubt for a price."

Randak lost all patience, in spite of Wandarr's efforts to calm him down. "You are fools then. We have done our best to warn you. We seek no recompense! Your safety is our only concern."

"Patience, Brother, they have not seen what we have, or endured the pain of loss…"

'Of course we haven't, because what you say isn't even real!" shouted another from the crowd. They could not see where the deep male voice came from but it was emphatic. "Off with you and your troubles. Vintar is neutral! Do you hear us? We are safe. We take no sides!"

The small group assembled began to laugh and jeer, "Go then, leave us. You are both deluded! Bother us no more with your tales of woe."

"Very well," even Wandarr began to feel as her brother, "We leave you to it then. You can discover for yourselves what Kolonth and his minions will think of your neutrality. Perhaps some other villages will have more sense!"

"Come Sister, let us not waste time on those who refuse to hear. Onwards, Jip, let us ride."

To the joy of the Randak and Wandarr, at least two whole villages took them at their word and already busily prepared defenses and strongholds for refuge while the warriors rode on to the next hamlet.

The roar of the Vintaran Falls echoed loudly, all the way to the little town nearest to the mighty dynamo of water. Randak and Wandarr shouted to hear each other at times, depending on the way the wind carried the sound from the rushing waters. Sadly, this last settlement, Luxton, also rejected their forewarning. The people unable to fathom why anyone would want to destroy their home when the beauty of the Falls was so glorious. Randak and Wandarr sadly moved on.

"Sister, why do we bother doing this?

"It is a good question, Randak. I know part of our mission has always been to warn, yet now more than ever, it all seems futile.

"Agreed, though at least two villages believed us."

"Yes, though I ask myself, was it worth it? I mean, even with the small defenses they were able to put together, do you think they will survive the onslaught of Kolonth's army."

"I know not, but sadly, it is not likely. Though they did plan for some places of refuge to escape to, so there is that."

"True, though I must admit I am not hopeful they will get very far once the enemy has found them."

"Randak, perhaps we were in error and should have forgone providing warnings and ridden straight to Narxa."

"I do hear you, Wandarr, but we did as we have always believed we must. What else could we do? If even a few lives are saved because of our words, be it not worth it?"

"You speak wisely, Randak. Yes, for certain their salvation is worth the effort no matter how many or how few. The rebuff from that one village was extremely harsh though. I cannot stop hearing their words of mockery. I must admit, though it is wrong, a part of me wants them to get what they deserve for their rejection of the truth."

Randak turned to see a few tears running down his sister's face and slowed Jip to match Nayr's pace. He reached out his hand to hold Wandarr's as they rode side by side for a short distance, until Wandarr unclasped hers, nodding her head in thanks.

Aiming Jip and Nayr, they rode in quiet contemplation towards the Millmarx. The Millmarx was a vast, marshy area in Vintar, famous for the unique plant life that it produced. The Millmarx plant earned fame over all of T'varin as a delectable seasoning which could be used in a wide variety of dishes, designed to appeal to even the most discerning palates. The hamlet to which Randak and Wandarr now galloped bore the same name as this crop. They were not quite to the Millmarx, two days' ride distant from their last stop, when they both halted their horses one after the other.

"One more land fallen to Kolonth," Randak looked back with sadness.

"I know, Brother. How long must this go on? Will anyone even heed our words anymore?"

"I wish I knew, Sister, yet we cannot give up. We must continue…"

"Peace, Brother, something tugs at my heart."

"What do you mean?" Randak looked into his sister's face, trying to read what she was thinking.

"You feel it too?"

"I feel something I cannot identify. A sort of premonition I believe."

"Like a tug on your heart, a strong pull to return the way we came?"

"Yes, yes, that is a good description. An overwhelming compulsion to revisit where we just were, the village of Luxton. But I don't know why. My heart pounds and my palms grow sweaty if I think of ignoring it and going forward."

Randak wiped the sweat from his forehead and saw Wandarr turn Nayr around.

"This strong urge, like an inner voice, whispers to me to make haste and I must obey. We must go back, there is something we must yet do."

"Since are both of one mind on this, let us take it as confirmation from T'var."

"I am with you, Sister." Randak moved Jip in the same direction as Nayr, and they were off.

"We will return to our last stop in spite of their rejection to our admonitions."

"Agreed, it is now two days' distant but I feel we have no choice. Look in the distance, Brother. Through the rising sun's rays, do you not see smoke ascending into the sky?"

"Yes, the damage is done but we still must go back, though I cannot determine the purpose of such a decision. Kolonth's troops may not be far. Perchance this is our mission; to meet them in battle."

"Perhaps," said Wandarr, but inside she felt a different purpose, a thought she kept to herself.

As they began their ride back to ruin and disaster, Randak attempted to lighten the mood. "You know, you are as hasty as I to respond to this compelling urgency. Yet, I thought I be always the impulsive one and you the thoughtful, patient, deliberate one, often the voice of reason, for me at least..."

"At the moment I may be both, Brother. True enough, you are more often the brash one for certain. Not a bad trait, though my duty is often to temper it."

They both laughed, but it was momentary, for as they drew ever closer, they turned their thoughts to what might be waiting for them ahead. Although they were in agreement on the need to return, they truly did not understand why they were so strongly compelled. Undoubtedly, they would only find the decimation and blackness left by Kolonth's soldiers. Regardless, they journeyed back.

Randak and Wandarr were already not far from Luxton, one and half days later. They pushed Jip and Nayr so hard that the way back became half a day less. They slowed their pace, not knowing if they might still find Kolonth's troops in the vicinity and were startled by a noise that made even the bravest quiver in fear.

They slipped from their mounts and stood perfectly still, straining to distinguish sounds above the roaring of the Vintaran Falls. Coming from far to the northwest, the ruckus could not be mistaken for anything else but the sound of a large army. At first, they thought the horde came for them. After a few moments of careful listening, the sound drifted away in the opposite direction until it could be heard no more.

The army marched away from them and as near as they could tell, it headed northwest along the River Brandor. They cringed, for it meant only one thing: Kolonth's armies now made their way back towards Mangloth, and would traverse the Rangdorrian Lands again, meaning their homeland would suffer once more under the oppressors' boots. The soldiers would undoubtedly engage in doing further damage to a land already defiled by their previous work.

"We must be near the edge the village we seek, if my memory is correct, though there are no signs of life left that we have come across so far."

Wandarr fought back the tears welling up inside at the thought of their own nation having to endure Kolonth's soldiers marching through for yet another time.

"Well, let's make for it whatever may be left," said Randak. So disturbed by the thought of what may be happening to the plains of his birthplace, he could barely think clearly, much less speak coherently. They both dismounted and now walked slowly onward.

Jip and Nayr seemed to sense their masters' moods, for they came close beside them and nuzzled their necks affectionately. Randak and Wandarr took comfort in this and thanked T'var for such faithful companions.

"So far there is nothing to indicate why we were drawn back," Wandarr was confused.

"Yes, I know Sister, this is strange indeed. There is nothing within the town, even going down the main street and calling softly solicited no response. There is no life here."

"I don't understand, Brother. Perhaps there is yet something to see ahead? Let's ride again though, just to be safe."

With a departing glance at ruined Lake Vintara in the distance, they turned and slowly rode on, looking for some sign of clarity. They had not gone far when they heard the unmistakable sound of weeping not too far from where the smoldering village lay in ruins. Approaching cautiously lest it be a trap, they found a young man sitting down with his face buried in his hands, sobbing freely.

The young man must have noticed that strangers stood nearby, for he shouted, "By T'var, have you not done enough? Have you now come to kill me too? Finish the job, foul ones, for you have left me nothing to live for. Go on while my head is buried and my back is turned and I am overwhelmed with misery. I greet death willingly. I am no more afraid of it, than I am of you!"

"Peace, Friend," said Wandarr, jumping off Nayr, she extended her hands, palms up to allay any fears.

The young man turned at the sound of a woman's gentle voice. The last thing he had expected was a kind voice and a hand extended.

"Who are you? Are you more of Kolonth's minions come to slaughter the rest of Vintar?"

"By T'var. Certainly not!" said Randak, angry at even the suggestion of being allied with Kolonth, dismounted from Jip and took a few steps towards the stranger. "We are merely two warriors of T'var, true enemies of Kolonth. We only intended to come through your land on an urgent journey. We did not think to find Kolonth's power released upon your homeland so soon."

"Alas, you are too late warriors, if that is truly what you are. The forces of that demon have been and gone and have left destruction in their wake. Our meadows, our farms, our lush valleys, our homes, our people - all gone. Most of our people slaughtered, the rest taken prisoner. I have no idea how far the destruction extends."

The young man stood to his feet and yelled into the sky, "Why did he not listen? We remained non-aligned. Our foundation of neutrality was as naught before them. They cared only for blood." He turned back to face Randak and Wandarr, *"Give Kolonth your loyalty, your allegiance to the true Master of T'varin or perish,* was their blood song. *We care nothing for your pitiful disengagement. With him or against him, that is your choice.* Then they let loose their carnage on a neutral people, with no enemies, or so we thought..."

"How did you escape?" asked Randak softly.

"I was out in a quiet place, meditating on T'var and returned to find…to find…this. I spoke to some of the dying I came across. Those who could still speak, with their last breaths, told me what had happened. Their tales all alike and all I held, died in my arms." The young man began weeping again, unable to continue speaking.

"We understand your heartache, friend. It is a sorrow fallen upon T'barth, Karnakon, even touched Glephas and one which now covers all of our own home, The Rangdorrian Lands as well."

"Please tell us, what is your name? I am called Wandarr and my brother here is called Randak. What may we call you?"

"My name?" the young man was surprised at the calming effect of Wandarr's voice. He looked up from where he still sat and Wandarr and Randak got a good look at him for the first time.

The young man, his face hard to describe for it was still wet from crying, was dressed in a light brown tunic which was open at the neck, with pants of a similar shade and short black boots. He did not appear to stand very tall, perhaps around five foot eight or nine inches, which still made him slightly taller than Randak. Wandarr took note of his lanky brown hair and slim build, but what fascinated her the most about him were his eyes. They were big and bright, in spite of the many tears he had been shedding and of a colour she thought might be hazel. His build slim, but muscular, what Randak thought must have been from the farm labour that so many Vintarans engaged in.

"My name," said the young man, as he rose to his feet, wiped his tears away with the sleeve of his tunic and walked towards them, extending his hand in greeting. "My name is Barak, and you must be the ones the messenger spoke of, are you not?"

Wandarr's heart leapt, without understanding why, while Randak immediately experienced a kinship and bond with this young man which he could not explain. Wandarr swore that as she shook Barak's hand, the Orbstar in her belt pulsed. The sensation so brief, she dismissed it and did not give it a second thought.

"Messenger?" Randak shook the man's hand in return. Barak described his meeting with the emissary of T'var.

"A Starborn Sentinel no doubt. But why refer to us? It knew we would be coming?"

"That explains the compulsion to return, Randak."

"Yes, but why unless…"

"Unless what?" Barak entered the conversation, hoping for clarity as well.

Randak's response surprised them both, as well as himself. "Barak, we are still travelling through Vintar and beyond. Would you like to join us?"

Wandarr stared at her brother, eyebrows raised, her head tilted, mouth slightly open ready to express her astonishment, but before she could speak, Barak answered, "There is nothing for me here. So long as one of you does not mind a partner with you on your steed. Why are you going further into Vintar though, when the Dark One's troops have gone back to the north? I listened to them while I was in hiding as they passed by where I had been meditating. They said their orders would take them to the far side of The Rangdorrian Lands to meet their Master. I am sure they spoke of Kolonth. They spoke of meeting him in a fortress tower near Kol on the border between the Rangdorrian Lands and Karnakon."

"Are you certain?" asked Randak.

"Quite certain," answered Barak. "I listened carefully to them until they were out of earshot."

"What can this mean?" Wandarr asked. "Could it be that Kolonth is not going to Narxa? Should we still head that way?"

"He is in our homeland, Sister. He dares to establish an outpost there! Who knows the way his foul mind works? Should we head to Narxa and he remains near Kol, we will have missed an opportunity to confront him. Better to keep him away from the Orbstar altogether, preventing him from ever making it to Narxa and finding it."

Wandarr lightly touched the Orbstar in her possession, thinking, but not voicing, *"Yes but does confronting him there not put this Orbstar in my belt within his reach?"*

Instead, aloud she suggested, "Perhaps the Averi has not passed the information on yet. Mayhap it is in Mangloth awaiting his reappearance and does not realize how urgent its prize may be for Kolonth."

"If true, that is good fortune, for we could bring an end to Kolonth at Kol, freeing T'varin from his madness, without any need to risk the route to Narxa," Randak spoke excitedly, finding great encouragement in his plan.

"Brother, I disagree! We **must** go to Narxa. That was our course. We should stay true to it. Else what was the point of obtaining the precious information from Glephas and the Barizons?"

"No, Wandarr, this course is better," Randak became more enthusiastic as he spoke, waving his arms as if to make his point stronger. "We can cut him off and face him directly. I will not be cheated of avenging our parents. He slaughtered them with the rest."

Barak watched the argument between the siblings grow in intensity and wisely stayed silent.

"We do not know anything about our parents for certain."

"Don't we? Even if not dead by his hand but imprisoned, I will have my vengeance on that monster."

"You have carried this weight too long, Randak. It is not your fault, nor mine. Is it possible your anger clouds your judgement?" Wandarr asked the question as gently as possible so as not to incense Randak, but it had the opposite effect, only aggravating him further.

Raising his voice, he made his determination clear, "In this, I will have my way."

"Brother, you know I will follow you wherever you go, even if I disagree. Please give some thought to…"

"Tell me, Sister," now Randak spoke softer, but slowly, his angry frustration still evident by the tone and deliberate slow pace of his words. "Tell me, what does your precious Orbstar say? Does it give any indication of what direction to go or decision to make?"

"No, Randak, so far, it has not spoken at all," Wandarr felt the jewel again and indeed, it remained obstinately silent.

"Then it is done. The discussion is over. Prepare to leave this place soon."

Barak was mystified by the whole heated dialogue, for he did not have context for much of what was being said. More importantly though, he absolutely did not like the way in which Randak spoke to Wandarr. He realized it actually upset him more than it should have, although he could not determine the reason why this was so.

He did clearly observe the pained expression on Wandarr's face as the two siblings argued and it touched his heartstrings in a strange way making him feel a need to defend her. He was about to say something along those lines, when Wandarr happened to give him a sideways glance. She must have gathered he was about to speak, for she shook her head back and forth and raised a hand to signify quiet, before she turned once more back to her brother.

Wandarr tried once more, "Perhaps if we give the Orbstar…"

"I said it's done. My decision on this is unwavering and final."

Randak turned away from Wandarr and stalked off by himself. He found a tree to lean up against and did so, still fuming that his sister would challenge his decision, and worse, do it in front of someone they didn't know.

Eventually his high emotions subsided, and he tried to reflect on why her disagreement bothered him so, and why his own response was so strong. *"And in front of a complete stranger as well, I probably sounded like a complete ass. Nothing to do about it now. I probably should apologize to Wandarr though."* He made that commitment, as the exerted emotional energy caught up with him and he found himself closing his eyes. *"A short nap may help my mood. Maybe I am just overtired."* His last thought before sleep overtook him, came unwelcome and unexpected. *"My parents, my fault. I wasn't there. I will do whatever it takes to avenge them. That will erase my guilt. All of it, everything is my fault."*

*   *   *

Wandarr watched her brother stomp off and realized she was now in the company of a person about whom she knew very little. *"How embarrassing to have such a family squabble in front of this man. My brother acted like a child. Hopefully I did not, or at least made a better impression."* She stared at Barak at a loss for words.

"Is your brother always this brooding? This moody? I should name him Moody Broody I think."

"Please don't," Wandarr laughed. "That would likely make him worse."

Wandarr and Barak sat down on the charred ground, both remaining quiet as they randomly stared around at anything but each other.

Wandarr finally broke the silence, though without looking at

Barak, "I love my brother, but I fear his judgement is being clouded by his anger, guilt and regret. He has always had a level of righteous anger against Kolonth and rightly so. But I fear he is crossing the line into vengeance and this is not good, for I think it may make him vulnerable in battle and perhaps in other ways too. He blames himself for the loss of our parents."

"I got that part," Barak finally spoke as he looked at Wandarr. "I am so sorry about that."

"As are we, for that, and for your losses and those of so many others. We seem to always be too late to help; here in Vintar too. He blames himself for all these failures as well."

"Yes, your brother seems to carry the weight of all of T'varin on his shoulders. I barely know him, yet even I hear that. Does he really need to do that? I mean shouldn't he just give that burden over to T'var?"

"Easier said than done, Barak. My brother can be as tenacious as Kolonth is relentless. Once his mind is set on a course and he believes he is in the right, he will not be deterred."

"So, in other words, he won't listen to reason?"

"Not when he believes his reasoning is sound."

"What did he mean by the Orbstar not giving any direction? I don't understand what you two were talking about."

"Ah, well the Orbstar is a longer tale in itself. Much longer. Simply put, though, sometimes choices and opportunities T'var brings our way are not always simply a matter of right or wrong, better or worse. There are times when the decision to choose one or the other is left to us, for neither choice is good or bad, though perhaps one at times may be better than the other but that is not always easy to discern. At times, T'var's commandments and directions are very clear and other times unclear or not clear enough. We then must make the choice using what amount of information, knowledge and skill we have, great or small, unintended consequences at times though there may be."

"You speak like a learned scholar of Glephas and as a true follower of T'var. I believe there is a great deal I could learn from you," Barak smiled at her as he spoke, some of his fresh grief alleviated. "I would surely like to accompany you both. Maybe I could even learn a few things from Sir Moody Broody." Barak looked around as if to verify that Randak was not within hearing, making Wandarr snicker.

Something else caught her attention besides Barak's humour. The informal comment of accompanying them, whether said in jest disguised as a request, or expression of a sincere desire, caused her a sort of joy she had not felt for a long time. She feared to dwell on it, for based on Randak's recent outburst, did not believe her brother would now consent to Barak joining them. Thus, she spoke once more to Barak about choices. "There is one choice I do know though, that I will make without hesitation."

"Oh? What is that?" Barak hoped she was going to say something about him joining them but heard disappointment instead.

"My brother and I will confront Kolonth face-to-face on The Island Land of Narxa. It is our destiny. I can by no means explain it, but I feel it and I know it to be true.

"Hold on," interrupted Barak. "I do not have any idea what you are talking about. I thought Narxa an old legend, without substance."

"That is the way many thought of Mangloth and Kolonth and look what it brought them."

Randak walked into the middle of their conversation, looking refreshed, if not a little sheepish.

"Tell me, Barak, how experienced are you with horses and swordplay?"

Wandarr gave her brother a hopeful look, though Barak's answer was disappointing.

"None at all, I'm afraid, though I have wished for a fine horse since I was a boy. Swords, not so much, but if it is of any help, I deem myself a fast learner."

"Well, that's something."

"Why do you ask these questions of me?"

"Well, if you are going to join us on our mission, then you will need training."

"Seriously, Brother? Training him? What has brought this about?"

"I have had time to reflect and if a Starborn appeared to him, there must have been more to it than just to tell him of our coming or so I surmise. What else could it be then, other then T'var's intention for Barak join us in our battles?" A little more softly, he added, "Also, I am sorry for earlier, I do apologize."

"In this I do not disagree with you, Brother; I believe you are right. Though, how do you propose we equip him? He has no sword and no steed. Accepted, thank you."

Randak nodded, affirming he heard all her words. "I have given thought to that as well. I will train him on Jip and with my Sonsword for now. Though I am not pleased this will delay us, he does say he is a fast learner, so we shall see how fast and how much of a delay. Beyond that, we will beseech T'var for aid and guidance since it seems he wishes us two to become three."

Barak and Wandarr exchanged smiles upon hearing Barak's response. "No fear, Randak, I will do my best and my thanks to you for this offer, which I heartily accept. If it gives me even one chance to exact some payback on those who have made my homeland a lonely, desolate place, it will be worth it."

*   *   *

"We have now come full circle," said Wandarr to Astar. "For such is the account of our expedition from T'barth to Karnakon and on to Glephas and Vintar ending with how we first came to meet Barak of Vintar."

"Of the rest or most of it, you are already aware. You are familiar with our forays against those loyal to Kolonth as we worked our back up into our homeland. Of the equipping of Barak, of our meetings with the Starborn Sentinels."

"Yes, your prowess precedes you," confirmed Astar. "But we have a tale too, one that fits within yours. We did not wish to stop you in the telling, but as you shared your account of Glephas and the Averi, you may have noticed the expressions some of our troops held, though I bid them be silent until you finished."

"What do you mean? You have a story to share as well?"

"Indeed," called out one of the Captains. "Our combined forces had just crossed the River Brandor, when a dark shape filled the sky overhead. We knew it for what it was, an Averi of immense size. It spotted us, perhaps because we were such a large group and moving, though we thought our white camouflage might have afforded us more cover."

Astar explained, "Our archers were quick though. As soon as the beast began descending toward us, both Bjorqarn and Astarian archers let loose a hail of poison-tipped arrows. The first volley was directed at the entire creature but when it fell low enough to be a better target, our archers concentrated all of their second barrage specifically on its legs. They appeared to be the most vulnerable part, since the thing was armoured almost everywhere else. Their aim was true and one of its legs took the full brunt of multiple arrows that found their mark."

One of the Bjorqarn archers finished up with, "The creature wailed in agony, loud as thunder, for the poison in those arrows works rapidly. It flew off in pain, but we knew not where it may have landed, nor did we wish to pursue it, as that would distract us from our mission. We thought perhaps Kolonth had somehow already discovered our group and sent the Averi out to destroy us but hearing your account, we now understand that was not the case. How fortuitous this was, for it caused the delay of the Averi, for which you previously had your suspicions but no explanation as to why that might be."

CHAPTER ELEVEN
TO ASTARIA AND BJORQAR

Thoroughly encouraged by the words they just heard, they continued to share with Astar more specific details of their travels as they rode alongside her towards T'barth. Now well on their way into that land, they already felt the approaching chill, in spite of the many layers of warm clothing they wore. After a time, the conversation shifted and they turned their attention to discussing possible strategies to employ once they reached T'barth and what lay beyond. Each contributed their ideas as to the best way of tackling the ice-covered wasteland and then trekking through the inevitable ice fields into Mangloth.

"Hush friends," said Astar. "Something is amiss. Do you not sense it?"

Heeding Astar's warning, a sombre lull fell as everyone strained their ears and eyes to detect the source of Astar's concern, yet there was nothing to be heard. No birds sang, no breeze blew, no creatures of the night found voices. The more they listened, the more their awareness grew of a deadness in the air, hanging like a heavy blanket, smothering any sounds of life.

"What does this mean?" Barak asked.

"I do not know. It is as if the whole land here waits in anticipation for some dreaded revelation. Perhaps a new horror of Kolonth's making is what we are about to face."

Astar's words made many of the soldiers draw their swords, as though to defend against the invisible menace lurking in the shadows, waiting to pounce on its prey. Wandarr felt it as well, though she sensed something different. She did not feel the uneasiness the rest of them did, but rather a vague familiarity about the dead quiet, though she did not understand why.

Two things happened almost at once. So fast did they occur, everyone jumped in disbelief. The shrill scream of an Averi overhead crashed the stillness. A chilling laugh, not quite human followed, for the flying monstrosity carried a rider. The assembled armies lacked the time to tremble in fear, for all of a sudden, three Starborn Sentinels stood before them. Clad in armour shining with the brilliance of the sun, they towered over the army, and none doubted they were of T'var.

They each spoke in turn. The middle Sentinel looked over the gathering, pointed to the sky where the Averi had been only moments ago, stating in a calm voice, yet one with volume akin to the roar of the Vintaran Falls, "Mangloth is not for you."

The second Sentinel gazed from Randak to Wandarr to Barak and back to Randak, "He seeks Narxa."

The third addressed the entire legion, "Astaria and Bjorqar are in great peril. Ride to their deliverance."

Their faces turned skyward and they vanished, leaving a distressed company behind. Astar and the Bjorqarn Captain, Jorkan, took charge and ordered everyone back in formation, before panic settled in completely.

"You heard the Messengers of T'var," Astar raised her sword skyward. "Our homelands are in peril, Mangloth is not to be our destination. Let us fly and may T'var guide us. We will cross the River Brandor to the east and then split up. Men of Bjorqar, to your homeland's protection and Warrior Women of Astaria, to our Motherland."

Astar turned to Wandarr, Barak, and Randak, "I know not what fate awaits us, but we would be honoured if you would join us."

"Well," said Wandarr. "Our destinations are at least in the same direction for now. Narxa beckons! What say you, Randak and Barak?"

"Let's move forward," said Randak, hungry for battle and tired of the cold flowing from T'barth. "Let us make haste." A silent thought haunted him momentarily. *"Did I make the wrong choice? It seems we are off to Narxa anyway. Wandarr was right; if only I had listened, we would be there ahead of Kolonth."* He looked at his sister, but she said nothing to indicate she was even thinking about their disagreement. *"No time for self-recriminations; I will yet come face-to-face with our enemy and make him pay for his atrocities; I will yet avenge our parents and all the others who have fallen as his victims. I will end him no matter what it takes."* The vehemence of his thoughts surprised Randak, as did the sudden chill in his arm. The former he dismissed as his righteous anger and the latter he attributed to the cold winds from T'barth. He ignored both and concentrated on the conversation at hand.

Barak nodded his head in agreement. "Perhaps we will be of more use in Bjorqar and Astaria. It sounds as though Kolonth's forces have invaded, well-laid plans notwithstanding."

"Onward," shouted Astar.

So saying, she turned her mount to the northeast and began galloping toward her homeland, her whole contingent following the command. Randak, Barak, Wandarr and Astar took the lead; four ahead of an army of hundreds. They rode as the wind, without tiring, spurred on by the Starborn Sentinels' commands. Many were already filled with fearful visions of what evil might be happening to their homes and loved ones. All matched the intense pace of the four leading the group, determined to reach the River Brandor without stopping.

After a day-and-a-half of travel without any long pauses, the River Brandor finally appeared. Astar conferred with her friends, and then announced, "We will make camp here for the night. On the morrow, we will traverse the River Brandor and then divide. Rest well, for we will need all the strength T'var can give us to face whatever lies in wait for us past the ice-covered river."

In the diminishing daylight, they created a camp on the westerly side of the river. Many fell into their tents exhausted, and those appointed to keep watch behaved more carelessly than normal, due to their overwhelming fatigue. The horses, thankful for rest at last, grazed in what little greenery they found and they too slept as deep a sleep as their masters.

Before all in her encampment were asleep, Astar took six of her warriors aside and spoke her concerns to them. "I fear our border towns, Woodworth and Alsa, lie too close to where Mangloth's forces will cross and may be in imminent danger, even as we sleep. I ask you, six of my strongest and fastest sisters, to bypass your rest and ride swiftly to ensure our people have fared well. If they have been attacked, seek for survivors. We will catch up with you, have no fear."

"Of course, my Queen, we are Astarian Warrior Women; your command is our pleasure to fulfill."

"Yes, we will only need a few moments to gather our things, ensure our horses are ready and we will be off."

"T'var go with you, my loyal sisters."

"And with you and our forces as well."

That deed done, Astar turned towards her tent but then saw the trio, the living Prophecy of Hope, were still awake and walked over to join them.

"All but us seem to have faded into sleep," Randak turned to Wandarr, Barak and the approaching Astar.

"Indeed, I am not ready for sleep yet either. My mind is occupied with the battle to come, what about you, Wandarr and Barak?"

"The same. I can't speak for Barak but I am not ready to close my eyes just yet either."

Barak looked into the night sky, "Agreed. I realize this is my first battle against such a huge number of the enemy. It's only been minor skirmishes up until now, but I am eager to help bring an end to this, to all of it. After what they did to Vintar…" Barak grew quiet.

"Yes," Wandarr picked up the conversation. "Though our ultimate goal is Narxa, we are committed to assisting in whatever way we can along the way."

"Is there anything else we are not thinking of?" Randak, ever the warrior, continued, "Our strategy is sound, but how may we supplement it? Do all know the contingency plans if something should not go our way?"

"All good questions, my friends. I do have some thoughts if they will not bore you. I will tell you now what I think will be of the most help."

They spent the next hour or more discussing Astar's ideas. As the night grew on, Randak started speaking less, seeming more quiet and tired than usual. The group was still deep in conversation when he excused himself and bedded down before the others.

"What ails your brother?" Astar asked Wandarr when Randak left to go to the tent he shared with Barak.

"I wish I knew," sighed Wandarr. "Of late he will not share his mind or his heart with even me. He is sullen and withdrawn."

"Yes, Warrior Moody Broody, indeed." Barak added, causing Astar to laugh out loud, "He is often brooding more so than usual these days. Though it doesn't show during battle, there is a tiredness about him too."

"Perhaps he grows weary of fighting at last," suggested Astar.

"Perhaps," agreed Wandarr, although she really did not believe that at all.

*   *   *

Kolonth flew forth on the back of his Averi, his thoughts rife with joy at how well his schemes were unfolding. The injury to the Averi had caused a delay, but not enough to concern him greatly. The information provided by the Averi overrode and more than compensated for delaying his journey to Narxa. The unanticipated pause allowed his precious source of travel the time needed to recover.

The information in the book did not just provide essential details about the chamber where the Orbstar might be found but also included information on other ways for approaching The Island Land of Narxa besides the using the Great Bridge. One of those routes was by sea, bypassing the Great Bridge altogether and landing on an untamed part of the coast. Specifics were limited but Kolonth thought the same directions could be applied by one approaching from the air and that is exactly what he intended.

His flight over the heads of his enemies was simply because they were on his Averi's flight path and in Kolonth's mind they were now quite inconsequential. He had long been aware of the approach of the armies from Astaria and Bjorqar and was amused at their audacious belligerence.

He cared not if they ever reached T'barth or Mangloth. Once he possessed his real prize, everything and everyone else left in T'varin would fall before him and fall quickly.

Now that Kolonth knew the truth of Narxa and what lay hidden there for centuries, he believed his victory certain. His Averi had received a choice reward for the wonderful gift it had brought Kolonth from Glephas. One that also helped its healing – many of the strongest prisoners were provided as fodder for the creature to renew its strength. For on its flight to Narxa, his Averi would be carrying a passenger as well.

Once the information about the Orbstar was in his possession, Kolonth decided to unleash his forces into Astaria and Bjorqar. With most of their strength marching to Mangloth, those lands' defenses were weakened. Kolonth knew his move was unnecessary, but it gave him pleasure to think of the havoc and misery which would ensue. He thought it unfortunate none marching into T'barth would be present to see the ruin of their homelands and laughed to himself.

Prior to flying out of Mangloth, Kolonth had commanded his battalions to march across the frozen River Brandor where it met the Astarian River and invade. His troops were to infiltrate the already-weakened forest barrier, adding potions designed to break down its wards completely, allowing them to either burn or freeze it, he did not care which. He still fumed over the impossible and inexplicable event at the Great Orchards of Karnakon.

Though Gruntlurch paid for his failure with his life, Kolonth's aggravation at the thought of that debacle remained fresh. He cautioned the military of his impending displeasure if the Astarian forests somehow escaped his wrath like the Orchards in Karnakon had and reminded them of Gruntlurch's untimely demise. They took his words to heart and as soon as they crossed the place where the rivers joined, began a rampage with no equal in all the history of T'varin.

They poured into Astaria, a rushing wave of annihilation. Kolonth's preparatory magiks which allowed the first emissaries into Astaria, had damaged the mystical barrier enough, that the Astarian Forest afforded little protection against the advancing hordes as they employed the potions Kolonth had provided them.

Crossing the border into Astaria, Kolonth's troops separated in half. One contingent began working its way southeast to Varin, the capital city of Astaria, which was situated on the edge of the Great Sea. The other half of the forces began moving south into Bjorqar and resolved to obliterate everything along the way. Both halves were under orders to inflict the same deadly punishment on both domains equally and without mercy.

The force entering Astaria looked forward to another victory of slaughter. Marching along they encouraged each other with memories of their most recent atrocities.

"Remember that last village we destroyed?" one of the less grotesque soldiers asked, though its forehead now bore a lopsided eye and where the eye should have been was a hole providing a look into what could have been part of its brain matter.

"Which one? There have been so many!" his compatriot smiled, licking all around his lips with his unusually long tongue.

"You know, the one where that family begged for mercy. The woman held on to her baby begging for its life even if we took hers."

"Oh yes, her screaming was almost as delicious as her squalling infant! Ha ha!"

"Yes and the husband and those two brats, his sons I suppose, all lost their heads about it!"

"As did she, of course!"

"Yes, we did make short work of that place, didn't we?"

"A bloody mess, like so many others! Quite rewarding it was and the Captain was pleased at the report, so pleased!"

"Now we have more fun coming our way. We will slaughter these damn Astarian, so-called Warrior Women to the last one and do worse things yet! Kolonth's orders were to do whatever it takes!"

"Our swords will taste lots of blood this trip, no doubt! I hope we run into more families like that…"

Their general shouted, "You two! Stop your chattering! Don't you know these cursed Astarians probably have spies about? Let's not be giving away our positions until we have to! Both of you, up to the front of the line with me! One more word from your mouths, even a laugh and I swear Kolonth will be less two soldiers. You hear me? Now move!"

In truth, neither Astaria nor Bjorqar were as unprepared as Kolonth's armies thought. Spies, well-secluded in the high branches of the Astarian Wood, knew of their approach long before they entered Astaria's domain. The general was right about spies being in place. Once the Astarians observed the enemy troops move to the crossroads of the frozen Brandor and Astarian Rivers, they immediately sent word about the invasion through their network of riders who rode stealthily and speedily on their errand. The news reached the Astarian capital Varin within three days and without delay, messengers also arrived in Bjorqar alerting their allies of the coming threat to their land, much of it likely focused on their capital Bjqa.

Once into Astaria, Kolonth's soldiers began torching everything in their path, yet so far, had found no living beings to torment and kill. The small hamlets they came across also seemed empty of life. They burned them nonetheless and assumed most of the people were in hiding and the actual warriors were likely all in the group foolish enough to make their way to Mangloth.

After a dozen or more times encountering the same absence of people in some of the larger towns, Kolonth's army began to sense something was awry. The half of the contingent carving a route to Bjorqar discovered the same lack of people. Outside of only one hamlet, which bordered both

Astaria and Bjorqar, did they encounter any challenge. A minimal and futile effort, their foes were dispatched without hesitation and they torched the place, a funeral pyre dedicated as a sacrifice to Kolonth.

The envoys from Astaria tasked with warning Bjorqar had ridden along the coast's pathway, one known only to those lands' most trusted messengers. This way avoided the jagged coastline and was the swiftest way to Bjorqar's border. A few leagues into Bjorqar, they began their hectic drive southeast to the central city, Bjqa, forewarning all other inhabited places along the way of the menace soon to be upon them. That is why only some of the settlements were unaware of the threat until it appeared.

Thanks to the Astarian spies and the swiftness of their riders, both Astaria and Bjorqar defenses were well-prepared. All understood that in the absence of the majority of their warriors, victory was unlikely but this did not deter them. Word of the ruin of the Astarian Wood only spurred on the Astarians' determination to battle with a rage unparalleled and a vengeance that any foe who survived, would long remember.

In both lands, anyone deemed old enough and capable enough armed themselves, ready to fight to the death. It went against the usual Astarian custom for their men to carry weapons since battles traditionally fell to the Warrior Women, however, all recognized these desperate times called for measures which outweighed normal practice. Bjorqar owned no such custom, but since most of their regular fighting men had journeyed to T'barth with the Astarians on the mission invade Mangloth, the majority of their women equipped themselves with whatever tools they had on hand which could suffice as weapons.

As soon as the news of the incursion reached Varin, their emergency contingencies fell into place across the country. Those who could not fight, fled to some of the caves lining the coastland, equipped with modest supplies. They were instructed to stay in hiding until someone came for them. If none sought them out, then after a lengthy amount of time, before their supplies were exhausted, they were to have scouts emerge after a few weeks to assess the situation and if possible, try to find aid.

"Father, will our warriors be successful?" a curly, blond-haired, five-year-old girl asked her father, who was still on crutches from a broken leg, the result of falling from a tree he had been trimming. Such bad timing. He reassured his daughter and her younger brothers, "Of course there can be no other, our Warrior Women will be victorious."

The Astarian and Bjorqarin leadership did their best to maintain order as people were being evacuated from the more populated cities and towns but it was hard for panic not to settle in here and there. These contingency plans had been reviewed repeatedly in the last few years and everyone understood the scenarios and was willing to do their part. But that was in theory, for they had not engaged in any practice runs, deferring that as too overly complex. Now that the situation was no longer theory but reality, the practicality weighed on many as a huge, terrifying burden. For some, the whole evacuation felt unreal and yet they could not detach themselves from the reality they faced.

Some of the outlying towns and villages had more concern due to their distance and availability from possible shelters, but that was overridden by the sight of their brave warrior women coming to assist and offer protection as they fled to safer refuges.

Some expectant mothers were more anxious, with their male mates staying behind to assist in the battle. They did not have anywhere near the training that the women did as per their culture.

"Trivent, do you really need to stay? I could use your help on this trek! I don't want to go into labour surrounded by a horde of Kolonth's brutes. If I wasn't expecting, I would be carrying my sword to battle and you would be evacuating with our young ones."

"I know Juliana, but I committed myself along with the other men. Do not worry, for we have had some training."

"Nowhere near enough! What are you going to do? Throw pots and pans at them? You are a better cook and probably wouldn't wish to part with those," she laughed, adding humour to an already tense situation.

"No dear, I think I will use garden tools instead. A rake or hoe in the eye or head can do wonders."

"Mother, Mother, we are ready," their two younger children, dressed in shorts and short sleeve shirts, ran out carrying knapsacks full of toys.

"Let us check those first before we depart. Delia, Trucoth, how many provisions did you remove to stuff your sacks with toys?"

"Not too many, Mother. Just enough to sleep at night with our stuffed wompas and a few shovels for the sand."

"Shovels? Sand?"

"Aren't we going on a vacation to the beach? That's what Father told us," the little girl stared up at her mother with her innocent, captivating blue eyes.

"Oh right," the mother looked at Trivent. "You know you didn't need to lie to them," she spoke softly. "They are brave and they are Astarian, bred to handle even the most…"

"Yes, yes, I know the drill, but still give a father's heart some latitude. Please."

He hugged his expectant mate, held both children tightly, and then they were on their way. Trivent watched them until they took a turn in the path, took a deep breath and then walked into his home. It was time to prepare his tools that would now serve as weapons in a most likely life-or-death battle.

Though the evacuations had some common themes across both

the lands of Astaria and Bjorqar, there were significant differences as well. Being a military culture, the Astarians were perhaps not only better organized but much more stoic in their approach. There were still concerns, fears, apprehension and worry, just as there inevitably was in their neighbour Bjorqar. Yet the Astarian's warrior culture led them to have the utmost confidence in a positive outcome. They could conceive of no other.

The young children, elderly, frail, sick and others incapable of fighting, were truly in the minority and when told of the necessity of evacuation, there was little grumbling or disagreement. Farewell scenes were repeated all over Astaria to a greater or lesser extent, depending on the population and their proximity to the Astarian border where Mangloth's hordes would undoubtedly make their entrance.

Astar's Advisory Council in the capital struggled with their concerns as they met to discuss the current state of things.

"With the bulk of our troops that were originally tasked with breaching Manglor still in T'barth, I'm afraid of what this may mean for us now."

"Did we make the wrong decision? Letting Astar and our strongest forces and allies convince us that they should be away like this?"

Their conversation grew intense, desperate, depressing, shifting to rejoicing when word came that the armies were on their way back.

"But will they be in time?"

"Of course they will. I know Astar. She will not forsake us. I believe even now, she rides with all haste."

In the village of Woodworth, farther removed from the larger cities and closer to the border, conversations were not so positive. The small populace, a mix of all ages, had started to gather in the town square to express their concerns and vent their frustrations. There was little stoicism among this crowd.

An aged grandmother's angry voice spoke above the grumbling, "Damn Kolonth and Astar and our unthinking leaders. Their plans were foolish, leaving us deserted like this. Now we have to run, before we are killed, eaten or captured."

"Eaten?" one of the younger women started to sob. "My children! T'var help us!"

"By T'var, that won't happen, will it?" asked a young man on the cusp of adulthood, his voice trembling with fear.

"Who knows? I hear Kolonth's troops are relentless, wild and untamed. The atrocities they have committed in some places unimaginable," one of the middle-aged men's words added to the people's despair.

"We must leave then. Fly as quickly as we can." The overwhelming thoughts of the horrors coming their way caused the group to lose focus on their military heritage and their pride. All else was overshadowed by their fears, truly one of Kolonth's greatest weapons.

"But where will we go?"

"We can't go west, that's already conquered. We can't go south, for they will no doubt be aiming for Bjorqar as well. If we go east to Varin, we will likely run into the enemy on the way."

"What hope do we have then?"

"Where are our leaders now? Have they abandoned us?"

By this time, the whole village had gathered in the town square, their desperation tangible.

"You are by no means forsaken, for we are here."

Two Astarian Warrior Women on horseback made their way through the crowd, their last-minute saviours. Hope began to grow amongst even the strongest naysayers.

"Gather only what you need. We have come to assist. There are tunnels built from long ago not far from here. They will provide you safe haven until this is over. If any among you wish to join us and fight after we have secured everyone else, you are most welcome to do so. We can use every free hand and bold heart that is willing."

Her fellow warrior offered understanding, "Some of you cannot do this, we realize and we certainly do not hold that against you. Our main task is to secure your safety. Rest assured, a number of our warrior sisters are engaged in this same endeavour across all of Astaria. It is part of the strategy developed long ago, for just such a time as this."

"See, here come the carts, driven by speedy steeds ready to take you to safety. Load yourselves and only your essentials on and we will make a hasty departure ensuring your safety."

Tears, moans, groans, elderly, injured and children crying about leaving their homes as parents told them they were all going on an adventure, filled the air. Once everyone was loaded onto the carts with what little they could bring, off they went to find safe haven in their designated place of refuge.

Unfortunately, none of them made it to safety. The ravaged remains of the people from the village of Woodworth, along with the bodies of their warrior sisters and the slain horses, were discovered by the warriors sent by Astar to search for survivors from the border towns.

The scene was horrific, more so because obviously Kolonth's Carnivores had been at work and not one soul, regardless of age, had survived the slaughter. The Astarians who discovered the site wept. Then they turned their mourning into something so ferocious and unyielding, that any of the enemy they next encountered perished within seconds. So they had sworn, their stoicism returned.

In Bjorqar, similar scenes sometimes repeated themselves during evacuations. Though without the discipline customary to the Astarian, and often lacking the same level of confidence in victory, for unlike their neighbour, Bjorqar had not developed as a military culture. In contrast, their military was relatively small in comparison to their general population, the complete opposite of Astaria.

Most Bjorqarns had pretty much ignored the military, seeing it as an outdated necessity that served no real purpose other than perhaps for show. And maybe to bolster some confidence that their leaders running the country knew what they were about.

Thus, in some places, very different scenes played out in the cities, towns and villages of Bjorqar, once the evacuation orders became known. Ironically enough, the orders and warnings were delivered by messengers from the very same military many thought served no purpose.

So, the mass departures to places of refuge began across all Bjorqar. Men and women alike crying, worrying, anxious for the safety of their loved ones. Children weeping because they were not allowed to bring much with them and had to leave their favourite toys behind. Many also cried as they watched their fathers and older brothers head off in a different direction. Sometimes the children heard their elders speak the name Kolonth. They didn't know why, but that name struck fear into their hearts and made them want to hold their parents and siblings tight and never let go.

People were carrying only necessary supplies but the ill, the lame, the slow, the very old and people with mobility issues struggled to keep up. Many worried that they might be left behind. Some even told their leaders to leave them so that others might be assured of reaching safety. An event like this had never happened in their lifetime and the sense of loss and grief for many was overwhelming as they walked away from their homes, some quiet, others murmuring.

"Momma, momma, why can't I bring my dolls with us?" the little girl cried.

"Only one, my dear, that's all we have room for and you will have to carry it. We must walk fast. We can't take too much, just what we will need."

"But where are we going? Why are we leaving our home? What's wrong? How long will we be gone? Why is Father not coming with us? He went the other way!" The little girl started to sob, upsetting her mother, her heart broken.

"There, there, sweet child. It will be alright. It's just a short break for a little time. We will be home very soon," her mother reassured her, not believing her own words at all.

An argument had broken out up ahead.

"He's too young, I tell you," a man's voice challenged the listener.

"No, we need everyone who is strong and capable. Your son may be younger than others, but he is also bigger and very strong for his age. We need him, Albrect. We need everyone if Bjorqar is going to survive this. Trust me, I know how you feel. My own son left to join the other troops not that long ago."

"But please, he's still a child," the mother's voice broke in.

"It's okay. Mother, Father, I need to go. I have to help. I understand. Please, stop arguing. I want to do my part, even if it means, well you know, even if it means that. T'var will protect and guide me one way or another. Don't you believe that?"

The son hugged his mother, took his father by the arm and they left in the opposite direction from the rest of the group, leaving the mother weeping behind.

Variations of this scene were repeated all over the countryside. Tearful farewells, younger children begging to bring their favourite belongings with them, sons old enough to engage in battle, leaving their parents and siblings behind, possibly forever. The designated leaders of the various villages, attempted to ensure everyone followed the instructions that had been laid out, though what hope anyone had left, dangled by a thread. Dread and loneliness, a pervasive gloomy cloud hanging over them all.

The fighters in both populations readied themselves. Evacuations large and small continued as more and more people poured out of the capital cities of Astaria and Bjorqar. Before she left, Astar had appointed leaders and they were well chosen, for they took control, making firm and wise decisions regarding strategy. They supposed Kolonth's troops headed for the capital expected to meet at least some minor resistance along the way. Based on this assumption, the first part of their plan meant clearing the people out of as many villages as feasible before the enemy forces' arrival. This way, they hoped their foe would become careless as they met no opposition.

Only three or four villages were allowed to keep a small remnant of people who would engage the enemy and then subtly withdraw without any substantial loss of life. Those who volunteered for this mission assumed their chance of survival to be minimal, but bravely recognized the greater purpose their sacrifice would serve in defence of their beloved motherland.

Accustomed to not finding any opposition as they marched through, the invaders had become very lax. Thus, when opposition did occur, it took the enemy forces some time before they could properly organize themselves to respond. By then, the attackers had fled and true to form, the villages suffered in consuming fire, as Kolonth's soldiers vented their infuriation at these inconvenient minor skirmishes. They hungered for true battle, facing a multitude of warriors to slash and kill. These bothersome incidents, annoying and unpredictable, caused their level of fury to grow.

The closer that Kolonth's hordes came to the capital Varin, the more uneasy they became. Instead of growing more cautious, in their vexation, they let their guard down all the more. The smoke coming from the villages situated only a few leagues from the capital thoroughly confused them. The sites were already burning and the invaders had not even reached them yet. Some wondered if this might be a sign from Kolonth assuring success, another one of his magiks worked up as a harsh blow for the miserable Astarians. Others thought the whole thing too strange and urged their Generals and Captains to lead around them and avoid approaching the areas lest it be some kind of trap.

No one could agree on what to do. Unable to reach a decision, in the end they divided; one contingent was given orders to go and secure Varin. They were not to waste any time with the fiery hamlets, but rather instructed to head north to skirt around them and once out of their sight, move south again into Varin and begin the first wave of attack directly on the capital. The other group divided again into thirds; each third assigned to go in and explore one of the three villages, annihilating any sign of life they found, before rejoining the forces on the other side where the high road led straight to the capital. This division worked in the Astarians favour much better than anticipated, and they implemented their defence plan with all conceivable speed.

Meanwhile, in Bjorqar, the people prepared to meet the advancing enemy. Unlike Astaria, with the exception of those too young or too frail to carry weapons and ordered to flee to the caves, not all the towns in Bjorqar were evacuated. Instead, the residents either armed themselves or assisted in digging a new channel, part of their counterattack plan; a contingency that had always existed but one never yet needed to be put to the test.

Long before the greater host left, preparations had already been made. Dams were constructed at strategic points along the River Qar which flowed from the River Brandor into Lake Qar and then out again down the Bjorqarvin River until it merged with the rushing Vintaran Falls. The barriers were designed so as to drive the flow of water further north into the upper part of Bjorqar. Those living on the edge of Lake Qar also did their part, with additional construction built to stop the flow of the river into the lake, intending to also push the water northwards. Water was to be the central means of fortification against their adversaries' fiery incursion.

While Kolonth's forces in Astaria wondered at the flaming villages lying before them, the assault force arriving in Bjorqar came to waterways where none existed before. They had begun their razing of the towns and setting fire to each area they passed through, yet the encroaching dampness mystified them, and hindered their efforts at setting Bjorqar ablaze.

About one quarter of their way into Bjorqar, the army began to realize something was different; the settlement they had entered appeared to be deserted but strangely, a new rushing stream ran through it. Out of nowhere, arrows started flying right into their midst and battle cries forced them to scramble in confusion. The army searched about for those concealed and saw nothing. They realized their enemy's subterfuge too late, for the Bjorqarns were secreted in the tall grasses along the shore of this strange new waterway.

Kolonth's troops attacked with a keen vengeance and not all the archers of this location escaped their wrath. Some survived by rolling into the cooling waters, where their comrades awaited them in boats, rafts and anything else floating close enough for them to jump on. They used makeshift paddles to propel themselves downstream.

Kolonth's generals cursed themselves for not paying more attention to their master's incantations for freezing things. Their foes would escape unless they remembered how to freeze the water, as had been done to the part of the River Brandor just below Mangloth. They wasted much time attempting to regain some semblance of order, the massive throng, furious at what was going on, now bent on bringing Kolonth's fury down upon everyone and everything in their path.

The generals found their voice, taking strict control of the enraged force before all fell into chaos, ordering them back into formation, reminding them of their ultimate goal and the importance of obeying Kolonth's directive. Hearing the inference in that reminder, the troops regained their composure and marched southward. When they reached the next village in their path, they found the same stream, though it had grown to almost the size of a river. Anticipating a similar attack this time, they searched the banks for any enemies hiding in wait. Adding to their confusion, no attack materialized for the community was deserted. At the next larger town, an annoying rain started which soon turned into a torrential downpour. The wind picked up and whipped the water into an uncomfortable fury.

The people of Bjorqar could not have asked for better circumstances. To many, this deluge provided a hope that perhaps their defeat might not be the outcome after all.

"This miserable rain will be the death of us before Kolonth's troops ever get here. It's so heavy, we are drenched right through. Look, some of us are already starting to shiver. Others are sneezing and shivering from the dampness in their bones and the downpour is so thick at times we can barely see! By T'var, can it not stop, at least a little?"

"Don't be so hasty, young man. Some of us elders can still recall a storm similar to this happening five or was it six decades ago?"

"It was six," another elder spoke up. "Along with its horrific result. I had never seen something so awful in all my life and I was probably just a bit older than you young folks now."

"That's right, Jomin. There were no barricades on either the Lake or the River back then. Nothing even close to the ones we just hastily constructed to fend off the current intruders."

"If it happens again now, like it did back then, it will grow even worse. During that time, the unrelenting torrential rain caused both Lake

Qar and its tributary to overflow and flood much of the territory. The foul weather resulted in many lives lost, farms ruined and whole villages swept away. I myself lost my cousins and a sister."

"And I an aunt, uncle and my grandmother."

"Wow, we didn't know it was that bad! What will we do if it happens like that again?"

"Well, young ones, this time we will use it to Bjorqar's advantage and flush out those damnable invaders in every which way possible! Mayhap this rain won't be the death of us and neither will they!"

"Maybe, just maybe, this is T'var's doing." At that, many in the group began giving praise to T'var at this turn of events and prayed that the rain would continue.

With the capital Bjqa now fortified, the most able-bodied people left in the city began to leave the capital in preparation for the next step of their plan. With some on horseback and others on foot, they moved westerly at a rapid pace. They refused to allow the rainstorm, ever increasing in its fury, to slow their progress. Their destination was the high place where the River Qar flowed into its lake. Here they would make their last stand against the invaders.

CHAPTER TWELVE
OF WOOD AND WATER

While the events in Astaria and Bjorqar unfolded, Kolonth reached the Island Land of Narxa astride his Averi. He thought he could see the ruins in the distance as they circled far above. He used the reigns to direct the Averi to land just beyond the ruins. The beast did as commanded.

"Well done, my loyal servant. Attempt to find some drink and perhaps a few small animals to feed on. Though I suspect this abandoned land is mostly barren for sustenance other than the water on its shores. I will call should I have need of you."

Kolonth left the Averi behind and marched towards his objective. He began his search for the mysterious underground chamber in the rubble of the Castle of Crystal. Kolonth trusted the information to be accurate and he anticipated that the Orbstar would soon be his. Why T'var had tossed it away those many ages ago, just after Manglor's loss, remained a mystery. Kolonth considered it to be an error made by a weak and foolish enemy and he intended to take full advantage of it.

The ruins covered a vast area but this did not daunt Kolonth, who strode into the midst of the rubble and debris scanning through them carefully, without worrying about the time it might take. He kicked fragments and broken pieces aside, seeking to uncover any hint or lead to assist him in his quest.

In the far end of the ruins, Kolonth noticed the outline of the top edge of a door. Covered mostly in moss and debris, it laid at an angle to the ground, propped up and held slightly open by shards of crystal and pieces of broken walls. He kicked away what he could and then knelt down trying to pull it open. It seemed to be stuck and uncooperative, so he found a piece of wood nearby and used it to pry the door completely open, convinced it might be the very thing to lead him forward. He was successful and once the door was fully ajar, he could see that it had been hiding a stairway that led into darkness.

Kolonth was truly excited now and without hesitation, began his descent. Not that darkness disturbed him but he used his magiks to light his way, for he did not want to chance missing anything of importance. The stairs ended in a corridor and farther ahead, he could see another staircase that would take him further down. This one too ended in a corridor, which he followed until he encountered another stairway, which also led him to another lower level. This was repeated numerous times and Kolonth wondered how these underground stairwells and corridors had remained intact, in spite of the ruined castle's age.

He passed many rooms as he marched through the various corridors and took his time to examine each one, but so far none were of significance. Kolonth was tiring of the repetition, as he followed another set of stairs down to the next corridor. Once he reached the bottom, he began his usual thorough examination as he walked this new hallway. It was then he realized that there was no new stairway to descend this time. He must have reached the very depths of the castle and unlike previous times, he discovered there was only one room on this lowest level. A chamber with a tiny bit of illumination within it.

"Could it be?"

He did not walk or even march but *ran* through the opening of the room and scanned all around it meticulously, his reward certain. Out of the corner of his eye, Kolonth detected the source of that faint glimmer of light, buried below shards of glass. Without hesitation, he raced to the place where he thought the Orbstar lay. Gingerly, perhaps the gentlest he had ever dealt with anything in his long life, Kolonth began lifting away the debris. At last it lay before him, the means to rule all; an Orbstar of T'varin.

Kolonth gloated. He laughed. He shrieked with his version of joy until the ruins began to tremble. Had his hollow eyes been capable of tears, he might have shed some. He stared at the Orbstar for a long time and studied its smooth surface. Though he lusted after it, he also recognized it was purportedly the weapon T'var used to murder his father.

He had come so far and it was within his grasp but he was not prepared to take a risk on something that was of T'var, lest it be a trap. He forced himself to peer at it without touching it, to see if he could discern any visions inside of it. After many hours of concentration, he finally reached out and took it in his hand and found it warm to his touch. It made a low humming sound as it began to come to life.

Kolonth searched his memories for all that he'd learned of the Orbstars; he wanted to be sure to use it properly. He was determined that the same fate would not befall him as it had his sire, which he believed resulted from Manglor's misuse of the Orbstar. Now, at last, he held the power of eternity within his grasp. In a day, perhaps two, maybe three if necessary, although he doubted he would require much time, he would learn how to control the Orbstar and T'varin would be his forever. Perhaps, he might even reach out and conquer everything beyond. The thought moved him and excited him, as his greed and pride became limitless. Kolonth clutched the Orbstar in his dark-gloved hand, sitting down in the midst of the wreckage to consider his trophy.

*   *   *

By the time Kolonth's troops split up, one force moving further into Astaria and the others marching southwards to Bjorqar, the joint Astarian and Bjorqarn forces led by Astar, along with Randak, Wandarr and Barak, had crossed the frozen River Brandor into Astaria. Seeing the pillaging and carnage in the burning Astarian Woods, they were inspired to race towards their enemies. The trail of their foes was not hard to find; they needed only to follow the path of destruction Kolonth's troops left in their wake. One led east towards the capital, the other south towards Bjorqar.

Having finally made their way through the forest, Astar turned to her Bjorqarn counterparts and said, "Friends and comrades in arms all, here we must part ways. We go to defend our motherland and you to your fatherland. T'var's good fortune be with you. We may yet see the end of this evil, though the price we pay will no doubt be dear. Onwards friends, let us fight for all of T'varin. *T'var! T'vari! T'varin!*"

The whole army, both Astarian and Bjorqarn, took up the cry and shouted it until if felt as though the very ground shook beneath them and their voices ascended high above the desolation laying before them.

The Bjorqarns separated from the Astarians and moved into position to advance when Barak raised his hand, signalling the group to stop.

"Wait!"

All eyes turned to him, wondering at his impetuous outburst but Wandarr and Astar anticipated what was coming, for they had seen Randak and Barak in close conversation earlier on in their journey. At first,

Wandarr thought perhaps Randak had shared with Barak the source of his discomfort. But when Astar told Wandarr what she had accidently overheard them discussing, Wandarr realized such was not the case. She was upset that they did not feel at ease to discuss their plans with her, yet she understood their reluctance grew out of concern for her welfare. However, that did not mean she liked what she was going to hear.

"They propose to go on to Narxa, alone," Astar said, turning to Wandarr as they rode alongside one another earlier in the day. "They are concerned for your safety. They think you will be safer with us, rather than facing Kolonth on Narxa."

"Foolishness! What nonsense!" fumed Wandarr. "After everything we have been through together. What madness possesses them to think like this?"

"I think they are only concerned with your safety, my friend," said Astar.

"Really! Do they not realize that no place is safe while Kolonth lives? I have a Sonsword and I have the Orbstar! What are they thinking? I should like to give them..."

"Hush, they approach. Perhaps there is something of the hand of T'var in their decision. Who knows?" said Astar.

"Besides, it will be good to have you take arms alongside us, if you will."

Wandarr was so perplexed that she acted quite out of character, quiet and sullen, more like her brother in one of his broody moody states as Barak might put it. Her demeanour made Barak and Randak wonder if perhaps she had discovered their intent. Following Barak's raised hand and tired of hesitating, Randak gained enough courage to ask, "What troubles you, my Sister?"

"As if you are not aware! Have you both taken leave of your senses?"

Realizing that Wandarr had caught them in their conspiracy, Barak and Randak turned their faces away, cheeks turning red, humbled with embarrassment. It only grew worse as she continued her rant.

"To leave me with Astar and go to Narxa yourselves! What of me? What of the Starborn Sentinel's message? Was it not to all three of us? How dare you even think of dividing us. Your plot is revealed, for Astar overheard you earlier and let it slip. She, at least…"

"We were only considering you and your wellbeing," said Barak meekly.

Wandarr started to say, "If that's what you want then, I will go with Astar," when she felt the Orbstar begin to pulse. Inexplicably, she sensed the Orbstar urging her in that exact direction. Whenever she thought of travelling with Barak and Randak into Bjorqar, the pulse stopped as though it were the wrong decision. More confused than ever, Wandarr's puzzlement showed on her face.

"What is it, Sister? Now you look puzzled."

"It is the Orbstar, I know not the reason, but it is urging me to go with Astar despite the destiny I feel awaits us on Narxa."

"Strange," thought Wandarr. *"My intuition tells me there is a specific time we are to be on Narxa and we must not arrive too early,"* though this she kept to herself.

"What about Narxa?" asked Barak. "I thought we must head for Narxa."

"Yes," agreed Randak. "But it would appear there may be some assistance T'var would have us lend to our neighbours."

"Very well," Wandarr said, giving in. "I will accompany Astar to whatever lies before us. Remember, you two must meet me at the Great Bridge in Bjorqar in three days time. Should either of you let anything happen to the other, you will have me to deal with."

All three laughed together at Wandarr's words but the laughter could not hide the premonition of danger which awaited them. Yet some inner instinct, perhaps the voice of T'var Himself, assured them they would all three be together on the legendary Island Land of Narxa in due time.

Thus, Wandarr did not act surprised when Barak announced that Wandarr would stay to fight with the Astarians and that he and Randak would ride and fight with their Bjorqarn allies far into Bjorqar before turning towards the bridge leading to the Island Land of Narxa. The men of Bjorqar rejoiced at the news of having these two mighty fighters join their ranks, as much as the Astarians delighted at Wandarr's presence. Hope rose anew, that something of their homelands and their peoples might yet be salvaged. So, while the Warrior Women began a determined ride east towards Varin, the primary city, the men of Bjorqar, now with Randak and Barak alongside, galloped swiftly south.

Deep in Astaria, Kolonth's divided troops moved to examine the villages and towns that the Astarians themselves apparently set on fire. No sooner had they entered, when they were surrounded by small bands of Astarians who hurled everything from dishes to tree branches and large rocks to heavy gardening implements in their way, followed by a barrage of flaming arrows. In each of the three villages, Kolonth's troops were surrounded by walls of flame. Though no strangers to fire and not fearful of it, the very fact of these ambushes was enough to sorely disorient them. Many of them ran wildly from the flames in all directions, resulting in them being both unprepared and suspicious when the Astarians vanished and the attacks ceased.

Disoriented and reeking of fire, what was left of the three troops emerged and in due course, joined up on the road leading straight to Varin. They waited a short time, believing they must still be ahead of the fourth group, heading north by going around the places on fire and who were supposed to rejoin them on this road but after two hours of trudging through the terrain, still no sign of their compatriots showed. Wondering if the fools must have either been ambushed or deserted and no longer caring, the remaining superiors gave the order for their troops to move out. Cursing as they went, they grew more anxious than ever to rend the capital piece by piece, to teach their invisible foes a lesson.

They did not understand that the Astarians used the disorientation to disguise the road to Varin and make another road seem like the correct way to the capital. In the chaos and in their haste and anger, they did not even realize they had changed direction, now moving north rather than east. Nor did they know reinforcements approached fast on their heels, as the larger Astarian forces, commanded by Astar, were less than a day's ride away.

In Bjorqar, the rains increased in intensity just as the returning force, along with Randak and Barak, crossed the Astarian border into Bjorqar but the troops did not let this slow them down. The commanders knew of the plan ready to be put into operation and thought the rains could only help, not hinder.

Though they rode swiftly, Jorkan explained the Bjorqarn strategy, "Randak, Barak, you must be wondering what the plan is for Bjorqar."

"Yes, actually though, it is unfortunate Barak and I might have to turn towards Narxa before seeing it unfold."

"Yes, Randak, I was thinking the same thing and it would be reassuring, Jorkan, to see that your plans worked."

"Yes," Jorkan continued, "the evacuation of our towns and villages are no doubt almost complete. Soon all the able-bodied fighters from everywhere, including the capital, will make their way to the high place where our River Qar flows into Lake Qar. Here our people will make their stand against Kolonth's minions."

"Well, I must say, if the Bjorqarn skill in waterways equals or surpasses your skills in battle, then the invaders have much to fear and I have no doubt of your victory. Don't you agree, Barak?"

"Yes indeed, but hold," Barak put his hands to his eyes to see better in the midst of the rain, "What is that movement ahead? Do I see foes, not many but stragglers perhaps?"

"Yes!" Jorkan, commanded his troops, "Everyone, be prepared. There may only be a few, but by T'var let them feel our wrath! They must pay for entering our lands with evil intent! Swords and shields at the ready. Formation for containment. Ride forward."

The Bjorqarns continued their advance and came across a small number of stragglers from Kolonth's forces. They guessed these individuals had become separated during the many ambushes in wait along the way in Astaria and now attempted to reverse direction, either trying to rejoin their troops or perhaps were simply deserters. Either way, they were easily dealt with and now all lay dead.

*   *   *

Kolonth glared into the Orbstar. He was beginning to understand some of its uses and properties but he was not pleased with the story that it told. In Astaria, the Orbstar revealed a multitude of Warrior Women about to surprise his troops, who for some unknown reason, did not travel towards Varin, but to the northeast edge of the Great Astarian Wood. In Bjorqar, Kolonth saw a torrential downpour which slowing his battalions there. The next vision showed him an entire area about to be flooded, his troops washed away and another vast array of Bjorqarn soldiers bearing down on his forces. Kolonth could not understand what had gone wrong, until he saw another face in the Orbstar. One that made him shake in fury with murderous rage. He understood now who owned responsibility for this turn of events. Incredulous! The interfering fool would not accept his inevitable defeat. Kolonth's wrath exploded with intensity. Infuriated beyond measure, he nearly threw the Orbstar against the dilapidated chamber wall in frustration but thought better of it.

"No matter," Kolonth muttered aloud. "If it is a final confrontation that is desired, so be it. And I know exactly how to bring him here."

Kolonth took the Orbstar in hand, focused all his thought on the location of his Averi where it patiently waited for him. Then he was there, or at least an image of him formed such that he stood directly before his massive pet. Eyes aglow with Kolonth's own fire of hate, teeth bared, it slavered in anticipation of its next assignment. It hoped that the payment for its success would be as savory as the last.

Kolonth stared into the Averi's eyes, and spoke a simple command, "Do not harm him. Fetch him here."

Immediately the Averi understood its Master's intent. With a shriek of delight, it arose into the sky, soared high above the clouds, and began riding the westerly wind into Bjorqar.

What Kolonth viewed in the Orbstar told a true account, but in his frustration, he stopped looking at what was being mirrored there. Had he kept his gaze fixed, he would have indeed seen more of his plans go awry as his troops faced defeat at every turn.

*   *   *

Wandarr and Astar directed the Astarian troops forward and soon they saw flames in the distance.

"Our plot is engaged," Astar said with a smile to Wandarr. "Now watch as our forces emerge and we wedge our enemies together and drive them north."

Wandarr asked, "How will the rest of your forces know we are here and why push them northward?"

Astar replied, "Do you forget how efficient we have become at sending messages inside our own borders? The others have known of our approach since we crossed the River Brandor. Not all of our spies have left their posts and we push the foe northerly for two reasons: we do not wish them to come too near Varin, so the capital may remain intact and we push them north as there may still be some power in the northeastern end of the Woods. It is where Kolonth's emissaries have penetrated the least. Know that the Wood is much larger than Kolonth's army. They will be lost in there for months and we will be able to deal with them at our leisure."

"You are far from unprepared, Astar. One would think you almost expected this."

"Not really, for Kolonth did not move as we expected, but in Astaria we have learned to be prepared for the unexpected."

Astar smiled as she spoke and Wandarr wondered how anyone could prepare for something they did not know was going to occur but she kept her questions to herself. All her attention was focussed on the impending battle as they drew in sight of their adversaries.

The troops of Kolonth maintained their movement northwards. They only realized their mistake when they met the remaining others who had been unable to find the way to Varin after skirting north around the villages.

One of the Generals called out to the other, "What are you doing here? Why aren't you in Varin as you were tasked!"

"We thought that is where we were going, you piece of trash! No idea how we ended up here? What about you? Your bunch look as confused as the prey of an Averi! Where are we anyway?"

"General, look over there, what is that?"

"What is what, you useless piece of…oh, I see some kind of shadows."

"Large shadows sir," the responder's voice became high pitched.

"By Kolonth! Those cursed Astarian women have led us astray!"

"See it's not just us! Your raiders have been tricked too and this isn't good. Don't you know what those shadows are?"

"Shades! We are right up near the Astarian wood. This is bad. They are supposed to have some mystical..."

"No, no, not anymore. Kolonth put an end to that. Their shadows may be looming over us but there is nothing they can do. They're as useless as some of you."

"But how did we get here? Troops, stay in formation or we'll have your heads. And stop your grumbling. We may not know how we got here but at least we know where we are."

"So you say but we have a bad feeling about this. This whole thing does not bode well and has the air of deceit. Attention everyone, both sets of troops, listen up. We are going to turn around and go back the way we..."

"Sir, do you hear that? I hear hoof beats," said one of the soldiers with keener hearing than most.

"I don't hear it but I can smell it," affirmed another.

"There it is, that large cloud of dust rising in the air, coming this direction."

"This does not bode well for us. Get in formation all of you and stop your whining."

Many yelled battle-cries, knowing the fight was about to be joined, yet understanding it would be short-lived.

"Sir, it looks like not all the true warriors moved on. Maybe we should reconsider withdrawing before they..." The soldier never finished his sentence, for his General's sword had swiftly dealt with his cowardly recommendation. If nothing else, the rest of the troops were motivated to fight for victory, rather than meet their general's blade.

They turned and in a poor state of what passed for battle formation, prepared to challenge, which is why they failed to see the other cloud rising in the west. Without warning, they were now crushed into a pincer movement between two very aggressive armies. Realizing they faced the actual contingent of Warrior Women and some recognizing the flash of Wandarr's Sonsword during the battle, they panicked and began scrambling to escape. Kolonth had told them this would be an easy conquest and the raiders who made up a good portion of the group lacked the fortitude for this heavy kind of fighting; they only wanted to burn, pillage, kill the helpless and ransack defenseless villages. They enjoyed bullying those weaker than they when winning a sure thing but this situation was not what they had expected at all.

The Astarian troops bore down on both sides and began forcing them deeper into the Wood. A few riders left formation and chased after stragglers who, in their confusion and fright of the Wood, tried other escape routes. Caught without effort, they found themselves forced back towards the shadows of the trees.

Wandarr discerned something unusual the closer they came to the Astarian Forest. Every time Nayr headed that way, as they joined the others in pushing the opposition northward, the Orbstar would vibrate in her belt, as if reaching out to something with which it felt a connection. Wandarr did not yet understand why it behaved in such a strange fashion. During a brief lull in the battle, when others seemed preoccupied with driving the horde further into the forest, Wandarr brought Nayr to a halt. Out of curiosity she took out the Orbstar.

She wished she had not done so, for it came to life straightaway. She did not vanish this time, as the Orbstar glowed in fury and throbbed in her hand until she thought it might burn her palm. She gazed into it and for an instant thought she saw a deep shadowy darkness, but it disappeared, replaced by a reflection of the forest. A stream of bright emerald light shot up above the battling crowd and headed towards the forest. It only went halfway before it was intersected by a returning beam of light of the identical colour that shot forth out of the Woods.

"Wandarr, why do you release the Orbstar?" Astar questioned the wisdom in doing so.

"I am not sure I am doing it, Astar. I think it is releasing itself. It is as though it possesses some kinship with the forest and is reaching out to it," Wandarr answered, still mystified herself.

"It's possible," explained Astar. "The Astarian Wood goes back into the Oldentime. Its mystical prowess and barrier have lasted up to now, until Kolonth managed to find a way to weaken it."

"That's it!" cried Wandarr. "The Orbstar is reinforcing the barrier again. At least at this end of the forest. Look!"

Wandarr pointed to where the forces of Kolonth scurried into the Wood. A greenish light continued to emanate from both the Orbstar and the forest, growing stronger in its brilliance as the beams met somewhere in between both. The defensive wall of trees appeared to have transformed into a huge contingent of Starborn Sentinels standing side by side, feet and arms spread open wide, holding hands as though forming a linked chain. At first, they appeared to be pale but the light from the Orbstar, merging with that of the forest, endowed them with renewed strength and the sweet aroma of lavender flowed across the battlefield.

This disturbing vision was far beyond Kolonth's troops' capability to handle. They now stood before Starborn Sentinels which most thought a myth, while the Astarian troops hemmed them in on all sides. This caused many of them to throw down their weapons and fall to the ground cowering in fear. Others ran headlong into the Wood but as they encountered the glow, they vanished into nothingness.

When the beam from the Orbstar, still held aloft in Wandarr's hand subsided, Astar smiled in victory and raised her voice.

"It is over," she proclaimed above the roar of troops. "Forces of Mangloth, it is time to surrender. Astaria is not yours, nor shall it ever be. Come Astarians, we have a few more foes to deal with, much damage to undo and lives to mourn."

She was about to turn to Wandarr and request her company onward to Varin, when she saw intense pain cut across her friend's face, Wandarr's smile of victory replaced by an agony that had not been there a moment ago.

"Randak!" Wandarr screamed. "N-o-o-o-o!"

CHAPTER THIRTEEN
THE BRIDGE TO NARXA

While the Astarians with Wandarr's aid battled for their homeland, upon the storm drenched terrain of Bjorqar, Randak, Barak and the larger Bjorqarn army swept down upon Kolonth's troops with a fury surprising even themselves. Sonswords glowing in the midst of the downpour led the way, pushing the enemy towards Lake Qar.

This was the first time Barak fought against such a large contingent and he found it both terrifying and exhilarating as his Sonsword cut through the foes without mercy. He was too focussed to speak but with every enemy he cut down, the cry, *"For Vintar! For Vintar!"* echoed in his mind.

At times, the battle seemed almost surreal. Though Barak and Randak had the protection of the Sonswords upon them as they cut a swath through the invaders, the soldiers of Bjorqar were not as fortunate. Barak saw Belsharn knocked off his horse and falling to the ground but had not time to assist, for he was immediately confronted by three of Kolonth's soldiers. His Sonsword sliced through them with ease, their half-bodies now bloodying the ground. He saw Jorkan take a wound to the shoulder blade of his sword arm and a number of his soldiers immediately surround their Captain in a long-practiced protective formation.

Barak turned to see where Belsharn had landed but had to maneuver away when Evad neighed in warning, lowering his head as a Carnivore lunged for Barak and then found itself impaled on his Sonsword; the energy of the sword pulsing with such rage the beast melted on contact. Barak still had no time to seek Belsharn, for in the midst of the pouring rain, grime and dust from the battle, he was suddenly confronted by two goliath-sized soldiers who did not appreciate what he had just done to the Carnivore. While others of Kolonth's troops ran the other direction when they saw the beast melt, these two, towering well over Barak even with him astride Evad, thought to put an end to Barak and his Sonsword.

"Come here little man! Let us see if you are brave with real soldiers instead of a mindless beast." They both waved their long jagged-edged swords. "Your pretty blade will make a fine gift for our Master."

"Bring it on!"

"Oh, we will. Prepare to…glurp glug…wha…." The first soldier wavered on his feet momentarily, as the sharp end of a Sonsword stuck out of his throat.

Randak's head poked out between the two giants as he shouted above the awful gurgling noise, "Thought you could use a little help." Randak gave the speaker a slight nudge with his Sonsword and the giant fell to the ground dead.

The second soldier made the mistake of turning to see where the voice originated and quickly found Barak's Sonsword stuck deep within his gut. He felt himself burning up from the inside out, finally collapsing to the ground, joining his partner in death. Barak gave Randak a nod and they rode into the battle, continuing their assault, now side by side. Less of the

Bjorqarns than the enemy fell but the groans of the injured and moans of the dying on both sides could be heard as blood, severed limbs and sometimes heads covered the battlefield; the smell of sweat amidst the grunts of those still fighting filled the air, as the aroma of death permeated the soggy landscape.

Still, this was a complete and unanticipated turn of events for Kolonth's leaders; they had assumed the fight would be with only what lay ahead of them and that they would march without much interference into Bjqa. Between the heavy rain, now joined by thunder and lightning, the unforeseen return of the greater Bjorqarn contingent and the frustrating skirmishes and ambushes they had encountered along the way, morale had dropped significantly. The troop's Generals and Captains recognized it all too well. Once, fear was the primary motivator for service to Kolonth but it did not engender loyalty. So Kolonth's Captains knew that unless something drastic and quick happened, they would all be washed away in the growing storm. The troops were already becoming unruly.

A less respectful soldier challenged Kolonth's leadership. "Well, Generals and Captains, this is a fine mess you have gotten us into, isn't it? Not only are we in the middle of this cursed storm, this has not been the easy invasion we were promised."

"Be silent you, little worm."

"Sorry, General." For emphasis, the soldier spit on the ground. "But I think you forget there are more of us than you and you-our great leaders-ha!- have probably led us to certain death. Chances are, we'll run into those lunatics with those glowing swords and that will be the end of us. You know, once they get going, nothing can harm or stop them."

"I suggest you stop talking right now if you value your pitiful life."

"What life, we ask you?" the grumbling started to spread.

"Listen all of you, you can stand and fight or you can desert us and crawl back to Mangloth and face Kolonth when you give him your report. Your choice, we don't care."

Small skirmishes had started to break out among some of the soldiers who attempted to stop the ones trying to leave, either through injury or threat of death. Things were getting out of hand, until one of the Captains, yelled, "Look over there in the distance. Help is coming. By Kolonth, we will be victorious yet."

The reprieve Kolonth's troops hoped for came suddenly and without warning. While they were still being driven towards Lake Qar, they saw another large mass afar off from an easterly direction coming to meet them. The thought that their enemies would soon be caught between two armies inspired them to fight against their current foes even more aggressively, but still the flash of unrelenting Sonswords began to wear them down. Some of them had encountered the Sonswords in battle before and the swords' imposing glow and the fierce, unyielding wrath of the warriors holding them was not something they could withstand.

Randak and Barak carved a path right through their opponents, laughing with battle fever upon them. They purposely took out those they marked as Captains and Generals so the forces became increasingly disarrayed without their leadership.

Above the torrent came a shrill noise which caused all the servants of Kolonth to stop and tremble. The huge, distant mass which Kolonth's soldiers had mistaken for their allies was revealed: a giant Averi appeared, low in the sky, right over the warring factions.

Heedless of wind or rain, it bore straight down from overhead, circled once, spied its target and dove. So swiftly did it move that Barak at first did not know what had happened until it was all over. At the creature's approach, he and Randak lowered their Sonswords to hide their glow, so as not to be discovered, hoping the creature would come close enough for them to drive their blades deep into its body. Randak, almost certain it was the same beast they had seen in Glephas, did not move. He realized too late he had made the wrong choice.

Both sides thought the Averi was going to land and challenge the warriors, which is what it trusted that all would think. No one expected it to swoop down, pick up its prey in its razor-sharp talons and fly back with its catch to its Master. But that is exactly what happened. Randak was taken, lifted up helplessly into the sky, his Sonsword fallen from his hand, now lying beside Jip, who was as confused about his master's disappearance as the rest.

Barak's scream of, "Randak, No-o-o-o!" was lost in the sounds of the storm and melee as Kolonth's forces now attacked with renewed vigour, encouraged by the appearance of their Master's pet. In one fluid motion, Barak dismounted, grabbed Randak's Sonsword with his free hand and thrust it into Jip's saddle bag. He remounted Evad before his enemies grasped what had happened and called to Jip, saying, "Follow me, Jip. To the Bridge."

Barak fought his way out of the cluster of foes around him with a righteous anger that forced them to give way before his wrath. The men of Bjorqar began to lose heart as the tide of struggle now turned against them. Many believed Randak was as good as dead and now Barak rode away from them mad with grief, probably to his doom. Their enemy sensed the hesitation and their murder lust grew as they killed more and more of the Bjorqarns.

The conflict carried on, drawing both the hosts of Mangloth and those of Bjorqar closer to the place where others patiently waited above Lake Qar. Those awaiting had no idea of what transpired north of them, for the army was still too far away to be seen clearly. They did not know their comrades had returned and they thought they were about to face

Kolonth's invasion force alone. When their lookouts came back with news reporting their troops were indeed returned, they rejoiced. Though when informed their side was losing, they thought it best to execute their strategy without delay. It was time to launch their contingency plan; they anticipated their comrades would comprehend what was happening and take appropriate action.

The Bjorqarns opened the dam holding back the water between the River Qar and Lake Qar. The waters, mixed with the still-steady torrential rains, began to flood across the area where soldiers on both sides continued to clash. Those fighting for Bjorqar saw the approaching deluge because they faced that direction but most of Kolonth's soldiers did not understand the danger approaching them until they heard the rushing torrent all too late.

The Bjorqarns turned and raced toward higher ground. Kolonth's servants mistook it for a sign of retreat and not until they turned and witnessed the cascade of water spreading into the vale, did they realize their error. The valley they battled in, below Lake Qar, was submerged and many perished.

Racing up, some of the foe escaped, only to find a new threat awaited them as the remainder of the Bjorqarns' might stood to defend their homeland. The raging current carried many of the enemy off, including those who tried to run, walk or swim their way out, only to discover the River Qar's banks continued to flood, pushing everything and everyone towards a watery grave.

In their haste to get away from the water and the enemies who stood towering over them on the high place near the western border of Lake Qar, many headed to the eastern side of the lake. This was the worst thing they could have done, since Lake Qar's waters had become a rushing torrent, pouring into the Bjorqarvin River where many of the soldiers became captives of the angry currents. The overflowing river persisted, growing in strength, rapidly pushing the few survivors towards the rocky rapids leading to the Vintaran Falls. Meeting the rapids was deadly enough, but reaching the Falls that dumped its massive waters and anything within them into the Great Sea far below, meant certain death for those who had not already perished in the unforgiving waters.

Most of the invaders were forced into the Bjorqarvin and drowned there, while the remainder crashed into the rapids' submerged rocks situated on the way to the Falls. A few escapees were caught by the Bjorqarn forces except for some who had scrambled to higher ground. That small group of the enemy headed northward again. Worn, weary and drenched from the continued rains, they crossed the frozen River Brandor and expected to make it back to Mangloth. Thanks to more Bjorqarns hiding along that route, none reached the capital and Bjqa remained secure.

*   *   *

Lightning flashed and thunder boomed as the Averi flew swiftly through the storm, Randak a helpless thread, dangling in its claws. He attempted to open his eyes a few times but it was impossible at the speed the Averi flew, for the wind and rain stung intensely. He had no idea where they were, but since the Averi had not yet dropped him to the ground far below, he concluded there was a destination to which he was being taken. It was difficult to formulate his thoughts or even speak to the creature, as if that would do any good. All he could manage to voice was, "T'var help me," but feared even that weak plea was lost unheard in the wind or drowned out by the incessant thunder.

"Finally, the storm stops and now the Averi slows. Maybe there is a way of escape if it lands. Let's see where we are though. Those ruins! This must be Narxa. I'm being delivered to Kolonth. No sword, no allies, no friends, only my wits. T'var, I need you now more than ever."

The Averi hovered a few feet above the ruins and dropped Randak where he landed unceremoniously atop the rubble. He scrambled to his feet looking for a way of escape but the Averi continued to stay in the air just above him, closing off any thought of freedom.

Randak looked up at the creature, thinking he might speak to it, when a voice erupted in his mind, *"Come, Warrior."* It made his head throb with a burning akin to a fever. His formerly wounded arm joined in the pain. *"The agony will cease as you follow my voice. Come."* Against his will, Randak's body began to move towards an opening in the rubble. Try as he might, he could not resist. For a moment he became an outside observer to his own movements. He tried to think, but his thoughts clouded over in a dense fog, his body and mind now captive to the voice's commands.

*   *   *

Wandarr glared at the Orbstar still in her hand. Astar stared at her intently.

"Take me to the Bridge to Narxa," Wandarr commanded.

Astar thought at first that her friend must be insane to be talking to the Orbstar, then remembered that this was no mere gem but a storehouse of unfathomable power, the stuff of myth made real.

Wandarr uttered the same words once more and placed all the feeling and intention possible into her effort. Astar watched in wonder as the Orbstar again came to life, shining and humming, immersing her friend in its radiance. Wandarr recognized that the power coursing through her body was similar to her experience at The Circle of Andivar and yet also felt very different. A burst of light broke forth from the Orbstar causing Wandarr and Nayr to vanish.

Astar knew that Wandarr did not just turn invisible again, she was really gone and somehow now stood at threshold of the Bridge to Narxa.

"King's Praise!" Astar muttered. "T'var be with you, my friend.

You shall need Him, I think."

*   *   *

Riding Evad in a frenzy, Barak raced headlong to the Bridge, oblivious to his surroundings. Jip galloped alongside. The downpour had slowed, at least in this part of Bjorqar and Barak was thankful for the chance to dry a little. He played the awful scene over in his mind repeatedly as he galloped towards his destination. Chastising himself for not acting more quickly, he let the guilt build, until tears welled up in his eyes. Driving all thoughts out of his mind of what might be happening to his brother-friend, he prayed to T'var for Randak's survival.

"Is it possible Wandarr somehow knows what happened?

"How soon will I find her?

"What will I say to her to ease her anguish?

"I will have to tell her this is all my fault.

"By T'var, what if Randak is, no I refuse to think like that."

So preoccupied in his thoughts, Barak did not appreciate how far he had come, or notice that the clouds had parted and the sun now shone. Thus, he failed to see the giant statues to which he now drew near. Neither did he see Wandarr standing before them until he was almost on top of her.

"Wandarr!" Quickly dismounting, he ran towards her.

"Barak!" Wandarr leapt off Nayr and covered the short distance between them. They immediately embraced, holding each other tightly, until Wandarr stepped away, her eyes wet.

"Randak needs us." She stared at the riderless Jip, confirming her worst fears.

"A great Averi, it plucked him from Jip right in front of me. I should have done something. I…it all happened so fast. I…am… I am… so…sorry. Should anything happen to him, I will never forgive myself." Barak felt tears forming, which now matched Wandarr's.

"Hush," said Wandarr. "I should have insisted on staying with the two of you. It is as much my fault. Enough. Let us go to Narxa. We will find him there; my heart tells me so."

"It's the dreams, isn't it? The dreams are coming true, or at least parts of them. He's in those ruins and in peril."

Barak jumped on Evad and called for Jip to come alongside.

Wandarr, however, stood before the entrance between the massive stone figures and said, "They will not let us go further. I tried to go onto the Bridge right before you arrived. I could not."

Barak took stock of the imposing statues for the first time since arriving. One was female, in the likeness of an Astarian Warrior Woman, the other male and by his garb, he was clearly a soldier of Bjorqar. Barak considered these stately, but daunting sculptures. "These are the Guardians of the Bridge! I think they must be the imposing figures from my dream, but I could not make them out then. I see them clear enough now though. It is them. Of that I am certain."

"Yes and do you remember the legend of T'var's last words to the Guardians?" asked Wandarr.

Barak thought for a moment.

"*Call me when the Warriors Three are in their time of greatest need.* The Prophecy of Hope!"

"Yes, but Randak is one of the three and in jeopardy. Yet for some unknown reason, we cannot go past these Guardians."

"Why not?" asked Barak, frustrated at Wandarr's obstinacy. He directed Evad forward to the Bridge and found he was unable to pass as well. He felt as if he and Evad had walked into an unseen wall. A thought occurred to him however as he considered this barrier.

"The Orbstar!"

"What of it?" Wandarr had not even told Barak that it was what she used to arrive at the Bridge. The second she materialized before the Stone Guardians she tucked it away, frightened and awed by its power.

"Well," Barak waved his hands excitedly, "The Orbstar can make you invisible. Perhaps there is a way of reversing it, using it to make hidden things visible. Maybe it will reveal the way to go through. Just like it showed you and Randak the way through the Glephoid Pass. Why not show the Guardians the Orbstar and see what happens?"

"I suppose it is worth a try," Wandarr hesitated. Cautiously, lest there be the same almost unbearable surge of power which she experienced when it transported her to the bridge, Wandarr once again pulled the Orbstar from her belt. Disappointingly, it stayed quiet and without any hint of the immense power it could display as she raised it up before the Guardians.

"Show me the door," Wandarr commanded. Nothing happened. "The Warriors Three are in their time of greatest need! Reveal the door!"

She spoke again, this time louder and with more authority. It was almost imperceptible, yet both Barak and Wandarr felt that something had changed. The silent giants did not move, nor did the Orbstar let out one flicker of light, yet they were encouraged.

"Let's try it now," said Wandarr with confidence, as she mounted Nayr and brought him alongside Evad.

The riderless Jip came alongside to join them. They approached the place between the Guardians where they had been repelled before. This time they felt no resistance. They rode through at a steady pace and once on the Bridge riding side by side, spurred their steeds into a gallop that would bring them out to the Island Land of Narxa.

The Guardians endured; silent, steadfast and aloof. Except as Barak and Wandarr passed by, a silent call burst forth from both figures. The call reached into the skies of T'varin, travelled far above Bjorqar and

The Rangdorrian Lands, Glephas and Karnakon and flew out across the ocean towards the King's Lands until it reached its appointed destination. A summons unable to be heard or understood by T'varin ears but the One who awaited it, knew what it meant: the time had come.

Barak and Wandarr galloped hard along the Bridge. They did not think they could push their steeds much further when a fog came out of nowhere and covered them completely. It was so dense that they could barely see each other and if not for the panting of their horses, they would not have known the other was nearby. It was an odd mist, some strange characteristic of the Bridge they thought, for it did not dampen their clothing.

They charged ahead for another half an hour when Evad began to excitedly whinny to Jip, who responded in kind. Looking more closely towards Jip through the fog, they could make out the silhouette of a rider upon him. Yet to their own amazement, they did not feel scared or concerned, only a mixture of peace and puzzlement. Talking about it later, they could only describe it as a settling calm resting upon them, in spite of the surprise visitor.

Initially they thought it was only their imagination but the more they glanced through the mist, they realized that they were correct the first time. If they listened carefully, they could hear a quiet conversation between the mysterious rider and Jip.

Abruptly the group was at the other end of the Bridge and on the Island Land of Narxa and the third rider was revealed. They had never seen Him in person before, yet still they knew Him. T'var stood beside them, smiling, though with a look of urgency in his eyes.

Barak was so much at a loss for words all he could say was, "Lord, are you riding Jip?"

He could see that T'var wore the same kind of shimmering robe the ancient stories spoke of. He had hair which was black and had bluish-green eyes the colour of pristine waters.

"That's odd, I thought the stories spoke of them as totally green." Wandarr worked at summoning the question she was fearful to ask.

"There will be time for questions later, Barak. Come! Randak is in great danger."

"T'var, is he? My Lord, is he?"

"No, your brother still lives and he needs us."

T'var pointed the way to the shambles of the Castle of Crystal, where they would find Randak and they galloped faster than they ever imagined in their rush to aid their friend and brother.

As they proceeded, a dark shape above cast a lengthy shadow upon them. Looking up, Barak shouted, "Averi! And a large one! This is the one that took Randak!"

Though even as he spoke the warning, Barak felt no fear. Their horses also stayed unusually calm, instead of bolting as one might expect them to do. The riders brought them to a halt.

"Indeed, Barak and he approaches swiftly. We have little time to spare but still let us see what he is about." T'var's words baffled them.

"What do You mean?" Wandarr asked.

The Averi circled, dropping lower each time, until it was directly overhead, now close enough that they could make out every detail of its serpentine body.

Surprisingly, T'var stared up into the Averi's abyss-like black eyes and spoke gently to the creature as though they were old acquaintances.

"Ah, my friend, I know you have been hard done by, your will corrupted by a dark force." The Averi continue to stare, its eyes filled with malice, but listening intently to T'var's offer. "How about we set that right and I send you to a new home where you might find more of your kind and those similar to you?"

Wandarr and Barak swore the creature smiled in response as if to say, "*Yes, I would like that,*" though it revealed all its sharp teeth, which was definitely unnerving for both of them.

"Do you see that, Wandarr? Its eyes are no longer black."

"I do. They have become a bluish-green now and almost reflect intelligence and maybe even excitement. But what does it mean?" she looked to T'var for a response, but He simply pointed a finger to the sky above the Averi, where an opening in the shape of a large hole appeared, and said, "Off you go! Enjoy your new home!"

The Averi did not even bother to look at them, speeding up and away through the rift, disappearing from sight as did the rent in the sky, closing as soon as the Averi was gone. Deep underground, Kolonth hesitated, for he suddenly felt a keen sense of loss but could not yet discern what it meant.

Wandarr and Barak really desired to ask T'var more about what just happened but were deterred from doing so, when T'var said, "Quickly now, let us ride!"

In what seemed like only moments, the group arrived at the ruins. Wordlessly, T'var dismounted, Barak and Wandarr following suit. Barak hesitated only a moment, retrieving Randak's Sonsword from Jip's saddlebag and then commanding their four-footed friends to stay.

They followed T'var to the edge of the ruins, where He waved His hand in a sweeping motion and similar to the rift in the sky only moments earlier, a doorway appeared. T'var walked through and motioned for them to follow. Once through, they looked behind them, but the mysterious entranceway was gone. They were now somewhere in what was left of the castle. They walked for quite a while through torch-lit passages and underground caves until they emerged in the wreckage of a chamber where they met both friend and foe. The air in the chamber was stale. Something else too permeated the air; the reek of an ancient hatred determined to devour everything in its sight.

Randak stood there, one arm limp at his side, helpless, staring into the face of Kolonth who held the Orbstar before him repeating, "You are mine! You are mine!!"

"Randak!" Wandarr shouted desperately trying to get his attention. "My Brother!

Wandarr turned to her King, "What has Kolonth done to him?"

Yet T'var remained strangely and frustratingly silent.

Barak shouted directly at Kolonth, "If you have harmed him, I swear..."

Kolonth gave the intruders only a glance and addressed Randak, "Ah yes, go greet your dear Sister."

Randak walked over to Wandarr and embraced her but his movements were stiff and awkward, like those of a marionette on twisted strings. When she tried to stare into his eyes, they were clouded and hard to read.

"What has he done to you?" Wandarr cried.

"Nothing, why nothing," said Randak weakly, hugging her tightly again.

As he did, he reached into the secret pouch in her belt and grasped for the Orbstar. Wandarr realized his intention and her hand reached the Orbstar first. She held it tightly but Randak seized her wrist and twisted the Orbstar loose. Barak was about to offer Randak back his Sonsword, when he witnessed Wandarr recoiling in pain, yelling, "Randak, what are you doing?"

Unbelieving, Barak saw the Orbstar in Randak's possession and watched helplessly as his brother-friend walked towards Kolonth, hand outstretched, the Orbstar laying in his palm, now freely offered to their greatest enemy.

CHAPTER FOURTEEN
THE VICTORY OF KOLONTH

Randak awoke from his bed, mystified by his surroundings. A knock on his bedroom door startled him further and he sat up.

"Yes, come in, what is it?"

A person he did not recognize responded, "The Imperator requests you join him as soon as you are dressed. The preparations you two discussed earlier this week will soon be ready."

"Yes, yes of course, I shall be along with all haste, thank you."

Randak had trouble identifying the strange being who seemed to know him so well. He looked at the man more closely, thinking that might help his memory, but to no avail. The man's short stature, long thin strands of gray hair on a balding head, sandalled feet and black cloak, with a hood that hid most of his complexion, did not help matters at all.

"Wonderful, Master. As you will see on your sofa, I took the liberty of laying out your armour and apparel. I shall wait for you outside your chamber. It will be my honour to escort our Champion, the Black Blade and Great Overseer of all our armies to the meeting."

"Yes, yes, of course, thank you."

Randak needed some time to himself. If for nothing else, to at least wake up and clear his mind. His bedroom was becoming more familiar to him, so he found his armour and began dressing for the meeting. He looked in the mirror above the sofa as he dressed and realized he now had graying hair and his face showed the weight of many years on it. The reflection definitely made him appear taller and more muscular than he remembered but perhaps that was just the trick of his still-tired eyes. He stared into the mirror a moment longer and then took a step back to see a full view of himself. He was so shocked at what he saw, he gasped, stepped back and tripped over a chair behind him, which crashed to the floor.

"Sir, are you alright? Do you need my assistance?" came the voice of the waiting attendant.

"Yes…yes…I mean, no…" Randak stuttered. "I am fine, just not quite awake yet, all is well now. I shall be right out."

He grasped the polished black sword that had lain beside his armour and stared at the image in the blade to verify what he had seen in the mirror. Still shaken, he placed it in its sheath. Randak was totally bewildered but decided it would be best to go to the meeting. He stumbled to his feet and then hurried out of the room to let the attendant take him to his meeting with the Imperator.

As Randak followed his escort, his mind and more importantly, his memory, began to clear. He understood now why the armour he wore bore a fiery red hexagon inside an icy blue circle on the breast plate. He knew why the sword in his sheath glistened pure black. He was a servant of the one true Lord and Ruler, the Imperator of all the world. He was about to meet with His Master, Kolonth.

Walking the many corridors and staircases provided Randak with time to search his memories and collect his thoughts. The chill of the building crept into his bones and while the stale air he breathed in was annoying, he was more interested in the paintings and murals on some of the walls as they walked to their destination.

The artwork depicted a series of various battle scenes from every land in the form of panoramas that at times stretched the entire length of some corridors. Each series revealed a sequence of events ending in the defeat of Kolonth's enemies and the victory of his armies over all the world. Averi flew above in the skies and shadowy figures marked with a circled hexagon, appeared randomly in some of the panels. The last tapestry caught Randak's attention for it portrayed the chamber where he had given the Orbstar to Kolonth. He wanted time to view the whole mural but his escort prevented that.

"We have arrived at the meeting room. It has been a pleasure to escort the Black Blade once again. Please enter, the Master awaits you."

Hesitantly, but with little choice, Randak opened the door and walked in.

"Ah Randak, welcome! I trust you slept well and are prepared for the next step in our plan."

"Yes, of course, Imperator," Randak bowed as he spoke. "To think that we are now going to extend our reach beyond the world of Kolonth itself is a great accomplishment! All because of your foresight, ingenuity and drive to secure freedom for all the lands, even those beyond our own world."

The words came easily to Randak as though they had been rehearsed, ones he had spoken before.

"Granted and thank you, though much of this success is due to you, my loyal lieutenant. It is because you saw the truth and acted well those many years ago, forsaking that Liar and Deceiver, the Pretender King and giving your loyalty to me. Without you doing the right thing, we would not have been able to accomplish all that we have. It is in no small part due to you that I have earned the name *Imperator*," Kolonth expressed his sincere gratitude to Randak.

"Thank you, Imperator, it is my honour to serve."

"We have accomplished so much, from bringing freedom from the Pretender's lies, to renaming this world to honour me, its true champion and calling it simply Kolonth was a stroke of genius. Partly your suggestion, as I remember."

"Was it? I had forgotten that. It seems so long ago. How many years now since our victory, Master? Time seems to have sped by too rapidly, my grey hairs are becoming greyer still."

Kolonth laughed, and said, "It has been almost one hundred years since the battle in that wretched chamber. My rule has brought longevity to the people. It is unfortunate that your sister and friend could not see the truth and perished there along with their false King or they would both be enjoying long lives. Only you discovered the truth and acted accordingly!"

Randak winced at that, saying, "Yes, I secured the Orbstar from Wandarr and turned it over to you, showing you my true allegiance. I was sick of the lies and half truths the false King and His followers kept spreading."

"Indeed," Kolonth nodded. "You were wise to see the truth that He hid from so many. That service to Him meant bondage not freedom. Slavery, not emancipation."

"Yes, if only Barak and Wandarr had listened and had not been deceived."

"Do you remember what happened next? After you gave me the Orbstar?"

"Yes, of course! You used the Orbstar to kill the false King. It pierced

His chest and He lay there, dead and gone forever." Randak was surprised at the question, as though his memory was being tested and thought it best to continue. "Yes! I did the right thing and freed this world from the evil fraudster's despicable plans to control everyone and everything. As you have said, the so-called King deserted His people by being absent from the world for over a thousand years or more. He only reappeared when He was in danger of losing one of His cherished Orbstars. It was only then that He reappeared, caring not for the suffering of the peoples of T'varin during all those years between. You put an end to that injustice once for all, my Liege."

"Excellent. You speak truly! And then, Randak? Do you remember what occurred after I ended the false King? I know it has been many years since it happened, but it is sometimes good to remember what moves us forward."

Randak continued to look around the room throughout the conversation. He noticed banners of all the conquered lands now emblazoned with the circled hexagon above their own flags and insignias. There were other signs of victory too, uniforms of leaders fallen in battle, some from Astaria and Bjorqar and other lands as well. These distracted him and he realized Kolonth had asked him a question.

Randak replied, "I am sorry, my Lord, I was once again admiring our spoils of victory so well displayed here. You asked me if I remember and I do. At the death of the Pretender, the chamber started to crumble. What was left of the entire ruins began to shake apart, falling in every direction. I remember a wall falling on my sister, with only her head free of the rubble. Most of her bones were broken from the weight of the wall and her lungs were damaged, making it hard for her to breathe. The Pretender's body was completely covered by the debris and could no longer be seen. Barak managed to get out of the way of most of it, but some still fell on him, crushing his legs."

"And then…?" Kolonth was very curious to hear Randak's answer.

"I walked to Barak and pleaded with him to swear his allegiance to you. I begged him to realize only the True Master could have used the Orbstar to defeat the Pretender. That you were the true King. If he would do so, I would free him, you could use the Orbstar to heal him and he could join us in victory. But he was stubborn and refused. I had no choice. I could hear my sister weakly whisper with her dying breath, *"Randak, please no...don't."* But what choice did I have? If nothing else, I could at least end his pain. I drove my sword deep into his chest. I let it rest there until he was gone. In fact, at your bidding, I simply left it there, for you promised me a better blade, more appropriate for your new lieutenant."

"Yes, I did, and you carry it well, Randak. The Black Blade; your new name and your sword's. You are the Overseer of all the armies of Kolonth. You are my Black Blade, so christened on the edge of the beginning of my new reign." Kolonth went on, saying, "The world of Kolonth and the people of all the lands are free and willingly do my bidding. See how they prosper and rejoice in their work and their play."

As he spoke, Kolonth moved his hands in a strange fashion, as if opening a curtain. Randak saw that which Kolonth described come to life in a host of images in the air before him. From Karnakon to Glephas, from The Rangdorrian Lands to Vintar and Bjorqar and on to Astaria, Randak watched as people worked, played and lived happily in prosperity and in service to Kolonth.

"See how content and joyous the people are to provide their services to our cause. Look how all their wills are focused on providing the food, machinery, weapons and everything needed to keep the vast armies you oversee well-fed and well-equipped. All are dedicated to supporting our cause, willingly and without fear."

"It is truly miraculous, my Lord. You have done so much for the people of this world."

"Yes, and now we will take this mission to other worlds. Starting with the home of that vile creature, Quad Razak, who attempted to betray me! Soon, at a midnight hour, I shall once again open the doorway to its world. Only this time, nothing will come through to our world, rather, under your captaincy, our invading forces will go forth into Quad Razak's domain and conquer it in my name. I will also provide you with the means to capture Quad Razak itself and hold it prisoner until I arrive to meet out my justice for its crimes against me."

Randak started when he heard the name Quad Razak and felt lightheaded; a memory was taking shape, one of a battle between Quad Razak, himself, Barak and Wandarr. Also, a memory of a venomous burning in his arm from the creature's flame.

"Ah yes," Kolonth interrupted Randak's thoughts before the memory fully surfaced. "You remember how the creature helped you by using its venom to ensure you could bear my mark. It buried itself deep within, in spite of the misguided efforts of your deluded friends. It was the first step in opening your eyes to the truth and setting you on proper path of loyalty to the rightful ruler of this world."

Kolonth's excited tone filled Randak's ears such that he could think of nothing else. "So it began, and now continues as we expand our reach. Are you excited, my faithful servant, to take the next step in fulfilling our mission? Our destiny to help other worlds find the same glory, peace and prosperity as we have been able to bring to this world of Kolonth?"

"Yes, Sire, of course! We shall be victorious! Thank you, Imperator, for the faith and trust you have placed in me. I, Randak, the Black Blade, your humble servant, am ready to do your bidding and fulfill the mission to which you have called me."

"Well said, Black Blade, well said, indeed! We have four days before we begin. On the fifth day, we will move out. I bid thee get some sustenance and rest; you will need to be in top form, as you call the troops together and ready them for the first incursion."

"Yes, I will, thank you, Master. I shall take my leave and return at the appointed time."

Randak walked slowly back to his room, the attendant once again in the lead. His mind wandered as he followed and he paid little attention to the route or his surroundings. He was back in his room in what he thought was a shorter time than what it took to go to the meeting.

He stripped off his armour, staring once again at the circled hexagon on the breastplate before he set it aside, shook his head, and laid down. Sleep overtook him quickly and a dream rose to the forefront. In his sleep, he began to relive the terrible scene in the chamber. The dream carried him to the part where he stabbed Barak, only this time Randak cried as he struck the deathblow. He didn't remember crying before. He certainly hadn't remembered that part during his meeting with Kolonth.

He was up early on each of the remaining mornings. His days were full, often lasting well past sunset, assembling the vast armies, ensuring all was in order. Randak was an excellent military strategist, one of the reasons Kolonth had trusted him with this charge. He knew Randak would have all well-prepared and in place for the day Kolonth would open the path to a new world. Randak had to admit that he was excited about the idea of stepping into a world completely different from his own.

At the end of these days, Randak was so tired that he would almost crawl back to his bedchamber, barely having the energy to remove his armour. Occasionally the attendant would help him, keeping a watchful eye on Randak for any sign of weakness, or other matters of concern that might need to be shared with Kolonth.

Each night as Randak lay in bed, he quickly fell into a deep sleep. As soon as he hit a certain point in his sleep, the same dream would return to haunt him and he would relive his actions in the chamber where he turned the Orbstar over to Kolonth. The dream was unrelenting and every time it returned, he would remember more details, adding to the weight of his burden, caused by his horror at what he had done. Yet the horror lessened each time he dreamed, for as he repeatedly re-experienced his actions, his heart grew harder. Each time he heard his sister, with her dying breath, beg him not to harm Barak, his emotions became more detached. Whenever he dreamed of stabbing Barak to death, his soul became hollow and empty, surrounded by a wall he erected to convince himself he had done the right thing.

On the third night, the dream added a new detail. Something about the Pretender, the false king. *"What was His name again? The supposed Lord of T'varin. Odd now that it's called Kolonth, not T'varin. T'var. That was it. T'var. Why is it so difficult to remember that name? T'var...T'var...but it's been so many years and T'var is dead. The true Master said it himself. T'var... Orbstar, something else about an Orbstar too... I did steal it from Wandarr and Kolonth killed T'var with it but..."*

Randak tossed and turned in his sleep, at one point kicking the bedcovers off, helplessly living through the scene all over again as the rest of the dream began to unfold exactly as it had on the two previous nights. He welcomed the day, if only to go through the motions of his duties as a distraction. He focussed what little energy he had on anything but the relentless night terrors that continued to haunt his sleeping.

On the fourth day, a few hours earlier than Randak normally would have retired to his chamber, Kolonth requested his presence on a matter of great importance. A little anxious, but confident Kolonth simply wanted the final update on the preparedness of the armies, Randak set aside his weariness and made his way to the same room he had met Kolonth in earlier in the week.

"So, my Champion, is the Black Blade ready for tomorrow? On the arrival of the midnight hour, at one minute past, the very beginning of a new day, we shall begin our new adventure of expansion!"

"Yes, my Lord, never better!" Randak said, wisely concealing his fatigue. "We are ready to extend your will beyond the world of Kolonth!"

"I would have expected no less from you. Now, in return for all your effort, I have a gift for you."

"A gift? Oh Imperator, That is not necess…"

"Yes, it is, faithful servant. To recognize all your diligent work, this is a gift worthy only of you. You will not be stepping into the new world tomorrow, Randak."

"I won't? But I thought…"

"Do not fear, my Black Blade. You will still enter the new world leading our armies, but not on foot."

"Join me on the balcony, where not only can we view the vastness of the armies you will lead, but you will also see your gift. Your chariot into the land which will soon be ours." Randak obediently followed behind Kolonth and peered out across the immense encampment. Now that they stood on the balcony, Kolonth raised both his hands to the sky and then shouted a deafening shrill sound, the noise so loud Randak winced and was tempted to cover his ears. Instead, once the sound ceased, he spoke to his Master once more.

"It is a marvelous sight, my Lord. This is a great gift to see my charge from so high, but I don't understand…"

Randak stopped midsentence as a black spot in the distance grew larger and larger until a great Averi flew before them. It circled around the tower in which they stood, and then hovered before them. Randak had the oddest feeling of discomfort but did not wish to show weakness before his Master, so steadied himself and stared at the creature.

It was almost as large as Kolonth's personal Averi, though this one was outfitted in armour that matched its green and black colouring. It possessed the usual broad wings that kept it airborne, along with deep, black eyes, razor sharp teeth and long, thick legs with claws capable of shredding anything it wished. Randak also noticed it had a seat fastened to it with stirrups and reins, so it could take a rider.

"For me, Imperator?? I'm… I'm…"

Randak was momentarily at a loss for words since he was having a hard time imagining himself flying on the beast, much less controlling and steering it.

"Honoured, I am sure."

"Yes, yes, honoured, indeed. This is what you meant when you said I would not be stepping into the new world?"

"Exactly, Randak. You are perceptive as ever! You will be flying into it as you lead our forces. I recognize this is short notice, but through my magiks, the Averi is well-prepared to be your ride. Fear not, your Averi will be as faithful to you, as you have been to me."

"This is a magnificent gift, my King, I am not worthy of this honour but I thank you indeed. I am excited that I shall soon fly into the new world that will soon be ours."

"Yes, you will! I called you away from your regular duties early enough to ensure you would have some time to practice flying on the Averi. I suggest you take advantage of the time. You will have no problem mastering this, but it will do the armies good to see you in the air now as they think about tomorrow's task. Kolonth lifted a hand up to the Averi, and it obediently landed on the ground close by.

"You may go now and bond with your new pet for it already knows your scent. I will watch you from the balcony here."

"Yes, of course, Imperator."

Reluctantly, Randak made his way down to meet the Averi. He wasn't exactly sure he wanted this gift, for Averi had always made him nervous. Of course, he couldn't tell Kolonth that; it would be seen as a sign of weakness and the Master could lose faith in him.

He summoned enough courage to approach the beast. He spoke to it, and it seemed to understand him. Randak noted that it sniffed the air as he approached, so it must have recognized his scent as Kolonth said it would. He wasn't sure how it knew his scent in the first place, but no matter.

After speaking to it for a bit, he cautiously petted its neck and examined the platform that held the chair and reins a little more closely. He then hoisted himself up, found comfortable positions for both sitting and standing and began his trial flight. Randak went slowly at first, though his confidence grew with each flight. At first, they flew low above the soldiers who cheered raucously once they realized the Black Blade was flying on an Averi. The flights grew higher and bolder with each round, along with Randak's comfort level. The last two runs took them the highest in the sky they been and even at that height, Randak could still feel Kolonth's eyes on him, though he couldn't see him.

Randak was certain that Kolonth was proud of him and he rejoiced at pleasing his Master so well. The final flight was done against the backdrop of the red glow from the setting sun, which was so thrilling and picturesque that Randak didn't want it to end. However, he did not wish to further tire himself or the Averi out as they would need all their energy and wits for the impending invasion. He skillfully landed the Averi where he found it, ordered the creature to wherever its lair was, commanding it to return to that very spot on the morrow. He stroked its neck one last time and then made his way to his bedchamber. After changing into his night-shirt, he collapsed into his bed once again, falling into a deep sleep almost immediately.

The dream returned with rapidity, but this time started out differently. Perhaps it was a premonition of the upcoming battle or so his anxious, semi-conscious mind thought. He was on a horse in the midst of a battle when suddenly an Averi, not the one that was his now, but one he recognized as Kolonth's, dropped from the sky, grabbed him in its talons and flew off, leaving a shocked Barak behind. Of course, this was the Averi that had delivered him to Kolonth in the first place. His sleeping mind recognized that he had not been carried to Kolonth willingly. In the dream the Averi disgusted him and not just the foul stench of the creature but the pure evil of it.

Randak stirred in his sleep at this strange beginning of the nightmare. He could feel the dream ready to start over. He did not want to experience his sister's death or his murder of Barak again; it was too much to take in. Yet deep down, past the barrier to his soul, was a desire to relive the dream, for each time it came, more was revealed about what truly happened in that chamber.

Maybe that was important. Randak was conflicted - he wanted to recall more and clear his murky memory but he didn't want to repeatedly relive everything either. Randak pleaded now, semi-awake enough to voice his fear aloud into the emptiness of his bedchamber, "Please no, not again, please no more, please make it stop."

CHAPTER FIFTEEN
RANDAK'S BATTLE

Kolonth's face contorted into what for him was a smile, expressing his pleasure at how well all was turning in his favour. *"This smells of sweet surrender and the bliss of ultimate victory!"*

Yet in the arcane dark of that ancient chamber, Randak struggled within himself as he once again relived his traitorous acts. An unbearable weight settled over him, forcing him to his knees. He had failed. Again. He had given in. Again. The dream was so real this time, even more so than all the other past nights.

It reinforced that those many years ago, he had wrested the Orbstar from Wandarr's hand and placed it in Kolonth's grasp, but the feelings that followed perplexed him. All was lost. All efforts wasted and it was his fault. They had come so far, fought for so long and all for naught. Now because of his weakness, caused by his festering wound, all their victories were worthless. In his sleep all these puzzling thoughts pounded upon him like numberless hammers and he the anvil. They hung and brooded over him, totally confusing him, driving him to despair.

Wandarr and Barak stood to one side, still in disbelief at Randak's treachery. They lamented that they had missed any forewarning that his injury would result in this, one they thought healed long ago on the Plains of Rangdorr.

"Barak, what's wrong with him? What has Kolonth done to him?" Wandarr was on the verge of tears.

"I don't know, but he is definitely not himself. He looks entranced. I am not even sure he knows we are here or even where he is. He appears oblivious to his surroundings, his eyes transfixed solely on Kolonth."

In anger and frustration, Wandarr screamed directly at Kolonth, "What have you done to my brother?" and was completely ignored. Kolonth spoke only to Randak.

"Brother-friend, it's Barak, can you hear me? We are here. Please say something." They continued to call to Randak but he acted as if he didn't hear them.

Wandarr turned towards T'var, who so far had not said a word. Tears filled her eyes.

"Is he lost to us? Can You help him? Please, please Lord, help him."

Randak appeared to be focussed on something they could not see, nor could they even begin to imagine what that might be. Kolonth's rant diverted their attention from Randak.

"The second Orbstar is now mine, as are you, Warrior." Randak could not hear him for he was still lost in his dream state. "You have truly joined me in my imminent victory. You now serve me and my dark minions as we triumph over T'varin once and for all. Oh, if only my sire Manglor were here to see my ultimate conquest!"

Kolonth's voice, loud and commanding, penetrated Randak's tortured dreams, making him remember all the wrong things in his life, all the misdeeds, all his past transgressions, all his many failures and turning over the Orbstar to Kolonth surfaced foremost in his mind as the worst of them all.

Each time Kolonth spoke, a new memory, real or imagined, thanks to Kolonth's powers of illusion, was dredged up, playing over and over again within the theatre of his nightmares, until Randak was lost in his own misery. Everything now was out of his own control as he was being dragged closer and closer into the mire which was servant to Kolonth.

Wandarr and Barak looked to T'var, the fear in their voices almost tangible.

"What is happening to my brother?"

Wandarr looked to T'var and back to Barak who echoed her concern.

"How can we help him? This place feels filled with fear, and Randak looks to be under a spell."

T'var spoke softly, "This is Randak's battle. He believes he is alone, but I have been knocking on the door. He need only open it a crack to realize he is not alone at all. But that is something he must do. I cannot do it for him."

Confused by the explanation, Wandarr was about to speak, when T'var put His finger to His lips, motioning both of them to be silent.

Randak believed that he was still asleep and dreaming in his bedchamber within Kolonth's keep, though a name from the previous nights' brutal remembrance broke into his thoughts through a whisper. Soft, faint, concerned, comforting, *"T'var,"* and then, *"Randak, it's not real. Trust Me. You are being deceived. It is all illusion. Awaken warrior. Awaken to the truth."*

Those few words were enough to begin to shake Randak free of the deception Kolonth had created. Randak struggled for words, but none came, for he was overwhelmed by his guilt, lost to a black hole sucking him into its emptiness, a hopeless abyss; the fabric of his being shredded into pieces as he battled to separate dream from reality; but unable to take back control, he kept dropping back into his nightmare. Still, the whisper persisted.

"Randak, hear Me. We are all here. Myself, Wandarr, and Barak."

"No, that's not possible! It's been almost one hundred years since I let her die and killed Barak."

"No, Randak, Wandarr and Barak still live. Randak, we have never left the chamber. It has only been mere moments since you gave away the Orbstar."

"Moments? No, that is not possible!"

"But it is the truth. The rest is false. A deceit. Kolonth's illusion."

Randak felt one small fraction of himself wanting to believe the voice in his mind but another part fought harder, urging him to believe in all that he and Kolonth had accomplished since the Imperator's victory in this very room. Allegiance to the Dark Master was his fate and Randak could no longer remember why following Kolonth was wrong. His arm swelled with pain, dulling his senses, clouding his mind, driving out T'var's words.

His arm kept throbbing in agony and as it did, Randak realized he would never be worthy to follow T'var; never worthy to even speak His name. Soon, he found it difficult to remember who T'var was. It was the dream all over again, the horrific things he did all about to happen once more.

Unwillingly he raised his head, yanked by some invisible chain, he opened his eyes wide and found himself staring into the gloating face of Kolonth. His forehead furrowed in anguish, attempting to fight off the inevitable reliving of everything again. Beads of sweat ran down his forehead, leaving trails on his face, now grimy and dirty, inside and out.

Randak felt his spirit slipping as he stared into Kolonth's soulless eyes, slipping into that deep, dark void. He must give in, give up all things right and true; all so distant, so unreal compared to how real all the years of serving Kolonth were. Those eyes bore into his soul, sucking his life force from his body, until his will would become totally given over into the core of Kolonth's darkness.

Helpless, he was locked into Kolonth's dark visions but for a moment he noticed something slightly different. Though he could not yet tell the difference between dream and reality, Randak vaguely remembered, before his treacherous act all those years ago, that T'var had originally stood beside Wandarr and Barak in the far part of the room. Yet now, T'var stood behind Kolonth, but Kolonth seemed unaware of Him. T'var stood taller than Kolonth and though Randak's gaze was locked into Kolonth's stare, with T'var now behind Kolonth, out of the corner of his eye, Randak could glimpse T'var's smile and His reassuring eyes. This had never been part of his dreams before.

"Is it possible the words I heard whispered earlier are true?"

"Yes, they are true. Clear your mind, warrior. Step away from the mire. From the illusion. Think! Do you really believe you would let your sister die and murder your best friend?"

"But I did, all those years ago. Kolonth told me and the dreams keep making me relive it."

"Illusions, Randak, Kolonth's web of lies and deceit. Open the door, Randak. Just a crack. You must break away from Kolonth's gaze. I can help if you will let Me."

A glimmer of hope started to blossom, enough that Randak shifted his gaze just slightly and suddenly he no longer felt trapped within Kolonth's stare, but rather afloat in the calming liquid blue-green sea of T'var's eyes. The door was open, just a crack, but it was enough.

"Look at Me for strength. Look to Me for forgiveness. Look to Me as your burden bearer. Look to Me, for My power can set you free! BE FREE OF THE ILLUSION! BE FREE OF YOUR GUILT! BE FREE OF THE PRETENDER AND TRUE DECEIVER! COME ALIVE! WAKE UP!"

The words were not said aloud but came directly from T'var. They penetrated deep into Randak's soul and surged through his entire being. He heard them as sharply and clearly as if they had been spoken aloud, driving into his spirit like a double-edged sword, slicing apart illusion from truth.

Kolonth knew that something was happening, but he mistook Randak's hesitation as a sign of one last valiant effort of resistance before the inevitable final capitulation to him. He remained oblivious to what transpired between T'var and Randak. Kolonth only saw a change in his pawn's demeanour when Randak tore his gaze away and looked past him.

Deep inside, Randak whispered to himself one word. Not just a word, a name. Only one name and it was a name of power, a name above all other names. "T'var."

That whisper resulted in an awakening and in the depths of his being, Randak said to himself, "T'var, You alone are my strength and my shield, to You only does my spirit yield."

It started as an almost imperceptible melody in his heart, escalating louder as it pushed away all the morbid thoughts, muck, deceit and debris of Kolonth out of his mind. No more a prisoner, he was liberated from the invisible chains with which Kolonth had bound him.

Randak gazed directly into T'var's face and saw tears in those unfathomable, deep calming eyes, a wetness falling as pools of liquid love. T'var was crying and Randak understood T'var wept for him. He knew in that instant that T'var knew exactly what he was experiencing. T'var felt as he felt. T'var knew the struggle within Randak better than Randak himself and now he tasted T'var's freedom and his personal battle was at an end.

Randak did not need struggle against Kolonth's illusion and deceit any longer. Randak would willingly surrender, though his surrender would not be to Kolonth, the illusionist and genuine deceiver, but rather to T'var, the true Lord of all T'varin.

From somewhere hidden down in the recesses of his being, from reservoirs of might far beyond his own, a powerful cleansing filled his body, mind and spirit. T'var's power and will, he now welcomed inside himself, allowing it to grow stronger with each passing second. A freedom consumed him, something he had not truly known since he was wounded. Now experiencing the truth, Randak's fury boiled over in righteous anger, as he stared Kolonth down.

"You are the real Pretender! The genuine deceiver! You had me believing I let my sister die and that I had murdered my best friend! Liar! Demon spawn! Deceiver!"

Wandarr and Barak could not believe what they were hearing, nor did they understand why Randak was saying such things. "What is he talking about, Wandarr? He hasn't harmed either of us." Barak felt a shiver go down his spine at the thought of Randak murdering him.

"I think Kolonth must have had him under a terrible spell. Somehow, he convinced him that he let me die which is awful and ridiculous. He would never, could never, allow that to happen."

Randak's outburst caught Kolonth off guard. He sensed events were turning against him but could not discern why or how. Randak was livid, more than he could ever remember being in his life. If his Sonsword had been closer, he would have grabbed it up and driven it deep into Kolonth's heart, just as the Deceiver had tricked him into believing he had done to Barak.

But Randak did not pick up his Sonsword, in fact something unexpected overcame him; the more T'var's love flooded his being, the more he saw the truth. "I should kill you, Kolonth. I dreamed of doing so for so long, that it has consumed me, consumed my life. Yet for so long, I blamed myself for our parent's disappearance and death. Then I blamed you, thinking that killing you would end my guilt. I see now that I was wrong. Wrong about so many things."

He looked at Wandarr for a moment before turning back to Kolonth. If true compassion could ever be reflected in one's voice, it was in Randak's at this moment. Absent of any hint of anger, malice or fear, Randak spoke clearly and directly to Kolonth as if they were the only two beings in the room.

Wandarr and Barak were both about to speak in turn until they heard T'var's soft voice, "Hold you two. This is Randak's moment of truth. Let him be for now. Simply watch and learn."

"I see you now for who and what you are and I pity you. You are still a child, pathetically seeking acceptance and approval from a father who could never and never will be able to give it."

Kolonth was so incensed and aghast at Randak's audacity, his face turned red in fury and it became worse at Randak's next words. "I forgive you. I forgive you, Kolonth, for everything. You don't deserve it but then neither do I. Yet that is the grace the King offers and I freely accept it. You could too."

"You? You pity me? Forgive me? I am not the one who is pathetic, you simplistic fool."

"You still can't see it, can you, Kolonth? Or maybe you refuse to. We have both been trying to attain, to earn a treasure that we sought. For me it was your end, thinking that would give me what I needed and for you, the Orbstars, thinking they would give you what you wanted. We were both wrong. They are not the real treasures. That line of thinking was as deceitful as the dreams you trapped me in. The real treasure is something that can't be earned or bought. Love. T'var's love. His mercy, his grace, his forgiveness. It is not earnable, not winnable, it just is. The real treasure is T'var. Not vengeance, not Orbstars, but Him. T'var." Randak turned away from Kolonth and looking into the face of His King, he smiled and then knelt, bowing before the True Lord of all T'varin.

Kolonth thought this moment would be one of the sweetest of victories but now he wavered. No one resisted his will for this long, especially not one injured so purposefully by him. Kolonth tried to focus on inflicting pain into Randak's maimed arm but he could not direct his mind on the wound, for it was gone and he was livid. "You sound like those useless priests of T'var and we all know what happened to them. You are all nothing more than blots on the pages of history and I am about to make a new…"

"*T'var Ish na ma sto, il a v al mor te so.*" It was as much of a shock to Randak as it was to the others present, except perhaps for T'var, for now Randak's tone of voice changed from anger to praise as he broke into song.

The words burned Kolonth's mind and he reeled in agony. This was a hurt he had not known for centuries, if ever.

"Stop!" Kolonth shrieked but Randak continued singing as Barak and Wandarr looked on in relief and T'var smiled with joy. The melody resonated within the chamber, growing louder as Randak raised his voice in song even stronger.

"Very well, fool," Kolonth shouted above the singing. "You think you may have won for now. The truth is that you are here only to perish at my hands. It is unfortunate Randak, for you could have been a great champion for me in my new kingdom. The dreams I gave you spoke true and now you have lost that chance."

Randak sang on, heedless of Kolonth's threats. If any could have translated, they would know the words as, "YOU ARE MY STRENGTH AND MY SHIELD, YOU DESERVE ALL MY HEART, ALL MY SPIRIT, ALL MY WORSHIP AND SO TO YOU, I WILLINGLY YIELD."

The words in that strange tongue with which Randak sung were as meaningless to him as they were to Kolonth but Kolonth's father Manglor knew them, for their existence predated the Oldentime. From the time before time, written in the scrolls of the sky as praise to the true King of T'varin. Kolonth recognized enough to know them as words of worship to T'var which scorched him, clouding his mind and intensifying his rage.

"STOP! STOP IT NOW! Stop your accursed noise, you miscreant!"

Kolonth's voice rose hysterical with fury, for the words Randak sang drove all the doom and despair right out of that dismal place. The heaviness which had settled over them all a short time ago lifted. Barak and Wandarr smiled as Randak stood tall, walked towards them, took his Sonsword from Barak and then embraced them both.

T'var smiled and turning to Kolonth asked, "You do not like this Oldentime tune, Kolonth?"

Kolonth paused for a moment as though concentrating on a vital task and then appeared confused. A combined look of terror and anger spread across his face.

"What have you done? Where is my loyal servant? My pet? You had no right! You will pay for this misdeed! You are do-"

T'var calmly interrupted, "The Averi is no longer yours to command. It is well out of your reach and safe. It has a new home and is now as free as Randak so…"

"Silence!" Kolonth roared back. "You will regret that action and you may think you have won this minor skirmish but you are mistaken.

Unlike my father, I now own two Orbstars, not just one and I possess the knowledge to destroy all of you and all of T'varin too, if I so choose."

"Only two, Kolonth?"

Wandarr, Barak and Randak were totally shocked when T'var miraculously pulled a third Orbstar out of thin air, holding it before them all. He turned to face Kolonth and to their dismay, asked, "Why not have the third?"

All three shared horrified expressions as their King tossed the remaining Orbstar across the room to an extremely startled Kolonth. Though none was more surprised than Kolonth himself, who managed to still securely hold the two he already had in one hand while he used his free hand to catch the third before it fell to the ground.

"Idiot," Kolonth began cackling with hysterical laughter. "You seek to deceive me as you once did my father. It will not work this time. You have sealed your own fate and now doomed all of your beloved T'varin as well. My victory is complete. Poor Randak. Now all that you dreamed when you were in my trance is about to become reality and you will perish with your sister, friend and your false King. Now, Pretender, all is complete as always meant to be. Behold the power of the Orbstars three. Forged in the fires of infinity, stolen by the Rightful Emperor of Eternity."

T'var interrupted Kolonth's ramblings, "Yes, it is true, Kolonth, Manglor long ago did assist in the forging of the Orbstars, as he once himself forged the Sonswords at My bequest."

The three glanced at each other astonished, for they had no knowledge of the origin of their swords until now.

T'var explained, "But though he turned the Orbstars over willingly, he continued to crave their beauty and their potency. He lusted after them until they led to his downfall and eventually his own eternal imprisonment. What of you Kolonth? Will you follow his path or will you choose differently? Would you take the gift of grace, of forgiveness and newness of life that I offer you?

T'var locked His eyes directly with His enemy, speaking with an authority that would not let go, yet with an unmistakable tone of mercy in His voice.

Kolonth would have no part of it. He broke T'var's stare and for a moment he appeared to hesitate. Perhaps something touched a part of his being buried down in the darkest caverns of his corrupted soul and for an instant, the trio thought Kolonth might relent. Submission was out of the question though, for Kolonth was determined to be the winner in this confrontation.

"Offer me, offer me?" Kolonth choking back his laughter. "You are in no position to offer me anything. It is I, Kolonth, Ruler and Possessor of the Orbstars of T'varin who will now do whatever I want. You murdered my father and now I will avenge him. What I choose is Your death!"

Kolonth held the Orbstars in his hands, palms open, two in one, one in the other, and concentrated on them with his unholy glare. Slowly they began to glow and rise from his hands until they floated up, hovering slightly above his forehead. The Orbstars began to shimmer brighter and brighter. Without looking at his enemies, Kolonth addressed T'var, "Now, prepare for Your life to end at my hands, as You finally pay the price for what You did to my father."

Randak and his companions held their Sonswords up as though to ward off any blows, although they knew instinctively the Sonswords' power paled in comparison to that of the Orbstars'. T'var stood perfectly still, as calm as a windless sea, fearless before the imminent annihilation facing them all.

T'var's spoke with a voice steady, smooth and tranquil, "Did you forget, Kolonth? I have already died."

This comment coupled with T'var's serene manner only infuriated Kolonth all the more. He screamed above the now-growing hum of the Orbstars.

"Then perish again!"

The Orbstars resonated with incandescent colours, shimmering in a kaleidoscope of splendour.

"The very fires of infinity will be Your own decimation forever, T'var!"

Kolonth was so enraged by T'var's attitude, Randak, Barak and Wandarr feared for T'var's safety as well as their own.

Speaking those last words, Kolonth glared up at the Orbstars and then to T'var. Obeying an inaudible command, they glowed with visible rage and each shot out a beam of coloured light which quickly combined into one stream of brilliant white shooting straight at T'var. T'var stood motionless, silent and fearless. Horrified, The Warriors Three watched the ray of light drive directly into T'var. They feared it would pierce right through Him just as Manglor's aim had found its target so long ago. However, as soon as the white light came into contact with T'var, it acted as if it hit something extremely solid and ricocheted, returning to its sender.

Kolonth glowered in anger and fear as the destructive force was reflected back at him. He found himself subsumed in the rush of light intended for T'var. Kolonth was weakening in the overflow of energy, though for a brief moment he thought to take control again.

Above the growing humming of the Orbstars and amidst the blinding light, Kolonth heard T'var's voice, distinct, crisp and cold saying, "No, Kolonth. No more. It is over. It is finished."

Kolonth tried to yell, but found he possessed no voice. In fact, as he looked down at himself to regain his balance, he discovered he no longer could hold together his shadowy body; it was becoming more and more translucent with each passing second. He knew too late, the same end which befell his parent Manglor, was happening to him. He consoled himself with the thought, though captured, there would always be a chance for escape and to challenge his enemy another time. When he felt Manglor's presence, still an internal captive in one of the Orbstars, Kolonth rejoiced, thinking that they could join forces to escape and conquer.

Kolonth could not anticipate what happened next, though. Consumed in the light of the three Orbstars, each orb sought to be the single receptacle of his prison. In a frenzied hunger, all three jewels reached out to absorb Kolonth, the three pulling him in separate directions, each seeking to have Kolonth to itself causing his form to be torn in three ways, his essence spreading out towards each of the hungry orbs.

The trio grimaced as Kolonth's form was ripped into three parts. It wasn't a smooth tearing, as each Orbstar pulled with eternity's might to have a piece of Kolonth. What was left of him was transparent and ethereal, torn and ragged; it too, was now being drawn up toward the whirling gems. Something so unexpected happened next that the three, almost in unison, exclaimed, "What?"

They fully expected what was left of Kolonth would also be absorbed and imprisoned inside the Orbstars. But to their astonishment, the final remains of Kolonth's torn form did not become imprisoned in the Orbstars like the rest of him already had. Rather, what was left of Kolonth's being bounced off of the three jewels as if they already had their fill of him and wanted no more. The Orbs now rejected the remaining malevolence that was once Kolonth, the rays ricocheted off the jewels as though hitting a brick wall and transformed into a cascade of colours which began flooding the area around them. While they shimmered, the glow increased in intensity and the ruins began to vibrate in rhythm to the multifaceted beauty now being produced by the Orbs.

CHAPTER SIXTEEN
THE ORBSTARS OF T'VARIN

Wandarr breathed deeply in awe, for she suddenly understood what was happening.

"Barak! Randak!" she said with excitement. "The Castle is coming back together. I can feel it."

"What?" laughed Randak. "You can't be serious! The ruins are... are... T'var, she is not right, is she? Can this be? But how?"

Totally amazed, Randak watched the transformation. The chamber they stood in, now bathed in the fullness of the light, ceased to be a dank room of fallen rock and moss-covered walls, but became instead a room newly refreshed and vibrating with a clarity it had not seen in centuries.

Barak hollered above the roar of rock and rubble being reassembled before them, "She is right, Randak. The Orbstars are using what they rejected of Kolonth to rebuild the Castle of Crystal. The whole place is coming back together as though it is being made anew."

T'var finally provided confirmation. "Yes, Barak. Come. There is more to see yet."

All of a sudden, T'var ran out into the hallway and up the newly formed steps. Wandarr was certain that He laughed as He ran. She wavered only a moment and took off after T'var, shouting to her comrades, "Come, slowpokes, if T'var wishes to race, let's not disappoint Him."

Open mouthed, Randak and Barak leapt after Wandarr in pursuit. They ran up and down the remade halls and corridors, in and out of rooms and up and down reassembled stairways for a long time. All the while they ran, they felt the hum and throb of the Orbstars, vibrating throughout the castle, which was bathed in a glorious luminescence as it was pulled back together. Finally, they stood at what they thought must be near the topmost height of the building and caught up to T'var.

"This is a merry chase you have led us on, my King," panted Barak.

"Surprisingly, I am only a little winded even after all those stairs," Randak said. "Where are we? Are we at the top of the sky?"

"Well, not quite, my good Randak, but certainly close," said T'var.

"Look out there," T'var raised His hands skyward and a multi-coloured, rainbow-like arch surrounding the Castle flew far into the sky. Gawking, the three warriors now understood their location; they hovered above the Island Land of Narxa, far above it, for the Castle of Crystal now floated in the sky. They looked out through the clear room they stood in, to see above them the familiar, though appearing larger in size, Orbstars, spinning, glowing, almost playing in a triad of delight. Wandarr was sure the combined powers of all three Orbstars made the building float. Randak was certain the three patterns of light the Orbstars tossed between themselves were the jigsaw of Kolonth's essence. They were both right. They all three looked at T'var in anticipation, positive that something wondrous was about to occur.

T'var looked up at the Orbstars, raised His hands to them and declared, "Now, let the end of Kolonth become the seed of T'varin's healing."

The Orbstars pushed the arrays of light they sent back and forth to each other, outward to the Castle. When the light hit the reborn Castle of Crystal, it was reflected back and scattered into another barrage which fell onto the land below with a radiance so bright, the three shielded their eyes against the brilliance. When their eyes finally became accustomed to the light, they fell before T'var, weeping in liberation and gladness because of what they witnessed occurring.

Below them, Narxa was being covered by a restorative, soothing rainbow, which gradually began spreading over the entire countryside. From their vantage point, they saw that everywhere the colours spread, the grass began to grow, flowers bloomed, rivers and streams gurgled and bubbled with fresh life. The transformation did not stop at the Island, for it spread across the Bridge and into Bjorqar. From there, it widened and stretched out to Astaria to the north and Vintar to the south.

Wandarr was not sure if this was due to some property in the Castle, or if what she saw was real but she swore the Castle started moving through the sky over each country, as the colourful arc expanded across all the realms. The works of Kolonth disappeared under the curative touch of the ever-widening rainbow driven by the Orbstars' light, shining across all T'varin through the Castle of Crystal.

Wandarr, Randak and Barak actually saw each nation transform as the myriad colours swept across the world of T'varin. The forests of Astaria thrived again. The rivers of Bjorqar and Lake Qar cleared from the fetid pools they had mutated into under Kolonth's spells. Barak cried out as he watched his homeland, Vintar, immersed in the healing light. He saw as pastures began flourishing, valleys and meadows shone again with lush vegetation and the swamplands came to life.

The next stop surprised them, for none of them had needed to travel to the narrow strip of land known as the Soutvold in their journeys, but they now saw that it too was immersed in the light's transformative healing power. The geysers and craters and the rocky land itself was consumed in such a powerful force of change, the entire Soutvold actually vanished from their sight. Although Randak wondered if one of those theories was correct when he thought he saw black shadows attempting to flee from the radiance, but quickly melting away as soon as it touched them.

The Soutvold continued to be bombarded by the ever-changing and now vibrating colours, some of them the trio couldn't even name, for they were not hues they had ever seen before. They did not know what to anticipate when the work was done but it was certainly not the end result they now saw before them.

"Oh my!" exclaimed Wandarr, "That is not what I expected."

"It's a vast parkland! Look at all the wild gardens, flowers of so many bright and wonderful colours. Some I think we saw during the change, but I don't even know what you would call them. This is utterly fantastic and unbelievable!" Barak was probably the most verbal and excited they had ever heard him.

"And look at the beautiful multicoloured fountains spread through-out. Maybe that's what the geysers turned into?" Wandarr guessed, cor-rectly.

"And look, you two, not just gardens but animals of all sorts," Ran-dak pointed below, "They are all playing and frolicking in this newly cre-ated-I don't know what to call it-sanctuary? I don't even know where those animals came from or what sort some of them are but I think it will be a safe place for all of them!"

T'var answered, "Yes, indeed it will be. Now look just above the parkland, for what comes next is a sight you and your sister will surely wish to see."

Wandarr and Randak clasped hands as The Rangdorrian Lands came alive again with fertile soil, the plains grew abundant with wheat and other crops. The Univer River looked clearer and Glephas sparkled anew at the colours' miraculous touch. All three stood beside T'var to watch T'barth become the next to be restored by the energy of the Orbstars. The ice liquefied so that the River Brandor could flow again and T'barth proper was restored as the hideous machine of Kolonth melted to nothingness under the light's onslaught. Randak was sure he even saw frozen corpses move again with life. Beyond the trio's sight, far below them in T'barth, two young brothers shook off the remains of their frozen state and ran to each other, hugging tightly in a tearful reunion. It was not long before they were joined by their parents and other T'barthians, now freed from their icy suspension.

The healing wave expanded from T'barth into Karnakon, revitalizing everything crushed, fried or frozen under the heels of Kolonth's troops. It was all as new. What all three noted more than anything else was, occasionally in the reflection of the Castle, they saw the expressions on people as the colours enveloped them. Some, incredibly happy to be covered in the light rejoiced, offering honour to T'var. Others demonstrated surprise, terror and sadness. They shook their heads and trembled as though they might drown or suffocate.

The three warriors were pleased to observe the demise of Kolonth's followers as the multi-hued spectrum reached them. Randak saw a small contingent of Kolonth's troops trying to outrace the Orbstars' light and reach Mangloth, get caught up and overcome. They looked to be drowning in it and Randak thought their mouths looked like they screamed in terror, but this was hard to tell, for as soon as the colours marked them, they melted into nothingness, almost in the same way as Kolonth.

The rainbow light found its way into the Glephoids and Randak gasped in recognition, for it headed right to where they once met the People of the Pass. The rainbow found where he and Wandarr had been separated and they both cried out as the mist-people merged into the brightness. They did not vanish, instead they morphed, changing from mist to solid individuals. Randak was sure he saw Hodie, but he did not have time to be certain for the colours swept around the people, picked them up and carried them to the north of Karnakon.

"Nomadia," said Randak astonished. "They return to their home, to Nomadia."

"Yes, Randak. They have ceased to be shadowy wraiths and are with substance once again," said T'var softly.

"What do you think will happen when the wave hits Mangloth?" Wandarr asked the other two.

"Watch!" commanded T'var.

The trio gawked, fascinated to see the translucent walls of the Castle reflect what was taking place under the influence of the Orbstars. They saw Mangloth before them, dark and dismal, an impenetrable fortress shrouded in mist and frost but only so for a moment. In a heartbeat, the colourful wave invaded, dancing in brilliance. They saw the whole domain of Mangloth begin to shake and tremble, attempting to fight off the inevitable. The border mountains shook, Lake Scugoll boiled in frenzy, the ice fields began to crack and turned to water, and the underground prisons burst open, revealing vast crevices deeper than any had imagined. The breeding pits dissolved at the rainbow's touch.

It was the dark stronghold they each focussed on more than anything else. Whether the fortress somehow understood that the Orbstars contained some of Kolonth or what happened next came simply from the Orbstars, no one could say for sure. Kolonth's citadel reached up to the rainbow before the colours ever connected to it and it began to shake.

Wandarr later described it as though it were coming apart at the seams, although Randak thought it looked more like it shattered into millions of tiny pieces. Barak could only remember the deafening sound which echoed across all of T'varin as the stronghold and the colours collided.

Soon all of Mangloth was bathed in an ocean of incandescence. Only, unlike the other countries where the varied hues painted their way just across the lands, in Mangloth, the outbreak of colour plummeted down far beneath the surface. For the decay inflicted by Manglor and Kolonth was heavy and their foulness sank deeply into the core of T'varin. The three stood beside T'var, staring in wonder as the spectrums of light churned and boiled in a turmoil of transformative ferocity. They watched incredulously as Mangloth began to change. The mountain ranges crumbled, Lake Scugoll widened, its fetid waters no longer churning, now turning into a healthy, pristine blue. The formerly icy fields turned green, lush in vegetation and the northern portion of the land began to take on a new vitality as well.

"All of Mangloth is healed," Wandarr rejoiced.

"Yes," said T'var, with happiness in His voice. "The land of Mangloth is no more, as is the Evil that inhabited it. Both now gone forever."

"So wonderful," said Barak. "What is it to be?"

"Yes," said Wandarr. "It is so beautiful now; it would be such a shame for no one to live in it."

"Ah," said T'var, with a beaming smile on His face. The mysterious tone in His voice made the three wonder if He hid some secret surprise. As if to confirm their suspicion, He turned to them and said, "Behold!"

T'var raised His hands once more toward the Orbstars and a new shade of colour burst forth from them. At first it seemed to be part of the arch, but suddenly it divided from the rest and began a separate journey far into the skies over Karnakon.

"What do you think is going to happen now?" Randak asked Wandarr and Barak in a quiet tone.

"I can't wait to see!" Wandarr's enthusiasm was contagious.

Abruptly the flow of light returned. They all knew it to be different in both form and density. The new wave of colour moved back over the former Mangloth, diving down into its centre. Touching the ground, it exploded in a cacophony of brilliance that blinded all but T'var.

"Great Lord T'var!" Randak exclaimed.

When the brightness subsided enough, they could see what had just occurred.

"How is this possible?" asked an excited Barak.

"This is their new home, isn't it T'var?" asked Wandarr, thinking she now figured out why the colour separated, where it went, and why it was different when it returned. "Oh Lord T'var, it brought them back, didn't it?"

"True indeed," said T'var. "Excuse me a moment, my friends. I have an announcement to make."

Barak was about to say, "Yes my Lord," when T'var vanished before their eyes and they all watched what now happened below in the renewed lands, through the window-like walls.

T'var greeted the Andini by saying, "No more are you out of time and out of place, the Orbstars bring you to a new home. Orchards and all, the Andini have a new land to enjoy and thrive in."

T'var's mighty voice resounded over the new country.

"Andini, your faithfulness is rewarded. The time of change has come and gone and you have survived it well. Now you have a new home. What was once a kingdom dedicated to wickedness, and the desolation of T'varin, is made new. It is now to be a land dedicated to the growth and prosperity of this world. Your people and your orchards are safe. Relocated here to take root and thrive. The need for the Circle of Andini is no more. Arise and be blessed and bless all that is around you. The charge I gave to your ancestor Andivar, I give again to you. Bear it well, faithful ones. Mangloth is no more. Welcome home to New Andivar."

The sound of cheering, clapping, laughing and more joyous noise than imaginable reached up into the Castle of Crystal where Barak, Wandarr and Randak joined in until tears of joy fell. T'var stood once again in their midst, joining in their rejoicing, laughing riotously Himself.

The cheering finished and they all felt exhausted. T'var turned to them and said, "Now one last thing before we return to the Island Land of Narxa."

"You mean we really have been floating in the sky over all the world?" Barak was astounded.

"As you wish, Barak" replied T'var, which was no answer at all, but it made Barak all the more mystified at what he just witnessed.

Barak thought to ask T'var what it all meant, when Wandarr directed them to what they failed to notice in their excitement at the re-creation of Andivar.

"The rainbow is gone."

Wandarr wanted to ask T'var what He was going to do next but His back was turned to them. They watched as He once again lifted His eyes up to the Orbstars floating high overhead, visible through the castle's glass ceiling.

"He's going to do something else now, isn't He?" Barak asked, directing his question to Randak.

"Yes, but what? He almost looks as if He is going to say something. To whom though?"

"Let's be patient," chided Wandarr.

The three were mesmerized, watching as T'var focused His gaze on the Orbstars which began to bathe Him in rainbow colours. The Castle's walls started to reflect multiple images of Him, as once again the colours of the rainbow increased in intensity. They noticed the reflections were all T'var and it appeared that T'var stood in all places across the world at once. He transformed into a huge figure; giant size, so that no one missed Him. His voice vibrant, authoritative and gentle, echoed everywhere and no one doubted its truthfulness.

"Hear Me, people of the eight lands, now made ten. I am T'var, the Deathslayer. T'varin has been remade and renewed. Nomadia and Andivar are now dominions unto their own. Kolonth and Mangloth are no more; their evil is gone. Their emissaries and all they wrought faded away along with the vileness they created. All has been made whole once more. Treat it well. Beware, lest a new darkness attempts to find root and seek your annihilation again. Follow My laws and leaders and it will be prevented.

"Now from each of your nations, I require two delegates whom you shall appoint to form the ruling council of T'varin on the Island Land of Narxa. To these ones, I give the charge of maintaining justice and peace for all of T'varin. My servants Barak, Wandarr and...Randak will form the inner circle of this council, as they have proven their unfailing loyalty and will lead you well. I must leave again soon, but I leave you in good hands. *T'var, T'vari, T'varin.*"

Randak, Wandarr and Barak glanced at each other, stunned at this latest revelation of T'var's. They were made for battle, not to rule, but they dared not question T'var's pronouncement. Randak momentarily wondered why T'var seemed to slightly hesitate before including his name with Barak's and Wandarr's in his proclamation.

T'var turned to the three and said, "Do not be afraid! Remember, I am always with you. You will do fine, in spite of your present doubts. Now it is time to return to Narxa. A wedding needs to take place and the guests will find it hard to attend if the hall for the reception is still in the sky."

"My Lord," asked Wandarr. "Whose wedding, may I ask?"

Before T'var could respond, Barak fell to one knee and grasping one of Wandarr's hands in his, interrupting, taking T'var's cue and saying to Wandarr, "Well, you know there wasn't time before and with all the fighting, I wanted to...oh well... Oh T'var..." Barak took a moment to stop stumbling over his words until he gained enough composure to speak his desire, "Wandarr, you know how deeply I love you. Since the war is over, I now humbly ask, if you would do me the honour of being my life partner, sharing our lives together as husband and wife?" Barak turned to T'var and Randak, who both wore comical grins and said in exasperation, "There, I said it! Are you both happy now?"

BEGINNINGS

Randak woke up in a cold sweat once again for the fifth time in as many days. The nightmare refused to leave him no matter how many different methods he tried to rid himself of it. It was always the same, with him back in that horrible chamber, the ruins around and Kolonth's icy glare holding him fast with unspoken words. *"You are still mine. You are still mine,"* forcing him to relive the illusion Kolonth had filled him with. Only whispering the name of T'var brought relief, making the terrifying dream vanish. Yet the memory lingered. Randak could still taste the bile in his mouth, the dust from that dreadful room and his arm throbbed each time he awakened.

Preoccupied with their wedding preparations, Barak and Wandarr failed to notice Randak's growing silence and increasingly sombre mood. With T'var's permission, riders from Astaria and Bjorqar were sent to Glephas to invite the Barizons, as well as to New Andivar, to request the presence of Sargon and the other elders. Wandarr thought about inviting some of the folk from Nomadia, including Hodie. After discussing the idea with T'var, she thought better of it when He explained, "A wonderful idea and very gracious, however the People of the Pass require some time to adjust before they will be comfortable among solid people again."

T'var himself came and went, appearing, disappearing and reappearing at irregular intervals. The trio did not question His comings and goings as it seemed so natural. They were certain that He attended to many other important matters and would be there when needed. The Orbstars floated above the castle, continuing to scatter their glow throughout the land, as the crystal walls provided a source of reflection stretching far off into the horizon.

In their spare time, the trio explored the renewed Castle of Crystal and each chose their quarters. Every apartment in the castle, for they were more like full living spaces than just bedchambers, was thoroughly equipped with bedrooms, baths, living rooms, even full kitchens; basically, everything one would need to live comfortably. More importantly, it appeared that the living quarters everyone picked were already specifically designed to consider their likes and dislikes. Favourite colours, pictures, décor, bed linens, curtains, cutlery and cooking utensils and even wardrobes, were customized to individual tastes. Later on, as people explored their rooms, whether governing delegates, guests, or permanent residents, they discovered how much more was already in place, truly making everyone feel at home.

Wandarr, Randak and Barak began to ask some of the people from Astaria and Bjorqar if they would consider joining them in the castle to help them organize things. The trio did not wish to refer to them as servants, but in effect that is what they were, though not subservient and all considered it an honour to be asked to work in the restored Castle.

Over the next two weeks, the delegates T'var requested from each land also began to arrive. Barak and Wandarr worked on wedding arrangements with T'var, busying themselves with where the guests would stay, how many and when, how the food would be prepared, what music to have and what felt like a million other details. While they were consumed with those tasks, Randak occupied himself with welcoming the new representatives, showing them their rooms and preparing them for the business of being the leaders of T'varin. This aided his sleep to a certain extent, as some nights his exhaustion overtook him and he collapsed on his bed, fell into a dreamless slumber and had to be roused in the morning.

One day Randak approached Barak and Wandarr, his face bearing a serious look. "Listen you two, I wonder if you might do a trade?"

They both looked at him confused, "A trade? What do you mean?"

"Well quite honestly, I am finding this work with the delegates and getting everything set up and organized, rather exhAustlyg." Randak neglected to mention the other thing that also tired him. "I was wondering if we might trade and as my gift to you both, I will look after the rest of the wedding preparations and you can take over the other business. I fear I am still more warrior than administrator and I truly think you both have gifts where I am lacking."

Wandarr laughed, "I don't know about that, but what do you think, Barak?"

"I think it is a great offer and a great gift and on behalf of both of us, thank you, Randak."

Barak hoped Wandarr would nod in agreement, which she did. He made a mental note to speak privately with Randak afterward to share just how much he was relieved to hear Randak's suggestions. For while Wandarr thoroughly enjoyed working on all the preparations, if he were honest with himself, he had to admit that lately, more often than not, he was becoming quite bored with the whole thing. *"I hope Randak knows what he is getting himself into,"* he laughed to himself. Taking Wandarr's hand in his, he walked away with her, leaving Randak with his parting words, "Do have fun, my friend."

Finally, the wedding day arrived. The great hall was adorned in perfect splendour in preparation for the wedding ceremony. It had been so long since any in T'varin had any time for something as glorious as the joining of two people in a lifelong partnership, that the excitement was both refreshing and overwhelming.

Barak and Wandarr had actually not seen each other for a few days, being so busy with the tasks they had taken on from Randak. Many people had contributed to the decorating and the dinner, plus offering a multitude of never-ending ideas; some good, others not so good and others, well, to be truthful, quite bad.

Randak, now fully dressed for the ceremony, had arrived early to check on everything and seeing all in order, he had gone to the room where he was supposed to meet Wandarr. With her not due for at least an hour, he paced back and forth in the room, reflecting on all the preparations, reviewing everything in his mind, to make sure he had not overlooked anything. Since everything had to be run by him for final approval, he was certain all was well. He wasn't going to let anything not be perfect. Standing before the mirror in the room, he examined his black dress pants and formal white shirt, ensuring the tie was properly secured and that his black dress shoes, a welcome break from the well-used riding boots he had worn through so many perils, were polished and free of any scuff marks. His Sonsword was sheathed, discreetly hidden by the black suit jacket he wore to complete the outfit. Seeing all in order, he took a deep breath, and tried to relax.

The whole affair had certainly kept him occupied and his mind off his nightmares, at least during the day. He now understood what Barak had meant by, *"Have fun."* He had listened to music tryouts of so many people willing to offer their talents, which included everything from a loud, off-key tenor to another bellowing out something akin to an operatic trage-dy. That singer hurt his ears. People also kindly offered to play instruments to accompany the vocalists. Some instruments Randak had never heard or seen in his entire life. Brass, wind and percussions he knew, but the odd shapes and deep or deafening noises that came from some of them were truly frightening and not a sound anyone would want at a celebration. Others were high pitched; one so much so, glasses started to vibrate to a noise that sounded like a squealing animal.

One of the women from Astaria offered her voice and he was so amazed at her talent that she saved him from listing to any more tryouts. Somewhere in there, even a magiks act showed up, offering to perform at the reception but he thought everyone had had enough of magiks of any kind for a while. Except maybe T'var, although Randak was certain you couldn't really call what He did magiks; T'var's power was something else entirely.

The decorators were superb, though and thoroughly excelled at their art. When people came into the great hall where the ceremony was to take place, they were greeted with an ocean of colours and a cornucopia of fresh fragrances from countless flowers dressed in bright blues, deep pinks, crimson reds and sun-drenched yellows, just to name a few. They adorned the halls and the backs of chairs and were scattered across the dining tables in the other half of the room. The great hall was a combination of seating area, dining area and dance floor; the perfect place for a large celebration.

Besides flowers, deep green wreaths of ivy tastefully hung on the walls and surrounded the room's large, tall windows. The powerful scent of the ivy and fresh cut flowers was incredibly refreshing after having to live through so much havoc across everyone's lands, where there had been a dearth of anything so colourful.

One thing Randak was confident would go well was the meal. For as soon as he took over the tasks from his sister and Barak, he made sure the chefs from the Centre of Learning in Glephas were asked to look after the wedding dinner. He told them to take their liberty and offer as many courses as they felt appropriate. He had no doubt they would outdo themselves, so was pleased when they responded affirmatively and noted they would arrive about two weeks ahead of time to begin preparations. He smiled when he thought back to the delicious meal that had been provided to them in Glephas and thought no more about that task.

The staff who were going to serve the meal were dressed in formal black and white and also acted as ushers to escort everyone to their seats. Although there were only a small number invited, Randak swore there were more people coming in than the room could accommodate, yet every time he looked the number of seats seemed to keep multiplying as they kept up with the growing throng.

Randak randomly peered out the door now and then and at one point, he saw T'var walk by and waved Him over. "Excuse me, are you doing that?" he asked, pointing to the chairs where another row had just appeared.

"Me? Such an odd question? What do you think, Randak?" T'var laughed.

Startled by an odd noise, Randak looked in its direction to see an instrument being tuned. When he turned back to respond to the question, T'var was gone once more.

Finally, everyone was seated. The air was full of excitement but as the music started to play, it brought everyone to a quiet, respectful silence.

Randak was at the back of the hall, standing just outside the room and could see Barak enter from one of the side doors at the front of the hall following T'var. Barak looked so nervous he was sweating. Randak almost snorted, trying to hold in a laugh. *What **is** he wearing? Is that a dress? No,* *not quite but honestly. Perhaps something traditional from Vintar? At least he can still wear his Sonsword with it."* Randak touched the handle of his blade as he heard a few small laughs and sounds of surprise from a small number of guests, but overall, everyone remained polite. *"Maybe they are just in shock."*

Randak realized how little he knew about the cultures of Vintar and the other places they had been, for their errands were always swift and often brought trouble. Definitely never enough time to explore or speak with the people about their customs. *"Maybe now that T'varin is restored, we will actually have the time for such things."*

"Randak, Randak, is it time?" A slightly nervous tremor in Wandarr's voice startled him. So focused on the sight of Barak, he did not realize she had entered the room.

He re-entered the room and stood there looking at his sister with a thousand thoughts racing through his head. He was about to walk Wandarr down an aisle and give his blessing to his best friend to marry his sister.

"Yes, Sister, almost. Are you ready?" He thought she might break out laughing when she saw how Barak was dressed, but then thought, *"Not my problem."* On the other hand, the flowing silk Astarian dress of pure white Wandarr wore was incredible and she was truly radiant; her veil simple, yet the elegantly designed tiara perfectly complemented the ensemble, creating a picture of beauty that made her brother proud. Astar, Wandarr's Attendant of Honour, wore a gown of splendor as well. Both women wore their swords with their dresses, which oddly enough, did not look out of place at all.

The music shifted, the signal for them to walk up the aisle. Astar first, followed by Randak and Wandarr. The crowd stood up upon the bride's entrance, arm-in-arm with Randak. As they began their march towards her groom, Randak heard the soft "oh my" from Wandarr as she set her eyes on Barak and knew she was trying not to laugh.

"Traditional Vintaran garb, I think." Randak whispered it to her in such a serious tone that Wandarr regained her composure as she walked towards her love.

Barak, smitten more than ever, could not take his eyes of his bride. Grinning and glowing with exuberance, all signs of nervousness gone. The music stopped as Wandarr and Barak now stood directly before T'var in the centre and Randak to the side.

"Who calls my sister to be his bride," Randak pulled out the ceremonial words of The Rangdorrian Lands from his memory.

"I, Barak of Vintar call her my love, to be my life-partner."

"Sister, do you consent to be this dre… this Barak of Vintar's life partner?"

"I do."

Barak thought Wandarr's smile was dazzling as she spoke the words.

T'var stepped forward and took Wandarr by the hand, bringing her closer to Barak who had stepped towards her as well. "Clasp your hands and face each other."

Randak moved and stood to one side of Barak and Astar to one side of Wandarr. A hush fell over the crowd as T'var spoke, His voice melodious, cheerful and jubilant. The couple stared into each other's eyes, oblivious to all the other eyes upon them as T'var welcomed everyone.

The actual ceremony, simple and profound, was performed by T'var Himself. Now that the couple stood before Him, He took out a white cloth, wrapped it around their clasped hands, and tied them together securely and then addressed the couple.

"Barak, are you ready to share your vow with Wandarr?"

Barak looked to the guests, then back to Wandarr and without hesitation, in a clear voice so that all could hear, he spoke his vow. "By the power of the love that brought T'var from heaven, I swear to love you with that same powerful love.

As the sun follows its course, mayst thou follow me as I will follow you.

As light to the eye, as bread to the hungry, as joy to the heart,

May your love and your presence be with me, as I swear my love and my presence will forever be with you.

Oh one that I love, 'til death comes to part us asunder and even then beyond that, still will you have my love."

T'var looked to Wandarr, nodded and without further prompting, looking deep into Barak's eyes, she spoke in turn, "You are my star of each night,

You are my brightness for every morning,

My love for you will never be forsaken.

You are the kernel of my heart,

You are the face of my sun,

You are the harp of my music,

You are the crown of my company.

Forever and again, always and for all time."

T'var spoke once more, "Now you are bound one to the other,

With a tie well nigh unbreakable.

Your final vows are made.

May you both continue to grow in wisdom and love,

That your marriage will be strong,

That your love will last,

In this life and beyond.

My eternal blessings now rest upon you.

Friends and honoured guests, I present to you Barak and Wandarr, partners for life."

All within hearing were overwhelmed with the powerful heartfelt vows Barak and Wandarr had pledged and spoke highly of them for days after. Their vows were not only eternal, but beautiful, for they each wrote their own and did not share them until the wedding day itself. Not one dry eye remained in the whole assembly before all was finished. Randak's eyes were probably the wettest, both proud and sad at the same time.

Just before the end of the service, T'var did something totally unexpected. With the whole congregation looking on, He lifted his hands, palms upward and said, "It is time."

Almost before the sentence was complete, the Orbstars appeared in His hands, two in the right, one in the left. The astonished crowd watched in fascination as T'var motioned to Randak, Barak and Wandarr. Up until then, Randak had stood with Barak, as Astar stood beside Wandarr during the ceremony.

"Your Sonswords, Warriors. Lay them before me."

Without questioning, the trio laid their Sonswords at T'var's feet, one straight and the other two at angles so the swords formed a triangle. Without warning the Orbstars once again hummed to life. Brilliance shot forth from the three gems and each Orb bathed its chosen sword in the fires of infinity.

"What does this mean?" Wandarr asked her brother and her new husband.

"I do not think it is over yet," offered Randak.

The trio watched as the Sonswords rose into the air, propelled by the intense power of the Orbstars. Unexpectedly, they and T'var no longer stood in front of the assembly of guests. Everything and everyone around them had vanished.

"T'var, where is everyone?" Barak asked, finding his voice.

"Where they belong," T'var laughed.

"It's us who have left, isn't it?" asked Randak.

"For a moment of time. We will return before the glow from the Orbstars, which enveloped us, blinded your guests and carried us here, is diminished."

"Why and where is here?" asked Barak.

Randak looked about and knew the chamber all too well. It had changed because of the restoration of the castle but he still recalled the bitter fight.

"It was here wasn't it, my Lord, the last battle against Kolonth?"

"Yes, indeed. Against Manglor too. Behold!" T'var pointed to a table that had been in the chamber, from time immemorial. A table which had seen the defeat of both Manglor and Kolonth. Wandarr wondered about the strange symbols on it and was going to ask T'var about them when He turned His attention to the Orbstars still held in His palms.

The blades floating effortlessly overhead began to glow more fiercely with the touch of the Orbstars. Another flash of light and the trio gasped as the Sonswords reappeared on the table, the glow fading. Barak was sure even the writing on the table looked different. Wandarr was certain it had been transmuted into other words. Randak was curious if the Sonswords would be given back to them and walked over to see if he could retrieve his.

He stopped as T'var said, "You need it no more, Randak. T'varin will now know peace for a long time. The Sonswords have served you well, but it is time to set them aside. They have each been infused with the power of an Orbstar and all three Orbstars have returned to their rightful place. They were never really of T'varin to begin with. The Sonswords of T'varin will rest here on this ancient table until they are needed and their time comes again."

"Who will need them, my King?" Barak asked, his curiosity getting the best of him.

"That is not your concern Barak. It is a story which belongs to others," T'var responded with almost a hint of chastisement in His voice. "It is time to return."

He smiled again and abruptly they stood in front of everyone. The recollection of what had happened began to fade, until they were uncertain it actually took place. The four of them returned, T'var finished the ritual, His smile joyous and contagious, matching the happy sound of His voice. "My blessing rest upon our happy couple and on all of you and of course upon the food and drink we are about to enjoy. Let us now celebrate the union of Barak and Wandarr. Let the festivities begin."

The reception was truly a glorious affair, with no small thanks to Randak. There were many speeches following the wedding dinner, followed by a celebration that would go down in history as one of the finest. Having T'var present definitely added another dimension to the gala. The dancing and laughter and love shared in the room lasted long into the small hours of the morning and Randak was thanked many times for the spectacular job he had done of choosing the right food and drink for all, with always enough to go around. As he hoped, the chefs from Glephas had outdone themselves, surpassing all expectations.

A small group of survivors from Barak's homeland of Vintar even managed to attend. The other visitors included those from Glephas, as well as guests from Andivar, Bjorqar and naturally a group of Warrior Women from Astaria. Some of the others who knew of the Warrior Women only from legend, found this a rare privilege. Of course, the Barizons and company, ever hungry after knowledge, plied the women with questions, until many of them excused themselves.

Guests were still eating, dancing and talking when Randak noticed that the bride and groom were long gone, off to a romantic retreat elsewhere on the island, before anyone else picked up on their absence. Looking out from over one of the balconies in the cool night air, he stared into the sky, inexplicably depressed and alone. So consumed with his thoughts, his finely-honed warrior's ears did not pick up on the interloper who joined his silent reverie.

The intruder's sigh caused Randak to turn in alarm and out of habit grasp for his Sonsword. He only turned halfway before he gasped, "T'var, You startled me. Forgive me, Lord."

"I don't believe there is anything left to be forgiven, my friend," T'var smiled, the glow in his eyes warming Randak's soul and driving out the loneliness. The sounds of the celebration drifted in and out of earshot with the wind, as T'var directed him to look at the clear night sky.

"Lovely, is it not? Yet despite the music and the beautiful canopy of stars above, something heavy weighs on the spirit of Randak. What troubles you, restless warrior?"

Unbelievably, after all he experienced, Randak debated whether to say anything to T'var. He felt vulnerable and the thought of baring his story made him more uncomfortable. Looking directly into T'var's face, he realized that T'var understood all along what troubled him and more than likely had for some time. This thought encouraged Randak to speak about what had been haunting him the past while. He exhaled, plunged in and began to tell T'var all about the nightmares, the fear and the pain so insistent on clinging to him, in spite of the salvation he knew was his.

"Ah," T'var said, after listening intently. "My dear friend, it is a truth that some wounds may only be healed in My Lands. The injuries from Kolonth go deep into your mind, more than just the physical hurt you endured. This grief is a burdensome thing."

"I know." As Randak said those words, he peered closely at T'var and once again saw enormous pools of love welling up in the form of tears. He finally grasped that T'var loved him beyond all imagining.

"What can be done?" Randak asked, as both once again stared into the bright starscape filling the night sky.

"You will come with Me, my friend. Barak and Wandarr will return in two weeks' time. Should the nightmares not cease, you will journey with Me. We will cross the Bridge together."

Randak thought he knew what T'var meant by those words but did not feel at ease to ask for a further explanation. He turned from his view of the star-filled night to say something else, but T'var was already gone.

Not until three days following his conversation with T'var on the balcony, did Randak's night terrors return. They were different. The scene was the same, the familiar noises, the identical smells in his nightmare, but the fear and his guilt were much more intense. A strangling and choking sensation continually gripped him in its dark clutches and only breathing the name of T'var vanquished it. The nightmares stopped until the fourth night before the newlyweds were to come home and then returned with a vengeance. Randak awoke each morning weary and haggard but despite that, he went about his duties faithfully, organizing the castle and meeting regularly with the new regents of T'varin. His fatigue was noticeable in spite of all his efforts to hide it. T'var checked in on Randak a few times during these days and He knew of the ongoing struggle without needing to ask.

The day that Barak and Wandarr were to return, Randak made a valiant effort not to betray his condition. He washed thoroughly, ate heartily and dressed in the brightest, freshest clothes he could find. In the late afternoon, the hoofbeats of Evad and Nayr could be heard approaching the Castle. Randak ran to the entrance to greet them. Reconnecting with them and experiencing their warm embraces as they met, made him realize how much he had missed them.

The trio, now reunited, spent a long time that night talking over old times and of their plans for the future. Randak purposely stayed up well into the early morning hours, hoping talking with his friends would tire him enough to sleep free of terror.

Wandarr later woke up to a chilling scream echoing down the hallway to her chambers.

"Randak, my Brother!"

Wandarr threw the bedsheets from her and with Barak in pursuit, ran down the hallway to her brother's room. They stood at the doorway of Randak's bedchamber and to their horror viewed a pale shape, shivering under a multitude of covers, one arm hanging limply over the bed, perspiration on his brow and his voice cracking with the words, "N-n-n-o-, Kolonth, n-e-v-e..."

"How can this be? Our vanquished foe still torments him?" Wandarr turned to Barak, tears in her eyes.

"Yes." T'var reappeared, a hand on each of their shoulders.

"How may we help him, my Lord?" Wandarr asked, trying to hold back more tears.

"Yes, T'var, what can be done? How long has this plagued him?"

"Too long, Barak," answered T'var sadly. "The pain is deep, mayhap too much so for here."

Softly, T'var walked to Randak's bedside and gently placed a hand on his brow. Randak breathed deeply and settled back into a much more relaxed state.

"Tomorrow, my friend," T'var spoke in a hushed voice, out of everyone else's hearing.

He ushered Barak and Wandarr outside the chamber into the passageway and said to them, "Meet me at the foot of the Great Bridge at sunrise on the morrow, all three of you."

Before either of them could question Him, He disappeared.

The rain poured heavily when Randak, Barak and Wandarr left the Castle. Evad, Nayr and Jip did not seem to mind though. They rode at a steady pace and the trio's destination came in sight as the downpour slowed to a light shower and the first rays of the morning sun were beginning to shine their way through the dark clouds.

They approached the Bridge slowly. No one spoke. Drawing near to the foot of the Bridge, covered in a dense mist, they glimpsed a figure walking towards them. Without a word they all dismounted and began leading their horses towards the person. Barak and Wandarr held hands and Randak walked slightly ahead.

It was T'var. He met them with a glow about Him which was deeper and brighter than usual. The drizzle continued, yet they warmed at the sight of Him. T'var extended His hand toward Randak and they understood.

Behind them, Evad nuzzled up to Nayr and then to Jip. Good-byes said to both, Evad broke into a gallop, rushed past T'var and kept going at breakneck speed across the bridge until he could be seen no more.

A shocked Barak looked to T'var, "Where has my…"

"Ah, Barak, do you remember when the Starborn Sentinel said Evad came from my Lands?"

"I do, my King."

"Now he returns home. He could not resist the call of My Lands. I know you will miss him, though."

"But he has been so faithful. We have been through so much together. What am I to do?"

T'var nodded to Randak who was engaged in his own conversation with Jip. His last words to his horse loud enough for all to hear. "Take care of him my friend. Yes, he is not as good a rider as I, but you can teach him. He is a fast learner."

Randak walked over to Barak and embraced him speaking into his ear, "No fear, Jip is yours now. A faithful friend who will look after you well." Barak returned the embrace, saying through his tears, "This isn't fair you know, you're the lucky one."

"I know, my friend, I know," said Randak, tears freely running down his face. "Take care, you who are more than a Brother. You are needed here."

Randak gave Barak one last strong embrace and turned to his sister. Wandarr was already weeping, unable to control herself. Randak hugged her tight, saying, "You will see me again. He will ensure it."

"Yes, yes," sobbed Wandarr, glancing up through her watery eyes and seeing T'var still waiting patiently. "I will miss you so much. Must it be this way?"

Randak squeezed Wandarr once more before stepping back and addressing them both.

"You and Barak have a world to restore. I have a new world to explore. I love you. I love you both." Without looking back, Randak began walking towards T'var.

All tears mingled with the drizzling wetness, as T'var and Randak clasped hands and began to slowly walk away deeper into the gradually receding mist, until they could be seen no more.

Barak and Wandarr embraced each other for a long time before they remounted their steeds and began to ride away. They rode home silently, tears still running down their faces. Jip, now Barak's faithful four-footed companion, a reminder of past times, both good and bad. He too, seemed to sense the emptiness that burdened Barak and Wandarr. The drizzle stopped and by the time the couple reached home, sunlight streamed through the Castle of Crystal and the multi-hued reflections began to drive away their sorrow.

Randak and T'var walked on in the mist. Randak felt different. At first, he thought he was becoming lighter, but then he decided that he was actually heavier, more real and solid than he could ever remember feeling. The dull ache in his arm was gone and he understood that it would never return. The memories of T'varin and Kolonth and all that had happened grew dimmer and an excitement began to well up within him that he could not explain. T'var's Land beckoned him and unclasping his hand from T'var's, he raced towards the music he heard.

Randak was not sure how, but he recognized the melody which gave him an overwhelming desire to join in the singing. The mist cleared and indescribable sights and sounds embraced him, crisp, pure and brilliant, even more so than the colours he witnessed through the Orbstars. Randak, filled with unspeakable and overwhelming joy, glanced back at T'var's smiling face and then ran towards the music. He did not know what to say, but he knew for certain the nightmares would be no more, for he was finally home.

THE END

ACKNOWLEDGEMENTS

For a story that was over four decades in the making, there are a host of acknowledgements I could make but I will try to limit it to just a few expressions of thanks.

A huge thank you to my family, especially my wife Beth who convinced me it was time to share this story with the world, and to the rest of my family and friends who continue to encourage my writing journey.

To those whose names may appear in the story in some form or another as a nod to their influences in my life: thank you Ryan, Dave, and JP for helping me live out some of the years I missed out on growing up. To Randy, my best and closest friend of college years, bless you!

Thank you to my editor and coach Paula Telizyn, whose assistance in bringing this story to its final version has been invaluable, and I am sure you will agree that the fantastic job she did on the maps also deserves a huge shout out.

Thank you to Shannon Wiedener for proofreading and ensuring my readers' experiences are not interupted by spelling and grammatical errors.

Thank you to my readers, past, present, and new for your continued support and feedback on my writing. I would also be remiss not to mention C.S Lewis, J.R.R. Tolkien, and Terry Brooks, who are among my favorite fantasy authors, and to whom I owe a debt of gratitude for how they have inspired me over the years.

Lastly and most importantly thank you to T'var, my allegorical Aslan, my Lord and Saviour Jesus, always my ultimate inspiration.

ABOUT THE AUTHOR

Barry M. Fellinger resides in St. Thomas Ontario with his wife Beth and. He enjoys spending time with his children and grandchildren, extended family, and friends. He also likes reading books from a variety of genres, watching superhero and science fiction television shows and movies, collecting comics, attending the occasional Comicon and relaxing in Sanctuary II, his comic book/man room for inspiration.

He has authored two sci-fi adventure books in his True Adventure Series for middle grade readers, The Almost True Adventures of Brandon and Josh and its sequel The Not So True Adventures of Brandon, Josh and Adam. Both books are available through online distributors in e-book and paperback formats. The first book in the series, The Almost True Adventure of Brandon and Josh is also now available as an audiobook.

For more information on Barry and his books where you will find updates on Barry's writing activities as well as his video series about Sheepy Weepy Wimpy Wompy, now called the Town of Meh, , please visit www.barrymfellingerauthor.com